Never Saw You Coming

HAYLEY DOYLE

D0319143

avon.

Published by AVON
A division of HarperCollins*Publishers* Ltd
1 London Bridge Street
London SE1 9GF

www.harpercollins.co.uk

A Paperback Original 2020

2

First published in Great Britain by HarperCollins*Publishers* 2020

ISBN: 978-0-00836575-2

Typeset in Minion by Palimpsest Book Production Limited, Falkirk, Stirlingshire

Printed and bound in UK by CPI Group (UK) Ltd, Croydon CR0 4YY

MIX
Paper from
responsible sources
FSC™ C007454
www.fsc.org

This book is produced from independently certified FSC™ paper
to ensure responsible forest management.

For more information visit: www.harpercollins.co.uk/green

Praise for *Never Saw You Coming*

'This very modern love story is quirky, fun and full of surprises. I loved getting to know Jim and Zara on their road trip and watching as their love/hate relationship developed against the background of a very real and vibrant Liverpool. Hayley's writing is funny and smart – a real breath of fresh air!'
Claire Frost, author of *Living My Best Life*

'Such a brilliant debut from Hayley Doyle! A modern day fairytale set against the backdrop of two enchanting cities. I loved it.'
Natalie Anderson

See what real readers are saying . . .

'I absolutely fell in love with this story!'

'A story to make you smile.'

'An excellent read! Zara and Jim are funny, frustrating, sympathetic, and very real. A must-read.'

'A perfect romance! Five stars.'

'An utter delight to read!'

'A lovely story about life, surprises, and falling in love when you least expect it.'

'Totally fun and entertaining.'

'Made me laugh out loud and want to cry!'

'A charming, layered tale.'

'Zara is a witty and impulsive female lead.'

'I absolutely loved this book from the very first page!'

'A book that makes you smile from ear to ear – for fans of Sophie Kinsella, Mhairi McFarlane, and Jill Mansell.'

'I feel as though I personally knew the characters, they were so well developed.'

Born in Liverpool in 1981, Hayley Doyle trained at the Liverpool Institute for Performing Arts, LIPA, and worked as an actress for more than a decade, including playing Ali in West End show *Mamma Mia!* She then went on to live and work in Dubai, where she founded Hayley's Comet: a children's theatre company specialising in musical theatre, acting and playwriting. During her time in Dubai, she was also a regular talk-show host on Dubai Eye 103.8, the UAE's no.1 English-speaking talk radio station. Hayley currently lives in London with her husband and their two children.

The truth is, of course, that there is no journey.
We are arriving and departing all at the same time.

— David Bowie

PART ONE

1

Zara

'I'm going,' I tell Katie over the phone. 'My bags are packed.'

I'm sitting at a waterside cafe drinking fresh mint lemonade, watching people ferry back and forth across Dubai Creek on traditional wooden water taxis, known here as *abras*. To my far right, the Burj Khalifa pings from the Downtown skyline like a giant pen, touching the cloudless blue sky with its tip. Katie was supposed to be meeting me, but as usual of late, she cancelled again.

'So, you're leaving Dubai,' Katie says, 'to go and live in some British city that you've never been to before, with a fella you hardly know?'

'Nick and I talk about living together all the time,' I say.

'And yet you haven't seen Nick for six months.'

'That's nothing when you plan to spend a lifetime with somebody.'

'Zara Khoury. You're not thinking straight.'

How patronising. It's not about not thinking straight.

It's about thinking off-course, doing something that's out of the ordinary. And there's nothing wrong with that, is there? How can wonderful things happen to us if we don't do wonderful things to start off with?

'Your daddy can't bankroll your love life,' she says.

'Oh, don't worry,' I reply. 'He won't.'

She doesn't respond, unless she's waiting for an explanation.

'I've got some savings, Katie. And a plan. I want to study again; finish my degree.'

'Right. You know what they say? Once a dropout . . .'

'Look, it's not just about Nick Gregory.'

'Ah, come on, Zara, don't kid yourself. It's *all* about Nick Gregory.'

The call to prayer filters across the creek, a beautiful and somewhat haunting melody that pauses me momentarily as I glance towards the mosques in the distance. Dusk will fall soon. Day turns into night so quickly in this patch of the world, the bold sun taking a break to allow an even bolder moon to rule the purple sky. I've never felt at home here, even though it's been the place I've spent the majority of my thirty years. I long to feel an urge to root down, but all I can feel is flight; a gentle breeze trying to lift me from this seat and take me far away. The scar sitting on my right cheekbone, the size of my middle fingernail and the shape of Australia, is no longer a reminder of what can go wrong, but a sign of what can turn out right.

'Believe me,' I say. 'This is all meant to be.'

Katie tells me she has to go; she has a meeting. I don't get wished a safe flight, or nudged to give her all the juicy gossip. She doesn't even mention the weather; and expats love to mention the British weather. She just goes.

As I intend to.

Tomorrow morning, I will land at Heathrow Airport. I'll go and buy that second-hand car I found online and drive two hundred miles north of London, to a city famous for its football, its accent and, of course, The Beatles. A place where they call something good *boss*.

'If only you could come here,' Nick says, often. 'You'd love it.'

Well, Liverpool, here I come.

2

Jim

'Unknown'.

I always answer my phone if the number's unknown.

It's one of my three life rules. Being up at six to get here, the Mersey Tunnel toll booth, for work at seven a.m. is another. This rule's partnered with navy pants, a V-neck pullover and high-visibility jacket, otherwise I'll lose my job. And the last rule's making sure my ma takes her tablets and climbs the stairs five times daily to keep her heart pumping.

Beyond this, I let myself be.

Except now, 'Unknown' flashes, skittering beside my hand, vibrating.

My phone lies face up on the small desk my knees are crammed beneath, next to a tattered paperback. Gene Wilder's autobiography; another Oxfam bargain. I've been at work for the best part of an hour, but this desk isn't mine. Tomorrow I might be put in the toll booth next door. Yesterday I worked three booths to my left. I watch my phone, itching to answer.

'Y'never heard of a barber, mate?'

It's the fella in the Ford Focus. He exchanges his quid for the correct tunnel fare every morning whilst listening to local radio, some crass breakfast show churning out the latest, not-quite-greatest hits. I've met with the overbearing stench of his aftershave many a time, not to mention the same old jibe about my hair.

'Have a good day, mate,' I reply, handing over the change. 'Nice one.'

And off the Focus speeds through the tunnel with an unnecessary rev. The next car pulls up; the window winds down; I hand over change.

'Unknown' continues to vibrate.

Christ. I always answer unknown numbers. Ever since my dad died eight years ago. Look, I don't want to delve into it. But seeing that word flashing before me reminds me. I hadn't answered the first time, had I? Or the second. And it was only on the third attempt I bothered picking up. It'd been the hospital, calling to ask for a Jim Glover, and I said, 'That's me.' The voice, light and female I recall, asked me to come and identify a man, thought to be Roy Glover, brought in dead on arrival. A heart attack on the Dock road.

But guess what?

There's a gleaming problem with answering my phone right now. You see, it's a sackable offence. I'm allowed to read. We all are. Books, papers, even a good old crossword. But phones? Nope. The use of mobile phones whilst working within the cage of a toll booth is a sackable offence. No 'three strikes and you're out'. It's an automatic lock-in.

'Unknown'.

I hunch over the desk, press the green circle, grumble, 'Hello?'

'WELL, SOMEONE'S STILL HALF ASLEEP,' the male voice belts into my ear. It's a harsh, nasal twang. I can't place it but it's an altogether familiar sound.

'Who's this?'

A flurry of laughter ensues, overpowered by a husky female voice.

'HEAVY NIGHT, WAS IT?' she asks, finding herself hilarious.

Shit. Noticing a lady waiting in her car beside my booth, I whip my phone beneath the small desk and dish out some change. Then, peeping over my shoulder to check there isn't another car behind, I bring the phone back to my ear.

'WE'VE LOST HIM,' the male voice says.

'I'm here,' I say. 'Who is this?'

'SHALL YOU TELL HIM, CONNIE? OR SHALL I?'

'OH, GO 'EAD, CARL, THE PLEASURE'S ALL YOURS.'

'Hurry up, I can't really talk.'

'JIM GLOVER?' Carl sings.

'How do you know me name?'

'YOU'RE LIVE ON AIR, MERSEY WAVE 103.4.'

'Y'what?'

Connie's husky laugh takes over. 'You're live on the breakfast show with Connie and Carl, Jim. Now's your chance to become a winner.'

'A winner?'

Stretching ahead of me, and behind me, is grey tarmac. That single word, winner, is not part of my daily vocabulary. The two simple syllables sound full and foreign in my mouth, my breath still fresh from instant coffee.

'You're head to head with Sophie,' Carl says. 'Say hi to Jim, Sophie.'

'Hiya Jim,' a crackled voice says, the slight echo confirming

8

that Sophie's using a hands-free kit from her car. And yet, who is this Sophie? And why is she – with me – live on the radio?

'Whoever answers this question first will become the proud owner of a brand-new BMW,' Carl goes on. 'Or, as Connie would call it, "a posh white car".'

'That's a bit sexist,' Sophie's voice says.

Her comment is completely ignored. The game that me and her are somehow a part of continues. Cars filter into the tunnel ahead of my glance, weaving their way from other booths. Any second now, a car'll pull up beside me and this game, this quiz, this radio prank, will come to a sudden end.

Why haven't I already hung up?

For every second I remain on the line, I'm begging to be fired. The joy it'll give Derek Higgins to demand that I see him in his office, to click his dry, swollen fingers as he orders me to remove my high-vis jacket. If reading is the perk of my role, then dishing out a P45 is Derek's.

'Jim? Sophie? Are you ready?'

We both mumble a *yeah*.

A mashup of the theme tunes to *Countdown* and *Who Wants to Be a Millionaire?* comes whistling through the speaker. Instead of waiting eagerly for the question, I can only focus on willing the banging in my chest to piss off. I'm breaking my boss's rule to adhere to my own, and it could result in me losing my job. Sure, rules are rules, but what about priorities? I should hang up.

'Okay; First one to say the correct answer wins.' Connie clears her throat. 'Name the author of *On Her Majesty's Secret Service*, *Dr No* and *Thunderball*.'

A gasp from Sophie tickles my ear. 'JAMES BOND!'

Bloody hell. My heart lightens. My knees are numb squashed beneath this little desk, my fingertips clammy.

9

'Ian Fleming,' I say.

A white van pulls up beside my booth, and with the efficiency of a robot, I hand change to the driver.

'Good fucking morning to you, too,' the driver spits. 'Rude fucking bastard.'

I sigh and take a breath, knowing it's now or never.

There's a good chance that Connie and Carl and the whole of Merseyside missed my muffled answer. Or perhaps Sophie heard it, and she's now ready to steal, to shout it out louder, clearer, stronger . . .

I blink. 'IAN FLEMING.'

And just like that, I win a brand-new car.

Connie and Carl play 'Congratulations' across the airwaves, singing the word 'commiserations' to Sophie, finding themselves unbearably funny.

I put my handset on loud speaker, drop the phone onto my knees.

'Stay on the line, Jim,' Carl says.

A horn honks.

Again.

'The producer'll chat to you in a mo.'

Four, maybe five cars have piled up behind my booth, the one in front honking away with unashamed clarity. Derek'll be making his way over any minute. With expert speed, I hand change to the impatient driver before he bombs it through the barrier. I recognise the next car. A Nissan Micra, silver, a sun-shaped sign stuck on the back window that reads *Be the Light. Namaste.* The girl behind the wheel passes through the tunnel regularly, never at a specific time of day. Sometimes, her hair's snatched up or curled all fancy like a Charlie's Angel, her wrists decorated with a bunch of bangles. Ed Sheeran sings through her speakers. Even now, in November, she never fails to wear oversized sunnies.

'Hey, you,' she says, rolling down her window and dipping her glasses to the edge of her nose. I give her a one-sided smile. She's a right chatterbox, this one, always trying to entice me out on the lash with her mates or making a remark about me looking 'cold' or 'hot' or 'tired'. Today it's 'worried'.

'I'm going for a few drinks tonight in Oxton,' she tells me. 'Fancy coming?'

Oxton. Pretty posh. Over the water.

A horn honks.

'Me best mate's having a party,' I say. 'Bonfire night, and all that.'

Another horn honks.

The girl pushes her sunnies up her nose with her middle finger, mouths, 'whatevs' and drives away. Another car pulls up. Then, another. My head's frazzled. Have I really, *really* just won a car? Come on, focus. I move fast, get the queue of cars to settle into a smooth, quiet rhythm as I wait for the producer to speak to me. I'm still on hold. And still trying to fathom how this has happened.

Last month's payday.

Yep, that was it. The day I signed my name.

I'd been sheltering from the wet drizzle, browsing around a discount book store. Fluorescent strip lighting and BOGOF offers surrounding me, I stood reading the back of a Truman Capote biography. My phone rang.

'Alright, Mam, what's up?'

'It's nothing, love. I'm okay. Honest.'

'You don't sound okay. What happened?'

'I was just making tea, that's all. Me mind must've

11

wandered. I forgot to concentrate for a moment. I burnt me hand. It just dropped, the kettle, it just dropped.'

'I'm on me way. Don't worry.'

I discarded Capote into the bargain bucket beside me and headed through town, towards Liverpool One to catch the bus to my ma's. Wind whistled through the city, a cold chill reminding shoppers that autumn was falling into winter. I was almost at the bus stop when I noticed a white BMW made entirely from Lego. It wasn't on the road, of course, but beside the shopping centre's crowd-pulling outdoor piano. Impressive. As were the two young girls holding clip-boards, approaching passers-by to sign up. Resembling a manufactured girl band, all petite with dark lashes and pouty pink lips, they wore bikini tops and hot pants, oblivious to the current climate.

'We only need three more names,' one of the girls shrieked.

I dodged out of her way, but her mate stepped in.

'Come on, sign up,' she said. 'We're not allowed on our break 'til the sheet's full.'

'I can't,' I said. Because I couldn't. I had to get to my ma's.

'Don't you wanna win a car?' both girls sang, like a kitsch pop duo.

A pen got thrust into my hand.

'What's the catch?' I asked, scribbling down my name and number as fast as possible. I never waited for their answer. I just legged it for the bus.

Had it been as simple as that to win a car? Really?

'Jim Glover?'

The voice from within my phone hollers around the toll booth.

'Yeah?' I reply.

The producer of Connie and Carl's breakfast show gives me strict instructions for how and when I can collect my prize. She's most unenthusiastic, as if me winning this car is a hassle her life can do without.

'You're totally serious, like?' I ask.

'Why did you take part if you didn't think it was serious?' she snaps.

Bloody hell. My whole morning's gone from boring to bonkers. I'm really trying to control myself here, but Christ, I've just won a car. What's the catch? Come on. Surely there's a catch.

'There's no catch,' the producer says.

She hangs up and the line goes dead. The rain outside has stopped, the sun stretching through the cold, windy air. Steam clears from the windows of my toll booth and a hint of blue sky frames the top of the tunnel entrance. I allow myself to smile, a wide, cheesy grin.

'Jim Glover?'

I stare at my phone. Who said that?

A rat-a-tat-tat sounds against the reinforced plastic window.

Derek Higgins.

His dry, swollen finger signals me to get out of the booth. 'Follow me.'

The office door swings on its hinge, creaking, a fault in the frame preventing the satisfaction of it shutting.

'How's your missus?' I ask.

'On a diet,' Derek tells me. 'But we need to talk about you, Jim.'

There isn't a clue in sight to prove that Derek has occupied this office for years. The walls remain white, the desk

13

uncluttered; a desktop computer and a single biro. A shift rota hangs beside a plain calendar. No family photograph, no football logo, no tea-stained personal mug. To those who don't know, it could be Derek Higgins' first day.

'You're going nowhere,' Derek barks, choosing to perch on the desk, his navy trousers bulging at the crotch, his navy socks not quite hiding his pasty calves. Offering me the only chair in the office with his hand, he removes his glasses, squinting. 'Nowhere,' he reiterates. 'And in a way, it's quite endearing. The fact that you're going nowhere.'

Now, I'm a tall fella. My growth spurt was quick and early – I was towering over my teachers by the time I started secondary school. I'm neither proud nor ashamed of my height, although my ma still nags me about my natural hunch. And yet here, in Derek Higgins' office, I feel small; worthless.

'You know what I'm gonna say, don't you, Jim?'

I nod.

'It hasn't been an easy decision for me. Lots of pros, lots of cons.' Derek holds out his palms like a pair of weighing scales. 'You're a pretty predictable character, Jim. Which is good on one hand, but . . .' He trails off. 'You're going nowhere.'

'So you keep saying, Derek.'

'Don't be offended. It's no criticism. It's the way you are. Most lads your age have either tried to get somewhere and failed, or actually gone somewhere, like down south, or –' he lowers his voice, '– *London*.'

I sit back into the office chair, letting my long legs spread.

'You're a good-looking lad, Jim. You are. I mean, you're not *my* type, if you catch my drift? But, you'd have to be blind not to notice you've got the looks. You're what my wife'd call a "dish"; a "bad boy". They all love a bad boy, don't they?'

Oh, Christ. I best brace myself.

'You could've been in sales, Jim. Retail. But you didn't go anywhere. You weren't one of those lads who did something soft, like . . . form a band.'

'I was in a band,' I mutter.

'What did you play?' Derek leans back and plays air guitar.

'Vocals. Lead vocals actually.'

'Exactly my point.' Derek clicks his fingers, such a strong, perfected click that its echo bounces off the walls. 'You never pursued it.'

'I was fifteen. Everyone's in a band when they're fifteen.'

'I wasn't.'

There were four of us in the band. Snowy, Griffo, Mikey, and yours truly.

Brian 'Snowy' Walsh – who got his nickname from his resemblance to Snow White; skin as white as snow, hair as black as ebony – played lead guitar. The drummer, Mikey Farley, was the youngest of six kids, so learning to play the drums was his only way of being heard. I was the front man and Phil Griffin was on bass. Griffo's dad was always away on business which meant that Griffo's mum went out with the girls a lot, so it was in their triple garage where we formed, rehearsed. The Griffins had a cook and a cleaner and electric gates. In fact, still do. None of us knew what Griffo's dad did, but we all knew he was raking it in. We drank a lot of his expensive spirits, wrote songs. We only ever performed covers. Led Zeppelin, the Stones, Chili Peppers.

'We used to do a boss cover of "Video Killed the Radio Star",' I tell Derek.

Derek sings a line, falsetto.

'Did you ever play The Cavern, though?' he asks.

'Once. Student night.' And it's true. The sweat does drip off the walls.

15

'Predictable,' Derek says.

'Or maybe I'm not so predictable,' I say, standing. 'I can't be arsed with this.'

'Excuse me?'

A horn honking outside startles us, ripping away my sudden confidence to storm out. I sit back down. Derek begins to pace the office and I realise, yeah, he's only being honest. I am predictable. Nothing I've ever done during eight years of working in the toll booths could've given Derek any other impression. My timekeeping's impeccable. My hair's always a mess. I only drink instant coffee from the machine. I chat to my colleagues, ask after their kids and buy them Mars bars when they're sick. You see, Derek didn't know me prior to my toll-booth days. He doesn't know about my old impulsive nature.

'You're right,' I say. 'I'm going nowhere. But maybe that's about to change.'

Derek pulls himself away from the rota and puts his glasses back on, glaring at me.

'Derek, I won a car.'

'A car?'

'Yeah, a car.'

'A real one?'

'Yep.'

'How?'

'On the radio. On the breakfast show.'

'Jesus Christ, lad. What sort of car?'

'BMW.'

'A BMW?!'

Derek loosens his tie a little further, wipes his brow. 'Congratulations, lad.'

'Cheers.'

16

The passing cars fill the dead air hanging between us, until Derek starts to laugh.

'What's so funny?'

'Oh, lad. I'm just imagining you driving around your neck of the woods in a BMW. I mean, it's not gonna last five minutes round there.'

The laughing produces tears and Derek removes his glasses again to mop them up with his thumb. He's got a bloody nerve.

'That's out of order, Derek. Out of order.'

But, is it? Maybe Derek has a point. The joy of winning is still boiling hot. I haven't had a second to think this through, let the cold water splash me in the face. I think about the flat I rent above Wong's chippy. The living room overlooks a dual carriageway flyover. Below my bathroom is a tiny back yard, just enough space for a wheelie bin. Where the hell am I going to park a BMW out there?

The bubble bursts.

'Look, Jim. You're better off selling the bloody thing and going on a spending spree.'

'What do you reckon it's worth?' I ask. I watch cars speed past day in, day out, but I don't know much about them. As a kid, I preferred my bike and my books. I passed my driving test years ago, like. I'm not soft. But I lost all interest in getting a car because I couldn't afford one.

Derek blows his lips. 'Twenty grand. More. I'm not a BMW man myself. More a Merc.'

'Twenty grand?!' Shit.

An hour ago, I was trying to read Gene Wilder's auto-biography cocooned in a toll booth. Now, I could be sitting on a small fortune. Derek Higgins' white office walls are suddenly leaping with rainbows and fucking unicorns.

'Sell it, Jim,' Derek tells me. 'I mean, where would you drive it anyway? You haven't exactly got anywhere you need to be, have you?'

Twenty thousand pounds. That's way more than I earn in a whole year. There's no need to worry about getting sacked. I'll be okay.

Actually, I won't just be okay.

I'll be grand. Twenty fucking grand!

'Anyway, Jim. Back to my original point.'

My shoulders relax. I take my hands out of my pockets. An intense warmth encases me for the first time in, God, probably over a decade. Since I graduated from uni. Christ, back then I had options, I had hope. But a new car is more solid than an English degree, isn't it? Holding my hand out, I smile, feeling a tingle of the old Jim Glover returning. I'll save Derek the pleasure of firing me and call the shots myself. I'll quit.

Derek doesn't spot my outreached hand. He opens a drawer beneath his desk.

'Surprise!' Derek says, handing over a letter. 'You're the Chosen One, Jim!'

'Y'what?'

I crouch over, resting my elbows on my knees, and skim the words to get the gist.

'You're sending me on a training day?' I ask. 'For card payments?'

'Yes, I am, Jim. Yes. I. Am. We have to move with the times. Not everyone wants to buy a Fast Tag for the tunnel and drivers are becoming more and more tired of using coins. You'll be our representative, learning how to use the card machine. You're the brainy one out of all the numpties here.'

'Love how you just described yourself as a numpty, Derek.'

'Watch it.'

'Do I get paid extra for going?'

'Oh, aye.'

This is officially my lucky day. I should go and buy a scratch card. I've never been promoted, never done the whole 'rounds are on me' down at the Pacific Arms with my mates. Would my dad be proud, I wonder?

'How much extra?' I ask.

'You'll be paid in . . . respect.'

'Ah, for fuck's sake.'

'Language, lad. I chose you 'cause you're smart.'

'I'm touched, Derek.'

'Don't be a smart-arse.'

The words *I quit* are tickling the edge of my tongue. I want to say it – scream it – but for some reason, they don't escape.

'Now, get back in the booth,' Derek says. 'Break's over.'

Predictably, I obey.

3

Zara

I've just landed in Heathrow Airport.

My teeth are brushed, my hair is behaving, likely due to
the expensive product I'd felt obliged to buy after treating
myself to a chestnut and blonde balayage. It was worth it.
My Lebanese genes are to be thanked for my hair, which
has a mind of its own, like my papa's. I ate a small cheese
sandwich offered to me before we started our descent and
now it's sitting in my stomach like a brick. For such a
frequent flyer, I can never seem to sleep on planes, not
unless I drink a huge amount of red wine. Last night, I
didn't touch a drop because I wanted to be as fresh as
possible for this long drive to Liverpool. I tried to rest, I
did, except I managed to get through three whole movies.
The sky here is low and thick and white. It will be lunchtime
in Dubai now, an endless blue rooftop stretching high
above the locals and expats, the sun shining its warmest
rays across the desert.

But I'm not here for the sky or the sun. I'm here for more than the whole damn sky.

I'm here for the universe.

I'm here.

I buy a UK SIM card for my phone from one of those machines in the terminal and call the guy selling me his car. We arrange to meet outside of Boots and he shows up like a taxi driver, holding a piece of crumpled paper with *Zara Khoury* written in bold marker pen. He reminds me to get insured, then mentions something about me having to go online to tax the car and hands me some paperwork. I'll go through all this in detail with Nick later. I handover my cash and the guy tosses me the keys – which, of course, I drop – and he tells me where the car is parked. A no-frills deal for a no-frills car.

Pushing a luggage trolley with two large suitcases, a holdall, a canvas tote bag and a mop – yes, a mop – I wander around Level Two of the airport parking lot, looking for my new car, shivering. God, I'd forgotten how damn cold this country is.

Nobody gave me a huge send off in Dubai, not even Katie. I'm not embarrassed or anything, I just don't think they got it. What I'm doing. Maybe if I was on the outside looking in, I wouldn't get it either. Or, maybe I just didn't know my friends as well as I thought I did. That happens when you move a lot; multiple settling-in periods. But I always listen to my gut. It will lead me to put down roots one day. I know it.

Anyway, if I'm honest, I haven't socialised much during the past six months. Work has dried up since the scar lodged into my cheek. Companies aren't keen on employing promo girls with something that isn't a beauty spot or a beaded jewel. At first, I hit an all-time low, but once Nick helped me to find some confidence again, I knew I had to hold onto my small pot of savings. I wouldn't be here today otherwise, looking for my new (well, used) car.

Where *is* it? I hope I haven't been fooled.

I can hear Katie in my ear, tutting. She's my oldest friend because she's lived in Dubai her whole life, consistently too, unlike me. She's Irish and belongs to the tight-knit, well-connected Kelly family who own a chain of Irish pubs planted inside big-brand hotels. One pub even has a cartoon drawing of a fish dressed up as a leprechaun framed behind the bar, something I drew back at uni before I dropped out. So, whenever I returned to the Sandpit, whether as a kid, a teenager or an adult, Katie was always there to jump back into the scene with.

It's a transient place, Dubai, people coming, people going. You're at the mercy of your sponsor or your work visa and when people feel like they've done a good stint, they're ready to move on. Or go home. It's a really easy place to make friends. Not so easy to keep hold of them. The most recent crowd I fell in with were better described as drinking buddies. A whole international mix, but predominantly South African or British, they were stellar at organising dhow cruises around the Omani Peninsula or thinking up group costumes for the Rugby Sevens: busy bees with feather dusters; Smurfs. Last year, a bunch of the guys dressed as human-sized fast food items and lay stacked on each other, swapping the order of the burger layers each time one of them needed to use the bathroom. I mean, it was hilarious. Katie's dating the lettuce now. I think it's serious.

Don't get me wrong, she was great when the scar on my face was new. No, *new* doesn't sound right. It makes it seem like I went out and bought something shiny. I think a better word is *raw*. But she got bored with me. I became a lot less up for it, a lot less fun. And Katie Kelly likes fun.

At least I had Nick.

'You have him on a screen,' Katie liked to remind me. 'You don't have him here.'

'That'll change one day,' I told her.

And that day has arrived. Today.

Bingo! I find my new car. A small Peugeot 106. Haggard, and much more *used* than simply a 'used car', it's the most hideous colour on the planet: not red; not brown; somewhere in between, like old dried blood. The pictures that guy posted online had told a different story. But, if this car gets me from A to B today, then so what? I love it. Plus, it'll give me independence, which is key when moving to a new place. I don't want to be too dependent on Nick, despite what Katie thinks.

I open the trunk and get a rush of excitement at the reality of what's happening.

'I need to see you,' Nick had told me yesterday via Skype. 'Now.'

'If only that were possible,' I teased.

Little did he know my bags were packed and waiting downstairs by the front door of my papa's villa. I told Nick I was going camping in the desert with friends, not to be offended if I didn't reply to his messages that evening, as it would be unlikely I'd have signal. He pretended to sulk, sticking out his bottom lip, then edged closer to the screen and realised something was missing from beside my bed.

'Where's the mop, sweetheart?' he asked.

It was downstairs, of course, with my luggage.

'Lulu found it in my room and used it to clean the floor,' I said, thinking on my feet.

'No way!'

23

'I know, right. Can you believe it? So it's drying out in the utility room.'

And now, I'm fitting that mop into the Peugeot, sliding it through the trunk and letting the handle poke through to the passenger seat. Its accessories – wigs, hats, novelty spectacles – are stuffed into the holdall. I was prepared for some drama getting the actual mop through check-in, expecting the odd glance from other passengers, but it's all been smooth sailing. My plan is actually going according to plan.

I settle into the driver's seat and make a phone call to get myself insured.

Then, I turn the key, start the Peugeot's engine.

I've driven a manual before, but not for years. I stall twice and hear my papa's voice saying, 'Why drive when you can catch a cab?'

By some sort of magic, I get the car going on the third try. Chugging out of the parking lot, the planes groaning overhead, I pull over into a temporary stopping bay to set up the portable satnav. I found it in a kitchen drawer at my papa's villa. It was there amongst old phone chargers and a toaster with a European plug socket, so I figured he wouldn't miss it any time soon. I enter the address for my final destination, one that's imprinted on my mind, my heart.

I set off and once I'm comfortably in fourth gear, I squeal in delight.

Nick Gregory is going to get the surprise of his life.

4

Jim

At three o'clock, when my shift at the tunnel finishes, I catch the bus to my ma's.

My family moved into this red brick terrace when I was five. Two up and two down, with a back yard and no front garden, we Glovers embraced the move, elated that we finally had our own staircase. The house hasn't changed much in thirty years, except for the addition of them slogan cushions with things like, 'Home Is Where the Heart Is' littering the settee. One whole wall is covered with family photos, mainly of our Lisa and Emma, my sisters. I'm not offended. They're a right pair of posers, all dolled up in high heels and massive feathers, dancing on cruise ships. Imagine me doing that? No ta. I find the opposite wall more appealing anyway, carpet to ceiling with bookshelves. We all love a good paperback. Well, me and my ma still do.

'Jesus Christ,' I cry, letting myself in. 'Do you really need to whack the central heating up this high?'

'Sorry, love, it's been on all day,' my ma says, swallowed up into my dad's old armchair, the telly blurring.

'All day?' I bend down to pick up the mail.

'Oh, calm down, will you? Go and put the kettle on.'

During the week, I clean my ma's house, make her tea, watch *The Chase* with her. I make sure the mobile hairdresser comes to set her hair. Thursday's usually corned beef hash, but I just swung by the Asda to get a couple of microwave cottage pies. I'm picking up my brand-new BMW in an hour. I'll have to give *The Chase* a miss and hope the excitement of my win isn't too much for her. She's got a chronic irregular heartbeat.

'There's no catch,' the producer had said.

God, I keep replaying those words over and over. Commercial radio stations are a bitch for pulling pranks on their listeners. How can I be so sure that this competition is legit? What happens if there's no car wrapped in a red ribbon for me to take home? I should prepare myself for another phone call in the morning, Connie and Carl laughing their arses off, informing me that I'm the biggest joke on Merseyside.

'Ethel brought some Jaffa Cakes round,' my ma says. 'Put them on a plate, love.'

I strip off my fleece and head into the kitchen. Clothes remain damp in the washing machine, a bowl with the dregs of soggy cereal sits in the sink. The bills, held up against the fridge by a novelty selection of magnets, are in the wrong place for me to ignore. Debts. My ma's run up a fair few since my dad died, not quite registering the way a credit card likes to work, to bite you in the backside. She's still paying for birthday pressies for our Emma's kids years after they've outgrown them, but she's too delicate to know, to be told. So, I take care of it. I glance at the mail: bills, more bills, and a postcard from Florida.

'What you reading at the mo?' I ask, placing a cup of tea and a plate of Jaffa Cakes on the little side table next to my dad's armchair. 'Anything decent?'

'It's upstairs on the bed, the name of it escapes me. Something about a family buying an old farmhouse in Scotland. The mother's gonna have it off with the recluse who lives on the other side of the loch. Obvious. Bloody good, though.'

I turn the heating down and perch on the arm of the settee, eat a Jaffa Cake whole.

'How's the Gene Wilder one going, love?'

'Great. He was really into the craft of acting.'

'You're the spit of your dad, loving all them real-life stories. I prefer the made-up ones.'

I wonder if my sisters are still passionate about reading. Their faces look directly at me from the wall – Lisa drenched in white lace at her Holy Communion, Emma's senior school portrait, the shoulder pads of her blazer shrinking her head to the size of a pea. And how they both look now, Christ. I haven't seen either of them in person since our dad's funeral. After their cruise-ship days, they settled in Florida and set up a dance school, the promise of a stateside get-together still in the pipeline. I bloody hate this shrine to them, their American teeth and blow-dried hair a lifetime away from the Scouse girls they once were.

Which reminds me.

'A postcard came today,' I say.

'Ooh, go and get it then, soft lad!'

My ma holds the postcard an inch away from her face, squinting, then after studying the sketch of Mickey Mouse holding a pumpkin, turns it around to read our Emma's writing.

'She says, "Tell Jim I've emailed him photos of the kids in their Halloween costumes".'

I never check my emails. My phone's data package is useless and I don't own a laptop. In fact, I only recently got Wi-Fi in my flat so I can watch Netflix, an outgoing which I know I can do without, but it feels worth it.

My ma's doing a little hmm. Hmm. Hmm.

'They don't half mention Jesus a lot in these postcards,' she says.

'You did bring us up Catholic,' I point out.

'Yes, I know, but since when did any of you talk about Jesus willingly? I had to bribe you all with a bag of cola pips to get your backsides to mass.'

A strong whiff of floral body spray floats into the room, paired with a voice that makes nails on a chalkboard sound like Mozart. I nearly fall off the edge of the settee. A large woman lingers at the bottom of the stairs.

'You're out of toilet roll,' Ethel Barton announces.

'Bloody hell, Ethel, where did you sneak in from?' I ask.

'Well, where else does your mother keep her toilet roll?'

For a woman turning eighty-four, she's made of the sort of steel that comes from surviving the Home Front as a child. My ma, a decade younger, wilts in comparison.

'Now, are you bringing your mother to our Yvonne's sixtieth tomorrow night?' Ethel enquires. 'Or do I need to pick her up? It's at the club, we've got a buffet and everything.'

'She's never sixty,' my ma pipes up. 'You wouldn't think she was a day over forty. Not a wrinkle or a grey hair in sight. And I'll get a taxi, thank you. Don't be ferrying me around. Jim goes the Pacific Arms with his mates on a Friday, don't you, love?'

'Still living life in the fast lane, Jim?' Ethel huffs.

Going the pub for three or four pints is hardly the fast lane, is it? During my uni days, yeah, I partied hard, blew my student loan and did soft things like shave my eyebrows off, but God, that feels like a bloody lifetime ago.

'Although you do look smart today,' Ethel says, heaving towards the table to pinch another Jaffa Cake. 'In that pullover.'

'It's me uniform.'

'Well, it suits you. I only ever see you in those t-shirts with the daft slogans on them.'

'Bands . . . they're not slogans, they're bands.'

'You're not a teenager, Jim. You're thirty-five,' Ethel exclaims.

'Thirty-three,' my ma corrects her.

'How's your job going? You've managed to hold this one down, haven't you?'

'Eight years,' I confirm.

'Still, we all had higher hopes for you than a toll booth,' Ethel says, mid munch.

My eyes wander up towards the framed photo of me in my cap and gown, hanging on the wall above the telly. My ma's looking at it, too. What a day. On the steps of Liverpool's Anglican Cathedral, my dad wearing his only suit, the shirt having been ironed twice that morning, his burly arm around my ma's slender shoulders. She wore a polka-dot dress and red lipstick, black shoes with little white bows on the toes. Such a bold outfit for a woman who's always chosen the shadows over the sun. 'First in the family to get a degree,' my dad had sung, gloating, as we all emerged from the ceremony.

'It's a shame you're not coming to our Yvonne's sixtieth, you know,' Ethel says, sucking the melted Jaffa Cake chocolate off her fingers. 'Our Yvonne's niece is about your age, unattached, works for the Civil Service. I mean, you'd be very handsome if you got your hair trimmed. You would, you know.'

'Oh, leave him alone, Ethel,' my ma sighs.

'There's lots of nice girls who work in the Asda, you know,' Ethel goes on, talking to me but looking directly at my ma. Then she looks outwards, as if addressing an audience much grander than two. 'They all know me in there, you know. They know I get your mother's bits and bobs for her, you know. They ask how I find the time to do me own shopping, you know. They really do. They're nice girls, Jim. They are, you know.'

'I know,' I say.

'He knows,' my ma says. Christ, she looks shattered next to Ethel's booming energy. Her dark greying hair is damp and fragile, her effort of mascara smudged below her eyes.

'But aren't all your mates married? Settled?' Ethel asks, taking one of her shoes off, followed by the other, cracking her toes.

'Settled,' I say, 'is when you have an argument with someone, and you find a way to reconcile. Or, if a problem arises, you resolve it. So, no, me mates aren't settled. One's married, two've got kids. I reckon that's the very opposite of settled.'

Ethel scoffs.

'Too clever for his own good, this one, isn't he?' she says.

I flick the standing lamp on, draw the curtains.

'Right, I need to get going,' I say. 'I'll speak to you later, Mam.'

'Everything alright, love?'

'Everything's boss. I just need to nip home, get changed for the bonfire—'

'He's got a date!' Ethel butts in.

'Not exactly . . .'

'Oh, that means he's definitely got a date.'

I rub my eyes, scratch my head. Maybe I do need a haircut.

'I had three children by the time I was your age,' Ethel

tells me, wagging her bloody finger in my face. 'In fact, it's borderline selfish that you haven't given your mother some grandkids who live on this side of the Atlantic. Three children, I had. Three.'

'There's two cottage pies in the freezer,' I say, kissing my ma on the cheek. Then she gives me a look – you know, the sort that only mothers seem to master – that suggests – no, tells me – to kiss Ethel, too. For an easier life, I grit my teeth, oblige. Ethel pretends to get all flustered and fans herself with the sudoku puzzle book lying on the settee, calling me a tease.

'Wish your Yvonne a happy birthday from me,' I say, opening the door.

'She doesn't look a day over forty,' my ma reiterates. 'I mean it.'

Cold drizzle hits me. I welcome its bite and zip up my fleece, my feet picking up a fast pace. I'm going to collect my prize. My golden chalice. It's like being thirteen again and beating Snowy on the Sega. Christ, it's better than that. I haven't been excited about anything for so long that I've forgotten how to be excited. Doubt's a fucker. It clouds my every right to be dancing on the moon, but let's be honest, it protects me too. Still, I was told I've won a car. This is Christmas morning, this is my twenty-first again, this is an ice-cold cocktail whilst lying on a beach somewhere in the Bahamas. This is my turn.

I'm halfway down the street when I hear my name being yelled. Ethel's standing on the step of my ma's house, waving her arms.

'Go and get us a four pack of toilet roll from the Asda, will you? It'll only take you five minutes if you run. Hurry.'

5

Zara

'You have reached your destination,' the satnav announces.

It's nothing like I've imagined. I double check the address, and yes, this pleasant but dull suburban close is Clifton Crescent. Nick's front door is in my view, third house along. Butterflies dance in my stomach. I know he'll be there because he works from home. Plus his car is in the driveway. He's sent me many selfies from that exact vehicle, recorded himself singing Queen songs to me from the driver's seat as he rested his phone on the dashboard.

'But it's a house,' I mutter. Not an apartment.

On my phone, I find the screenshot I took of Nick's address below his email signature; Nicholas Consultancy, The Loft, 6 Clifton Crescent. Well, this is it. And it's big, for a British house. Semi-detached with its own garage, the roof extension, which of course must be Nick's office, clearly in view. Why had I thought he lived in an apartment? Hadn't he told me that? A long front lawn spreads beneath a large bay window, well kept with a neatly trimmed hedge and a miniature wishing well. The front door has a cute plaque that says 'Welcome to the Mad House'.

I adjust the rear-view mirror and give myself a check.

No smudged eyeliner, no goop in the corners of my eyes. Good. I grab my make-up bag and top up my lip gloss, a peachy pink. My scar is still more prominent than my long nose, the first damn thing I see whenever I catch a glimpse of my reflection. But that doesn't matter. If anyone can see past that scar, it's Nick Gregory.

Oh my God. I can't deal with the fact that I'm here. I'm actually here!

I'm too excited to move. I want to relish every little detail. It's like the moment where you receive a beautiful gift wrapped with a bow: although you can't wait to open it, you also want to savour it as a mysterious box.

It's bang on four o'clock; starting to go dark. How is the day almost over before it's even begun? Mind you, it's already eight o'clock in Dubai. What would I be doing if I was there, instead of here? Thursday nights are the start of the weekend. Restaurants are filling up, taxis difficult to hail, the traffic moving slowly around Mall of the Emirates. A twinkle of party-time dancing in the air. Not for me, though. Not anymore. I'd be curled up in my PJs by now, watching *Grey's Anatomy*, waiting for Nick to call me on Skype. Nine-ish was usual for us on Thursdays; five-ish for him in Liverpool.

I take out my phone. I've got three messages from Nick.

It's almost Fri-yay!

I hate it when he says Fri-yay.

Haha, I know you love it when I say that.

Haha.

So, what you up to today? And how was camping? I miss you xxx.

Thrilling. That's what this is; absolutely thrilling. Nick thinks this is just a regular day for me, four thousand miles away from him, and yet here I am, outside his house. Everything we have talked about for months is about to start. Now.

I type my reply.

Hey, hey! Camping – meh! Sorry I've been off the radar. Phone issues. Boring! I miss you too xxx.

Agh. He's read it already. And he's typing.

'Come on!' I sing out loud, psyching myself up. 'Let's do this.'

I open the door and get out of my little hatchback. Pushing the driver seat forward, I lean into the back seat and grab my army jacket; authentic – apparently – US Army, with badges that have seen better days sewn along the sleeves; I love it. It's a fond reminder of hopping from festival to festival with an awesome group of people a couple of years ago, partying in green field after green field after green, muddy field. We covered quite a distance, from Suffolk to Budapest, although it kind of rolls into one. Shame we've all lost touch. I slip the army jacket on over my denim pinafore and grey t-shirt, patterned with silver stars. I've thought about my outfit carefully. And yes, I'm a bit cheesy, but really, the stars are aligning.

I open the trunk, slide the mop out. Everything else can

remain inside the car for now. The mop and I are the same height, neither likely to be described as tall. The bow tie has fallen into the boot, so I fix it back around the edge where the handle is visible below the mop's head. I place a pair of cheap aviators into the mop's ropey hair.

'Hey, you,' I grin. 'Shall we?'

And throwing my shoulders back, I march up Nick's garden path, past the wishing well, and ring the doorbell. The mop stands beside me, proud, like a centurion's spear. How totally British this house is; the bricks, the grey and white painted door frame, the stained glass patterned panels. I take a deep breath, my future about to become my present.

A little girl with tatty braids and wide blue eyes answers the door.

'Oh, hello!' I say, startled.

Another even littler girl hangs off the bigger one's legs. Both are dressed in sparkly tutus over what looks like bottle-green school uniforms, tiaras hanging out of their messy hair. They look from me to the mop and back to me again.

'Hey kids,' I smile, aware of the shake in my voice. 'Is Nick here?'

'Mummy!' the littlest one yells. 'Is Nick here?'

The older girl just continues to stare.

'Who's Nick?' the little one asks.

'Mummy' appears, throwing a towel over her shoulder. A navy-blue baggy tracksuit hangs off her curves. With black shiny hair cut into a short bob, her baby pink lips curl beneath a neat button nose.

'Nick doesn't live here,' she says, clear, with an air of confidence, unless it's her accent that gives that effect. She looks down at her little girls and pushes out her bottom lip, pulling a perplexed face which makes them giggle.

'I'm so sorry,' I say, checking out the house number again, scanning Clifton Crescent. 'My mistake, I guess.'

'Yep. Your mistake,' the woman says.

'Her mistake,' the littlest one says.

Turning to my domestic pal, I give the mop an awkward smile and catching my reflection in the aviator lenses, I feel my face flush. I'm totally lingering on a stranger's doorstep, and there's nowhere to go other than back to my crappy car to readdress the situation. Maybe the satnav's directions were wrong. The wishing well didn't feel very *Nick*. There might be many Clifton Crescents on the outskirts of Liverpool. All it takes is one wrong letter to make one big error.

'Come on, girls,' the woman says, and ushers them inside. 'It's Thursday, which means?'

'Egg and chips at Nana's house!' the girls cheer, jumping up and down.

'Let's go and get ready then.'

'Sorry . . . bye!' I say, but the door slams shut.

Except, wait. This car, here beside me on the driveway, it's just *like* Nick's car. But, God, what do I know about cars? If it's got four wheels and a roof, it's the same as the next car with four wheels and a roof. I take in my surroundings. There are three, four, five cars all parked on driveways in this close that are kind of similar. Totally similar. Well, practically identical.

I back away. The sign, 'Welcome to the Mad House', is making me feel most unwelcome. The gravel stones on the path are noisy beneath my suede sneakers. I just want to disappear; my whole presence feels so unnecessary, so misplaced, outside this neat yet bland house. The older of the little girls is at the front window now, watching me and the mop. She hadn't spoken, but her eyes are wide, inquisitive. She waves, and I instantly feel like less of an intruder. I return the wave and mouth, 'Sorry,' again, pulling a funny face that says *silly me*. The little girl smiles, her big teeth wonky, not quite the right fit for her small mouth yet.

The mop slips back into its place in the trunk, poking into the passenger seat via the car's interior, and I open the driver's door, wondering what my next move should be. I've got no reason to look back; it's the wrong house. But, without intention, I do it anyway.

And there he is.

Standing upstairs, peering from behind the curtains of the front bedroom.

I blink, my heart pulsating, and I stop dead, frozen between an open car door and the driver's seat. It's definitely him. His round, thick shoulders, that cream knitted sweater he wears whenever he feels the cold working in his roof office. His hair, styled specifically to look slightly messy on top.

'Nick?' I whisper.

Except Nick doesn't live there. So who is that man?

6

Jim

'Just sign here, here and here.'

I'm trying to pay attention, but there's a massive distraction in my way.

A brand-new BMW M3.

A five door, nineteen-inch alloys, three litre turbo engine, high-performance saloon. The interior is fitted with black leather racing seats, a nine-speaker sound system, built-in satnav; the dashboard's made from black carbon fibre and chrome. The seats are heated.

The producer tosses me the keys.

'It's all yours. Congrats.'

I climb into my car. *My* gleaming white car. The soft heated seat engulfs my body and I take my fleece off, chucking it onto the back seat, feeling the sheer comfort of the leather close to my skin. The powerful rev of the engine is euphoric.

Driving away from the studio's underground car park,

the producer's scowl gets smaller and smaller in my rear-view mirror. I focus on the road ahead like I've never focused before. No traffic signal can be ignored, no other driver taken for granted.

Cruising down the Dock road, I turn up side streets and drive in circles, bringing myself back onto the Dock road again. Tunes blast from the speakers: Daft Punk; The Doors; a bit of Bowie. I swing by my flat above Wong's chippy, park around the corner and run like the wind to get changed, throwing on the first t-shirt and jeans I lay my hands on. Getting back inside my car is like receiving a huge hug; I can't bloody believe it. I run my fingertips over the interior features, the music pumping. It's not that far to Snowy's. I'm going to cruise, take my own sweet time.

Twenty grand. Derek Higgins reckons that's what I'll get if I sell it. How much will it cost to take my ma to Florida to see my sisters? Does she even have a passport? I do, but it's never been used. Neither of us have ever been abroad.

Actually, with twenty grand, I could work for free for a while, become an intern. It wouldn't be irresponsible of me to do that with twenty grand in the bank, would it? Even at my age? Like taking a step back to go forward, starting over again.

After my degree, I got a job in the mailroom at a publishing company, home to a whole host of local lifestyle magazines. My plan was to start by sorting letters and move into writing features, maybe even become editor. Only, a problem swamped me: competing with those who could afford to work for free. Thanks to their smug faces, any chance of escaping stamps and pigeonholes was as likely as me finding a golden ticket in an invoice. I wasn't like them, you see. The way I was brought up, you worked to earn, even if it meant a pittance, and I wasn't going to suck up anyone's arse for free whilst scrounging off my hardworking family. So, even when I arrived early and stayed late, just to make contact with the editors, I was dismissed like an opened, redundant envelope. I was the mailroom fella. Why would they give me a shot? So I thought fuck it. And quit.

'But, you've got a degree, son,' my dad had said.

'A lot of people have degrees, Dad.'

'You got a First.'

'It doesn't mean I'm qualified for much, though.'

'But surely it qualifies you for something?'

'And I'll find something soon, Dad. Promise.'

Oh, Dad. I'm sorry. Salty, hot tears well up, but I blink them away, swallowing hard.

Fireworks are beginning to explode across the city. From the comfort of my driver's seat, I watch as mini rockets dart through the sky, whistling, fizzling. Even if I keep the car, this is still a new start for me, isn't it? I mean, driving to work every day in this awesome beast would at least get the day off to a bloody great start.

I turn into Snowy's road, crawl up beside his house, put the handbrake on. God. Even *that* feels good.

'It's yours?' Snowy's hands are plastered to his neat black hair. He loves new stuff. Trainers, tablets, the latest smart telly. Situated in a new-build development, his whole house is a show home minus the plastic fruit. He gets a new car on a lease every two years, but not one in this sort of league.

'It's mine.'

'So, you're saying you gave two birds in town your phone number and now suddenly you're the owner of this fucking beauty?'

'You couldn't write it, mate.'

'You fluky bastard.'

Circling my prize, Snowy's jaw is so far dropped that his usual smiley, squinting face is unrecognisable. He runs his index finger across the bonnet.

'She's exquisite,' he says.

'Quite. I just can't believe I've got me own wheels,' I say. 'For years, I've sat stationary, watching everyone else driving, going through the tunnel, wondering where they're going . . . and now, I'm going somewhere.'

Snowy laughs. 'You're a deep fucker, mate,' he says.

'And you, Brian Walsh, are blessed with the intellectual capacity of a jellyfish.'

'What you got against jellyfish, eh?'

'Oh, I didn't say they don't play a sophisticated role in the ecosystem.'

'Okay, you've lost me now. As per usual. And I need a drink. Got some tins on ice in our new freezer.'

'Can't drink, lad.' I jangle my keys, dangling them like a carrot. 'I'm driving.'

We snigger, before pushing each other back and forth, the odd mock punch thrown in, until we both hug unashamedly. Neither of us has a brother, but that's okay, we've got each other.

'It couldn't have happened to a better fella, mate,' Snowy says, his grip still tight.

'Cheers.'

'I mean it, Jimbo. If anyone else pulled up outside me house having won a dream car for doing absolutely fuck all, I'd be fuming, mate. I'd wanna rip their smug head off and feed it to the dog. But, you. You, Jimbo. I'm over the moon for you. I am. Truly. What did your ma say?'

41

'Haven't told her yet.'

'This is boss. Just so . . . *boss*. Fucking hell, mate, you're making me cry here.'

I don't admit that I nearly cried earlier. It's different for Snowy, who blubbers often and always quite comfortably has, and who's now blowing his nose on a fresh, clean handkerchief from his shirt pocket.

'You soppy get,' I say.

'Fuck you. Anyway, why don't you leave the car here tonight? Get smashed.'

'Nah, I'm off work tomorrow. Doing the Sunday shift instead. Double time.'

'All the more reason to get smashed, then. What's wrong with you? You pregnant?'

'Look, I don't wanna waste me day in bed hungover.'

'Ah, yeah. It really sucks to be you,' Snowy chuckles, pulling a stupid face. 'I mean, you're a boss drunk. A riot. But you're a fucking bastard with a hangover.'

'Fuck off.'

'Ah, you're the worst, mate. The worst! You act like someone's done a massive shit in your head and you're all like, "oh, woe is me," and then the next minute you're like the monster coming over the hill, a scary motherfucker.'

'We're getting old. Can't handle it anymore.'

'Speak for yourself, I'm always fine the next day.'

'You're a one in a million, lad.'

'I know I am. Now, come on, Jimbo. Let's get inside. The burgers should be done.'

'Who has a barbecue in November?'

'It's bonfire night.'

'It's fucking freezing, mate.'

'It's an indoor barbecue.'

'Oh, so you mean you're grilling burgers and sausages inside? That's not a barbecue.'

'Ooh, did someone lose his sense of humour whilst driving a BMW?'

'Have you got onion rings?'

'Ha!' Snowy laughs. 'Have we got onion rings? We've not only got onion rings, but we've got corn on the cob, spicy chicken drumsticks, garlic bread – with cheese – and for those who think they're too posh for a burger, we have hummus.'

Any excuse for a party, Snowy has it. Even as the dad of three-year-old twins, there's always a reason for some sort of shindig. These days, the occasion gets tweaked to suit the kids, until they conk out, and then old-school partying begins. You see, Snowy used to be a tour manager, gigging all over the world, until fatherhood forced him to pack it in. He doesn't half crave that lifestyle, though, and loves to drag us along.

The twins and a bunch of local kids are sat, crossed arms and cross-legged, on the patio in the back garden, wrapped up in coats, hats and scarves like Christmas pressies. Us lot, the grown-ups, stand around, all waiting for the firework display to kick off. A couple of older kids clamber onto the roof of Snowy's new shed for a better view.

'If anybody dares to touch the fairy lights, there'll be no hot dogs,' Snowy announces.

'And if you cross the line, there'll be no fireworks,' Mikey adds, indicating the imaginary line with his arms. He's a high school music teacher now, and my God, he loves to use *that* teacher voice. Although it doesn't take him long to sneak through the house and admire my new car. I follow him.

He whistles, sizing it up. Then, he looks at me and back to the car again.

'You'll get fifty for this, Jimbo,' Mikey says, sipping his drink. 'But, don't drive it anywhere. If you're selling it, sell it now. Once you hit a hundred miles, its value'll drop to about forty-five.'

Hold on. What the . . . What the actual? Fifty. Grand. What the fuck?

Now, I'm never sure whether Mikey knows what he's talking about or if he's a complete bullshitter. Still wearing his school 'uniform', Dumbo flying across his tie and his striped shirt tight around the middle, Mikey's rarely seen without a glass of whiskey in one hand, a ciggie in the other.

'I was gonna get meself one of these,' Mikey continues. 'But the missus was giving me grief. Said it wasn't right for the kids. What did she expect me to do? Ring Noddy, see if he's selling his little red and yellow car? I said to her, I don't think your spray tan's right for the kids, but I just got more grief. You're a lucky man, Jimbo. A bachelor with a bimmer.'

'Rolls off the tongue, doesn't it?' I say.

Mikey loves to bitch about his family, but Christ, he'd be lost without them. The only married one in the gang, his wife is Victoria and likes to be called Tori. They had one of those massive weddings in a castle in Ireland and are still paying the bill seven years on. His two young girls – ballet obsessed, gymnastics obsessed – put a few extra lines on Mikey's forehead, but they still manage an all-inclusive family holiday twice a year. I'd swap my life with Mikey's in a heartbeat.

'You want my advice?' Mikey asks, pausing long enough for me to blink. 'Don't sell it. Don't give this baby away to anyone. You drive this around and you'll have a bird in no time. A classy bird, too. I mean, my Tori's classy, but she's got a dirty mouth. Gets it from her ma.'

'Mate. It's not exactly me life goal to get a girlfriend who only wants me for me wheels.'

'Well, what is your life goal?'

Good question.

BANG! Red and blue fizz above our heads into white glittering droplets. *Oohs* and *ahhs* echo from the back garden. I look at my car, then back at Mikey.

'How'd it go with Tori's mate?' he asks, and sticks his tongue between his teeth like a right sleaze. 'Tapas, eh?'

Shit. I was hoping Mikey had forgotten about that. He leans back, resting against the BMW. I kind of wish he wouldn't.

'She was nice,' I say, putting a strong downward inflection on the 'nice', a way to bring this chat to an end before it begins. 'Where's Griffo tonight?'

'Working. But, don't change the subject, gis a bit more juice than that. Come on, what happened after the patatas bravas? Did you double dip in the garlic sauce? She's been after you for ages, according to Tori. What's her name again . . . ?'

'Rebecca – well, Becca – I presume her full name's Rebecca.'

'So, not much talking then? All action?'

'No, Mikey. Leave it.'

'Such a prude.'

But I'm not a prude. You know what I am? I'm embarrassed. Yeah, I went on a date with Tori's mate, but we didn't go to the new tapas place for a meal. We just went there for a drink. It was all I could afford and as much as I fully support equality, I can't let a girl pay for anything on a first date. Look, I know I'm old-fashioned in that sense, but so what? It's how I was brought up.

'Seeing her again?' Mikey probes.

'Nope.'

Mikey pushes himself off the BMW, tutting.

'I suppose she wasn't "The One",' he says, making inverted commas with his fingers whilst still holding his glass and ciggie. 'You're so hard to please, Jimbo. Yeah, you've got the whole sexy look going on, but who you holding out for? Salma fucking Hayek?'

'Nah, she's too old.'

'Ha. Well, I hope you let Little Miss Becca down nicely. We don't want another girl in Liverpool crying herself to sleep over Jimbo Glover, do we?'

I hadn't needed to let Becca down nicely. I'm not soft. The way she sipped that Rioja when I told her what I did for a living, well, let's just say I'm glad she didn't choke. Girls like Becca want a fella with their own desk. Not one they share with other toll-booth workers. To throw her a lifeline, I told her I still lived with my ma. A white lie, but the final nail in the coffin.

'You have a seriously warped opinion of me, don't you, Mikey?'

'Let's go and get a top up,' Mikey says, rattling the ice around his empty glass.

Inside, passed out on the pastel-pink sofa in the lounge, are Snowy's twins, still in their warm coats and woolly hats, the CBeebies bedtime story glowing from the telly. Snowy gets the tequila out. I decline. God, I feel so boring. And guilty. Guilty for all the times I laughed at the designated driver or rolled my eyes at how dull people were for bringing their car. At least Snowy had raised a good point. I won't have to cope with a rotten hangover tomorrow.

Something as cold as ice clasps the palm of my hand.

'Looks like you need some sort of pick-me-up?' It's Helen, Snowy's girlfriend, one hand holding a bottle of opened prosecco, the other holding mine.

She's not dressed for a cold bonfire night. Her tight jeans are ripped at the knees, a loose Oasis t-shirt hangs off one shoulder revealing a red bra strap. Long, thick, red locks bounce over her other shoulder.

'I'm not drinking, Hel—'

'Ah, shut it, Jimbo. We ALL know you're not drinking; you're DRIVING. Show off.'

Her lips, a little smeared, match her lingerie with shocking power, but the rest of her face is fresh, clear, rosy. Helen has flawless skin. Snowy and Mikey are stumbling by the breakfast bar trying to force the contents of a tequila bottle into a giant water pistol.

'I feel like I'm standing in a zoo, looking at all the animals behind the bars,' I say.

'That's why I NEVER drive,' Helen says.

'Didn't know you could drive.'

'There's a lot you don't know about me, Jimbo.'

I sip my Coke, like a loser. 'No way, Hels. I know everything about you. Twenty-two years, you can learn a lot about someone in that time.'

'Fuck me, Jimbo. Is that how long we've known each other?'

'Yep. Since Year Seven.'

'Year Seven was TWENTY-TWO years ago?'

'Do the maths, Hels.'

'I was shit at maths. God! I still *feel* twenty-two.'

'Well, if it's any consolation, you look about twenty-three.'

Helen lifts the bottle of prosecco and swigs. 'Charmer.'

'On a good day, I mean. On a bad day, I reckon you look about twenty-eight.'

Her hand is still in mine.

'Come with me,' she says.

No. I tug my hand away and shove it into my jeans pocket.

I'm not going anywhere with Helen. With a few drinks down me, yeah, I always follow her, listen to her. She bloody loves an antisocial one-on-one. But it feels very different tonight. The blend of bright kitchen lights and my being fully aware of everyone in the room makes slipping away awkward. And as innocent as it is, being sober doesn't hand me an excuse.

A squirt of liquid hits me between the eyes. Snowy's got the tequila gun in his hand, killing himself laughing. He throws his head back, aims for his own mouth and shoots a blast of tequila down his throat, then turns the gun back on me as his target.

'Mikey said you blew Becca off,' Snowy shouts over the music.

Helen playfully hits my shoulder.

'Who's Becca?' she asks.

'No one,' I say.

Snowy squirts me again, this time getting me right in the eye.

'Ah, pack it in, mate!'

'Not "The One"?' Snowy mocks, which pisses me off.

Mikey snatches the gun and gives himself a shot, followed by a whoop.

'The One, or not The One, *that* is the question,' he says, and shoots Snowy.

Helen puts the bottle of prosecco on the table and walks off, heading into the lounge to check on the twins. I watch as she removes their coats, holding their little limbs like delicate china. The boy, Rocco, turns his body into the sofa and curls up tight, determined to slip right back into the deep sleep that his mum's just disturbed him from. Helen bends her knees and sweeps the girl, Maisie, up into her arms.

Just before she reaches the stairs, Helen's eyes catch mine. So, I creep into the lounge, take Rocco in my arms and follow her.

In Year Seven, because our surnames both began with G, I had to sit next to Helen Gladstone for all lessons except music. It took me until Year Nine to ask her to go out with me.

Helen was my first kiss. According to Helen, I was her second. We went to the pictures every Saturday night until we were old enough to start trying to get into pubs. Helen's mum called me the son she never had. My dad loved her. She even came to Rhyl with us every summer. It took Helen a whole year to let me touch her boobs, then, on the eve of our final GCSE exam, we lost our virginity to each other in Helen's dad's shed. Helen left school and went to college to do nursing. I stayed on to do my A Levels. During my first year at uni, we were careless and Helen fell pregnant. She wanted an abortion.

Neither of us ever said out loud that our relationship was over.

We didn't need to.

And now, Helen and Snowy's gorgeous little twins are conked out, with me and Helen tucking them into bed, together, as friends.

'We need a bigger house,' Helen whispers. 'These two can't share forever.'

'You've only just moved in,' I whisper back.

Helen slouches down into a bean bag. The twins' room is spacious, maybe because the furniture is so small. A gentle lamp with a soft blue bulb calms the room, making me sleepy. It's only about seven o'clock.

Tapping the bean bag, Helen invites me to sit beside her.

'Remember when we used to think Fleetwood Mac followed us around?' she mouths, a hint of sound escaping her red lips.

'They did.' I smile.

'Everywhere we went, one of their songs was playing.'

'That random pub in Southport.'

'Exactly.'

Simultaneously, we both whisper the lyrics of 'You Can Go Your Own Way'.

'I wish we hadn't,' Helen says, bringing her knees up to her chest.

'What?'

'Gone our own way.'

I let out a small laugh, and Helen follows, cringing at herself.

'Sssh,' she says. 'I'm being serious.'

'You're pissed, Hels.'

'Patronising.'

Maisie begins to stir. I hold out my hand, gesturing Helen to stay sitting as I drag myself up, placing my hand on Maisie's tummy. I've seen Helen do this numerous times. Snuggling further into her bunny, she settles. Raven haired, just like her dad, Maisie's a real-life little Snow White, whereas Rocco's got his mum's fiery hair and freckles.

'Don't be sad, Hels,' I whisper. 'You've got a gorgeous family here.'

Helen replies with a sigh.

'Come on, Helen. Get up. Let's join the party.'

'I chose the wrong man, Jimbo.'

'No, you didn't. Don't be a drama queen. You didn't choose anyone, it wasn't like that.'

'You're saying I had no choice?'

'I'm saying you didn't have to choose. It wasn't like me and Snowy were about to duel and you swanned over to decide who you wanted. Me and you were kids, Helen. You and Snowy happened years later. A lifetime later.'

'He doesn't understand me, doesn't give me what I need.'

'He makes you laugh.'

'He makes everyone laugh.'

'I'm going downstairs.'

I'm already by the door, tired from whispering, when I feel Helen's breath on my neck.

'I don't love him, Jim.'

'Well, I'm sorry for you. I am. But it's not my problem.'

She twists my shoulders, forcing me to turn to her, face to face.

'It is your problem.'

'Since when?'

'Do you remember the last time we slept together? Before I got pregnant with the twins?'

'It was long before that, and you know it.'

'So, you *do* remember our last time?'

'Stop it.'

But, she stretches onto her tip toes and kisses me. It's so soft, so entirely familiar, that, shit, I allow it to happen. My arms naturally wrap around her waist, one hand reaching to the small of her back. The fruity, acidic taste of her tongue is strong, making me all too aware of how sober I am.

Maisie wakes again, this time calling for her mummy.

Breaking away, Helen doesn't hesitate in going to her girl. I get out, head straight to the bathroom, lock the door and splash my face with cold water. I rest on the edge of the bath, plastic crabs and seahorses in a rainbow of bright colours stuck to its sides. Pressing my palms into my eyes, I rock forward, my hair falling across my face, annoying me, itching me.

What a mess.

Today was supposed to be a good day; the best – the start of something new.

I know she offers it on a bloody plate sometimes and Christ, it's getting tiresome, but how could I let myself kiss Helen? And while she's drunk?

That's what scum do.

I flush the toilet and open the door to be met on the landing by Snowy, toothy grinned, thrusting his hips to the beat of the music coming from downstairs.

'Mate,' Snowy cries, unaware of his kids trying to sleep. 'I'm buzzin'.'

'Keep your voice down, will you?' Helen emerges from the twins' bedroom.

Snowy keeps thrusting and shimmies his way towards his girlfriend, circling her whilst pulling that face kids do when they're told off for being 'silly'. I can't help but find him funny, my bonkers best mate, and even Helen plays with her hair and cackles.

'I'm buzzin',' Snowy repeats. 'But, I'm also bursting. See ya later alligators!' And he plants a loud kiss onto Helen's cheek, not forgetting to slap her on the bum before disappearing into the bathroom.

'Let's just get the fuck downstairs,' I say.

'Agreed,' Helen says.

At the bottom of the stairs, swigging a bottle of Perrier water and admiring a set of three framed Jack Vettriano prints, is Griffo's dad. Griffo's dad doesn't drink alcohol, despite having a fully functioning bar in his house: draft, premium spirits, the lot. I've never asked him why he doesn't drink. He's not the sort of man you ask questions of.

'Alright, our James.' He nods.

There's always a light on when it comes to Griffo's dad, never a moment when he switches off, looks caught unaware. His name's Richard. But I don't call him by his name because I once overheard him say to someone, 'You don't get to call me Richard. You don't get to call me anything. Got that?' The way he spoke was sinister, his teeth gritted, his lips doing all the talking. So, although I've known him since I was a kid, he's always just Griffo's dad.

'Hey,' I manage.

'Popular these, aren't they?' Griffo's dad says, nodding at the frames.

I shrug. Well, I know Helen loves them.

Griffo's dad places a strong arm around my shoulders, his pumped muscles encasing me like giant bubble wrap. Christ, I always feel like such a scruff-bag beside this man. My old t-shirt, printed with a fading camper van, is creased and noticeably poked with holes next to his Ralph Lauren polo shirt, his smart suit jacket tailored to perfection. Although I washed my hair yesterday, I'm aware of its stench in comparison to the shining shaved head beaming beside me, expensive aftershave thickening the air between us.

'The lads tell me you've got yourself some wheels,' Griffo's dad says.

'Some random stroke of luck . . .'

'Well, you gonna show me or what?'

And it seems Mikey wasn't bullshitting about the value of my car. According to Griffo's dad, it's actually worth fifty-four thousand quid. The sound of the numbers spoken out loud knocks the breath out of my body. I'm fucking shivering, although I feel hot, clammy.

'Depends when and how you want to sell it, though, James. Your problem's getting that sort of money for it when a buyer could just go and pick their own straight from a car showroom. Then again, you might get lucky, might find someone who'd rather deal with the seller direct. You got lucky once, why can't you get lucky again? That's my outlook anyway.'

Griffo's dad gives my shoulder a small squeeze.

'The more you drive it, the more it'll lose its value. Just bear that in mind, James.'

'I need to take me ma for a spin. At least.'

'Of course you do. I'm just giving you advice, lad.'

Advice isn't all he gives me either.

Griffo's dad offers me fifty grand in cash if he can buy the car tomorrow.

'Cash?!'

'I only deal in cash.'

'Deal.'

We shake hands, although fuck, I'm shaking all over. I feel my phone vibrate once and take it out of my pocket. No, it's not my ma. It's just a text, thank God, from Helen.

Jim. I'm so so sorry about b4. Don't know what I was thinking. H xx

Oh Christ, Griffo's dad's still talking to me, going through the terms of our deal, making sure neither party is unhappy with the offer on the table. I'm trying so hard to listen to what he's suggesting, but all I can hear is *fifty grand, fifty grand, fifty grand, fifty grand* . . .

'You don't want any dickheads scratching the doors 'cause they've nothing better to do,' Griffo's dad says. 'And you want that whole fifty, don't you?'

I swallow, nod.

'Now look, Jim. I'm not saying you live in a shit hole—'

'I do live in a shit hole.'

'Stay in a hotel tonight. A good one. Valet park the car. You can afford it.'

'Bloody hell. I can, can't I? Well, I can tomorrow.'

'We made a deal. You can afford it tonight,' Griffo's dad winks. 'And enjoy it.'

His Perrier bottle empty, Griffo's dad rejoins the indoor barbecue and I feel my phone vibrate again.

Sorry I do know what I was thinking but didn't explain right. Sorry. H xx

Then, again.

Let me explain . . . U went ur way I went mine (FLEETWOOD MAC!!!!!!!!!!!!) I honestly honestly thought we were 2 different. I thought u were gonna move on and get some high flying job. I never thought ud stay here!!!!! U wer 2 clever 4 someone like me. Lifes so unpredictable

Christ, Helen. I can't be doing with this drama, not tonight. I get inside my car, decide to go and surprise my ma. This party isn't doing me any good right now and I need to be on the ball tomorrow to meet Griffo's dad. I've not even started the engine when my phone goes nuts, buzzing.

Sorry!!!! Pressed send by accident. I know we've talked

about all this b4 but I'm so miserable and so confused. I love the person Snowy is. But I'm not IN LOVE with him. U told me I went after him 4 an excitin life. U were right. I did. I thought I'd get 2 c the world and go on all those world tours with him. How stupid. I never got 2 go anywhere. I should've just stayed with u. H xx

Judging by the fact u haven't replied I'll just say SORRY 4 bein a soppy drunk. H xx

Forget all I said. Let's pretend the kiss was 4 old times sake haha. H xx

7

Zara

At least I have my own room, even if it is in a hostel.

Once I left Clifton Crescent, I screamed as I drove, completely bawling my fucking eyes out. Well, wouldn't you? It's not like anybody can hear you when you're driving down busy roads, trucks overtaking you, tyres crashing through rain puddles. I just kept driving, onwards, onwards. When I came to crossroads or junctions, I turned whatever way I felt, mostly right. Just because. I had nowhere to go, no place to find.

I mean, I'm at a hostel now. In downtown Liverpool. When I realised I'd driven myself in a huge circle, I pulled over outside a high school, all closed up for the day, not a student in sight. I checked my phone, praying for a message, a missed call, an explanation. Nothing. Nick wasn't even online. He's always online. I bashed the steering wheel over and over, and not because I'd seen that in movies. It was a solid, genuine kneejerk reaction to stopping and not having any reason to get out. If I'd been in a house, I probably would have thrown something against a wall, to feel it hit, to hear it break. I howled, my head resting on the wheel. Then I blew my nose, wiped my face with my fingertips. I had to create a plan. Nobody can drive around the suburbs in circles forever.

I looked for hotels on the satnav and followed the routes. Five hotels, I tried. Five. All of them were either fully booked or extortionate. It's a busy time, apparently, so the various hotel staff kept telling me. There's a big football game on this weekend and Kylie is playing some venue called the Echo Arena tonight. But I don't know anybody in this city other than Nick and I needed a bed. I needed to stop, reset, breathe. And God, I needed to get out of that fucking Peugeot. So, the satnav finally led me to this hostel.

'I never want to be on my own,' I say quietly, opening my purse, digging out my card.

'No problem,' the young girl behind the desk says, monotone, scrolling through her phone with one hand. A sign on the wall behind her says *Ask _____ for help*, the name *Ida* scribbled into the blank space with a marker pen. Ida – presumably – is petite, but in a different way to me; a shirt buttoned all the way up to the top, an undercut in her hair, not a trace of make-up on her gaunt, freckled face. 'You want a bed in a shared dorm?'

'God, no!' I cry, horrified.

Ida, who speaks with a Scandinavian lilt, seems to be taking a selfie, pulling a blank, serious expression from behind thick, square spectacles.

'But, you never want to be on your own?' she asks, gazing at her own image.

'I was thinking out loud. I didn't want to be on my own *tonight.*'

'Okay . . .'

'I mean, I wasn't supposed to be on my own. And it sucks.'

'Well, like I suggested, you can have a bed in a shared—'

'No way, I'll be thirty-one next month.'

'Whoa . . .' Ida puts down her phone. 'That does suck.'

'Thanks.'

We stare each other out. Ida, clearly at ease with this. Me, pretty freaked.

'Do you have parking?' I ask.

Ida clicks away at the mouse, yawning into the computer screen behind the desk. Then, she stretches her arms up high and yawns again, a loud, satisfying noise accompanying the whole motion.

'Sorry, what did you say?' she asks.

'About parking. My car's outside and I don't think I'm supposed to be parked there.'

'No.'

'No, what?'

'No, you can't park there.'

'So, where can I park?'

'Don't know. I don't drive.'

Well, this is just great. Just. Great. All of my material belongings are packed into that car like badly stacked Tetris blocks – ALL of them – except for my ski wear which currently resides at my papa's villa in Dubai. Every shoe, every earring, every trinket is right here. My coffee mug decorated with a pink and silver 'Z'. A small collection of Trolls from my teen years. My yoga mat. Two bottles of Shiraz which I should be drinking right now, in celebration. A brand new A3 sketch-book, tucked between the layers of my clothes.

And, of course, the mop.

'Are you okay?' Ida asks. The concern in her voice, on a scale of one to ten, zero.

'No, not really.'

'Room fifty-two. Fifth floor.' Ida slams a chunky key ring on the desk. 'Oh, and I forgot to mention, the lift's broke.'

Snatching my room key, I shuffle out of the hostel. I'll just have to grab my overnight essentials once I find a legal place to park. The cold feels bitter between the fine rain and wind sneaking around the city's cobbled side streets. Fighting tears against the miserable night air I smooth down my hair, for – what a surprise – it's finally starting to frizz.

I climb behind the wheel of the Peugeot and drive in circles, circles and hey, more goddamn circles. A multi-storey parking lot close to what looks like the shopping district will have to do. About a fucking mile away. I park up.

'Tonight wasn't supposed to be like this,' I say out loud as I open up my suitcase, aware that I look like a mad woman. But there's nobody to see. My voice echoes around the empty lot. I know I shouldn't, but I look at my phone. I've got two emails and one Whatsapp. I open the latter. It's from Katie.

Are ya there yet? Followed by an emoji of a plane.

I can't possibly reply to that right now.

The emails are junk, irrelevant.

Wrapping my army jacket close around my body, I head back to the hostel with my toothbrush, clean underwear and a stripy shirt for beneath my denim pinafore tomorrow, all stuffed into my canvas tote bag. In the distance, bangs echo through the sky. I'm reminded of Dubai where hardly a week goes by without some sort of firework spectacle. The walk is slightly uphill, past a host of pubs, packed to the brim with what looks like a mixture of students and regulars, karaoke blaring from behind the steamed-up windows. Groups of students are huddled inside the various bars, all wearing their coats and drinking pints. Earlier today, I would have seen these people as potential friends, or classmates, my application to study here in Liverpool still in process. Now, they're just loud and in my face, a blatant reminder of the path I'll no longer go down.

If Nick didn't live there, then who did?

It was him . . . It was . . . with another woman. And two kids.

Halfway up the bustling street, I see a church ahead, lit with colourful floodlights and lasers. As I approach, I notice that not only is the church missing a roof, but the inside is hollow, shrubs and greenery growing around its frame. How utterly spectacular! If only I had my sketchbook with me. I'd love to capture this moment, even with a few strokes of a pencil. Sure, it's raining, but the raindrops could add character, give the sketch some extra life. But no. It's locked up in that multi-storey parking lot with the rest of my things.

Anyway, I won't even have any use for the stupid sketchbook. Not now. Not after what happened this afternoon at Clifton Crescent.

I think of those little girls.

They both looked like their mom; almost like three sisters. I'm *all* father, something which definitely disappointed my mom from the word go. Today, the younger girl was a bundle of chaos and cuteness, but the older girl, she seemed – I don't know – sad? Okay, maybe not sad, but tense. I was about her age when my parents finally called it a day. We were living in Singapore then. I'd just settled into school. I sometimes think about the friends I made, wonder if I'd still be friends with them now if social media had been around back then. Would I know the names of their kids? See what they wore on their wedding day? Perhaps been invited to some of those weddings? Or would they just be names that 'like' a photo now and again, or wish me a *Happy Birthday, hon!*?

By the time I arrive back at the hostel, my whole body feels battered, bruised with exhaustion. I know it's not actually possible for a human heart to break, a lightning crack down its centre, but it's the only way I can describe the feeling in my chest, beside my lungs, trapped behind my ribcage. It hurts. It really fucking hurts.

The room itself isn't too bad, though. Pine desk with a matching chair, a clean sink and mirror, a single bed with fresh folded sheets. Folded. Oh, God. I've got to make my own bed.

I pick up the white bed sheet, hard and crisp, and shake it open.

No. I'm just too tired.

There's nothing I want to do right now. And I mean it. Nothing.

So, I flop down onto the bare mattress, not even pausing to remove my army jacket or my suede sneakers, damp with the splashes from the outdoor puddles. The sheet's creases are harsh, lines as sharp as rulers, but I cuddle it against me. It can act as a giant tissue.

I haven't cried over a guy like this, ever.

Sure, I cried over Zein (I know – Zein and Zara – believe me, that's as cute as it got). Another lifelong expat, he was a first-class engineering graduate and we were on and off for years; usually on when we were both in Dubai. When he suggested a ski weekend in Beirut, I'd just been offered a promo job and couldn't say no to the money. I mean, if I wasn't paying my papa back for the wasted tuition fees after I dropped out of university, I would've gone. Except, I was. Paying my papa back. And, guess what? Zein fell in love on the slopes of Mzaar.

Fate. They're married now and have a son. I've always told myself that was beautiful because if it happened to Zein, it will happen to me. It happens to all of us.

But I've been single – well, 'dating' – ever since.

I check my phone.

Nick is online. Oh my God, he's online. And yet he hasn't messaged me. Did he see me? God, of course he saw me. Unless he's blind, something else he might have miraculously forgotten to mention along with the whole house and the whole wife and the two whole fucking children. I can't help myself. I type.

What happened today? Send.

I wait for the tick. The two ticks. They don't turn blue. He hasn't seen it. He's no longer online. He'll reply as soon as he sees it, though. I know he will. His head can't handle leaving it until later. He's the most efficient replier since the internet began. Nobody replies more quickly than Nick Gregory. You'd think he had nothing better to do. Oh, we've joked about it a million times over. It's one of our things.

Come on.

Where are you?

I hold my phone close to my chest, too afraid to check again and yet not ready to let go. I think of the mop in the Peugeot. Oh, what a fool I am.

I wish I hadn't left those bottles of wine in my suitcases now.

I grab my purse, go down five flights of stairs and run past Ida. There's a store opposite and I buy their finest bottle of screw-top red. Five pounds ninety-nine. Back in my hostel room, I turn the lamp on, but there's no bulb inside. The main light will have to do. Well, it's either that or total darkness. Besides, I've unscrewed the bottle. This isn't a party. I swig as the harsh light beams down on me, like the sun when you're desperate to find shade. I swig some more. The wine is tart, dry, coating my teeth and landing in the pit of my empty stomach with a heavy splosh.

In the corridor, I can hear Spanish voices, fast talking, full of song.

My sobs grow thicker and slower, until I'm so drowned in disappointment that I drop my phone and, thankfully, fall into a deep, deep sleep.

8

Jim

Pulling up in front of next door's house, just to throw my ma off a little, I decide not to use my set of spare keys and ring the doorbell instead.

'M'lady,' I say, mocking some sort of posh accent. 'Your carriage awaits.'

My ma wraps her baggy cardigan across her body and rolls her eyes. 'You been drinking? Get in, you daft sod.'

'Nope. I haven't been drinking and I'm not coming in.'

'Y'what?'

'You, m'lady, are coming out.'

'Get in, soft lad. And what's all this "m'lady" stuff? Get in, I'm freezing.'

'Go on, go upstairs and put on your best frock.'

'It's gone eight o'clock. I'm watching *Corrie*.'

'Bloody hell, Mother! I'm taking you out.'

'Out? Why?'

'I've got a taxi waiting,' I fib. 'He's waiting on the corner.'

'You serious?'

'Best frock. Now. The spotty one you wore for me graduation.'

'I'll never squeeze into that.'

'The jumper with the sparkly stuff—'

'That's me Christmas top.'

'Well, it hasn't got Father bloody Christmas on it, has it?'

'No.'

'Go!'

The front door slams in my face and I return to my car, grinning. Closing my eyes, I imagine Griffo's dad handing me a briefcase filled with notes wrapped in wads of a hundred quid. A strong handshake. Like in a film. What the hell am I going to do with it all? After pouring the lot into an empty bath tub – of course – and climbing inside; smelling it, crunching it, flicking it into the air?

Fifty. Grand.

My phone vibrates again. I know who it'll be.

I rally shouldn't mix me dunks. I do love Snowy. He's the bather of my kids. H xx

Maybe I'll bugger off to South East Asia for a few months. That's where people go, isn't it? Angkor Wat and war museums, partying in giant donuts floating along the Mekong? Or is thirty-three a bit too old for all that? Will I look like that loser who still hasn't found his way? Around nineteen-year-olds, cocksure they've found theirs?

Ah, shit.

I feel soooooooo guilty. I really move Snowy. He's a good man. H xx

Christ's sake. I'm just going to keep ignoring her. Helen's lucky to be with Snowy. They've always had my blessing.

Through the rear-view mirror, I see my ma coming, the street lamps reflecting off the sequins on her top. Good, her handbag is hung over her arm. Her pills will be in there. Sitting on her shoulders is her red anorak, slung around her like a cape.

I jump out, opening the passenger door for her, and bow. She gives me an impatient slap across my head and bends over to peer inside the car, looking for a driver perhaps, before standing up straight again. A rocket squeals, bangs pattering out low in the sky above us.

'What's going on, Jim?'

'I'm gonna tell you everything.'

'Oh, Jesus.'

'No need for any "Oh, Jesus"; this is a genuine surprise. But if we stand out here all night, we might be struck dead by a firework and we'll miss our chance. Get in, I'll explain everything.'

I gently help her lower herself in before settling myself behind the wheel.

'Oh, love. What'll the neighbours think?'

I honk the horn – twice – and my poor ma jumps, a strange little yelp escaping her mouth. Off we drive. Sleepy streets lead towards a main road of struggling shops and many chippies, a pub on every corner. Rows of houses scattered amidst derelict warehouses, a disregarded part of the city that yearns for redevelopment. I feel bad calling this place a shit hole. It's where I grew up, where my dad and my ma did their best, where – despite the negative press and lack of aesthetics – I've always been safe, welcome.

'You're looking at the dashboard as if it's some sort of nuclear weapon,' I laugh.

My ma, the woman who always knows what to say, even at funerals, is silent. The racing seat swallows her and she sits back, her head pressed into the seat, eyes wide, frog-like, as if she's sat at the top of the Big One at Blackpool Pleasure Beach. I'm going twenty miles an hour and yet her knuckles are white, gripping onto her handbag.

'Tell me you didn't steal it,' she mutters. I notice she's wearing lipstick, a rosy pink that shimmers on her thin lips. 'Actually, if you did steal it, tell me the truth.'

I pull over, a little too sharply. We both jolt.

'Mam. You're sitting in this car with me. *Me*. Your son, James Anthony Glover.'

She shoots me a weary look.

'I've never stole anything in me life. You know that.'

Her eyes narrow. 'Is this something to do with Griffo's dad?'

Oh, bloody hell. It wasn't. But now it is.

Turning the ignition, I sigh. 'I'll take you home.'

'Don't do that.'

'Well, you don't seem to wanna let me indulge in surprising you, so . . .'

'Oh, don't be daft. Look at you sulking.'

'I'm not sulk—'

'You are. Your chin's gone all chubby and your lips are pouted.'

'Stop it.'

'Look, I'll shut up. I'll keep me big mouth zipped.'

'Nah, forget it.'

'I most certainly will not forget it.'

'Eh?'

'I want me surprise.'

68

'You do?'

'I do.'

'Oh, bloody hell.'

The tinkle of a piano sounds through the speakers. I turn up the volume and drive onwards. Elton John's voice serenades us and I catch a glimpse of my ma's face softening, her eyes closing into a smile.

'Ooh, I love this one,' she says, singing her own version of the words to 'Your Song'. 'Doesn't it remind you of our Emma's wedding?'

I smile. It does. The last time all five Glovers were together in one room, dancing, laughing, alive. The relief it had given my ma when our Emma had announced she would be getting married in Liverpool, bringing her American fella and his folks to her home city, was priceless. It made up for the holy shock of our Lisa eloping to Las bloody Vegas.

We turn onto the Dock road and as much as I want to put my foot down, feel the beauty of the power behind the rev, I remain as cautious as a learner, as sensible as an instructor. We cruise past the Liver Birds, then the Albert Dock floodlit beside the Wheel of Liverpool. Rockets sparkle across the sky, gentle bangs echoing from all around.

'Your dad would've loved this,' my ma says. 'He'll be looking down on us, leaning against them pearly gates, grinning from ear to ear. I can just see it.'

I try to see it, too, but to me, it's a scene from one of those biblical films from the Seventies, bellowing voices and beards, nothing that resembles something real, something true. I wonder how clear the images of my dad in heaven actually are to my ma, for although a lifelong Catholic, she doesn't believe in God. Or the church. Or even the Holy Communion she takes each Sunday morning when she goes along with

Ethel Barton and her daughter, Yvonne. She goes out of habit, of course, and pretends to believe out of guilt. She regularly admits to both.

'You hungry?' I ask.

'Hungry? It's almost me bedtime.'

'You don't fancy some supper?'

'You mean like tea and toast?'

The Titanic Hotel is one of the finest on Liverpool's waterfront, and highly recommended by Griffo's dad. An old rum warehouse in Stanley Dock shining with redbrick class, it has a vast, grand, and surprisingly cosy industrial feel. The lobby opens out into a spacious, thriving rum bar. Long wooden tables and modern hanging light fixtures surround us as we sit up on high brown leather bar stools.

'Are you sure you wanna sit here, Mam? There's a nice couch by the window.'

'I love sitting at the bar,' she says, her tiny feet dangling down, swinging. She's wearing her black shoes with the little white bows on the toes, the ones she bought for my graduation. 'I always used to make your dad sit on the high stools with me.'

'Ah. I didn't know that.'

'We did go on the odd date, you know. Once or twice, like.'

We order a cocktail each; I decide on a mai tai, my ma a pina colada. Melted ice dribbles onto my t-shirt and it strikes me how scruffy I must look right now. My knees are poking through the rips in my jeans.

'I mean, look at this place.' My ma lowers her voice. 'Who would've thought people'd pay to stay somewhere called the Titanic? And it's confusing 'cause it feels really posh, doesn't it? But it doesn't look anything like that ship that Jack and Rose fell in love on. It looks more like a warehouse.'

'That's because it is – well, it was – a warehouse.'

'Can you believe I'm drinking a pina colada?' she giggles. 'Wait 'til I tell our Lisa and our Emma about this. They're phoning home tomorrow night, you know. Isn't that marvellous?'

I raise my glass. 'Cheers.'

'Am I allowed to ask what this is all about yet, love?'

I give a little hum, teasing her. Then, I tell her the whole story. Starting with the phone call that morning in the toll booth to walking into the offices of Mersey Wave 103.4 to sign for my prize.

'They gave me a free bottle of water,' I add.

'You can get free water from the kitchen tap, love.'

'And then, there it was,' I say, holding my arm out as if the car's behind the bar. 'No red ribbon or anything like I imagined, but I can live with that.'

My ma looks into her pina colada, shrinking into the bar stool's wide leather back.

'I'm pleased for you,' she says, not sounding pleased at all. 'Just be careful.'

'I can drive. I've driven the bloody van every time Snowy's moved house.'

'I don't mean that. I mean be careful with your luck.'

'What do you mean?'

'Remember that woman who won the Pools? It brought her nothing but misery. And all those lottery winners in the paper, they go on about how winning was the worst thing that ever happened to them.'

Rubbish. My dad keeling over on the Dock road is the worst thing that's ever happened to me. Nobody more than my ma should know that.

'I'm gonna sell it,' I say. 'And take you to Florida.'

'What? America?'

'Well, what other Florida is there?'

'You can't do that.'

'I certainly can do that.'

She purses her lips, wafting away something invisible between us with one hand.

'No,' she says, but she's fighting back a smile.

'You've been desperate to go to Florida ever since they moved,' I say. 'Don't deny it.'

'And I'm not letting you waste your money on that. It's a bloody fortune.'

'It's not a waste. It's far from a waste. You'll get to meet your grandchildren.'

Her eyes are wet with tears, her voice shaky.

'But I have met them, love,' she says. 'I've met them on the internet, on the screen.'

It's just not in her nature to accept something so expensive, so big. Even when I buy her M&S bath sets for Christmas, she always demands to know why I bother, and instead of saying thank you, she tells me how she makes do with the stuff from the Asda perfectly well, the peach melba shower gel. But, really, she absolutely loves the M&S set.

'Well, you're gonna meet them in person,' I say. 'Get real hugs. *Real* ones.'

'I think I need a lie down. Will you take me home, love?'

'Well . . . I was gonna get you a nice posh room, so you could enjoy them massive hotel beds and soft pillows, get a cooked brekkie in the morning.'

'I've got soft pillows at home. And what am I gonna sleep in? This Christmas jumper?' she snaps, then places her hand on her heart. 'Oh, I'm sorry, love. But, I don't want you spending a penny of that money on your old mother tonight. I want you

72

to spend it on yourself, or a nice girl. That's what you should be doing. Not worrying about getting me a room on the bloody Titanic. You know I can only sleep in me own bed anyway.'

Yeah, I should've known that.

'Now, that's enough of getting all emotional for one night,' she says, straightening her Christmas jumper. 'Who the bloody hell do we think we are, eh? Getting carried away like that. Anyone'd think this was an episode of *Corrie*. You can't tell I've been crying, can you?'

I shake my head. No.

'Right. Good. Now, get me a taxi, please, love.'

'I can give you a lift,' I say, but she's already on her way through the lobby. 'I've got a car, remember?'

'You've had a drink.'

'Are you sure you don't wanna stay? I'd love to treat you.'

'You're taking me to Florida! Let's not go over all that again. And you got me a pina colada. Besides, I left me pills at home.'

I know she's not telling the truth, that they're in her handbag.

'I'll give you the cash for the taxi tomorrow,' I promise.

Rockets still squeal above and in the distance, a smoky ghost dancing across the city. I turn around and reenter the Titanic hotel. The barman asks me if I'd like a table this time. I agree and order a pint, the sharp sweetness of that mai tai still hanging on my tongue.

'Will anybody else be joining you?' the barman asks.

'Maybe,' I reply and take out my phone. There's a couple of girls' numbers, sure, but only ones that it hasn't worked out with and I haven't bothered deleting. Scrolling through my contacts, everybody I care about is at Snowy's party. They'll be shitfaced by now. And—

9

Zara

Outside the multi-storey parking lot this morning, the street is littered with carefree students and fried chicken takeaway boxes. I'm drained. Sure, I slept, but not soundly.

'You can't park there, love,' some guy announces.

I know I can't park *there*. And the way he calls me 'love' isn't affectionate, rather like 'shove'. I ignore him and re-jig my bits and pieces around my second- or possibly third-, fourth- or fifth-hand little Peugeot. I'm struggling to fit the mop across the back seat. I knocked it last night when I got my clean underwear out of a suitcase and it's poking me in the ribs as I try to drive. I need to get away. Today is a new day and all sorts of wonderful things might happen with the right attitude. For a start, Ida wasn't working this morning to give me a half-assed condescending look as I left the hostel.

'Did you hear me, love?'

I continue to struggle with the mop. Why can't I position it right?

'Yes, I heard you,' I say. 'I'm really sorry for ignoring you.'

'I just don't want the bizzies to catch you, that's all.'

'What's the "bizzies"?' I ask, trying to be friendly, dropping the mop again. The guy is drinking tea out of a polystyrene cup and dressed like he has just wandered off a building site.

'The police,' he says.

'The police?' I ask, trying a different angle. I knock my holdall with my knee and its zip splits open as it falls across the wet gutter, its contents spilling into the murky rain puddles. The guy watches as I scramble to retrieve the hair-dryer, a couple of my sketches, a pair of novelty spectacles. 'Why are they called the "bizzies"?'

'Dunno. Just something we say.'

'Must be a Liverpool thing,' I say, managing a smile. 'Like the way you all say "boss" if something is good.'

'You American?'

How did this damn mop ever fit inside this car? How? I don't understand. I flip it around, try again. The guy sips his tea and continues to watch me struggle.

'Not quite,' I answer. 'Sort of. I mean, I have an American passport.'

'Boss.'

'Is it?'

The guy blinks. Twice.

'Look, love,' he says. 'You need to get off them double yellows.'

'I'm going as fast as I can,' I yell. I didn't mean to yell.

The guy holds out his polystyrene cup. 'Hold this.'

Giving me a gentle but definite shove out of the way, he bends inside my car, opens the sunroof and positions the mop to poke out of the top. Then, he takes his tea back and walks away, not forgetting to wish me all the best.

Finally, I can get on my way.

I climb inside and turn the key. The satnav comes to life and I tap in Heathrow Airport. I've booked myself a flight back to Dubai because I can't figure out a better solution – I just know I have to get the hell out of Liverpool. Any other people I know in this country are just acquaintances, Facebook friends. So, it's a toss-up between going back to my papa's villa, or making the effort to go stateside to stay with my mom, and the latter is too much of a big deal. I'm in no great hurry, though. My flight doesn't leave until tonight, so I give the radio a try. Good, it works. I pull away from the hostel and start driving through the busy streets of Liverpool's city centre.

Nick never replied to my WhatsApp. He still hasn't read the message or been online, and I last checked five minutes ago. The harsh pain in my chest can only be released through tears, so fuck it, I let them come.

The radio crackles, this old banger of a car not equipped with much of a sound system. Elbow's 'One Day Like This' has just started, and oh, I love this song. The intense string section sets me off even more. I want to listen to it happy, exactly how I imagined I'd be today. I've spent the last six months living for today, never expecting to wake up in a backpacker's hostel all alone. I know I'm torturing myself with these thoughts, but I can't help it.

I'm not even paying attention to the satnav. I need to focus.

What was that?

Should I have turned?

Ah, great. Yeah, I should've turned off that complicated excuse for a roundabout. Except, hold on. Why can't I u-turn? Why? I'll have to take the next turning and come back around. The satnav is 'recalculating'. But, whoa, what's going on?

There is no turning. All that lies before me is a one-way trip into a huge tunnel.

'What the actual . . . ?!' I cry.

There's no going back. The tunnel swallows me whole and all I can do is put my foot down to keep up with the other drivers going forty miles per hour, which feels pretty fast in this crappy car. Elbow is replaced with awful fuzz.

'How long does this thing go on for?' I shout, banging the wheel.

It's not as if I can stop, get out, ask anyone.

Opening my mouth, I take a huge breath and hold it. Disappear.

I was six years old, sitting in the back seat of a yellow taxi. Sandwiched between my parents yelling at one another, passing blame like a game of ping pong. I made an excellent net.

We were edging into Manhattan, moving slowly, immersed in a long tunnel.

'Why can't I go back to work?' my mom cried. 'How is this fair?'

'You've no idea how good you've got it,' my papa told her.

'Your opinion, Samir. Not mine.'

'My opinion matters most.'

'Why?'

'Because it's practical.'

I decided to hold my breath. My theory was that if I didn't breathe, then I wouldn't be alive, which meant I wouldn't be there. I'd be invisible. And my parents could say what the hell they liked to each other and I'd never know, never be a part of it. I wouldn't be in their way, the root of all their problems.

78

'You're a fucking snail, Samir.'

'Don't use that sort of language. Not in front of your daughter.'

'She's your daughter, too.'

'And why am I a – what do you call it – snail? A snail? What ridiculous metaphor are you going to hit me with now? Seriously, April.'

'Ridiculous?'

'That imagination of yours is dangerous. It stops you from getting on with your duty.'

'My duty? As what? A wife? A mother?'

'Yes, April. My God, yes. Exactly that. This conversation is futile.'

My face was starting to pulsate. Would they notice if I went pop?

'You're a snail, and I'm the trail. Think about it, Samir. It's not ridiculous. It's accurate.'

My papa laughed and the tunnel came to a bright, sharp end. He nudged me, playfully, and it forced me to release, take a fresh breath, come back to life. Although I didn't like how I felt. I was hot, sweaty and I wanted to cry, but my papa was laughing and I didn't want him to stop. Laughter was so much nicer than shouting. My mom bent forwards and reached out her hand, touching the taxi driver's shoulder gently.

'Sorry you had to hear that,' she said to him.

'No problem,' the taxi driver said.

'A snail!' my papa gasped. 'Whatever next?'

And although my mom wasn't laughing with him, I do remember letting myself smile. I imagined my papa as this big grumpy snail, my mom a glittering trail dancing behind it. Maybe I was hiding inside the shell. I didn't know what 'ridiculous metaphors' were, but whatever they were, they were my favourite thing about my mom.

God, that awful fuzz. It shakes me back into the tunnel, forces me to breathe out.

I try turning the radio off. I can do without the unpleasant noise. But, the damn thing won't turn off. Is the button broken? Or am I pressing the wrong one, turning it up instead of down? A horn honks, startling the crap out of me.

'SHIT!'

The other car swerves close beside me, the passenger yelling a series of insults from behind the closed window. It doesn't take a genius to lip read, 'YOU CRAZY FUCKING BITCH!'

'I'm so sorry,' I yell back, but the other car speeds off.

The radio will just have to remain on. I sob again, possibly with guilt at almost causing a crash, or simply picking up where I left off a few moments earlier. Heartbroken. And this is so unlike me, which makes me even more annoyed. The eternal optimist, that's who I am. I love an uplifting quote, even if they are a bit five years ago now. Yesterday I posted, 'Be the reason someone smiles today'. It still got about thirty likes. Katie wasn't one of them.

'Oh, thank God,' I sigh, smiling and wiping my dripping nose with my sleeve.

There is light. Actual light at the end of the tunnel. And to top it off, Elbow has returned, still singing, the violins now in full force. It's either a particularly long song or the tunnel was much shorter than it seemed. But, neither matters. I'm out.

I drive into a queue of cars, all waiting to get through some sort of toll booths.

'Throw those curtains wide . . .' I sing.

My heart still feels so heavy, but it makes a difference to

sing, even if I do sound terrible. I tap the steering wheel, resisting the urge to break down all over again. There will be a sign towards the highway – well, motorway – soon, a way of getting back on track. I pay the tunnel fee and put my foot down. I approach a roundabout, continue straight.

'. . . ONE DAY LIKE THIS A YEAR'D SEE ME RIGHT . . .'

Yes, I'm starting to feel a little better, just a little. So, I sing louder, and for the shortest moment close my eyes, take a deep breath . . .

And FUCK.

I fly straight into the back of the car in front of me. Even the damn radio cuts out.

10

Jim

The plus side to waking up in a posh hotel with a head as heavy as a bowling ball is, without a doubt, the pillows. And the duvet. Just the crisp, white sheets in general. They all feel like delicate fairies kissing my abused body.

The down side is being woken up by the bedside phone ringing. And ringing. And ringing. Until I muster up the energy in my arm to reach over and answer.

'Mr Glover? Checkout was fifteen minutes ago. Please vacate the room or you will be charged another night's stay.'

Fuck. That means I've missed breakfast, too.

Grabbing a complimentary water, I swill my mouth to stop it from feeling like a dried-out raisin. I'm still dressed, which softens the blow of not having time to enjoy the walk-in shower. The thought of taking my clothes off to wash and then getting back into dirty clothes is exhausting.

How much did I drink? I can't remember getting into this room.

Reaching into my jeans pocket, I take out my phone. Dead. At least I'm off work today, but shit, this means I'll be spending my day off in absolute hangover hell. And, fuck! Oh, fuck, fuck, fuck. I'm meeting Griffo's dad at noon. What time is it now?

I scour the room. The sun shines brightly through the warehouse windows and creates a mirror across the bedside table clock. Squinting, I try to read the time, my eyesight blurring. I close one eye and focus with the other. No use. I swap eyes. Oh, bloody hell, I just want to know what time it is. Everything today is already very, very difficult and I've only been awake for five minutes. Snatching the remote, I manage to get the telly on.

Thank God for Sky News. It's twenty past eleven.

I'll just have to rock up at Griffo's dad's house like this. I could get a Big Mac on the way. Maybe stop off at the Asda and pick up a deodorant and some chewies. It's not as if Griffo's dad'll be shocked – or give a flying fuck – what state I arrive in. Our deal is all about the car.

The carpet beneath my feet is spongey. I enjoy the sensation, appreciating my last moments in this plush room.

Then, the room phone starts ringing again.

I pick up my socks and shoes, my fleece, my wallet, and dart out in my bare feet.

Even waiting for the lift is tiring. My forehead is attracted to the ground; my sinuses are not appreciating my movements. The lift doors open and I shuffle inside, the lights and mirrors over-friendly. I'm pleased to be alone.

Ding!

A couple waiting on the fourth floor join me.

'Jim,' the lady says. 'Morning.'

'Morning,' I say, wondering how the bloody hell she knows my name.

83

'Heavy head this morning?' the man asks.

I recognise his voice, his accent. Scottish. Alan. Alec?

Yeah, that's it. I was speaking to Alan/Alec and his wife last night in the rum bar. They're here in Liverpool for their silver wedding anniversary, doing the whole Beatles thing. I bought them a bottle of champagne and helped them drink it. They're both broad and loud, squeezing my personal space, causing my chest to ache. Rosy cheeks and tips of noses confirm they have hangovers too, but their cheeriness agitates me. I just want to get out.

'How did it go with the girls?' Alan/Alec asks, rubbing his hands together.

'Ooh, spill the beans, Jimmy,' his wife chuckles. She'd been calling me Jimmy; that part is coming back to me, too. Nobody's ever called me Jimmy before last night. 'Do tell.'

Tell. If only I could recall.

'Look at Jimmy's toes, Al,' she says, noticing my bare feet. 'He thinks he's Paul McCartney.'

Ding!

Ground floor.

And as the doors open, there they are.

Loose curls, bronze tans and all shades of denim, there's no mistaking the girls from Belfast here for a long hen weekend. I seem to recall there being more than only three of them, but maybe their charisma felt greater than three, or my vision duplicated them. Lounging by the reception desk, they spot me. And my bare feet. I can't work out if they're giggling or hissing. What did I do, besides buy them drinks? Hungover or not, I won't be the bastard to ignore them. I sit down on a strangely low designer chair, my thighs feeling tight, my back needing to crack, and put on my socks.

'Morning,' I smile. God, I'm fumbling. Doing two things at once is verging on impossible. 'Hope you had a good night?'

The three girls reply saying, 'Grand,' as if their voice boxes are made of ice.

A haze of events drill through my skull, rattling like a steam train. I play them over and over in my mind, like watching a bad-quality movie on VHS. There was singing, and L-plates, and the barman asking the girls to keep the noise down. It was cold, we were outside, smoking . . . I was smoking? Oh fuck. That explains my heavy chest, the fur on my teeth, and on her tongue . . . whose tongue? The L-plates . . . the bride-to-be . . . she was dragged away, laughing. Or crying. I bought her a drink, then another. She cried on my shoulder, literally. Did I chat football with the barman? Football? Me? I forgot my room number. I must've tried to guess it. Oh God. There were corridors, and walls, and at one point I was on my hands and knees crawling. Did I knock on someone's door? Oh, Holy fuck.

Those girls are definitely hissing.

At least they got free drinks out of me.

Through blurred vision, I check the hotel bill handed to me in a fancy card. The total to pay makes tequila-tasting vomit shoot up and hit the back of my throat. Swallowing, I have no choice but to hand over my trembling credit card. After what seems like hours of holding onto the edge of the reception desk in silence, five words ring in my ears.

'Your card has been declined.'

It takes a difficult surge of brain power to work out how to rectify this, but I manage. I ask if I can split the bill by paying with debit card and credit card, to which the answer is, 'Of course, sir.' Before relief can register, the words come back to haunt me with an extra tagged on at the end for free.

'Your card has been declined again.'

Various attempts are made at trying various amounts, until both cards work. Ninety-four quid is paid by debit, the heftier balance maxing out my credit card. One massive conclusion comes crashing down upon my heavy, heavy head; I am officially broke. What had I been thinking? Blowing such an obscene amount of money in just one night? Yeah, I'm sitting on the edge of fifty grand, but it's not in my hand – or my bank – yet.

I must be way over the limit. Yet driving feels acceptable because some amount of sleep has occurred between the bender and now. However, if the police pull me over . . .

It's almost noon. I'm going to have to swerve my Big Mac, which makes me want to weep. Griffo's dad lives on the Wirral next to a golf course, meaning that to get there, I have to pass through work; the Mersey Tunnel. God, I really need some sunnies. Even the darkest cloud in the sky is too bright for me today: my bed is calling my name; my curtains eager to be closed. How fantastic it'll be to wake up tomorrow, rested, sober and fifty grand in credit.

Elbow's 'One Day Like This' is playing on the radio. The urge comes over me to take a deep breath and sing. It distracts me from the stale alcohol fizzling along my veins, saves me from throwing up. My voice is huskier than usual, more effort required to get the notes and words out, but it feels good.

The entrance to the tunnel is fast approaching.

How strange to be doing this, driving my *own* car towards it, into it.

Immersed within the tunnel, the radio crackles, signal lost beneath the River Mersey. I stop singing and decide to concentrate. The darkness of the tunnel and its artificial lights are adding to the intensity of my hangover and I have to prepare myself for the daylight that'll hit me any moment.

Boom.

I glide towards the toll booth, the very one where I answered the unknown number yesterday morning. Gayle Freeman is on the booth. It's not until I throw my change into the bucket that she recognises me, her eyes and mouth resembling bright marbles in my rear-view mirror.

The Wirral seems sunnier than Liverpool. Patches of grass in the centre of the oncoming roundabout greener, tarmac smoother. Traffic is sparse, tranquility on the other side of the water. The radio signal is clear again, Elbow's serenade returning, their epic ending going on and on, sounding divine through the nine speakers.

'*THROW THOSE CURTAINS WI-IDE . . .*'

I approach the roundabout and cruise around it, another coming up ahead.

A silver people carrier whizzes past, coming so fast out of nowhere that I'm relieved to brake in time at the junction. Pangs of dehydration shoot through my skull. I want water – no, a Coke – so, so bad.

Then, just as I manoeuvre into first gear, I feel an outrageous force.

The shock jolts me forward and I stall. What the fuck?

My knees empty, a hollow sensation. Attempting to gather myself, I feel my palms become sweaty, yet my hands are cold, shaking. Adrenaline is shooting through my whole body, the panic pounding in my already aching head. It's cushioned by the sudden appearance of the inflatable airbag. I raise my eyes to glance in my rear-view mirror.

I can't work out the make of the car.

Small, perhaps a hatchback, maroon.

Some sort of wooden pole is sticking out of the sunroof and the whole bonnet is too close to the boot of my car. Far, far, far too fucking close. The driver is still inside, but the driver's head is planted down onto the steering wheel.

No. Please, please, NO!

I have crashed.

Just moments away from Griffo's dad's house.

PART TWO

11

Zara

I hear a crass swear word or two.

'What have I done?' I whisper to myself, repeating the words over and over.

I lift my head upright, open my eyes wide. A mist floats between where I'm sitting and the car in front. The driver's door is swung open and I realise the swearing must be coming from the driver himself.

Thank God he's alright.

'Are you hurt?' he asks, knocking on the windscreen.

'I don't think so.'

'What's your name, love?'

I wind down the window.

'Zara Khoury.' Why I give my whole name, I've no clue. If anything, I should have given a fake name.

'Zara? Can you feel your legs?'

'My legs?'

'Yeah, can you feel your legs?'

'Why?'

'I dunno.'

'Why are you asking me if I can feel my legs?'

'That's what they say, isn't it?'

'Who's they?'

'The paramedics.'

I can feel my legs. Unless I'm hallucinating? That's what happens in *Grey's Anatomy*, isn't it? The crash victim is lucid, talking, laughing, lucky to be alive. But the reality is the opposite; they are actually moments away from going into cardiac arrest, or the victim looks down and sees that her legs aren't even attached to her body any longer, they've been sliced off in the crash and are lying in the middle of the road.

No. I'm okay. Shaken, yes. But definitely okay.

The other driver is bending towards me, his arm through the open window as he reaches down and opens my door. I take a deep breath. This guy is being kind, he is rescuing me even though this is my mistake, my fault.

I know I should say sorry.

But I don't.

Why can't I just admit to being wrong, apologise and calmly try to sort this mess out like any other adult? I'm lucky. My Peugeot, already in a sorry state, doesn't look much worse than before the crash, but a collision like that could have easily sent me flying through the windscreen. A scar already sits beneath my right eye, burnt into my cheekbone, doesn't it? Worse things can happen than admitting to your mistakes.

'Give me your hand, love,' the guy says. What he's saying is helpful, but he doesn't sound helpful. His hand is reaching out to me. 'Come on. Zara? You need to get out of this car.'

'Why?' Of course I have to get out of the car.

''Cause it's dangerous.' He has a very strong Scouse accent, stronger than Nick's. Each word is meaty, full of flavour. 'And unless you can't move, Zara, and I need to somehow call an ambulance, then you need to get out in case – I dunno – the cars burst into flames or something.'

'*What?*'

I leap out of the car and run to the other side of the road, watching our smashed-up vehicles through splayed fingers. My car does not explode into flames. Nor does the guy's. I allow a moment to self-check. No pain. Good. The guy also seems completely unharmed. Pissed off, but unharmed.

'Christ, I thought you were seriously injured,' he says.

'I'm okay,' I manage.

He isn't coming near me; rather he's backing away. It's hard to make out how old he is, or what he really looks like, his brown shaggy hair masking his face as he sits down on the sidewalk a good distance away from me. His legs are long, his knees pointing to the sky like arrows through his ripped jeans. He's staring ahead at his car through strands of hair, motionless.

I really want to say sorry. I mean, this guy has fallen victim to my personal mess, hasn't he? I was unfocused, too emotional to be driving. I straighten up and decide to break the silence, to apologise.

But. Panic rises. Fear takes its hold.

'You slammed on your brakes,' I find myself saying, accusing. 'It wasn't my fault.'

'It was *your* fucking fault!' the guy cries out.

'No, it wasn't. It was an accident,' I attempt.

'So it was MY fault three seconds ago, but now it was an accident?'

'Don't speak to me like this. You don't know me.'

'No, I don't. Thank fuck.' The guy pauses, then spits. How appalling.

Then, he lifts his hand, his finger now pointing right at me, like the tip of a knife.

'And actually,' he scowls, 'I *do* know you.'

'What? How?'

'I know that you're the fucking idiot who smashed up me car.'

'You slammed on your brakes.'

'Girl. That's a lie. An outrageous lie.'

'I didn't see you.'

'How did you not see me? Are you gonna tell me you're blind now?'

'Don't be stupid.'

'I'm not stupid. I'm livid.'

'God, stop shouting!'

'I don't normally shout, you know. I never raise me voice.'

'Well, you're certainly raising it now.'

'I don't care.' And the guy releases some sort of feral howl, lifts his fist and punches it hard into his other hand, repeatedly. 'You've fucked everything up.'

'Like what?'

'Like none of your fucking business.'

I dare to smile. 'Don't worry. Your insurance will cover all this.'

'No. *Your* insurance will cover all this.'

'Your face is so red.'

'Is it?'

'Yes.'

'Good.'

'I've never had a *stranger* speak to me like this before,' I cry.

94

'Well, it must be fucking wonderful being you.'

'You're horrible. You're actually horrible.'

'No, *you're* horrible,' he snarls. 'For ruining . . . everything.'

'Please stop shouting. You're gonna lose your voice.'

The guy turns his back to me. 'I can't even look at you.'

'Why? Because I've made you late for some sort of lucrative business meeting?'

Well, that's shut him up. The guy falters, takes a step back.

'How did you know?' he asks, still unwilling to face me.

'The car.'

'What about the car?'

'Only flashy businessmen drive cars like yours.'

'Is that right?'

'Yeah,' I sigh. It's so obvious. 'And you're really scruffy.'

'Thanks.'

'You're welcome.'

A cold breeze circles around us and I fold my arms across my chest. The guy is scratching his shaggy head, perhaps impressed, or taken aback, by my sharp intuition. At least that's one thing I can be proud of.

'So how does me being scruffy make you think I'm a flashy businessman?' he asks. 'Don't I need a suit? A poncey briefcase?'

I tut, roll my eyes. 'No, they're fake businessmen.'

'Y'what?'

'The ones with the real money go to meetings in their scruff.' I start to walk towards him, but the guy flings out his arms signalling for me to keep my distance. 'They're the owners of the companies – or their dads are – which is most likely your scenario. Am I right?'

'Spot on.'

'You've got so much money you don't need to care about

95

your image. But you want to be seen driving an awesome car, because you can.'

He twists around to look me right in the eye. He has pale grey eyes, like unpolished diamonds. There's a flicker, a glint. 'You're some sort of expert in this field, are you?'

'I know a thing or two.' I shrug.

'Can you stop talking now?'

'Because I'm right?'

'Because you're giving me a fucking headache.'

I know a thing or two about businessmen. My papa is one.

The kind who wears the smart suit and carries the brief-case and always wants a better car: he's somebody else's bitch. He spends his time complaining about how many hours he's worked compared to the CEO who drives around in his BMW and never shows up on time to meetings; never dresses appropriately.

'Why don't you just quit?' I once asked. I was about sixteen. The newly shaped Khoury family were out eating dinner together – a rare event – whilst on a long weekend in Sri Lanka, a short flight away from our residence in Dubai.

'He can't quit, Zara-Baby,' Marina, my papa's wife, said.

No matter how many times I asked politely for the hyphenated 'Baby' to be dropped from my name, Marina, a six-foot-tall Russian blend of beauty and severity, chose to ignore me. So I just died a little inside every time I heard it. Thank God I didn't spend much time with Marina or I would've been fully dead by the time I was seventeen.

'He has responsibility. He has family now.'

'He's always had family,' I said.

I could never bring myself to think of Marina as my stepmom. Still can't. It's not because of anything tragic.

My own mom is alive and well, living in the States, busy painting watercolour landscapes of lighthouses and baking cookies. No, the real drama is more excruciating, more soap opera. Marina is only seven years older than me.

'Can't you just get another job, Papa?' I asked.

He sipped his beer, sucked on a marinated prawn.

'Zara-Baby, life is not easy,' Marina said, just as Sammy started to throw a tantrum. I stood up, on instinct wanting to take my baby brother into my arms, cuddle him and give him his bottle, sing the song about the dog called Bingo. But before I could get to him, my papa told me to sit back down and clicked at Lulu, our Filipino maid, who was eating dinner at the table behind us. Marina took Sammy from his high-chair, his chubby legs kicking away, and kissed his forehead before passing him to Lulu.

'Goodnight my precious Sammy-Baby,' Marina said.

'Night, Sammy Bear,' I said. 'Night, Lulu.'

'Listen, Zara,' my papa said, wiping his mouth with the napkin. 'You don't understand because you haven't had to work hard for anything. You're going to have to find a good man to marry who will take care of you. And if you don't manage that, what are you going to do?'

'I'll take care of myself.'

'How?'

'I'll get a job.'

'Doing what?'

'I'll try different things, see what makes me happy.'

'Wrong.'

'Okay, well, maybe I could illustrate books, you know, for kids?'

Marina laughed, sipped her wine.

'And I'd like to eat croissants and sit on the cobbles of

Montmartre writing my memoirs, but hey, I live in the real world,' my papa snapped. 'Zara, some people are born into money. Some have to work for it. Now, you might think you were born into money—'

'I don't.'

'Don't interrupt me. People like us, we have to work for it. The nice villa we live in, your school fees – and don't get me started on what it cost me to send you to that boarding school – it's my job that pays for all that. Without my job, what would you do?'

I could feel a mosquito tickling my ankle.

'Papa, I just meant that you always seem unhappy. You're on a plane more than you're at home, you work long hours, you hate your superiors. You're a smart guy, so why can't you get a different job? Something that makes you happier?'

'I told you, it pays for everything. End of conversation.'

A gentle breeze whistled through the balcony of the resort restaurant. I gulped my juice.

'Well, Marina could get a job,' I said. 'And that would pay for all her beauty treatments.'

'I have a baby to look after,' Marina laughed.

'No, you don't. Lulu looks after him.' I turned to my papa who was now using the napkin to dab his forehead. 'It's just a suggestion, Papa. But that would save you some money, wouldn't it?'

I was more than aware that I should have kept my mouth shut. Within moments, I was alone at the table, my papa and Marina choosing to go for a walk without me. I was told I could order dessert and put it on the room tab. Instead, I swigged the remaining dregs of my papa's beer, Marina's wine.

The next and final evening of the trip, our little Khoury family did not eat out together. Marina went to bed early with a headache. My papa met a colleague at a nearby resort for a business dinner. I sat with Lulu as Sammy slept in his cot, doodling on my homework and wondering if I would ever know where I belonged.

At thirty, almost thirty-one, years old, I still don't know where I belong. It certainly isn't on the approach of a roundabout somewhere in between towns in the north west of England with this scruffy guy and his pompous car.

We haven't spoken for a while.

I'm not good with arguments. They never fuel any sort of fire within me, just leave me feeling as though I want to break down into tears. But, I'm holding it together, perhaps still in shock at causing a crash, destroying this guy's car.

Yes, I did cause it. There's no escape from that.

It's time to own up, to get on with the inevitable.

Turning my head, I look across to the guy. Oh my God. He's quite literally shaking. He didn't seem like the type to cry, but what do I know? He looks on the verge of a melt-down. Maybe if he was short, overweight, a bit sweaty and spotty, I'd be more comfortable with him being upset, but this man is – in all honesty – handsome. Rugged, even. His clothes are a mess, and yet they hang off his body at all the right angles. I should stop gawping.

Plenty of cars have driven past since we crashed. All drove slowly around and went about their business, leaving the situation between me and this guy firmly between me and this guy.

Another car appears. It slows and the window winds down.

'Everything alright?' the woman asks me. The guy's still staring into the ground. 'Do you need any help?'

'We're fine,' I find myself saying. 'Thank you.'

The fewer people involved, the better. It's going to be a tiring ordeal as it is, having to take responsibility for this mess, no doubt pay for damages. I hate myself for contemplating asking my papa to help. I could call him, now. No. I absolutely will not ask my papa to help. I can fix this on my own.

'You sure?' the woman asks.

'We're fine,' the guy says. He gives a strange smile. Just one corner of his mouth moves, the other remains tight with anger. Then his head slowly drops back down and the car drives off.

Here we are, back to where we were.

I shiver. It's bitterly cold and my pathetic excuse for a coat is still on the passenger seat of the Peugeot. The north of this country is so damn bleak, way more than the south.

'Look, I'm sorry,' I say, walking towards the guy, offering my hand.

But, he doesn't accept, doesn't move.

'It *was* my fault,' I go on. 'Completely. I'm really sorry I tried to blame you. I could make an excuse for myself and say I was scared. I mean, I was. I am. Scared. But, it was so wrong to try and pin any blame on you. I drove into your car because I wasn't concentrating on the road ahead. In fact, I was crying. I had a terrible day yesterday . . . and then I tried to sing along with this stupid song on the radio because I thought it might make me feel better, because . . . well, I didn't want to feel alone in my car. How stupid is that? I thought that by singing – and crying – that I would somehow feel, well, not alone. Anyway, I'm sorry.'

The guy turns, looks at me. For a sharp moment, his gaze slips and falls upon my scar, silently asking – as most strangers do – *How did that happen?* Then, our eyes meet again. His, pale grey, have a tinge of blue; a contrast to my oversized brown ones. He doesn't quite have a beard, but there's more than just stubble, as if he always has the look of needing to shave.

'I'm sorry,' I say again.

'I guess we all make mistakes,' he says, a faint smile appearing from one side of his mouth, less strange than before. Quite pleasing, actually.

I hold out my hand. The guy takes a step closer, accepts.

'We should contact my insurance company,' I sigh. 'My phone's in the car, unless, could we use your phone? Sorry.'

He reaches into his pocket and pulls out his phone.

'Dead.'

I'll have to get my phone from my car, but as I inhale, my hand stays gripped to the guy's. Our eyes lock tight, and I can see a red rawness surrounding his, so I squeeze his hand further. As if the wind has just changed, my heartbeat picks up its pace.

The guy tries to pull away, but I keep my grip.

'Say something else,' I say.

'Y'what?'

'Say something else. Keep talking. What's your name?'

'Jim. Why?'

'Keep talking.'

'Let go of me hand!'

A realisation dawns on me. I release Jim's hand and pull away.

'Jim?' I say. 'You're drunk.'

I know too many guys like Jim.

Of course this Jim guy has been drink-driving. With a flashy car like that, wow, he must believe he's invincible. No harm could ever touch darling Jim, could it? If Jim wants to get all boozed up and spin his wheels, let him. Jim makes up his own rules.

Like every other fucker.

I don't want to look at Jim a moment longer. But, I have to hold his gaze. I have to win this one.

'I'm not drunk.'

'You are. You're wasted. I feel like I've just inhaled an entire shot of whiskey.'

'Look, love. I'm not drunk. I'm just a bit hungover.'

'A bit hungover? Oh, come on. And after I apologised like that. It *was* your fault. You slammed on your brakes.'

'Don't start all this again.'

'I'm calling the police.'

'And tell them what? A drunk guy reversed into your car at a quiet junction?'

'Awesome idea, yes. I think I'll say exactly that.'

Jim's eyes shrink, hatred boring through his pupils. His pale skin must squeal at the sort of sun I'm used to, thousands and thousands of miles away from this spot of tarmac. The bitter air between us hangs still.

'You know what?' Jim says, breaking the silence. 'Go 'ead. Phone the bizzies.'

And he bends over, catching his hands on his knees, and bows his head. I wonder whether he's going to be sick, but there's no retching, no coughing. Instead, just a man defeated. He's admitting his mistake, taking responsibility. How noble. Giving him a hug suddenly feels like the most natural thing to do. I edge closer, reach out my hand and hover it over his back.

'Please,' he says, his head still low. 'Let's just get this over with. I'm done.'

I'm done.

What does he mean, he's done?

Then again, there's no point in trying to work out the

logic of a drunk person. Perhaps he, too, had a bad night. Probably lost a heap of cash at some casino. Or maybe his wife has kicked him out. He's not wearing a wedding ring.

Focus, Zara.

I turn my attention to the small mountain of mess so carelessly thrown into the smashed-up little Peugeot. How am I going to get all of that stuff back to Heathrow without a car?

I could dump the mop. That would help.

No.

I open the driver's door and slip into the seat. Turning the key, I try to start the engine, but it cuts out, again and again. I honk the horn by accident, then lay my head onto the wheel, a dead weight.

'What the hell are you doing?' Jim flings my door open and grabs my arms, ripping the strap of my denim pinafore, dragging me out. He starts yelling something about the dangers of trying to start a vehicle in the state it's in. 'One minute you wanna get me done for drink driving and now you wanna fuck off and pretend nothing's happened? You're a mental case. Of all people on this earth I could've had a car crash with . . . Jesus Christ!'

'Please stop shouting.'

'I'm not shouting.'

'You are!'

And something unexpected occurs. Jim laughs. His whole face looks so different when he cracks a smile; less pale. I catch onto his infectious tickle and here we are, together, laughing until I get a stitch and Jim chokes, coughing up part of what he describes as a 'hangover'. We sigh, long and hard, my high pitch against his low. I pull my stripy top over my hands and wipe my cheeks, dirty mascara marks smudging the white cuffs. I remember the rip in my pinafore and touch it.

'Sorry about that . . .' Jim points to the rip.

'It's okay. I've got a little sewing kit somewhere in one of my bags.'

'And a broomstick,' Jim adds, looking at the sunroof.

'It's a mop.'

'I won't ask.'

'Good.'

A passing stranger might even believe we're friends.

'Jim,' I say. 'I know you've had a shock, so have I. The crash was frightening, horrible, and I wouldn't wish this situation upon my worst enemy. Not that I have a habit of making enemies, and if I do, I don't ever mean to. But, what I'm trying to say is, Jim, I need you to give me some money.'

'Y'what?'

It's the perfect solution. Jim's recklessness caused the crash and I don't have time to waste sorting out my car. I'll just leave it right here, pile all of my belongings into a taxi and get to London. Courtesy of Jim. Then Jim can get on with his day however he wants. Buy a new car. Whatever.

'I can't take all that stuff on a bus or a train, it's too much. I'll have to take a taxi.'

'And you're expecting *me* to pay?'

I nod.

'And you're just gonna abandon your car and do a runner?'

'Guess so.'

'That's illegal.'

'I'm leaving the country. What does it matter?'

My plan had been to just dump the car at the airport, deal with any minor consequences of that another time, another day.

'I haven't got any cash on me,' Jim says, reaching into his pockets.

'Come on. Would you honestly rather I get the police involved? Tell them you've been drink driving?'

Jim growls and tugs at his hair. He takes a step back and looks at his BMW, walking the length of it and back again. With caution, he inspects the trunk, hovering his fingertips over the damage. Then, he bends down to look at the wheels. He repeats the same on the other side. Then he sits himself behind the wheel. What is he doing?

'Come back,' I cry, 'or I'll have to call the police.'

Jim starts the engine and an aggressive crunch emanates as metal separates from metal. Now all I can do is wait for him to leave me behind.

Not the most unfamiliar sensation.

Like that time I missed the boat back to Dubrovnik. I was the only single friend amongst couples, and at the harbor, I realised I'd left my backpack by the rocks where we'd all set up camp for the day. Thinking I had time, I ran back. The boat left without me and I had to pay an unimpressed guard a small fortune to take me back on a speedboat. The other couples thought it was so cute, *so Zara*. I thought they'd just left me behind. Then there was the whole family thing. My mom getting that new husband, and of course, that new daughter. And my papa getting that new wife, who gave him what he'd always wanted. That son. That takes being left behind to a whole new level.

And now, in Liverpool, the rain feels like vicious ice chips, spitting upon my frizzing head. I fish out my army jacket, not that it provides me with much warmth.

Jim is sitting, stationary, revving away.

Leaning against the undamaged trunk of my otherwise

wrecked car, I scroll through the numbers on my phone. There must be someone I know who can help me out. Or is calling the police my only option? What would I say to them? 'Oh, a drunk guy ahead of me halted and I drove into him . . .'

Papa.

My finger lingers over his number. Other than transfer a loan into my account, what could my papa do aside from be disappointed in me? On the other hand, I don't even have an overdraft. What will happen when I reach zero? Perhaps a bit of extra emergency cash from my papa wouldn't be such a bad thing.

When I was a kid, he made me pay for snacks from the kitchen cupboard with my pocket money. 'You can't always get what you want for nothing,' he would say as I handed over a few coins from my little beaded zip purse in exchange for a bag of Cheetos.

No. I cannot ask him.

Self-loathing rises in me, and I begin writing a text. I use different language for every contact in my phone; some get *xxxxx* at the end, some get a crude one liner that displays friendship more than a string of hearts. I can swap numbers with a new buddy in a bar and get the messaging banter perfect the next day. Yet, having known my father for thirty whole years, I still don't know how to message him. It's the simplest of requests; call me asap.

Hovering around *Hi there, Papa*, I hear my name.

'I was testing it out,' Jim shouts over, his window sliding down, referring to his car.

'What for?'

'To see how the engine runs.'

'Is it okay?'

'It's boss. Except for the fuckup called the boot.'

Jim gets out and opens all the doors of the BMW except for the crumpled-up trunk. He's right. It is a fuckup. What used to be a slick behind is now an ugly mess. The once smooth, shining edges are now dull, jagged and scratched, and although my bonnet got a bashing, the dint doesn't look that out of place, unlike the angry dints on Jim's car.

Despite the bitter weather, Jim is sweating. He lifts the bottom edge of his t-shirt up to dab his brow. There isn't an ounce of fat hiding beneath his skin. No sculpted ab muscles either. I bet he eats like a king and works out like a sloth. He cups his hands to his mouth and breathes into them, following with an unpleasant sniff.

'Delightful,' I mutter.

Jim sighs. 'I stink.'

'Again. Delightful.'

'You're right. I'm wasted.'

The urge to do a little victory dance is almost too much, but I don't budge.

'Please don't call the police,' he says.

'But—'

'Not today. Please, not today.'

Then, Jim opens the trunk of my Peugeot and begins to unload. With minimal effort, he lifts both suitcases and wheels them over to his car. Returning, he collects more of my things, slinging my canvas tote bag over his shoulder and struggling with the broken holdall.

'Christ, what the hell's in here?' he asks.

'Toiletries, electronics – you know, laptop, charger—'

'I don't actually wanna know.'

'So why did you ask?'

'Are you gonna stand there and watch, or give us a hand?'

One of my sketches flutters from the bag and I manage to catch it with both hands. It's a personal favourite, of the mop wearing shades and dancing on a disco floor, a glitterball spinning above its 'head', with a little white cat dancing beside it, arms outstretched in the 'Night Fever' pose. I scrunch the sketch up into a little ball, embarrassed for having even bothered to sharpen the damn pencil in the first place. I'm totally stumped. My entire life is slung on some random British roadside.

'Grab the rest of whatever you need,' Jim says. 'I'll give you a lift.'

'A lift? You mean a ride?'

He doesn't respond. He's rotating a suitcase and angling it on the back seat. I heave the holdall up, sliding it behind the passenger seat. Jim won't take me all the way to London, will he? He's drunk. He's a stranger. There's no way this can end well. A luggage tag falls from a suitcase handle and he picks it up.

'I presume you're going the airport?' he asks.

I nod. This is highly irresponsible of me.

'John Lennon or Manchester?'

'Sorry?'

'Which airport?'

'Oh . . .' It hadn't occurred to me to book a flight from anywhere other than Heathrow.

Jim slots the second suitcase into the back seat, rocks it to test its stability, then shuts the door.

'Is that everything?' he asks.

'Not quite,' I say, making one more trip over to my car, my attention on the last remaining item. It's still sticking out

108

of the sunroof. I should leave the mop with the Peugeot – it's redundant. Then again, I could have easily left the mop behind at the hostel. So why didn't I?

Well. To leave it here is accepting that it's over.

And I can't.

Crouching, I remove the mop. The aviators clatter to the ground and I bend down, picking them up and placing them on the mop's head to bring it to life once again. In the shades, I see my own double reflection. My scar. The damp weather makes my hair look so dull, so dark. That damn balayage such a waste. Why did I fork out on a blend of expensive colours for nobody to care?

Unless he does care.

I never gave Nick a chance . . . I just presumed . . .

Oh, God! I've presumed so much since yesterday and that's all it is, a presumption. What if I've somehow been mistaken? There's a reasonable explanation for everything, isn't there? My interpretation of the situation could be completely wrong. And if there's one thing I have, it's time. My flight doesn't leave until tonight. This mop will not be left stranded on a roadside with the blood-coloured car. It's going to come with me and demand an explanation. I haven't come more than four thousand miles with a heart filled with good intentions to have a door slammed in my face. This isn't the end, it can't be. There are answers to be found and there's only one way to find them.

I carry the mop to Jim's car. To my surprise, he's already opened the sunroof in preparation for its arrival.

'I don't want that mop marking the interiors,' he says.

This makes me smile, and the weight pressing me down since last night lifts a little. My hopeful heart is returning to its regular beat.

'So, where do you need a lift to?' Jim asks.

I don't mention anything about London or Heathrow airport. I don't want to run away anymore. The crash has allowed me to stop, to pause, to gain clarity. There's always good to come from bad. I follow enough influencers on social media to know they can't all be wrong, they can't all be telling lies about their balanced lives or simply pretending to be happy. Maybe they really are happy. And if they are, I can be, too. I refuse to be beaten. I'll stay in Liverpool as planned, get the facts straight.

Nick's postcode is stored in my memory. Jim enters it into the BMW's built-in navigation system. And back we go through the Tunnel.

13

Zara

The journey through the tunnel is about as enjoyable as peeling my big toenail off. The radio signal crackles and fizzes, but Jim doesn't bother to switch it off. His odour has become more apparent. The mop's positioning isn't tight, so it rocks from side to side creating an irritating tick. Jim shows no sign of wanting to strike up a conversation. And to top it all off, I really need to use the bathroom.

When daylight hits us again, Jim stretches his long arm behind and grabs the aviators from the head of the mop. Confusing. I don't know why he needs shades on the most miserable day of the year, but each to their own, eh? Why doesn't he have his own designer pair? These aviators are super cheap rip-offs from Patpong night market in Bangkok, bought about four years ago and very obviously fake. It's a miracle they're still in use.

'Got any change?' he asks, holding his palm out to me.

Taken aback, I fumble through my army jacket pockets and

find a few pound coins. Jim snatches them from me and throws them into the basin, overpaying the tunnel fare. Then, he removes the aviators, tosses them into my lap and speeds off.

'Why did you do that?' I ask, digging my nails into my seat.

He doesn't bother answering.

'Jim?'

I spot a cafe, demand he stops.

'You need a double espresso,' I say.

'I won't argue with that.'

The cafe is more of a sandwich shop, in an industrial block of factories and offices. Jim sits down on one of two wooden chairs at the single table for customers, making it clear that I'm buying. Fair enough. I mean, he is giving me a ride. Most people are ordering meaty baguettes dripping with thick mayonnaise. I get one for Jim – bacon and egg – then plonk myself down onto an empty chair, placing two polystyrene cups of coffee on the table. I push the paper bag, leaking with grease, towards him.

'For me?' he asks, his eyes lighting up.

'I couldn't eat a thing.'

He thanks me. Twice. He looks much nicer when he smiles. Although I'm horrified when he opens the baguette and drowns the contents with thin, brown sauce, squeezed from a brown plastic bottle that looks as though it's been sitting on this table since 1972.

'Excuse me,' I say, taking myself off to the single bathroom.

My hands are shaking. Yes, it's cold, but my nerves are shot. There's no mirror in here either, so I put the lid of the toilet seat down, sit and touch up my mascara, eyeliner, concealer and lip gloss using a compact. The frizz in my hair will just have to remain. There's no winning against this drizzle.

Jim hasn't even asked me where I'm going. Sure, he asked for an address, but hadn't he presumed I was going to the

113

airport? Maybe he thinks I'm going on vacation, that he's giving me a ride to a friend's house. It's kind of him not to ask about the mop – what bizarre excuse would I invent? That I'm going on a bachelorette weekend and the mop is part of a game? Or I guess I could pretend that I'm an actress and the mop is a prop for my one-woman show. One that I've written, of course. These musings are a damn good distraction for what lies ahead. It won't be long until I see Nick again, perhaps within the next thirty minutes.

I allow his full name to settle in my mind for the first time since last night. Nick Gregory. I recall his voice from our previous chats, smooth and drawn out, never in a rush to get anywhere. It's different to Jim's accent, only tickled Scouse around the edges of certain words. I need to give him the chance to explain. How unfair that I bolted off. He's never seen me behave like that before. I wonder how I seemed? Angry? Disappointed? Childish? Any of those reactions would be enough to make him step back, give me space. If he's done nothing wrong then I'll struggle to forgive myself for spoiling what should have been a wonderful surprise. Not to mention what a bad judge of character I've been.

Adding an extra coat of mascara, I pinch my cheekbones, an old-fashioned trick, but worthwhile. Answers are imminent. I might as well look my best – or as good as possible within the circumstances – when I get them.

Jim is already waiting for me in his car outside by the time I emerge from the bathroom.

'How do I look?' I ask, pulling at my seatbelt.

Jim shrugs.

'Do I look different than before?' I ask.

'No.'

'Not better? Even slightly?'

'Slightly.'

'You're just saying that.'

Jim says nothing.

'Are you not wondering where I'm going?'

'Nope.'

'Even though I told you I was going to the airport? And where we're going isn't an airport?'

'Nope.'

'Glad to see the coffee has perked you up, Jim.'

Six months ago, I was at a ladies' night in Dubai with a group of girls for Katie's birthday.

Sixty-eight floors high, the rooftop bar – aptly named Sky High 68 – was a current hotspot for midweek partying. Large cushioned sofas created sociable L-shapes amongst small infinity fountains, changeable neon colours zooming from the one long bar. The music was more a series of calm, futuristic sounds playing alongside a monotonous beat, the zesty smell of shisha sprinkled through the hot night air like sweet sherbet, doing a fine job of masking the copious amount of cigarette smoke. Pink cocktails flowed, all free for ladies, of course. The place was a meat market.

True, the look of the bar was impressive, each corner of the floor pristine, but it lacked a soul that I won't ever give up searching for. It made me miss those laid-back bars in Vietnam, Cambodia and Laos, with their power ballads and their many, many lanterns. If only I could have found some sort of job there; some reason to stay, to be needed. Promo work in Dubai could be fun, at times lucrative if I landed the right event, but it was ad hoc, inconsistent, and depended upon the weather being cooler – just hot, as opposed to burning like an angry furnace. At least the quiet times gave me the chance to escape, to travel.

'Shots!' Katie announced.

I cheered alongside the girls, but made a swift exit to the ladies' room before having to neck sambuca. Locked in a cubicle, I scrolled through my phone. Nothing. Why hadn't George been in touch? The last exchange of messages was so promising, the proof in words right there on the screen. Okay, so he wasn't my dream guy, but we'd enjoyed numerous hilarious dates that included a lot of alcohol and a lot of mutual appreciation for *Stranger Things*. We also had pretty wonderful sex. Often. So, why the silence?

Ah fuck it, I was going to break the goddamn silence.

Hey You . . . at Sky High 68 with the girls. You out tonight? x

Delete, delete, delete.
I tried another approach.

Just bumped into a girl at Sky High 68 who is the double of Winona Ryder . . . Delete, delete, delete.

I reapplied my lip gloss. Maybe a shot was a good idea after all.

As I left the ladies' room, the hot desert air hit me hard after spending so long inside the cold air-con. I took a breath, adjusted myself and felt my heart begin to race as I caught sight of someone across the bar. There was no need to text, to wonder, to speculate. There he was.

'George!'

He turned. His shirt was crisp, white, and tucked with precision into his slim, black jeans.

'Hey babe,' George said planting one, two, then three kisses on my cheeks. I don't know why he went in for three. He's English. 'How's it going? I didn't expect to come out tonight – I was working late. We've got a big event starting next Sunday, been in meetings all day. I'll be project manager again, which is nuts because my role never started out that way.'

I was baffled as to why he was educating me with this drivel.

'Who's your friend?' another guy asked.

George put his arm around me and gave me a little shake, like a tambourine.

'Oh, this is Zara. Zara this is . . . everybody.'

I gave a half-hearted wave and rocked back and forth in my high heels.

'What's going on?' I asked turning to look at George.

He made a huge effort to create a blank expression across his wide, clean face.

'George. I was under the impression we were having *fun*.'

'We did have fun.'

'Yeah, exactly. We are.'

'So what's your problem, Zara?'

'I don't have a problem. It's just that we've been having fun for five months—'

'You're counting?'

'No! I'm just good with dates. A wasted talent.'

'Sure.'

'And I was just wondering when we were, I dunno, gonna meet up next?'

'Hmm. Hadn't thought about it.'

'Okay . . .'

'What? Is that not good enough for you, Zara?'

117

It wasn't good enough for me, no. But George was being quite aggressive, a side that I hadn't witnessed at all apart from when he yelled at taxi drivers for taking a wrong turn.

'Look, babe,' he said, lighting a cigarette. 'I'm in the middle of a work thing here.'

'Sorry.'

'Sure.' He gave my bare shoulder a hard, but subtle squeeze. I brushed him off and took a step back. George was not as good-looking as I made out and his voice was definitely higher pitched in reality, as if stuck behind his nose. But we had definitely been having fun. Nothing bad had happened between leaving his place on Saturday morning and now. A couple of texts, a touch of interaction on social media, nothing to suggest things were over.

'Why are you treating me like this?' I asked.

'Babe. Not now.'

'Yes, now. Why not now?'

'Zara. You're drunk. Fuck off back to your mates.'

'Why are you being so mean? What did I do?'

He came in closer, his spiced scent overpowering, his cheek resting against mine.

'Look, babe,' he said. 'You're not my girlfriend.'

I jerked myself away.

'Well, thank God, if this is how you treat girls,' I said.

'Will you lower your voice?'

'No. I've nothing to be ashamed of.'

A petite blonde bounced over to join us, her figure designed for lycra, the volume of her locks unaffected by the outdoor heat. She introduced herself as Amanda from Australia. She seemed hungry for gossip, eager to know who I was and how I knew George, or Georgie, as she referred to him.

'Georgie knows EVERYONE,' she said, continuing to bounce.

118

I made a pained effort to bounce back. 'We haven't known each other long.'

'Oh, are you guys dating?' Amanda asked. 'Oh, yay!'

George said, 'No,' as I said, 'Sort of.'

'Oh, shame! You guys have amazing chemistry. Just saying!'

Another guy put his arm around George, offered him a drink. George turned his back on me.

'So, how long've you been in Dubai?' Amanda asked. The first question every expat asks another when left alone to make small talk.

'On and off since I was a kid,' I said. 'But, I've lived all over ... Singapore, Hong Kong, New England, actual England, sort of, for school and uni ...'

Sometimes, I wish I could record this story to play aloud to new people I find myself chatting to, saving me from repeating it. My story is exhausting, unspecific. There's no strength in its background, no meat to its middle. The present is an ongoing maze.

'I was born in the states,' I went on, Amanda chewing on her straw.

'Cool. And what do you do?'

Another inevitable question I struggled with. I didn't really do anything.

'I can doodle,' I laughed, avoiding an answer. 'But I just like to party.'

Oh, God. How my own words made me cringe.

'Who doesn't?' Amanda clinked her glass with mine. 'You're awesome. Hey, Georgie! Zara. Is. Awesome.'

George touched the arm of the guy he was drinking with. 'Excuse me,' he smiled. Then, he clasped my hand and pulled me across the bar, next to the entrance. Ping! The elevator doors opened and a small group of beautiful people embraced the rooftop with gusto. George took a long drag of his cigarette and blew the smoke sideways.

'I don't want to do this,' he said.

'Do what?' I asked.

'You're NOT my girlfriend.'

'Yeah, I heard you the first time.'

'So why were you making a tit of yourself just now?'

'I wasn't making a tit of my . . . you're a total bastard.'

'Excuse me?'

'You heard me. You took me out and led me on, now you're just tossing me aside.'

'How did I lead you on?'

'Well, I mean, I wouldn't have slept with you all those times if I'd have known.'

'Known what? That I didn't want to marry you and have children with you?'

'God. This is so harsh. I'm not that kind of girl, George.'

'You've got a pretty high opinion of yourself, haven't you, babe?'

'Fuck you, George.'

'Keep your voice down.'

'In case your precious colleagues hear what a total dick you are?'

'I said keep your voice down.'

'Why? Is it Amanda's turn tonight? Are you worried she won't fall for your charm?'

'Stay the hell away from me, Zara. I mean it.'

The next moment happened so swift, in fact, so slick. George, his face as hard as stone, lifted his hand and stubbed his cigarette into my right cheekbone. The lit end twisted in deep, the motion fast but the moment long. Then the elevator doors pinged open again. George stepped in, the doors sliding shut just as I fell to my knees. The pain was so sharp, so intense, I couldn't find the strength to scream as I emptied my lungs with one long, heavy breath.

I remained crouched over for what felt like some time, all my concentration keeping me quiet, as though I might just disappear if I stayed down there long enough. My hands were pressed into my cheek, wishing the burn away. Echoing around me were the sounds of laughter, of air kissing, of ice clattering in glasses, people enjoying other people. The beat from the speakers thumped along, pulsing across my forehead, creating a dull ache.

I couldn't go back past the bar now. Not only because this incident would ruin Katie's birthday, but because I was too afraid to slip past George's crowd, to be stopped by Amanda. What would they say about my hand pressed against my cheek? How could I lie and conceal the fact that the person responsible was their old buddy, Georgie? Oh God, what would he do to me if I told them the truth?

The bare skin on my back felt warm, and it wasn't the night air. It was somebody's hand. I was going to get told off for blocking the entrance, asked to leave. But, as I slowly began to unravel, the hand on my back kept me steady and another hand helped me to standing. I lost my balance a little in my heels.

'Are you okay, sweetheart?'

Sweetheart. Such a simple word played like a string quartet in my ears. I kept my eyes closed. The man's hand touched my bare shoulder and with such tenderness, he asked if he could take a look at my face, to see what 'that horrid prick' had just done to me. He'd seen the whole thing and regretted not moving in sooner.

'I didn't want to interfere,' he said. 'I'm so sorry.'

He was definitely British, but I was unsure of his accent, perhaps Northern.

I wanted to speak, to say, 'Don't be sorry, it's not your fault,' but I was still trapped inside my own mind in my shock. Allowing my eyes to open, I looked at the man. He was medium height – tall next to me – and fair haired, a little freckly, with a smile that invited me to feel at home. His cheeks were dimpled, his brow damp, his shirt creased with the heat. I guessed that he was either new to Dubai or here on business.

'We should speak to the manager,' he said, his hand still stroking my shoulder. 'Get them to call the police.'

'No,' I found my voice. 'We can't do that.'

'Why? You've been attacked, sweetheart.'

'Honestly, no. Forget it. I won't be seeing him again.'

'But—'

'I'm serious. There's nothing the police can do. It'll look like I was asking for it.'

'No way.'

'I'm a girl in a bar, I've had alcohol, I'm dressed like this,' I sighed. 'Believe me, it's not worth the hassle.'

The man's smile dropped. 'I'll go downstairs now and see if I can find the prick.'

'You won't find him. Look down,' I said, my head tilting to the rooftop balcony. Below the hotel were twelve lanes of traffic, a spider of a junction just yards from the entrance. 'You see how busy it is down there? He's gone.'

The man mopped his brow with a napkin.

'Well, can I get you something?' he asked. 'A drink? Some water? Something stronger?'

'Water. Please.'

He returned in seconds with a pint of iced water. I put my hand into the glass and grabbed a few ice cubes, pressing them against my cheek. The ice melted quickly between my finger-tips, dripping down my dress, onto the floor. The man took a clean napkin from the side of the bar and wrapped up the remaining ice, and without asking, held it up against my face.

'Is it bad?' I asked.

'No. It's actually like a beauty spot.'

'Oh, come on. You don't have to be so nice. I can take it.'

'Okay, it's quite a red and raw beauty spot . . . but that won't last long.'

I laughed, and then began to cry. The man brought me close to him and hugged me tight. This simple act of kindness from a stranger was the truest form of comfort that I'd experienced in a long, long time.

'Do you want to get out of here?' the man asked. 'I mean, I can't say I know the area, but do you want to go for a walk?'

'And get some fresh air?' I managed to joke.

He laughed. 'I hear the air conditioning in the lobby is out of this world.'

'I should go home.'

'You live here?'

'Sort of.'

'Alright for some. This time tomorrow I'll be back in Blighty.'

'You here on business?'

'How did you guess?'

I pressed the ice deeper into my burn. 'You seem a little overwhelmed by the heat.'

The man cracked another smile. 'Am I that much of an amateur?'

'I've seen worse.'

'Look, can I at least see that you get home okay? I'll get a taxi with you?'

'That's kind of you, but no, I'm fine.'

And I did feel fine, within reason. This man's calm presence had to get credit for that.

'Well, at least give me your number,' he suggested. 'And I'll give you mine. Then text me when you're home so I know you really are fine.'

As I took my phone from my bag, the man held the napkin full of ice against my cheek, keeping the fresh wound cool. At the far end of the bar, I could see Katie and the girls helping themselves to a bottle of vodka served with sparklers, the bar's signature birthday treat. I wasn't going to be the person to bring the mood down. I'd take Katie for lunch next week, apologise for leaving so abruptly.

'Well,' I said. 'Thank you for . . . I dunno, saving me.'

He blushed, which I found rather sweet. 'You're very welcome,' he said.

I headed towards the elevator, pressed the button, waited. In the last few minutes, whilst enduring unbearable pain and complete humiliation, I had felt lighter than usual, a gentle atmosphere of safety encompassing me.

I heard the man's voice again.

'Are you sure you don't want me to come with you?' he asked.

The elevator pinged open.

'No,' I said. 'I'm not sure.'

'Well, shall I come down to the lobby with you, and then, when you're safe inside a taxi, you can decide whether or not you want me to go with you?'

I smiled. 'Yes.'

As the elevator doors closed, the man put his arms gently around me.

'What's your name?' I asked.

'Gregory. Nick Gregory.'

14

Jim

I look across at Zara. She's gone pale, taking deep breaths.

'Do you need me to pull over?' I ask.

'What? Why?'

'You look like you're gonna be sick.'

'Likewise.'

'Look, just don't be sick in me car, alright?'

For some reason, this makes her laugh and she has the cheek to give me an 'aye aye captain' with salute.

'Boys and their toys,' she says to herself, all smug, although loud enough for me to hear.

I'm seething, but I don't respond. It's sounds daft, but yeah, I want her to think I'm just a boy and this BMW is my little toy. Not her, specifically. I couldn't give a flying fuck about what she thinks. But in general. I want the whole world to think it. I want it to be my truth. I want to be genuinely only annoyed that my car's had a bash up and it's going to be a pain in the arse to get it sorted, but life goes on. It'll get sorted. Worse things happen at sea and so on.

But. FUCK.

This isn't my truth, is it?

For me, this is a shipwreck. I'm a grown man with a lost chance, not a boy with a toy. Not that it's easier being the latter. Not in my experience, anyway.

My sisters are both older, Lisa by seven years and Emma by five.

Growing up was like watching a telly show where they starred as a double act, me always on the other side of the glass, admiring, listening. Whatever I suggested – playing MouseTrap, watching *Fraggle Rock* – it got dismissed with a big ruffle of my hair and an 'Ah, he's so cute,' sometimes from Lisa, mostly from Emma. They were a force. And I was blown away by them.

My ma took on three cleaning jobs to pay for their tap and ballet lessons. I was dragged along, but not to dance. I was too young to be left home alone. I had to sit and wait amongst the other mothers and bored siblings, in the cloakroom of the church hall, the tinkle of an out-of-tune piano seeping through the wall. The newsagents across the road became my saviour.

It was there I found a hobby.

I'd seen an advert on the telly for a magazine about maps of the world. Each week, the edition came attached with a little clear bag of plastic pieces and stickers, all part of building your own globe. Collecting all twelve editions meant completing the globe, the final piece allowing it to spin on its axis. My pocket money had gone up from one to two pounds since Emma and Lisa began dancing, my dad sneaking the extra quid my way with a wink and a shush behind my ma's back. And the magazine cost just that: two pounds a week.

So I began collecting.

Every Tuesday, as Emma and Lisa fought their way to be first into the church hall, I'd stop, look, listen and think, cross the road and buy my magazine. Then, curled up beside the metal radiator, its paint chipped and peeling onto the cold, tiled floor of the cloakroom, I'd read it from cover to cover, completing the wordsearch, the spot the difference, the weekly quiz; one time on rivers, another on mountains. Keeping the little clear bag safe in my coat pocket, I waited until I got home to build my globe, slotting the new piece into place.

During week seven of the collection, I went to Snowy's after school for tea. Snowy was allowed out on his bike before mealtimes and gave me a 'seater' as we rode through the estate. Snowy pulled up outside the off-licence. We both went inside, Snowy scratching his skinny ribs and complaining about being ravenous.

'But your ma's got the tea on,' I said.

'Me ma's stingy with the potatoes,' Snowy said. And he bought a Toffee Crisp and two cans of 7Up. 'You should get some fodder, mate, or you'll be starving.'

I had my two quid, all ready to buy my magazine the following day. A packet of crisps wasn't going to break the bank. I could ask my dad for it when he got home. So, I chose some beef Space Raiders.

'10p, love,' the girl on the till said.

I handed over a quid, got ninety pence change.

That night, after Snowy's ma dropped me off, I found my ma and my dad in the kitchen arguing. My dad told me to go up to my room. I took the glass from my sock drawer, and turning it upside down on the carpet, ear to the glass, I listened through the floorboards. They weren't arguing. They were talking about Maggie bloody Thatcher. My dad had lost his job, again.

The extra 10p was never asked for.

At the newsagents, I picked up the seventh edition of the magazine, took it to the counter. Keeping my fingers crossed behind my back, I handed over my money. I believed that a stroke of luck, or kindness, might just be on my side.

'You're 10p short,' the lady said.

'I haven't got it.'

'Why's that?'

'I bought some Space Raiders. Yesterday.'

'Well, you'd better choose something else,' she said. 'Something you can afford.'

So, I chose a comic. And a can of Coke. And enough penny sweets in a paper bag to take me up to the exact amount I had to spend; one pound and ninety pence. I sat beside the radiator and read the comic, ignoring the dot-to-dot and feeling sick from all the sugar.

The following week, the newsagents were only selling the eighth edition. I'd never get the seventh piece to my globe. So I gave up collecting the magazines and started reading paperbacks instead. I kept my globe – just over half of it, unable to spin on its axis – on my shelf, most countries visible, the Pacific Ocean entirely missing.

The dancing lessons paid off for my sisters. When Lisa landed the job dancing on a cruise ship, Emma followed a year later. Both girls sailed all four corners of the globe before settling in the port they started in; Fort Lauderdale, Florida.

And it sounds soft, but I've felt forever 10p short.

* * *

128

Now, Zara's picking at her nails, little flecks wafting about my car like fucking dandruff.

I swear, if any of that touches the interior, falls onto the leather—

BEEP!

'What the fuck's your problem?' I shout at the driver behind, scowling at him through my rear-view mirror.

'You can go,' Zara tells me.

'Y'what?'

She points to the traffic light. It's green. She was right. I can go.

Shit.

I give a wave to the driver behind. My bad.

15

Zara

Jim's breath is heavy as he drives, regular huffing going on and the odd sigh, the scratching of his stubble. I'm trying to remove my pale blue nail polish. It started by peeling off both thumbs, but I can't handle the inconsistency of my nails not matching. It makes me feel off balance. With care, I drop the bits of dried polish into my lap, for despite the battered trunk, the inside of Jim's car looks – and smells – as good as brand new.

The Electric Light Orchestra sings through the speakers about Mr Blue Sky. A few songs follow that I've never heard before and as much as I want to listen, I'm restless.

'So, are you from Liverpool?' I ask.

'Yeah.'

'Do you live around here?'

'No.'

'So, you live closer to the city than the suburbs?'

'No.'

'This is my first trip to Liverpool.'

Jim doesn't reply. It could be my paranoia, but I think the music has become a little louder. He taps his fingers on the steering wheel, playing along with the beat of the song. I press the button to open the window and with care, throw my bits of nail polish out into the passing air. Once the window shuts again, the tension magnifies.

'Where are you from?' Jim asks, with a pained expression as if he's yanking out his front teeth.

'The States. Originally.'

Jim raises his eyebrows and continues to tap the wheel.

'So, what is it you do?' I ask, running my fingertips lightly across the shiny buttons on the inbuilt stereo, the swanky navigation system.

'Do you have to touch that?'

'I'm guessing you run your own business. Or you work for your dad.'

'Right. Yeah.'

'So come on, are you some mysterious entrepreneur?'

'How did you guess?'

'I'm good at this sort of thing. I'm a professional people-watcher. I've spent a lot of time in airports and living with people I barely know. So, what's your success story? Is it something to do with IT? Or selling data on the internet? Not that I know anything about that sort of shit. But that's how most dudes I know make their dollar and drive around in cars like this.'

Jim shrugs, elaboration clearly not his strong point. A barrier of ice forms between us again and I can't bear the ache swelling in my forehead. I'd rather talk to anyone than be left with my own thoughts; I'm just not good with them. And now, I've got the chance to have an actual conversation with somebody, after the emptiness of yesterday, of last night.

'So, you probably invented some kind of adhesive picture hook and made a small – or large – fortune,' I muse. 'Or you're a drug dealer.'

Jim continues to tap the wheel in time to the song on the radio, some Nineties hit that's all intense drums and angry vocals. I can't remember the name of the singer or the song. The lyrics keep repeating over and over.

'I guess that was pretty offensive, huh?' I admit.

'What?'

'Me accusing you of being some sort of drug dealer?'

He laughs. Not exactly from his belly, or even as if he's been tickled. Still, a jovial flash. He checks his mirrors, he indicates, changes lanes. The ice has melted just a little.

'I don't have a job,' I tell him, whether or not he wants to listen. 'Currently.'

He nods once.

Out of the passenger window, rows of semi-detached brick houses pass us by, all identical in shape, in size, the front doors and front gardens presenting a glimpse of individuality. Life here would certainly be different to anything I've ever been used to, but what does that matter if I'm happy? If I'm loved?

'I've had loads, though,' I go on. 'Jobs.'

'Boss,' Jim says.

'Once I had to dress as a cheerleader to promote these new overpriced hot dogs and guess what?'

'You never got a free hot dog?'

'I never got a free hot dog.'

Jim returns to his tap-tap-tapping.

'Would you mind not doing that, Jim?'

'Doing what?'

'That tapping.'

'Why?'

'Because it's making me really anxious.'

He stops.

'Thanks. I'm just nervous.'

He doesn't ask why.

'I don't know what I'm doing. I've had the most awful twenty-four hours . . . well, twenty hours, to be precise. God, it hasn't even been a whole day since everything fell apart. It's funny how time plays tricks on you, isn't it? Like how some days just go by in a flash, and some drag on forever, like everything you thought can change in the space of just a few hours, minutes even. Do you know what I mean, or am I just chatting shit?'

'I know what you mean.'

'I can shut up if you want. It just feels better to talk. Makes me less nervous.'

Jim still doesn't pry.

'Don't you think it's worth trying to get answers though, rather than spend your life wondering? I do. I'd rather just know. I'd rather get the facts. Move on. Otherwise there'll always be a niggle, a sort of unsettling buzz in my brain. And also, there's two sides to every story, right? I like to think that most people in the world are good people, that there's always an explanation for their actions. I might seem like a terrible person to some people – like to you, I'm sure you think I'm a terrible person – but, despite my faults, I'm not. I never *mean* to hurt anyone, or annoy anyone, it just seems to come across the wrong way. Like when my friend Katie threw a baby shower for her sister. All the girls were cooing over the bump and Katie said to me, 'What do you think, Zara?' and

133

I said, 'Wow, it's huge!' Which was the absolute worst thing to say, apparently, except I'd worked with a woman once who got upset whenever people told her that her bump was tiny, she was so anxious that she'd have an abnormally small baby. Okay, that's a really bad example, but—'

'I don't.'

'You don't what?'

'I don't think you're a terrible person.'

'Oh. Thank you.'

The city sights are long behind us and the rundown independent shops and warehouses have disappeared, replaced by more appealing rows of houses with an almost quaint cottage look about them.

'You familiar with around here?' I ask.

Jim shakes his head in disapproval, as if he's just sniffed a fart.

What's his problem? This place seems pretty nice; there are even horses in the field we've just passed. I bet he lives in a huge apartment, ultra modern and gleaming with sharp greys and blacks and whites. A real bachelor pad.

We stop at the traffic signal. A red light. If only Jim would talk to me, engage with me, keep things moving.

'I guess we're both just having a bad day, huh?' I say, in an attempt to sound upbeat.

It sort of works. Jim laughs.

'Can you remember your worst bad day?' I ask.

'You serious?'

'It helps.'

'How?'

'Because, Jim, it reminds you that things aren't as bad as they seem right now.'

'Quite the philosopher, aren't you?'

'Mine's when my parents split. I mean, it was so obvious for months, but, God. The news hit me like . . . whoa. I can't even imagine them being together now, but that day sticks in my mind as being fucking awful. I knew I was about to lose a lot more than just a set of parents. And I was right. Gut instincts, eh? Are your parents still together?'

Jim's eyes glance across at me and back to the road ahead.

'Oh, Jim. Forgive me. Please. That was not appropriate.'

'Me dad died.'

I close my eyes, try to disappear.

'I'm so sorry,' I whisper.

'It was a while ago. But it doesn't feel like a while ago.'

I tell myself to shut up. Just shut the fuck up. Now.

'What happened?' I ask. Why? Why did I just ask that? What's wrong with me? 'Actually, no, you don't have to answer that—'

'Just keeled over.'

'Oh, my.'

'He was going the pub, couple of mid-week pints, the usual. Never made it as far as the pub. He said, "Ta-ra, see you later", picked up his keys from the little dish on the mantlepiece, took his coat, even though it was July. And that was it. The end.'

I don't respond.

'His heart was beating, then it wasn't,' Jim goes on, quite matter-of-fact. 'Just walking to the pub. That's all. Fuck me, there's nothing like finding out that's happened to make you sort your shit out. Accept your responsibilities.'

Well, maybe that explains the expensive car, Jim having to take over his dad's business. I hate how quickly I judged him. I should apologise, but it doesn't feel right to do so, or to say anything, really, so I reach out to place my hand gently on Jim's forearm, his hand resting on the gearstick. But I don't get the chance to fulfill my intention as Jim moves to indicate left. I doubt he even noticed what I did, and to save myself possible embarrassment, I tap the gearstick in pretend admiration and then clasp both of my hands together to prevent any future urges.

'Ha!' Jim laughs, a cynical burst that startles me. 'Christ, I don't know why I just told you all that, love. Ignore me, I'm probably still a bit bollocksed. Spouting shit. Sorry, like.'

Fleetwood Mac perks up through the speakers.

'*You can go your own way . . .*'

'Oh, I love this song,' I smile.

It might only be from one side of his mouth, but I'm sure that Jim's smiling, too.

'Me too,' he says.

'Wait!' I see the edge of Clifton Crescent. 'Pull over.'

Jim complies, the roads of this suburban neighbourhood quiet, plenty of space to park.

'I just need a minute,' I say.

Pulling the mirror down from above the passenger seat, I check my tired complexion, my teeth for misplaced lip gloss. I'm actually trembling. Yesterday afternoon I'd felt like a kid unable to sleep the night before her birthday. Now, my spirit is darting all over the damn place. Jim turns the engine off and blows his lips out. Leaning back in his seat, he folds his arms and closes his eyes.

I check the clock. Lunchtime. At least those little girls will be in school.

'Do you wanna hand?' Jim asks, his eyelids remaining shut.

'With what?'

'All your stuff.'

136

All my stuff. Of course, I need to take all of my belongings out of Jim's car so he can drop me off and get on with his life. Maybe there *was* a huge misunderstanding yesterday. I'll see Nick and everything will work out exactly how I planned. He might have been trying to call my Dubai number, which won't be working because I'm here. Trying again might be the best decision I ever make.

'Okay,' I say. I'm ready.

Jim springs out of the car. With the same energy, he opens the back doors and heaves out one of my suitcases.

'Jim, stop!'

'What now?'

'Can you leave everything where it is please? For a few minutes more?'

Folding his arms again, his hair hanging over his narrowing eyes, he lets out a tired sigh.

'I'm just collecting something from a friend's house,' I lie.

'You're lying.'

Shit. If Nick's answers aren't the ones I'm hoping to hear, I'll have to ask Jim to take me to a train station, or a pub, or any place where I can figure out how to get to London in time for my flight.

'Listen, love,' he says, shaking his head. 'You seem to be having some sort of personal crisis. I don't wanna judge, but please, don't drag me into it. You're asking me to do you favours, but, Zara, you've gotta admit that this is all a bit weird. I'm a total stranger. You seem like a nice girl, so I wish you all the best. What happened to us today sucks arse, but look, I'll have to leave you here. I don't know you, and you don't know me.'

I know that he's only trying to be nice. The anger in his voice has gone. He's speaking complete sense. Yet, with Nick's house behind me and Jim's smashed-up car before me, I feel like I'm lost in the woods, stuck in a place I've been warned not to explore. Nick's forthcoming explanation isn't something I can predict, but Jim, so far, is an element of safety. He's brought me this far without any serious trouble.

And Jim's also wrong. He's not a total stranger, not anymore. He removes the last of my things from his car and returns to the driver's seat. I run to the driver's side and press my hands against the window. It rolls down.

'Jim? Before you go, please tell me what you see when you look at my face.'

Jim's face falls with an apology.

'I know you see it,' I say. 'Tell me what you see.'

He looks right at it. 'A scar. A ciggie burn. A pretty bad one.'

'It's six months old and it knocked the fucking wind out of me. But, I was helped by a kind stranger, who became a kind friend, and more. He gave me the confidence to get out of the hole I was in, to get on a plane and come here—'

'Why are you telling me this, love?'

'Because the man who helped me lives in that house over there. And I'm scared that he isn't who he said he was. I need to believe that the last six months of my life haven't been a complete lie. And you were wrong, Jim.'

'What about?'

'You said you don't know me. Well, you do. Honestly, there isn't much more to me than what you already know. And I know more about you than anybody else in Liverpool, so call it weird, call me fucking psycho or whatever, but I'm asking you to wait with my things, just for a little while longer.'

'How much longer?'

'Can I get back in the car?'

Jim flicks his head as if to say, go on then.

'I'm not gonna lie,' I tell him, getting into the passenger side. 'I'm totally freaking out. Oh, God.'

'Okay, just breathe.'

I obey, but not without a struggle. The panic is unreal. I close my eyes, knowing that I'll have to retrace my steps from yesterday. The breathing is helping; Jim's advice is sound.

'I just need another minute or two,' I whisper.

'Well, I'm also gonna close me eyes then,' Jim says. 'Don't mind me.'

16

Jim

She's quiet.

I don't want to blame Zara for the headache I've got, but Christ. Every time she speaks, she might as well take a little hammer out and batter my brain. Every passing second is like I'm standing on an escalator, walking up the one that's moving downwards. If I run, it only speeds up. I'm stuck; I can't get off.

So, this moment of calm, this miniature window of tranquility, I'm all in.

In fact, I can feel myself nodding off.

Ah. This is nice. A little kip's just what I need. Then I can say *adios* to this maniac and drive to Griffo's dad's, a bit more perky, head a bit clearer to explain why I'm so late. I know I won't be getting fifty gr—

Stop.

I'm not ready to acknowledge this yet.

I'm swaying. My eyes are closed, my body still, my head

against the seat. And yet, I'm swaying. My whole everything sways, it swarms, it's drowning in a black ocean of giant waves and I've forgotten how to swim. Or, no. I'm just too weak to survive it. I'm going to be sick. Oh God, if I keep my eyes closed, I will, I'll vomit. Breathe. Just breathe, fella. Focus. I'm going to have to open my eyes and stop this merry-go-round spinning. But, I want some time, I want some sleep. It'll help me out when I finally get the chance to see Griffo's dad, especially since my phone's dead and I can't ring him. If I can just get some kip, I can apologise without yawning.

Apologise?

Griffo's dad isn't the sort of fella you want to apologise to.

Oh, fuck this day. Fuck. It. All.

17

Zara

I hadn't planned on inviting him back to my papa's villa.

Plenty of taxis were waiting outside the hotel and Nick still had his arm around my shoulders. I didn't want to break free from his safe hold, to sit alone in the back of a car with a strange man driving me home who would simply see me as a drunk girl leaving a bar. And I know, Nick Gregory was a strange man, too. But Nick had witnessed the whole incident. Even if he wasn't the only person to see what had happened, he was the only one who acted upon it.

We talked the whole way, just like two regular people who had hooked up, and his cute accent and bad jokes made the ache in my cheek somehow ease.

It felt natural to invite Nick in for a drink.

He told me to find a first aid kit and helped to clean then fix a Band-Aid over my injury.

Nobody was home. My papa had taken Marina with him on a business trip to Singapore, plus Sammy was away at school. I opened a bottle of wine, grabbed two glasses and took them into the garden where Nick was already making himself comfortable on the hammock.

'I can't believe you live in a house with a swimming pool,' Nick said.

'It's hardly a *swimming* pool. More of a pond without fish.'

'Beats the puddles in me garden at home. This is boss.'

'Boss?'

'Oh, I mean good, great, amazing. Liverpool slang.'

We chatted for a while, small talk and more bad jokes. We came up with a feast of insults that would suit that vile bastard George. I was amazed at how much I could laugh about somebody who was so awful to me just hours ago. As I was about to get a second bottle of wine, Nick attempted to get out of the hammock.

'Can we go inside, sweetheart?' he asked, failing to sit up with any hint of elegance.

'Struggling with the heat?' I smiled.

'Amateur.'

He held out his hands for help and I was more than happy to assist. I'd kicked my high heels off and he was much taller beside me now as he came to standing. He lowered his head and cupped my face in his hands, then gave me a soft kiss on my sore cheek, below the Band-Aid.

I pulled away.

'I'm sorry,' he said.

But, what did Nick have to be sorry for? He'd been nothing short of wonderful since George had attacked me. Nobody could have made me feel more cared for. What's more, he had cut his night out in Dubai short to take me home and make sure I was completely fine. Nick had treated me with respect, something I hadn't experienced for the longest time.

I tilted my head away, exposing my left cheek, the one that was untouched, unscarred.

Nick bent over and kissed that side instead.

'We should go inside,' I said.

'That would be more comfortable,' he smiled, relieved.

Over plenty more wine, we sat in the kitchen and talked until the sun started to make an appearance. We both agreed that Reese Witherspoon was the sweetest person on the planet. We didn't understand why people chose to have a dog, but totally got the need for a cat. Nick took great interest in the brightly coloured sketches pinned onto the fridge of various animals surfing, and chuckled, asking where they came from. He wanted to get some for himself.

'They're mine,' I admitted. 'Well, I drew them. For my little brother, Sammy.'

'Impressive,' Nick said. 'Talented as well as beautiful.'

'He likes to surf.'

Things became a bit silly and we danced on the white-tiled floor to a string of cheesy eighties songs blaring from my laptop. Nick grabbed a mop and displayed some bizarre moves that had me aching with laughter. We playfully touched each other's fingers. I sat on his knee and cuddled into his chest. It didn't occur to me that this time with Nick would ever come to an end.

'I need to go,' he said.

'I don't want you to go,' I said, panic rising.

'Me flight's in a few hours, sweetheart.'

Nick had built a wall around me, one that was made of silk pillows, twinkling with blue lights. He had wrapped me up and protected me from the pain, and now he was leaving. That wall was already beginning to fall down.

'If it makes you feel better, I don't want to go either,' he said.

'Then stay!'

'I can't. I've got to get back.'

'Why? You told me you mainly work from home. Work from here.'

I know I sounded desperate, but he was leaving, and without him, I was exposed. I had nothing to lose.

'Fine. I'll come to England,' I said.

'You're welcome any time.'

'I will. I'll come . . . today! I can fly out today. Why the hell not?'

'Yeah, why the hell not? But, sweetheart, you won't see me in England.'

'Why?'

'Once I get back, I've got a lot of work to do and then I'm on a few more business trips. It's a crazy time of year. Honestly, just relax. Let's keep in touch.'

'Yeah, I know what that means.'

'We can Skype.'

'Sure. Because that always ends well,' I said, then bit my lip. 'I'm being ridiculous.'

Nick laughed and tickled me under the chin.

'I get it,' he said. 'You were attacked tonight; you're not okay. But you will be.'

'What if I won't? What if I see him again? What if I meet another guy and he . . .' I couldn't fight the tears and my loud sobs revealed that I was actually pretty drunk. We'd knocked back a lot of wine and I hadn't eaten dinner. 'I've just really enjoyed talking to you.'

'So let's keep talking. Technology is a magical thing.'

'Ha. When it works.'

'It will work. Please don't cry. I've done such a good job of making you feel better and now I'm gonna leave and me

last memory will be of your beautiful little face like this.'
Nick scrunched up his face and pretended to cry like a baby,
which did make me chuckle. 'Yes! Still got it. Actually, I've
got an idea.'

Nick picked up the mop, his former dancing partner, and
grabbed a pair of broken sunglasses that happened to be
lying in the empty fruit bowl on the table. I watched,
confused, as Nick stood the mop upright. He slipped the
sunglasses into the mop's head, which was level with mine.

'Ta-da!' he sang.

I swayed, attempted to steady myself.

'This is Nick,' he said, as if he were introducing a friend,
an actual human being.

'That's a mop.'

'No, when you take the sunnies off, it's just a mop. But
shh. The mop is very sensitive, he gets sad when he's just a
mop. Because when you put the sunnies on . . . ta-da! He
becomes Nick. And anytime you wanna talk to Nick, he's
here for you. You can tell him anything, everything, nothing.
He'll listen to you.'

'You've actually gone mad.'

'Come on. Play along with me.'

'Okay . . . erm. Hi Nick.' I waved at the mop.

'Hullo,' Nick said, shaking the mop's head. 'And now, I'm
gonna hide behind the fridge and you're gonna hold the
mop . . . Okay. Can you see me?'

'No, you're behind the fridge.'

'Wrong. I'm with you.'

'Oops. Silly me. I forgot you can magically transform into
cleaning equipment.'

'If you put a bow tie around Nick's neck, he can take you
to the ball.'

'And on the stroke of midnight, I'm guessing Nick turns back into being just a mop again?'

Nick came out of hiding and took me – and the mop – in his arms.

'I know it's not ideal,' he said. 'We met under strange circumstances, and although what happened to you tonight was horrible, you are possibly the most beautiful woman I've ever met. Ever. And you like Wham! And A-ha. And you live in a house with a swimming pool! But the reality is, I don't live here. I have to go home. So, if you need me, call me. And if you can't reach me, talk to our shaggy friend Nick here.'

And that's when our lips met and I let him kiss me.

The desert sun rose high and fast, making it clear that last night was history: a memory. Its rays fired down onto the tired, dusty pathway that led from the villa to a taxi that would take Nick on his journey back to England. I watched him drive away, the sun burning my bare feet. At my side was the mop, tight within my grip. And I held on tighter. Tighter. For as soon as I let go of that mop, I'd be all alone again.

'I'm ready,' I say.

Jim's eyes are still closed.

'So am I,' he says.

'What for?'

'You to get out.'

'But, you'll wait here, with my things, yeah?'

'Do I have a choice?'

'I'm leaving the mop,' I decide. 'I can do this alone.'

As expected, Jim opens his eyes, but only to shoot me a glance that confirms I sound completely crazy. I throw a quick smile his way, straighten my pinafore and my army jacket, smooth down the frizz of my hair one more time. I'm doing this.

'Welcome to the Mad House,' I mumble as I ring the doorbell.

Its chime hangs in my ears. My gaze goes up towards the front bedroom where I had – without doubt – seen Nick looking down on me yesterday.

Nick doesn't live here.

Footsteps sound from afar, and then closer, closer, coming down the stairs. The door opens. It's him.

'Nick!'

'Oh, sweetheart,' he sighs.

My feet, so cold inside my suede sneakers, feel light. I bounce up onto my toes. Nick seems tired, older than he looked on my laptop screen, as if six years have passed rather than six months. Apology is written all over his face, his dimples present, but not from his regular smiles.

'I told you I would come,' I say.

'I didn't think you actually would, though,' he says.

'Why? I did everything else I promised. I went to my friend's wedding, remember? Even though I heard that George might be there? I promised you I would go, you made me believe I'd be okay, and I am. I'm okay. Why did you think I wouldn't come?'

'You didn't tell me you were coming yesterday.'

'Because it was supposed to be a surprise. For your birthday!'

'Come inside,' Nick says, opening the door wider.

I practically leap through the front porch and skip into the hallway. Falling into his arms, I expect Nick to catch me, to return the embrace. He takes hold of my hands instead, removes them from around his neck, squeezes them and lets go. I've never noticed a ring on his left hand before, and thank God, there isn't one today either.

I want to ask what's wrong, but I'm afraid.

'I'm in shock, sweetheart.'

'Good shock or bad shock? Actually, don't answer that.'

Framed photographs of the two little girls are arranged across all of the walls: small cherubs sitting on furry white rugs; toothless smiles in green school uniforms. There isn't a single picture of Nick to be seen. Certainly no wedding photograph; not within my view. Perhaps the little girls are his nieces and this isn't his house. Except it is.

I'm willing my instincts to be wrong. Please, please, be wrong. Let the children be his nieces, his cousins, his best friend's kids, anything but his own. Please. I can feel tears waiting in my eyes.

'Tell me I was mistaken, Nick. Tell me I jumped to conclusions yesterday. And if you tried to call me, I'm sorry, my Dubai number isn't working here in the UK. I bought a new SIM, but—'

'Zara, stop. How did you find out where I live?'

'Easy. Your emails.'

Nick's face is so blank that I hardly recognise him. His regular laughter lines are invisible, his expressions dull instead of bright. I take my phone out of my army jacket pocket, show him the screenshot of his address printed in small letters below the company logo for Nicholas Consultancy. My eyes catch his and I never thought it possible to witness the blood drain from somebody's face, but it does, and he gulps, as if he's swallowing a hard, dry rock.

'And I knew you worked from home,' I say. 'Is this your home?'

He nods.

'Do you want to show me around?' I try, my voice quivering.

'Not really.'

'What?'

Instead, Nick cups my face, pulling me close, and kisses me. His hands move to the back of my neck, down my back, and I throw my arms around his waist naturally, although more on instinct than with passion. Moving me towards the stairs, I fall back and Nick kneels, his hard crotch pushing against me. He kisses my neck, my chest, nuzzling his head across my stripy top.

'Wait . . . Nick . . .' I say. 'Let's talk.'

'All we've done for six months is talk.'

'Well, I didn't just come here for sex!'

'So why did you come?'

His words stab me like an ice-cold dagger.

'To start our life together,' I say, instantly ashamed at how that sounds in the still air of this beige hallway. All this time, I thought I was seizing a wonderful opportunity, but in reality I was just taking a risky gamble. 'You know how much I want to complete my degree and you told me that Liverpool has a great university—'

'You say you want to do a lot of things, sweetheart. Last week you told me you wanted to climb Machu Picchu.'

'And you said you wanted to climb it with me!'

'Why didn't you tell me you were coming? I could've booked us a nice hotel in town, had the champagne on ice.'

'I don't want a nice hotel, I just want to be here, like we'd talked about.'

He covers his face with his hands and murmurs *okay* over and over to himself.

'You want to be here,' he says, quietly, 'and you are. So, please, let's stop talking.'

He moves closer and presses his lips against mine once more. Lifting up the skirt of my denim pinafore, he runs his hand inside my thighs. This should be a fabulous moment – it's all I've spent many nights thinking about as I've tried to fall asleep over the past months. Except, in my mind, Nick wasn't so rough.

'Stop,' I say, trying to push him away.

'Come on . . .' he mumbles, his face heavy against mine.

'No.'

Placing my hand on the banister, I haul myself up to standing. I fix my army jacket, which has fallen off my shoulders, and straighten my haphazard pinafore. But Nick's closing in on me again, his scent wildly different from the one I remember. I don't like how he's breathing, panting.

'Nick, stop. Please.'

'Agh,' he says, gasping from arousal, pushing me away. 'Look what you're doing to me.'

This isn't how it was supposed to be. But, then again, Nick has a point. We haven't seen each other in the flesh for six months, we've only spoken about what it would feel like to touch one another, and God! How we've spoken about that. For hours upon hours. We have been gentle to each other with words, and then gentle on our own bodies with our own fingertips, watching one another caress ourselves across a screen. Nick has seen every inch of my skin – not only have I opened my heart but also my legs to his view, my confidence soaring at how fucking sexy he's made me feel from four thousand miles away. I've watched his cock grow hard in his hands, talked him into a climax, and listened as he brought me to multiple orgasms before the camera.

151

'Tell me I got it wrong,' I whisper, desperately.

The innocent faces from the photographs on the walls are closing in on me, their sweet round eyes all too similar to Nick's. Yesterday, I was convinced the girls looked like their mother, but now, the truth is too difficult to ignore. As much as I want him – of course, I want him, I love him – this doesn't feel right at all.

'You got it wrong,' Nick says, coming close to me again.

Surely I'm about to have everything I've ever wanted. A partner. Someone to brunch with, to watch movies with, to sleep with. What's more, he isn't looking at me down the lens of a camera: he's right here, right now, needing me, wanting me. He begins to unzip his jeans, teasing me by pulling on my denim strap.

I think of Jim, waiting for me in his car. What would he make of me lingering in this strange house, my long-distance lover trying to fuck me without as much as a proper hello? But, why am I thinking of him? Some guy with a BMW and a bad attitude?

So I close my eyes tight. Lean in. I want everything to be okay, to be what I've been led to believe. I'm not feeling it, but I want to. The disappointment is overwhelming, so I try to ignore my gut, tell myself I'm tired. I move closer and allow my lips to meet Nick's again.

'Greg?' says a calm, female voice.

Nick pulls away from me and stumbles into the banister as he reaches for his low zip. The name, 'Abi,' trickles out of his already drooling mouth as my attention flies in the direction of the doorway where a woman stands smiling at me. We've met before. Yesterday. When she politely, but firmly, told me that Nick does not live here. She's wearing a baby pink tracksuit today, her black bob still shiny.

'Greg,' Abi repeats. 'You know what time it is.'

Nick throws himself against the front door, his fists pounding the pinewood frame. Abi plants her hands on his shoulders and steers him away, turning him towards the stairs. As if I'm a ghost, utterly invisible, she gives him a hefty push up the first few steps.

'It's time for you to pack your bags,' she says, as if telling a child to go and brush his teeth. 'Now. Right now. You've got exactly fifteen minutes. Then leave this house, keep walking and don't ever come back. I'm filing for a divorce.'

My lungs tighten sharp with each breath, as if an elastic band is being wrapped around them. I have to get the fuck out of here.

'Where are *you* going?' Abi asks.

It's a struggle to get to the door. Although just feet away, I can't get through it. As if stuck in a nightmare, one where limbs feel like lead, feet defeated by quicksand, I just cannot coordinate my fingers to find the door handle and pull. Once again, my army jacket is sliding off my shoulders, but now it's Abi grabbing it with both hands, pulling it off in an attempt to stop me escaping. Wriggling my arms free, I open the door, run.

The grey white sky is brighter than I expect. I hear Abi call out 'Oi!' and she's behind me. She yanks the straps of my pinafore, pulling me backwards, like a toddler in reins, and the sudden force makes me cough. I'm pushed onto my front, thrown down onto the garden path like a bag of trash being hauled into the garbage shoot. Face down to the ground, my lips take in the taste of tiny, rain-soaked stones. A claustrophobic warmth presses down upon me and Abi's breath is hot in my ear.

'You're not the first,' Abi says. 'Or the second, or even the third.'

153

I push back, but it's no use.

'You're not special. I know you probably think you are, but you're not.'

'I don't—'

'Shut up.'

Abi's fingers weave into my hair and she pulls hard. This time, it hurts. I cry out.

'I'm sorry,' I say. 'I had no idea. I had no . . .' But my lips taste more stones.

'That's what they all say!'

Then Abi releases me. I sit up, spitting the dirt from my mouth. I wait for her to say something else, to come at me again, but instead she starts to cry. This is not only my worst nightmare, but it's clearly hers, too. With every sob, every moan, every inch of lost dignity, I connect with her more. We've both been burnt, both been duped, we're both kind of in this shit together. So, I touch Abi's back, guiding her upwards. Without a second thought, I hold her. For a beat, both of us relax within each other's embrace, and there's a short silence.

'How long?' Abi asks.

'Six months,' I admit.

'Six months?! That's not possible, he's hardly left the house.'

'Oh, it's not what you think—'

'You have no idea what I think.'

'Of course, I'm sorry. But, we were only talking online, we never—'

'Online, eh? Well, that makes it alright, then, doesn't it?'

'Maybe?'

'Maybe.' Abi's eyes widen, then she raises her voice. 'Oh, yeah! "Maybe" my arse!'

Abi shifts, pulls away, our moment of sisterhood now passed. She's growing taller, slowly, towering over me. Closing my eyes tight, I prepare for pain, but, Oh! I'm being elevated instead. First my hands are pulled, followed by my arms, and then my feet are dangling in the air as I flop at the waist from up high. I'm on the move, my whole body bouncing further and further away from Abi, from Nick Gregory . . . well, Greg. Clifton Crescent becomes smaller and smaller, as if I'm flying on the back of a slim drone.

Around the corner, I'm lowered to stand on my own two feet. My knees are shaking, my palms chafed, a ladder runs down my black tights revealing scraped skin. A continuous thud hammers away in my chest, unbearable and ever so present.

But I'm safe. Jim has saved me.

18

Jim

A massive part of me is hoping I'm still in the Titanic, in that massive bed, having a massive fucking nightmare. I open the passenger door and stomp back round to my side of the BMW.

'Get in,' I say to Zara.

She doesn't move. She not only looks like the victim, but she's acting like one, too. I mean, yeah, it mightn't have been polite of me to get involved; whatever was going on over there is Zara's mess. But I can't just watch someone get the shit kicked out of them, even if I'm dealing with a loose cannon here. With Zara. This girl I've had the pleasure of knowing for a grand total of, what? An hour and ten minutes? Christ, that's not even the length of a film. Still, I imagine she was taught not to get in a car with a fella who commands, 'Get in.' I certainly wouldn't want any daughter of mine to comply.

'Zara, love. Get in the car.'

'It's okay, you can leave me here,' she says.

'Jesus Christ,' I mutter.

My whole face itches. I crouch down to look in the wing mirror. My eyes, no longer stinging rouge, are framed with purple shadows. This hangover is kicking me in the face.

'What you doing now?' I ask, my attention drawn to Zara who's lugging her bags and suitcases out of my car. Her haste is impressive. She slides that bloody mop out and, holding it upright, stops and lets out a moan.

'What's up?' I ask.

'My jacket,' she says. 'My favourite jacket, my army jacket. It's lying in the hallway of Nick – I mean, fucking *Greg's* – house.'

The mop falls from her hands, the wooden bounce of its handle echoing through suburbia. Zara sits on the largest of her suitcases, reaches into one dress pocket, and then into the other. She's patting herself all over, like she's trying to zap a wasp.

'Fuck!' she yells at the top of her voice.

The bungalows opposite seem to shudder. I shoot my arms out, as if the 'whoa' that escapes me stands a chance of calming her down. I'm guessing her phone was in her jacket pocket. She's going to need that.

'Do you want me to go and get your phone back?' I ask.

'You'd do that?'

'Well, I wouldn't recommend you going back to get it, love.'

'Don't laugh at me!'

'I'm not—'

'You are. You're dying to laugh at me.'

And I do laugh, unintentionally. Shit.

'Look, Zara, do you want me to—'

'NO! God, no!'

'Okay, okay, calm down.'

'God, I need to eat something,' she mumbles.

Is right, love. Me too. That butty she bought me in the cafe was good, but not enough. Between sad, winter-drained rose bushes and painted wooden fences, everywhere around us is beginning to grow a little halo of light-headed fuzz. I'm so hungover, I think I might faint. Zara's pacing is making me dizzy, back and forth she's going, and Christ, it's giving me anxiety. I need to get out of here, away from this soulless little pocket of nowhere, some brick estate smack bang between the city and the motorway. I didn't even see a pub close by on the way. The nearest thing that isn't a cul-de-sac is a retail park with a Next and a Costa and PC World. Just what everyone needs. A smart shirt, a mocha and a Mac.

'You can go,' Zara informs me.

'Can I?'

'Yes. Just go.'

'I'm released then, am I?'

'Don't be such an asshole. I'm not in the mood.'

'Oh, I'm the arsehole?'

'This has got nothing to do with you.'

'Yep. You're right. This has nothing to do with me.'

'Stop being so sarcastic.'

'Stop being so bossy.'

'I'm not bossy.'

'You are.'

'I'm not!'

'You are quite possibly the bossiest little madam I've ever met in me life.'

'Well, forgive me for forgetting how super sweet your life is, Jim.'

'Okay, I give up. I've stuck around. I've listened to your shit. I've tried to help. I'm done, Zara. I'm completely and utterly done. You want me to leave you here? Fine. You can find your own way to wherever, whatever. I've got me own shit to deal with.'

I get inside my car. Then, noticing one of her bags, a flimsy material thing with some sort of cartoon print on the front, I open my door – yet again – and go to hand it over to her.

'You left this on the back seat,' I say.

She reaches out to accept the bag, but whoa, I get the distinct impression she's about to vomit. Her tanned skin turns white as a bloody ghost, her huge brown eyes gloss over. Her hand misses the straps of the bag and it crashes to the ground. As does Zara.

And now, I'm sitting in a rocking chair, in the dark corner of a house that resembles my nan's, God rest her soul. A rose-pink lampshade decorated with dusty pink tassels stands beside me, the light on, giving the feel of evening, not lunch time. The floral wallpaper is busy with oval frames of sheep dogs, of birds, of horses. The cushioned chair I'm sat on gives off a musty scent. A huge golden clock in the shape of the sun hangs above a grey-green tiled fireplace, its electric fire giving off the sort of intense heat that my ma'd give a thumbs up.

I mean, seriously. What the fuck am I doing here?

Zara stirs. She's lying on the settee like Sleeping fucking Beauty. She falls back down as quickly as she tries to sit up.

'Sip this,' Mary says to her, and a china teacup is thrust towards her lips.

You might be thinking *who's Mary*?

Don't worry. I'm thinking the same bloody thing.

19

Zara

'Sip this,' a soft voice says to me.

The warm, sweet liquid tickles my throat and I gulp a little more. Sugar in English breakfast tea is delicious.

An older lady is standing over me. She takes my hand in hers. The bumps of veins feel smooth and comforting against my fingertips, like the crepe paper I used to make costumes during summer camp as a kid. I glance at the lady, taking her in from head to toe. Slippers that match her many lampshades encase her feet, but she isn't short of glamour. Eye shadow and lipstick bleed into her ageing skin, small gold hoops dangle from her ears. This is like being served tea by Elizabeth Taylor's sister.

'Am I dreaming?' This would be so typical of one of my insane dreams.

'You're not dreaming, queen,' the lady says. 'You fainted outside me house.'

'Queen?' I ask, still a little parched, despite the tea.

'Just a term of endearment,' the lady laughs. 'Where's this one from? You talk like you're in a film, got one of them American accents, haven't you? Here you go, queen. Eat a biscuit.'

As I munch on the biscuit, half awake, I try to figure out what brought me into this house, why I'm here at all.

'That was quite a commotion you created out there,' the lady says. 'I'm Mary, by the way. And I won't bite. You don't look very tasty.'

I cough up a little bit of biscuit. Mary laughs, a hearty but raspy laugh, roughened with years of smoking.

'I'm only kidding, queen. Jesus Christ, you look ill. And I bet you've got a lovely tan when the blood comes back to your face, you've got that gorgeous sort of dark skin, haven't you? You wanna thank your lucky stars you haven't got Irish blood swimming around your bones, I only have to think about the bloody sun and I fry. Where are you from?'

I'm having some difficulty answering questions.

'Do you remember where you're from? Oh Jesus, queen. Do you even know your name?'

I nod. 'Zara.'

'ZZZara? Or SSSara?'

'ZZZara.'

'Very posh. Like Zara Phillips.'

'And I'm half American, quarter Lebanese, quarter French, not that any of that means anything. I can't even speak French. It just explains the skin thing.'

'Ooh, the state of you. Very exotic.'

'Not really.'

'Do you wanna tell me what happened, queen?' Mary asks, taking a seat in a cream armchair moulded to fit her slender frame. A tabby cat jumps onto her knee and nuzzles in. The TV has been simmering with mild laughter and information

161

about how to win thirty thousand pounds plus a holiday to the Maldives, but mutes as she points a remote at it. The large wall clock tick, tick, ticks.

Blinking a few times, I come into a comfortable sitting position. My canvas tote bag is hanging off another cream armchair, my holdall is on the seat with my laptop poking out through the broken zip. Both suitcases are in the centre of the room, the mop lying by their side. I'm warm, I'm rehydrating, I feel – hope – that I'm safe. It'll do me good to talk, to make sense of everything that has just happened.

'You see, queen. When the kids are on their school holidays, they ride their bikes up and down this road and make a right racket. But, they're not on their school holidays, are they? When I'm just sat here watching a bit of Philip and Holly, I'm not expecting to hear shouting and screaming coming from out front. That chap filled me in, said you're a nice girl who'd had a bit of a bad morning, so I couldn't leave you outside. Do you wanna tell me what's going on?'

My mind can't move on from the part where Mary mentioned 'that chap.'

Jim? Where is he? Well, at least he hasn't left me completely alone. As far as bad situations go, I could have definitely woken up in worse places than Mary's English den. Jim could have left me on the street. Abi might have been watching from Clifton Crescent and come running after me with a knife.

Oh, God. Abi! Nick! No, not Nick. Fucking *Greg*.

'I fell in love with the wrong man,' I say.

'Don't we all?' Mary sighs. 'Go on. Spill.'

I tell Mary about how I met this man in Dubai who told me his name was Nick Gregory. Without going into detail, I spoke about our long-distance love affair and how I'd flown over here to surprise him for his birthday.

162

'I just found out today that he's married,' I conclude.

Mary leans in closer. 'You only just found out today?'

'Yes. His wife beat me up outside their house.'

'But, hold on a second, queen. You honestly only realised today that he was married?'

'Yes. I've got the bruises to prove it.'

'No, I don't doubt you got a beating. But I doubt you didn't know he was married.'

'I'm not lying, Mary.' I stand, but a head rush sends me back down again.

'Listen, queen. I've done a lot of cruising over the years. The Med, the Caribbean. And when you're sailing the seas on a ship, my God, the world seems like such a big place. Sometimes you have to get through one hell of a storm just to reach a spot of calm, sometimes you have to avoid the storm and endure a longer journey to see any hint of dry land. But, Zara queen, me daughter lives in New Zealand. And I love the bones of her. I can't bear the fact that she doesn't live down the road from me anymore. So, when it gets too much, I go and see her. And I've got her in my arms in just over one day. It's not cheap, but it's worth it.'

'I don't understand what you're getting at,' I say, hoping I don't sound rude.

'Flying makes the world a much smaller place. Why did it take you six months to come and see him?'

'I wanted to come sooner, but he was working on a large contract and wouldn't have had time to see me. Then, he was supposed to come to Dubai on business again, but that was cancelled. Then, he had a family wedding and lots of duties, and it was a couple of months ago that he had this horrid bout of tonsillitis so he didn't want to pass it . . .' I trail off.

'You're saying your entire relationship developed over a computer?' Mary asks.

'Uh-huh.'

And other than those selfies in Nick's car, I never even saw beyond his 'office'. Although I don't tell Mary that. I might as well borrow one of Mary's lipsticks and write STUPID across my forehead. It probably won't make me look any smarter if I tell Mary how I'd believed that my love for Nick was old-fashioned, as if he were away at war and we were writing letters to one another, except our exchanges were on messenger chats instead of paper.

Messenger chats. Oh my God, he must have set up a bunch of social media accounts under his fake name. Then again, it only takes seconds to create one, doesn't it?

'So,' Mary says, waving her arm. 'Where does this fella fit into all this?'

'What fella?' I ask.

Mary stands. The cat jumps down and darts from the room. 'Him.'

I twist around to look over my shoulder and see who Mary is pointing at. A shrill yelp escapes my throat. Sitting in a large wooden rocking chair, half shadowed like the Phantom of the Opera and reading a tattered old book, is Jim. He glances up, looking between me and Mary, not at all impressed with having to suddenly become a part of our conversation.

'How long have you been hiding there?' I cry.

He sighs, he stretches, he yawns. He closes the book, keeping his index finger sandwiched between the pages, and leans forward, his elbows resting on his knees. A slight shake of his head answers my question; he's been there the whole time.

'Why didn't you say anything?' I snap.

Jim looks at Mary, perhaps for help.

'He didn't have anything to say,' Mary says. 'How's the book?'

'Yeah, it's not bad, Mary,' Jim says, that smile appearing from one side of his mouth. 'I don't mind this sort of crime thriller stuff now and then. It's like crack on paper.'

'But it won't kill you,' Mary laughs.

'You're not wrong there,' Jim laughs, too.

'Take it with you.'

'You sure?'

'I won't be reading it twice. Do you wanna top up?' Mary lifts the teapot from the oval table beside her armchair. 'Another biscuit?'

'Oh, go on then. You've twisted me arm.'

I sit frozen on the edge of the sofa, my hands hanging onto my chest. What's going on here? Jim and Mary are acting like the best of friends, completely at ease within each other's company. Now they're talking about the book again, and other similar ones they've read, and I'm just getting lost listening to them, for they've somehow switched their chit-chat onto the area of Liverpool where Jim is from. Apparently Mary used to live down that way, going back about forty years. Jim says she must have done alright for herself, to get a house up this way. Mary says it was the only perk of being married to an accountant.

'I thought you'd gone,' I whisper.

Jim and Mary stop chatting.

'What did she say?' Mary asks.

'She said she thought I'd gone,' Jim says.

'Gone where?' Mary asks.

'Dunno. I think she thought I'd just got off, like.'

'Why would she think that?'

Nobody answers Mary's question. I smile at Jim, my way of saying thanks. He didn't just 'get off', or however he wanted to put it. Jim actually smiles back, that one-sided smile of his.

'And now you're awake, queen,' Mary says. 'Can you tell me why the bloody hell you're carrying a bloody mop around with you? I asked your friend here as he was carrying you through me front door, but he said he didn't know.'

'Well, I told her I wouldn't ask,' Jim says. True to his word, he hasn't.

'I mean, it's not unusual for a girl to be dragging a couple of suitcases around. But a mop?'

I hold my china teacup out for a top up and tell them my story. The elaborate details are discarded, a dumbed-down version of how I've been telling it before yesterday. Mary's wrinkled, painted face seems to grow a few more grooves as she listens. Jim sits quietly in the rocking chair, listening, not opening his book once while I speak.

'I wish you would've told me that story sooner,' Jim says, when I finish.

'Really?' I ask.

'Yeah, 'cause I could've warned you that Nick was a right plank.'

Mary breaks into a cackle.

'My heart is shattered,' I say, aware that I'm on the brink of yelling, but I'm furious. 'I know I seem like a crazy person, carrying a mop around like a security blanket, but it became a thing . . . like a joke. A private joke. Just between us. We'd video chat and the mop was always there with us like this extra person and I'd dress it with a silly hat or a wig and . . . oh, you don't understand.'

They clearly don't.

They're crying tears of laughter, Mary smudging her eye shadow and Jim pressing his thumbs into the corners of his eyes. They both keep apologising because they know their uncontrollable fits are offending me.

'And you brought it all the way from Dubai?' Mary asks.

I nod. 'I've flown so much in my life, it's almost like taking the bus. But this time was different. I had purpose rather than just bobbing back and forth.'

'Bloody hell, queen. It would've been easier bringing a camel than a mop. At least you could've rode on its back.'

'You know what, I don't have to listen to you guys mocking me,' I say. Enough is enough. 'Thank you for taking care of me, thank you for the tea, thank you for lending me your ears, but—'

'Oh, sit down, queen. Bloody hell, she's a dramatic one, isn't she?' Mary cocks her head and rolls her eyes at Jim, who seems to be really enjoying rocking back and forth in that chair.

'I'm not being dramatic,' I say, admittedly loaded with drama. I take a breath. 'I was under the impression that Nick was the person I'd spend my life with. He said those actual words, "We're going to spend our life together". What was I supposed to think? That really, he meant, "Oh, I'm secretly married and have two daughters"? Everything I own is squashed into those two suitcases. I booked a one-way ticket, for God's sake. That's how positive I was. No. That's how tricked I was.'

Jim stops rocking. The cat reappears and finds Mary's lap again.

'Anyway,' I say, calm, starting to feel the benefit of a decent cup of tea. 'I've booked a flight back, tonight. This trip is over. Almost. I just need to get to the airport. If I miss my flight I'm screwed.'

'What time's your flight?' Jim asks, both he and Mary looking up at the clock above the fireplace.

'Ten.'

'Oh, plenty of time,' Mary says. 'Do you wanna cheese butty?'

'No. I don't have plenty of time.' I swallow. 'I've got to get to Heathrow.'

'Well, don't let me stop you,' Mary says, her attention switching to the cat, stroking with verve. 'You both better get going soon. How far's Heathrow? That's London way, isn't it . . . maybe four, five hours from here?'

A thick pause sits in the centre of Mary's sitting room. Then, the cat, just about to drop off, is shaken awake, hissing, as Jim stands with gusto, the empty chair continuing to rock away.

'LONDON?' he shouts.

'What are you shouting for?' Mary asks.

'He always shouts,' I inform her. 'Although he thinks he doesn't.'

'I DON'T,' Jim shouts.

'You must bring out that side in him,' Mary says, trying to comfort her pissed-off cat.

'Thanks, Mary,' I huff.

'You didn't know you were taking her to London?' Mary asks.

'I thought I was taking her to John Lennon, or Manchester.' Jim paces the room and has a good look at the pictures on the wall. He clears the shaggy curls hanging over his eyes, pushing them back past his forehead. 'I know now,' he says.

Did I just hear that right?

'You'll take me all the way to London?' I ask.

Jim folds his arms, his focus remaining on the pictures.

'If you let go of the mop,' he says.

Well, of course I'll let go of the mop. What a stupid suggestion. Why would I want to carry this pointless mop around with me any longer? It symbolises the most catastrophic waste of time and an abundance of lies, lies, lies.

Then again.

Being without the mop means going back to who I was six months ago. What will I do with all the hope that's been growing within me, blowing up like a balloon? I don't want it to burst and disappear into thin air. Every minute, somewhere in the world, two people fall in love. So, when's it my turn? My heart is honest. I'm not cynical enough to have presumed Nick was lying. If I discard the mop, will it turn me into a cynic? Or strip me of my confidence? What will happen if I let go?

The cat is sleeping, snoring and purring in unison.

'I could do with a new mop,' Mary says. 'Or I could sell it on Ebay. If that mop's from Dubai, it's probably gold plated and worth a small fortune. Today could be my lucky day.'

I sling my canvas tote bag over my shoulder and pick up one suitcase. Jim follows me, lifting the second suitcase and the broken holdall. The mop stays flat on Mary's thick carpet, a dead man awaiting his burial.

'No, Mary,' I say, watching Jim load up his ruined car. 'I think today is *my* lucky day.'

20

Jim

Lodged deep within my soul, a glimmer of hope had been shining. Today was supposed to be *my* lucky day. You see, as I was sitting in Mary's rocking chair, I thought about getting my car to Griffo's dad, with minimal mileage, and maybe he'll tell me that the boot can be fixed. An easy job. Common, perhaps. It might still be worth something. And something is better than nothing. I've promised my ma Florida. There's no way I can take that away from her, not if there's the tiniest chance that Griffo's dad will give me *something* for this car.

Except, ha. Oh, ha fucking ha. Now, now I've been roped into going across the whole country, being some skivvy taxi driver, and for what? What's in it for me? Why didn't I say no? Who does Zara think I am; Robert bloody De Niro? But how could I stand in Mary's house after drinking her tea and eating her biscuits, after taking her paperbacks and using her loo, and look like the bastard who won't help the damsel in distress? Knowing women like Mary, she'd beat me senseless with that mop before sending me on a guilt trip that'd take years to return from.

'I can't thank you enough,' Zara says, pulling the seatbelt across her. 'Road trip!'

I sigh. This is absurd.

'Plus, I get to travel in style. Your car is so comfortable, Jim.'

With my foot on the accelerator, a harsh rev unleashes my need to swear.

'How's your hangover?' she asks, grinning.

God, I want to wipe that grin off her face.

'How's your love life?' I ask. Result.

That was a bit mean, wasn't it? The girl is broken, her ripped clothes making that deep scar on her face more prominent for some reason, and her long hair, so lush with loose curls this morning, is now a mass of frizz. I glance across at her, petite like a little doll, shrinking into the black leather seat. One leg is crossed over the other, a huge ladder in her black tights exposing smooth, bronze skin. She clearly gets to enjoy the sun. I dislike myself for eyeing her legs longer than necessary. Oh, so what? She's pretty. Doesn't mean I have to like her. And she's sulking after that last comment; her enormous, dark eyes studying her lap.

The traffic's not moving fast. We hit three reds in a row. A flashing light from behind the steering wheel distracts me.

'Shit,' I say.

I'm almost out of petrol. And there's nothing like a fuel strobe to trigger a bout of anxiety. Hitting the wheel with my fist, I shut my eyes. I hate how something as simple as filling a car up with fuel is a massive ball ache. Only hours ago, this would've been the least of my problems. In fact, with fifty grand in my pocket, I couldn't even begin to imagine having a problem. Now, I'm drowning in them.

'Do you go to London often?' Zara asks.

'Oh yeah. All the time,' I say, totally relishing in my own sarcasm.

'Business or pleasure?'

Heavy rain patters down, blurring my visibility. I'm going to have to tell her that this 'road trip' is about to end. Very, very soon. She might cry, and I'll feel like a right dick. But, I owe her nothing and the sooner our ordeal is over, the better. I can't afford to fill the tank up. It's as simple as that. The flashing light is urging me to speak up, begging me to get rid of Zara and get to Griffo's dad's before the car comes to an embarrassing halt.

The windscreen wipers go into overdrive. I pull into a slip road and park up outside a row of shops consisting of a newsagents, a betting shop and a takeaway called Pizza Perfecto that isn't yet open for business. I tell her simply that I can't take her to London and give her no excuse. I feel one hundred per cent shitty. But I remind myself that if Zara hadn't pissed on my chips, then I wouldn't be pissing on hers. Christ, there'd be no chips to piss on at all if she'd just been watching the bloody road this morning.

I wait for her tears to come. Instead, Zara starts to rub her hands together.

'It's freezing in here,' she says. Taking the liberty of fidgeting around with the various dials and buttons beneath the radio, she finds the heating and turns it up full blast. She's completely ignored everything I've just said to her.

'Zara?'

'Yeah?'

'Did you hear what I said?'

She nods.

'I can't take you to London,' I reiterate, my words delicate.

'I'm not stupid, Jim. I knew you weren't going to take me.'

'You did?'

'Yeah. I mean, why would you do that? Really? What's in it for you?'

I'm stumped. 'Nothing. Exactly.'

'It'd be weird if you did that.'

'It would.'

'So just drop me off at a train station. If it's not too much trouble.'

But, it is. It's indeed too much trouble. Driving from the outskirts of Liverpool to Lime Street station means hitting Friday traffic, which also means not making it to Griffo's dad's without having to fill up. And the way she said *if it's not too much trouble.* Christ, it's wound me up in corners I didn't even know I had.

No matter what way I look at it, I've got two choices: I can either ask Zara to pay for the petrol, which is humiliating, or I can swing by my flat and take the money from the biscuit tin.

And both choices suck.

It sits on top of the microwave in my kitchen.

Technically, it's not even a biscuit tin. It's an empty Quality Street tin, the last chocolate eaten sometime between Christmas Day and New Year's Day twenty-odd years ago. As a kid, I used to put my spare change – or my slummy, as my dad would call it – in there, because it was more transparent than a piggy bank. I liked to see my money, not guess how much might be in there. That way, there was no disappointment. Back then, the slummy saved would be spent on my favourite magazine, or with enough will power, games for my Sega; *Sonic, Golden Axe.* They were replaced by hardback books, videos, and eventually DVDs, my vast film collection still presented across three shelves in my bedroom (in alphabetical order, too).

These days, the slummy is saved for less entertaining essentials such as bleach and toilet roll, a pint of milk. I dip into the biscuit tin more often than I'd like, so I'm not holding out for a miracle, just enough to keep my dignity intact. There might be enough in there for a bit of petrol, but nowhere near enough to get my ma to the airport, never mind bloody Florida.

'Where's the train station from here?' Zara asks when we pull up outside the chippy, the busy flyover rattling overhead and sheltering us from the rain. Wide eyed, like Alice in bloody Wonderland, I'm guessing that a girl like Zara isn't used to places that are so unattractive.

'It's not around here,' I say. 'I just need to nip in and get something.'

'Nip in where?' Zara looks around frantically across the dashboard.

'There,' I point to the chippy.

'Wong's Fish Bar?'

I nod.

'Why? Are you hungry?'

I can't tell her this is where I live, but honestly, I do not understand why. There's nothing to be ashamed of, nothing whatsoever. The flat I rent is decent. Small. My leather settee purchased on Ebay is in good nick; wooden blinds; an impressive wall of bookshelves. A turntable sits on a second-hand tile-and-teak coffee table with a collection of vinyl filed at its side. I'm no slob, and other than not changing my bed sheets as often as I probably should, the place is clean. But, from the outside, I know it looks like a crack den. And no matter how many scented tea lights I burn around the place, the smell of grease from the chippy can't be masked. Why do I care what Zara thinks? Christ, she thinks I'm some 'mysterious entrepreneur', a joke almost worse than today itself. Maybe that's it; I can't pretend that I don't like the notion of being somebody I'm not. Somebody successful, somebody who has it all. Anything's better than the truth.

'Starving,' I tell her.

Well, I'm not lying. Except something from Wong's? Ah, bollocks. The novelty of that wore off about four days after I moved in. But I say, 'And you should eat before your journey.'

'From there?' Zara asks, horror bleeding from her voice.

I'm quick to defend. I'm fond of Mr and Mrs Wong and their antisocial kids.

'Best chips in Liverpool,' I say. 'You can't leave without trying them.'

'We're kind of in a hurry . . .'

'You'll be sorry.'

Zara flashes her perfect teeth, smiling from her mouth, not her eyes.

'Okay. I'm up for anything,' she says.

'Wait here.'

I'm parked on double yellows, but there isn't another space free. Switching on the hazards, I dive out of the car but not before warning Zara to stay put. I don't trust her not to wander off, so I give her a job; to watch out for traffic wardens. She accepts her challenge with a small salute and I run into Wong's.

'Jimbo!' Mr Wong cries, his blend of Chinese and Scouse always sounding on the verge of tears. 'Long time no see, lad.'

An acute waft of vinegar and chip fat hits my nostrils.

'Can I go through the back, mate?' I ask.

'You forget your key?'

'Something like that.'

175

'Jimbo!' Mrs Wong appears, always sounding as though she's telling me off.

'He forget his key, love,' Mr Wong cries.

'Stupid.' Mrs Wong folds her arms.

I ignore her and fly past, through the kitchen and out the back door, ajar to carry away the smell of cooking. I grab the spare key from under the mat, there for the Wongs' antisocial kids to let themselves in and watch Netflix on my telly.

Taking the lid off the biscuit tin, I see a sea of silver and copper; about fifteen quid's worth, I reckon. It'll take me too long to count all this out. I open the cupboard below the cutlery drawer, take a carrier bag from the stash. Emptying the coins into the bag, I shake it to check there's no holes, then tie a knot in it. I catch my reflection in the full-length mirror hanging in the hall beside the bathroom door. It won't hurt to change my t-shirt. It reeks of smoke, stale booze, body odour. I throw the carrier bag of coins onto my bed, unzip my fleece and take off my t-shirt, scrunch it into a ball, chuck it into my wash basket. I grab a clean t-shirt, one I won from the Pacific Arms pub quiz, a local brewery advertised across the chest. I put my fleece back on.

Shit. Zara'll wonder why I'm wearing a different t-shirt.

I drop the plastic bag, zip my fleece right up to beneath my chin. That's better. I ruffle my hair a bit and retrieve the bag.

Oh, double shit. The bag rips. Coins splatter across the carpet. There must've been a bloody hole in it after all. Falling to my knees, I attempt to collect the coins but can't hold onto them without some slipping between my fingers. Blood rushes to my head. I see stars, black spots. Snowy wasn't half right about how I handle hangovers. Suddenly the idea of salty, greasy chips from downstairs isn't such a bad one.

I go back into the kitchen, pour myself a glass of water. I

catch a glimpse of the collage hanging on the wall, photos arranged all slapdash, yet thoughtfully planned with an online template, made by Helen – a joint gift from her and my mates – for my thirtieth birthday. Most of the photos were taken during our teens and twenties, boozed up, boggle-eyed and effervescent. Hats played a big part: all of us wearing sombreros and drinking tequila; all of us in Santa hats or sparkly devil horns. Christ, I was broke back then, too, except it didn't seem to matter the way it does today. An unwise arrogance allowed me to enjoy the lack of cash, the start of debt, almost as if there was a poetry attached to it, a beauty that portrayed me as more interesting because I had more shit to shovel. These photos are bursting with stupidity, but in truth, they were packed with potential.

'Bastards,' I mutter, giving the collage a sly look. 'Smug little bastards.'

Mikey Farley's aged a lot, his hairline creeping backwards at a pace not to be envied, and Griffo – who's always looked older, a middle-aged fella by the age of twelve – looked trimmer back then, less bloated, fewer chins. Helen, with radiant red hair on every photo, her sharp blue eyes alive, hasn't changed a bit. Neither's Snowy. And they still hit the hard stuff regularly. How do they manage it with two kids? But, God. Helen's texts from last night. She'll be in a world of pain today, her paranoia sending poor Snowy around the bloody bend.

I take the empty biscuit tin into the hallway, opening it once again. Bending down, I pick up the coins and put them back where they belong. I'll just have to take the whole tin with me.

'That was quick,' Zara says.

I give a sigh, relieved, and tug on my seatbelt.

'Where are the chips?'

'Huh?'

'The best chips in Liverpool?'

'Oh. Yeah.'

'Are they in that?' She points to the back seat where I've just slung the biscuit tin.

I rub my eyes with the palms of my hands.

'Jim?'

'What?'

'Are you okay?'

'The chips are cooking,' I say. 'I was just checking you were alright.'

And back I go into Wong's, and this time, for chips. I ask Mrs Wong if I can owe her later, expecting her to bollock me, but she says, 'On the house.' I presume this is due to my Netflix generosity. Then, she asks me if I want salt and vinegar on my chips, and still chuffed about the free fodder, I say yes. She hands me two hot paper packages which I hold against my chest and inhale the delicious, yet – ah, shit – overbearing smell. If anybody knows how much this particular smell lingers, it's yours truly, the fella who lives above a chippy. What a dickhead. I'm about to expose my car to this awful stench, giving Griffo's dad another excuse to knock further pounds off. I can't ask Mrs Wong for fresh freebies. And I'm going to look like an even bigger dickhead returning to Zara a second time without chips.

'Why you dithering?' Mrs Wong asks.

'I'm not . . .'

'You are. You dithering.'

I never dither. I'm not a ditherer. I look at the clock above the extensive chippy menu, listing dishes from English stodge to Peking duck, and it's bang on two. I try to work out how many hours it'll be before today is officially over.

'You still dithering, Jimbo.'

Through the raindrops dancing down Wong's windows like fat wriggly worms, I can see the ridiculous state of my car. Nobody needs perfect vision to see its faults. Christ. Even a blind man'd be able to see it's ruined.

'I'm not dithering,' I say again, and run through the rain, back into my car.

I toss a portion of chips into Zara's lap. The rip of paper is satisfying and we eat in silence, the sound of the rain and the traffic rather therapeutic. I'm guzzling the hot chips, the potato burning the roof of my mouth. But, the sooner I eat, the sooner we can get on our way.

'Can you put the radio on, please?' Zara asks.

'Yes, your highness,' I say, not actually intending to say that out loud.

She doesn't react. The atmosphere hangs between us like frost on a slippery path.

Perhaps she's been crying? The tip of her nose is red raw, her eyes misty, black smudges kissing that scar. But, hey, it's Friday! Friday, Friday, Friday! The radio is so kindly reminding us, its upbeat vibe barging into my car. A phone-in is taking place, callers going live on air to say the most exciting thing they're about to do this afternoon, this evening, this weekend. Each caller is trying to outdo the previous, and if I hear another, 'Whoop whoop,' I might smash the radio up with my bare fist. The Black Eyed Peas come on singing about how tonight's gonna be a good night.

'You finished?' I ask.

'Mmm. They were tasty. Thank you.'

'You haven't eaten much.'

'I'm worried about the grease staining my clothes, making them smell.'

I bite my bottom lip so hard it's probably going to bleed.

Snatching the wasted chips, the paper, the plastic forks, the crappy little napkins, I nip out and toss it all into the bin outside Wong's, give Mr Wong a friendly wave, get in my car and speed off.

The smell isn't actually so bad. Plus, the food seems to have put Zara into a bit of a coma, all five chips she consumed. Her head is resting against her seatbelt, her eyes closed, heavy. I can tell she's not asleep, her frown's too deep, her lips too tightly closed together. Still, I won't dare disturb her.

'You having a giraffe, love?' the girl on the till at the petrol station asks me.

She's caked in make-up, her eyes two black buttonholes in a tangerine face. Intimidating spikes grow from her finger-nails as she snarls, counting the change I've poured from the biscuit tin onto her counter. I try to help her out.

'Move your hand,' she says, already at the end of her short, short tether.

A fella behind starts whistling. The hole I'm falling down is getting deeper, the ground sucking me into the dregs of River Mersey puddles. I want a wave to come and wash me away. I don't know how I can sink much lower.

'You're 10p short,' the girl shrieks, like she actually can't believe it.

I'm that kid in the newsagents all over again.

The fella behind stops whistling.

'Here you go, mate,' he says, tapping me on the shoulder. He places a twenty-pence piece on the counter. I scoop up ten pence to give him his change, but the fella waves his hand. 'Ah, forget it, mate. No probs.'

Words can't find their way into my mouth. I hope my gracious nod and pathetic sigh of relief is enough for the fella who's just saved my arse, witnessed my demise. I back away, sort of waving, sort of hoping to disappear in a puff of smoke behind the display of Pringles.

'Don't you want your empty Quality Street tin?' the girl with the tangerine face shouts.

I pause, just for a second.

'Nah,' I say. And get back into my car. 'Shit.'

I flop my head onto the steering wheel. The stink of chips has seriously lingered.

At Lime Street station, there's nowhere to park.

The temporary parking bays aren't only full, but a big queue of cars trails behind and the longer we sit in that, the longer I've got to listen to Zara. She's perked up. I can't decide what's more intolerable; the radio or her questions.

'Is Liverpool always this busy on a Friday?'

'Why does Britain have such terrible weather?'

'Do you get snow here at Christmas time?'

'Have you ever been stuck in traffic in LA?'

'Haven't you been to LA?'

'Is it always this windy?'

Her accent's bearable, a cute mash of not-quite English and not-quite American, but that doesn't mean I want to talk to her. She reapplies something onto her lips, another coat. I glance across at her and watch her pout, then wipe some dried sleep away from the corners of her eyes with her pinky.

'I like trains,' she goes on. 'They're a bit of a novelty to me. The mode of transport I've taken least in my life.'

I indicate, move left and drive past the queue.

'Do you?' she asks.

'Do I what?'

'Like trains?'

'Yeah. When I was, like, six.'

I drive past the main entrance to Lime Street station, its wide steps scattered with people scurrying to dodge the torrential rain, another umbrella blowing inside out with each gust of wind. On the opposite side of the road, St George's Hall stands proud, unafraid of the storm dancing so vigorously around its grand pillars. The main road is chocker, bumper to bumper, and I unfasten my seatbelt, leaning across Zara to see if I can make out what the holdup is. A coach, plus a couple of buses, perhaps.

I lose my balance a little and put my hand out to steady myself. On Zara's leg. Just above her knee. I feel like a right prick. She lets out a sort of, 'Ooh!' and I turn towards her saying, 'Soz.' My hair's falling across my eyes, partially stunting my vision, but I can't doubt how pretty she is. Those thick lashes accentuate her dark eyes, like that posh chocolate that comes wrapped in cardboard with gold writing. Her skin looks tired, yet natural. I reckon she'd look gorgeous all dressed up for a night out. But, Christ, she's had a shit day. I have to give her that.

'I think what you did was pretty brave,' I say, honestly.

Zara twitches, like a wild animal on its guard. I edge the car forward. The lack of conversation between us suddenly demands a filler. I'm over-analysing the leg grabbing; no, the leg touching; no, well, whatever it was. The total accident.

'Really?' Zara asks.

'Yeah. It was ballsy. Not that you need to know what I think—'

182

'No, I do. I'd like to know, actually.'

'Well, it shows you're not afraid of failure.'

'But I did fail.'

'Failing's better than being afraid of failure, don't you reckon? It's active, not passive.'

Zara frowns as if this requires a lot of thought, which is cute.

'So you don't think I'm a psycho?' she asks, eventually.

'Oh, yeah. I reckon you're a total fucking psycho.'

And we both laugh, cheeky grins mirroring each other.

'How did you track him down?' I ask.

'It was so easy. His email signature had his company name and address beneath it.'

'Jesus, he was asking to be found.'

'Although, now it's obvious his name is actually Greg Nicholas. God, even saying that name out loud makes him sound like a total stranger. Like who the fuck is Greg Nicholas?'

I want to tell her that he's someone just not worth her time anymore, but instead, I shake my head, slowly. He's not worth my words. Besides, I need to watch where I'm driving. The coach has moved on, which means the cars in front are going forward. I turn right past the Empire Theatre, then right again into the much quieter side street and park up outside the stage door. Opposite, the side entrance to Lime Street station is beneath a shelter, opening out onto a busy taxi rank. Zara can go in that way.

'Do you mind helping me with my bags?' she asks.

I do a swift check around for traffic wardens. Nobody would dare to roam the streets in this sort of weather, not even Rita the Meter Maid. I turn off the ignition, release my seatbelt.

'Yes, your highness,' I joke.

183

But, neither of us move. We sit still, our seat belts unfastened, our urge to get out at level zero. A bucket load of hailstones smash against the windscreen, this side street a wind trap, as my car rattles. Amidst taxis and cars honking horns, yelps and squeals of those caught outside echo through the weather. A gang of women are huddled under the small shelter of the stage door, and through the haze of my steamed window, I can see they're all dressed in identical black t-shirts and trousers with a bright pink sash. One wears a white veil and a pair of L plates. None are wearing a coat, their hands shielding their hairdos. Shit. They're not those girls from Belfast, from the Titanic last night, are they? Then again, Liverpool's a haven for hen parties.

I look at Zara. Her head is pressed back against the headrest, like mine. She raises her eyebrows, slides her eyes in my direction. I return the eyebrow raise and we both let out a simultaneous sigh.

'After three?' I suggest.

'After three,' Zara nods.

'One, two . . .'

And on three, we fling our doors open, Zara struggling with her side and scrunching up her face to push against the wind. I slam mine shut and, hunched over, run to assist her. Already, I'm drenched, the hailstones battering onto my fleece, my thighs sticking to my jeans. Zara emerges, and we both shift her belongings from the back seat onto the road. So much rain is dancing into the gutters that huge puddles have appeared, the ground unable to soak up the water. My canvas trainers squelch. My toes are cold and damp inside my socks. The women on the hen do start singing, badly.

'She's gettin' married in the morning . . . Ding dong the bells are gonna CHIIIIME . . .'

They sound like gremlins being strangled.

Zara can't shift her suitcase, it's stuck in a whirlpool of water, and she drops her broken holdall into the puddle. I pick it up, thrust it into her chest and tell her to run.

'I'll get these,' I say, gesturing her to get inside the station.

A taxi hoooooonks, the driver's hand unmoving from the horn. Zara has run into the road without looking where she's going. The honking continues and Zara stands there in the rain yelling about being sorry. I tell the driver to do one. The grease from those chips has settled in my stomach and I burp. That's better. Using all my strength, I hoist Zara's suitcases from the gutter and get them safely into the station.

Zara's beneath the timetable board, searching for information on what time the next train to London departs. Her head tilts to the side and she's wringing her long hair out, water dripping around her soaked feet. She takes off her tiny shoes – small enough to fit a doll – and pours water from the heels. Inside my trainers, my feet wrinkle in slush. I trudge the bags over to her and rest my hands on my knees, shaking out my wet head like a dog.

'Have I got panda eyes?' Zara asks, breathless.

'What's that?'

She points to her cheekbones and bats her eyelashes, drawing imaginary circles around them with her fingertips. Her makeup has run giving her a couple of black eyes, one much more prominent than the other.

'No,' I tell her. 'You look great.'

Zara blinks. 'Thanks.'

I give another shake and water trickles down my nose, sprinkling Zara. She looks down at her wet clothes and she bends over and laughs. I laugh, too. You've got to hand it to the weather. My side aches with a stitch, yet I'm still laughing, and for a moment, I could give this girl a hug, wish her well for the remainder of her trip.

Zara straightens up, pulling the band from her hair and using it to harshly scrape it all back and tie a knot onto the top of her head. Her whole face is now unmasked, bright like the moon.

Except.

'You missed a bit,' I say.

And I reach out, taking the few loose strands dangling down the side of her face, tucking them behind her ear.

'What time's your train, then?' I ask, removing my fleece, flapping it dry.

'Well, it says 14.47.'

'Perfect. Time to grab a butty from the Upper Crust.'

'No . . .'

'Burger King?'

'No . . . it says 14.47 . . . Cancelled.'

I stop flapping and look up at the board. She's right. The 14.47 to London Euston is cancelled. As is the 14.39 to Manchester Piccadilly. And the 14.42 to Newcastle. And the 15.47 to London Euston, too.

'Maybe there's something wrong with the board?' Zara ponders.

I'd presumed the hectic rush within the station was an amalgamation of the weather and a Friday afternoon, but I notice now that this isn't general train station bustle. The place is utter chaos. Queues of passengers are crammed together, all demanding refunds at the desk, phones pressed against their ears or fingers tapping frantically, all trying to find alternative ways of getting to where they need to get to.

An older couple, complete with overnight bags and matching beige raincoats, stop the fella pushing a trolley

186

fitted with a bin, the fella who keeps Lime Street station clean and tidy. They're demanding some sort of explanation. The fella picks up an empty crisp packet with a helping hand grabber and mutters something to the couple.

'A tree?' the wife exclaims. 'You're telling me we can't get back to Manchester because there's a tree on the line?'

The poor fella shrugs, trying to get on with his job.

'A tree?' she says again. 'How can a tree cause this much disruption?'

Her husband offers the handle of his overnight bag to his wife and rolls up his sleeves.

'Tell me where this tree is,' he says. 'And I'll move the bloody thing with my bare hands.'

Me and Zara look at each other.

'Must be one hell of a tree,' Zara says. 'I'll have to take a taxi.'

The problem is, the whole of Liverpool seems to have had the same idea. The line waiting for black cabs is expanding and Zara runs ahead leaving me to follow behind with the cases, a slave to her actions. She waves, calling me over.

'Here you are, your highness,' I say, out of breath.

'Why do you keep calling me that?'

'This line's moving quickly. You'll be home in no time.'

Zara sulks. 'Home.'

'That's where you're going, isn't it?'

'My papa's villa is certainly not home.'

What the bloody hell's her problem now, eh? Just the thought of a villa in Dubai is uplifting.

'So you're gonna get a taxi all the way to London?' I ask.

'Are you stating the obvious?'

A man standing in front of us whips his head around. He's

stout, balding, with steamed-up glasses and a soggy newspaper tucked beneath his armpit. He looks as knackered as I feel.

'A taxi won't take you all the way to London,' he says.

'Why not?' Zara asks.

'You're best getting them to drop you off at Crewe, get the train from there.'

'But, what if another tree falls on the line?'

'What if the sky comes crumbling down?'

'Good point.'

The man returns to wait for his taxi.

'It's gonna cost you a fortune,' I tell her. 'Just to warn you.'

'Well, what choice do I have, Jim?'

'Don't snap at me.'

'I'm not snapping.'

'You are. Your highness.'

'You think I'm some stuck-up spoilt little princess, don't you?' she cries.

Well, right now, she is acting a little, how can I put it? Grand? But, I can't be bothered to elaborate. She's leaving. I've got my own problems to sort out. A mountain of them.

'I'm not, you know,' she continues. 'I'm not a princess. At all. And I know why you think that. You're as cliché as every-body else. It's because you know I live in Dubai. You just presume I live in a palace with servants and camels, that I'm about to be married off to some mega rich sheikh . . .'

'Well . . . are you?'

'NO!'

I'm holding back a sly smile. I fail.

'You don't believe me, do you?'

'I didn't say anything, love.'

'You still think I'm a princess.'

Christ. I'm not going to entertain this.

188

'Just because I went to boarding school doesn't mean I'm a princess.'

I raise my eyebrows, dare to give a little whistle.

'I went to school with actual princesses. I was like dirt on their shoe in comparison.'

'Me heart bleeds.'

'And I was expelled.'

'Right.'

'Anyway, that's beside the point. I'm just sick of people presuming I'm someone I'm not. I don't have a job, and – believe it or not – I really wish I had one, and I don't have much of . . . anything. And! I have to pay my father rent for a room in a villa he gets to live in for free from his company.'

The man with the soggy newspaper turns around again, adjusts his glasses.

'For free?' he asks, gently.

Zara nods. 'For free.'

'Can you afford a taxi all the way to London?'

'What choice do I have? Thanks to that damn tree.'

A waiting black cab honks, impatient. The man's now at the front of the line. Zara's next, her black cab turning into the rank and crawling up beside us. The driver steps out to assist with the bags.

'Going the airport, love?' he asks.

I open the taxi door.

'Your carriage awaits,' I joke. 'Your highness.'

'You're an asshole,' Zara says.

'It's been a pleasure.'

The driver settles back in his seat, and looking through the glass shield, he barks at Zara to 'get a move on'. There's no need for that; she hasn't been taking her time. If anything, quite the contrary. As she gets in, I'm still holding her canvas bag, swinging it from its straps. I look properly at the cartoon image printed on one side. It's a meerkat sat in a jacuzzi. It's pretty funny, actually. Zara leans across from her seat and snatches it.

'Why so tetchy?' I ask.

'Doesn't matter.'

'Ah, come on. Is this some cult foreign cartoon you're into?'

'No. I drew it. Okay?'

'What? You drew it? The meerkat?'

'Yes. And the hot tub, and the . . . everything. It's my design. My cartoon.'

'Ooh, get you. It's good,' I admit. 'You got others?'

'I love how you wait until now to spark up a conversation, Jim.'

Zara pulls the twisted knot on top of her head and her hair falls loosely down her back, around her shoulders. The driver knocks on the glass shield. It's time to go.

'See ya later, your highness,' I say, and close the door, giving the roof of the cab a tap.

'Bye, Jim,' Zara says through the open window. 'And thanks.'

I'm free.

Approximately thirty seconds later, I'm not even out of the taxi rank, psyching myself up to run back through the rain, I hear Zara yelling again. Only this time, it's not directed at me. She's back at the front of the line, the driver placing her luggage around her.

'Please take me,' she's begging.

'You've wasted me time, love.'

'I've done nothing of the sort. You're a taxi driver, you take people where they need to go and you get paid for it.'

'I'm not taking you all the bloody way to London.'

'Why?'

'And how am I supposed to get the bloody hell back from London?'

'Drive?'

'You know what that'll cost me in petrol? In time? Me and the wife are going to a silver wedding tonight. I won't make it back for last orders.'

'I'll pay for your petrol, your time. Just take me. Please.'

'No.'

'Please.'

'Bloody tourists.'

Another driver steps out of his black cab.

'What's the hold up, mate?' he asks.

Zara's driver stretches out his arm and points a finger right in her face.

'This one here wants me to drive her all the bloody way to London.'

'Well, you can't do that, mate.'

'I bloody well know.'

'Listen, girl, he can't take you to London. Now move.'

Those waiting in the queue are having a gander, standing on their tip toes to get a good view, muttering mixed opinions on whether or not this girl should be taken all the way. Some woman shouts, 'Don't be a lousy get, take the poor girl!' Another questions why on earth anybody would ever want to go to London in the first place. A few agree. And yet, there's Zara, struggling with getting her bags onto the pavement whilst still pleading, asking the next taxi driver, then the next. Nobody's helping her. And why should they? Nobody knows her.

Except me. I've known her for about four hours now.

'Excuse me, mate,' I say, jumping in front of the first taxi, another passenger now in the back seat and the driver about to exit the rank. I wave my arms, the brakes of the vehicle squeaking from the rain. 'You can't just leave this girl stranded.'

'Jim, what are you doing?' Zara asks.

'You can't treat her like that, mate. Have a heart, will you?'

The taxi honks his horn and moves forward a little, threatening.

'Don't be such a tosser!' I shout.

The driver steps out. Shaved head and shaved chin, he's equal to me in height, but three times the build, tattoos across his knuckles. I very nearly shit myself.

'Who you calling a tosser? You fucking gobshite.'

'Eloquent choice of words, mate,' I say.

Variations of horns honk, drivers hang out of their windows. Some are quietly trying to see what the problem is, and others aren't so polite, vomiting the most vulgar vocabulary. The driver squares up to me, his round, hard belly pressing into my ribs. On instinct, I push back.

Somehow, Zara gets herself in between me and the driver. Well, she is small enough to appear from nowhere, and she muscles in, trying to break us apart. I place a hand around her waist, an attempt to keep her away from our spat, but the driver grabs the strap of her dress and throws her against the brick wall.

A small gasp escapes the onlookers.

'I'm fine, I'm fine,' Zara says, shaking off the gravel, but her voice is trembling.

This is bang out of order. I take hold of the driver's sweat-shirt and swing a punch with my free hand right across his jaw. A larger gasp now filters through the taxi rank, a couple of cheers and a round of applause from the hen party huddled in the stage door opposite. Fuck. My hand aches. I'm by no means a fighter, and, in all honesty, I'm panicking. The driver's eyes are bulging, his round head becoming very red. His tattooed fists curl tight, his browning teeth drip with riled spit. Another driver barges in, holding the first driver back and telling me to fuck off.

'Go fuck yourselves,' I say.

My knees are quivering. Either I'll have to swing another punch or await my own beating. I haven't had a fist fight since I was ten and some lad nicked my cola pips in the park.

'Stop this,' Zara says. 'None of this is going to get me to London.'

And, great. A couple of police officers have spotted the incident and are stomping towards us all. I back off, hands up high. Both drivers get into their respective black cabs, drive off. They even manage to get willing passengers. You can't blame them in this weather.

'What was all that about?' a police officer asks. She's female, much younger than me.

'A misunderstanding,' I say, chancing a smile.

The second police officer strolls into the rain with confidence, as if immune to getting wet. Zara shivers.

'Where's your coat?' the young police officer asks.

'Uhm. In my suitcase,' Zara says.

'Why aren't you wearing it?'

'I like the cold.'

'You look a little lost. Are you with this man here?'

I find myself placing my arm across Zara's shoulders. 'Yep, she's with me.'

'And everything's okay?'

'Everything's fine,' I say. 'It's them taxi drivers you should be talking to, not us. They started it.'

'How so?'

'Erm . . .'

It's impossible to sound like an innocent citizen when facing the police.

'Jenny?' the second police officer calls from the other side of the road.

The tingling ache in my fist subsides. But, the adrenaline pumping in my chest beats stronger. Zara squeezes my arm. I follow Jenny's head, turning in response to her partner. A complicated knot sitting behind my belly button, the one that started with the crash four hours ago and has been feeling tighter, tighter, tighter as this bloody day progresses, tightens again.

'Excuse me,' Jenny says and goes to join her partner.

Beside the stage door of the theatre, beneath a huge poster advertising the forthcoming pantomime starring Jane McDonald and some fella from *Hollyoaks*, is my BMW, being inspected. Both police officers are drawn to the boot, one bent over and scanning the damage, the other taking down some notes. I watch, willing for the car to be left alone. Jenny is reading the number plate aloud, speaking into her radio. Her partner looks at the bonnet, the perfect undamaged bonnet, rain water its only enemy.

'I didn't mean to park it there,' I say, indicating the weather by holding out my palms, a prayer for it to let me off the hook. 'Desperate times, you know . . .'

'So this is *your* car?' the policeman asks.

Shit. Shit, shit, shit. They're not going to take it away, are they?

'I'm just running some checks,' Jenny says.

She's mid twenty-something, I reckon, but could pass for sixteen, the sort who gets annoyed that she still gets asked for ID buying a bottle of prosecco in the Asda. It's not cool or attractive being as cute as a squirrel, and this girl must've fought hard to get her warrant card and wear that hat. But, I can't feel sorry for her. She's making me take a breath test, standard procedure, apparently. Twelve hours have passed since my binge, but my nervous system isn't enjoying having to comply, to wait, to wonder if today's truly going to become much, much worse.

'You passed,' Jenny's partner, the policeman confirms.

That sounds like good news. Yet I pause, afraid to get excited by an answer that I maybe misunderstood. If I passed, what does that actually mean? That I passed and I'm drunk? Or I passed, meaning I'm not drunk?

'You're fine,' the policeman says, kindly.

I embrace the rainfall. But Jenny's still checking my number plate.

She tells me she's just discovered that this BMW M3 isn't insured. Okay, I know I never read the small print when I signed for the car yesterday, but for fuck's sake, who reads the small print? I'm buggered, aren't I? It's over.

'Keys,' she says, holding out her hand. And she confiscates them like a swiss army knife being taken from the bad boy in school.

'You'll get it back,' she says now, daring to tap my arm. 'Once you get some insurance and pay the impounding fee. It's only two hundred pounds.'

'Just bear in mind,' the policeman adds, 'it's twenty quid a day on top of the release fee, so you mightn't wanna leave it too long. Got it?'

'Loud and fucking clear,' I say, then, 'sorry.'

The penultimate scene from a horror movie is more pleasant than watching the recovery truck arrive, the monstrosity taking over the whole street. A man shorter than Zara rubs his hands together with glee as he takes my place – MY PLACE – in the driver's seat. He manoeuvres the BMW onto the truck, the hazard lights flashing a burnt orange, a burst of colour too intense for such a miserable afternoon.

I know my lip is quivering. 'Bye,' I mumble.

The truck slowly turns right past the Empire Theatre and as the mangled boot begins to disappear from sight, I fall to my knees in the empty spot where my car had once been. I squeeze my fists, my eyes, every muscle keeping my torso warm to save myself from screaming. Christ, even at my dad's funeral I kept my shit together, giving my ma and my sisters the freedom to cry as much as they needed to. But, honest to God, I feel like crying now.

'I'm sorry,' I mutter aloud, perhaps in preparation for what I'll have to tell my ma. The distance to Florida is now so much further than a mere 4,200 miles away. So much fucking further.

And, where the hell am I going to find two hundred quid? Or more! Not to mention the cost to get the bloody thing insured and fixed up? Winning this car has become a financial catastrophe on a scale that me and my humble life can't handle. Bloody hell, I'm sobbing. I am. I'm sobbing! It feels weirdly good for a split second, a quick release. What had my ma said about winning?

'. . . And all those lottery winners in the paper, they go on about how winning was the worst thing that ever happened to them.'

How right she was, and how quickly I'd dismissed her.

My jeans are soaked with rain, the pavement rough beneath

my knees. Fucking hell, I'm in the gutter, quite literally. I can't blame Jenny. The young girl's only doing her job, which is more than I can say for that bloody taxi driver. I like people who work hard, live an honest life, like my dad did. So I can only blame one person for this, and she's there, on the opposite side of the road, sheltering from the rain, sitting on one of her enormous suitcases and shivering like some abandoned orphan. She drove her banger into my gem of a car and then blamed me for being drunk. And, afraid of the consequences, not wanting to seem like the big beast next to the little beauty, I've let her get away with it.

Well, not anymore. Zara's going to pay. Yep. She's going to pay the two hundred quid plus to get my car from the pound, pay for insurance, the lot. Every fucking penny.

Of course, there's going to have to be something in it for her. That's how deals work, isn't it? And I'm going to have to somehow stop her from hitchhiking a ride to London, hopping on a coach, finding a way to Crewe to get a train, or simply saying no. So, I'm left with one option. The hen party are still contemplating when to 'run for it'. I can hear a few of them saying, 'Not yet', one being the bride, so she trumps the lot. I approach them.

'Ladies,' I say, smiling. Dying inside.

They whoop. One of them starts singing 'It's Raining Men'.

'Can I borrow someone's phone?' I ask. 'Please.'

One woman takes her pink sash off and hooks it around my neck, yanking me towards her. Her eyebrows are severe, her lips plumped up, huge. She smells of gin in a can.

'Alright. If . . . you take your top off,' she howls, to which the others all, of course, howl back.

I'm too tired to protest. And wise enough to know I don't have a choice.

'Hold out the phone,' I say. 'So I know you're not having me on.'

The sashless woman takes her phone from her little gold handbag, holding it up high.

'Go 'ed lad,' she says. 'Off, OFF, OFF . . .' And so the chanting goes.

I unzip my fleece, a little slowly, (maybe) giving the girls a thrill. They squeal. Maybe I could become a stripper. I lasso my fleece over my head, gasping with cold, and throw it at the bride who catches it with a giddy amount of enthusiasm. Then, I lift the edge of my local brewery t-shirt, give a stupid wiggle, and with more self-loathing than I imagined was ever possible, I strip it off. The phone is tossed to me amidst wolf whistles.

Thank God I catch it, clean, and I open the browser, type Griffin Enterprises and find the only number ever used to get hold of Griffo's dad. Nobody – not that I know anyway – has Griffo's dad's mobile number. Not even Griffo. Apparently. Griffo's dad's secretary answers. She puts me through to Griffo's dad, who sounds as though he's on a building site somewhere.

'James?'

'I can't begin to apologise for not showing up today.'

'You in trouble?'

'Not trouble. Not exactly.'

'Well, are you or aren't you?'

'No. I'm not in trouble. But I need a favour.'

'Fifty grand for a car not a big enough favour, our James?'

'The car . . . it's gone.'

'What? Stolen?'

I hate lying to Griffo's dad. When we were teenagers we lied to him about taking his best whiskey from the cabinet.

Later, he topped up the bottle with soy sauce without us knowing. The next time we went for a sneaky sip, all four of us puked.

'Yeah, it got stolen.'

'So how can I help?'

'I just need to borrow a car. For a day. You'll get it back tomorrow.'

Griffo's dad pauses. In the background I hear clanging, metal on metal.

'Fine,' he says. 'Get to my house. There'll be a vehicle for you there.'

'Oh, God. Thanks . . .' I hesitate, never knowing what to call him. 'Will it be insured?'

'Do you think I'm a fucking idiot, James?'

'No. No. Sorry.'

'Twenty-four hours, James.'

'Twenty-four hours.'

So, I'm going to make Zara pay for everything. And in return, I'll take her all the bloody way to London.

21

Zara

Jim is talking to me.

Not grumbles or mumbles or a simple yes or no. Actual sentences. What's more, he isn't giving off that Jim thing where when forced to speak more than two words, it's as though speaking is like passing gallstones. He is coherent. Melodic, even.

'I have an offer for you,' he says. 'One that you can't refuse.'

My laddered tights itch the back of my thighs and I wriggle on the suitcase I'm sitting on. Jim is dressed again, having done some bizarre striptease for a hideous bachelorette party across the road. Disturbingly, he'd looked pretty hot in doing so. I spotted him half-naked, chatting on the phone, and nothing about his behaviour made an ounce of sense. Now, he's back in my space. By choice.

'I want you to hear me out,' he says.

'I'm listening.'

'Good. Because you should.'

Who does he think he is, speaking to me this way? Hardly

200

a word from him all day as I sat just inches away from him in his squeaky posh car, oh, except to tell me how much I needed to eat a paper bag full of greasy, fatty fries.

Today, all I needed was a friend. Okay, so it's not ideal that it's the guy I catapulted into, especially since I can't help feeling pretty awful about it. But Jim has been my companion for the majority of today. Being in such close proximity to another human for – what? – four hours, it's only polite to engage in conversation. To be kind. To be nice. Unless you're a total psychopath. Or sociopath. Jim shows signs of both. Every now and then, I get this pocket-sized blast of him being this nice guy, a kind of down-to-earth philosopher, and then he'll turn, like the aftermath of a bad storm, screaming eerie silence. And now. Oh, now. Now, Jim wants to talk.

'I'm gonna to make this very simple for you, girl. There's no negotiation. I want you to pay for damages caused to me car. It's only fair. You crashed into me. And I want you to pay for me car to be released from the pound—'

'How much is that going to cost?'

'Two hundred.'

'Two hundred pounds?'

'Yeah.'

'Why can't you pay that? I don't care if you get your car back or not.'

'It's your fault the police took it away.'

'How?'

'Because it was parked illegally.'

'I didn't park it.'

'No. But I only parked there so you could get on a bloody train.'

'Surely someone like you can afford two—'

'I asked you to listen, Zara. Will you let me finish?'

I fold my arms but almost lose my balance on the suitcase, so I steady myself with my hands. I can tell I've annoyed Jim by cutting in on him, but he's being so unbelievable with his demands.

'Go on,' I say.

'So, you'll pay for the damages. And to get me car back. And . . . five hundred quid.'

'WHAT?'

'You heard.'

'Are you mad?'

'Not at all. I'm gonna take you to London. Now. Soon.'

'I don't understand.'

'I've got another car. We'll go and get it, then I'll get you to the airport.'

'But what about the car in the pound?'

'That'll take too long, we can't risk the time, especially with Friday traffic.'

'So, why five hundred pounds on top?'

'If – and I use the word *if* hypothetically here 'cause we both know there isn't a taxi in Liverpool who'll take you all the way to London – but, *if* you were to get a taxi, it'd cost you more than two hundred quid. Easy. Then, you'd have to pay for the driver to get back. So, five hundred. You pay me. I get you there. Deal?'

The rain begins to calm, to spit.

Math was never my strong point, but I try to work out the figures in my head. If I stay overnight in Liverpool tonight, even in that cheap hostel again, with food and a few much-needed drinks, that will be about a hundred pounds. Then, I'll have to get to London tomorrow, somehow, *and* book another flight at full price. The costs are soaring as each raindrop falls from the sky. No matter what way I look at it,

Jim's right. He's making me an offer I can't refuse. Unless I decide to just bum around in Liverpool for the next chapter of my life, something I believe that the universe is advising me not to do.

'Time's ticking, love.'

How dare Jim be right.

And as for the damages: well, yes. I am liable. A niggling worry has been eating away at me that if I didn't somehow rectify this, then karma would come back to haunt me. My savings were to spend on my new life with Nick. Now that's gone, they're simply for a rainy day. And God, that just so happens to be today, doesn't it?

'You'll get me to the airport?' I ask. 'All the way? And on time?'

'I will.'

'And then this is over?'

'Yeah.'

I hold out my hand. All thoughts of building a little nest will have to disappear, for now, until the universe sends me the next positive sign.

'Deal,' I say.

'Deal,' Jim agrees.

He keeps my hand within his grip and waves his free arm at a black cab, which surprisingly stops, despite us not waiting in line. I guess I'm going to see where Jim lives, which will be interesting. I love seeing people's homes, although it always makes me daydream about what my home will look like when I'm in a place where I truly belong.

Inside the cab, we sit together on the backseat and grasp the suitcases between our knees. Ridiculous as it is, I suddenly miss the mop. It seems so far away now, and so long ago since I held it. Oh God, my mission has failed in all its forms, hasn't it? I'm only realising that now, somehow. Jim gives his address to the driver, and the driver whistles before repeating a word Jim said; 'Caldy'. That must be the name of the town we're going to.

'Is that the house next to the golf course?' the driver asks.

'Yep. Sure is,' Jim says.

Holding back tears, I try to feel good about the progress we're finally making. But, as the taxi crawls through the rain-sodden streets, up a hill lined with small pubs and even more kebab takeaway places, I spot the hostel where I stayed last night. Through a window dancing with a million raving raindrops, I see large posters for club nights plastered against cafe walls and bus stop shelters promising the biggest party on the planet. I wonder where the Tate Liverpool is, not that I'll be paying a visit anymore. The plan to finish my degree here is now in the past. Taking a turning into a more sophisticated area of town, I see an intimate Indian street food restaurant beside a bustling wine bar with wicker lanterns and fairy lights, vibrant and pretty, even on a miserable Friday afternoon. Oh, these are the kinds of places I would've loved to socialise in, talking the night away over lots of wine and nibbles. I think about the friends I was looking forward to finding, the ones I'll never meet.

'I missed out a small part of the deal,' Jim says, jolting me back to reality.

'What?'

'You're also paying for this cab fare.'

Un-fucking-believable.

We go through that tunnel again.

The cab driver isn't much of a talker, whistling along to the songs on the radio, and Jim is having forty winks. Then the radio crackles with interference and the driver switches it off, discontinues his whistles. Wow. It's so lonely in the back here now, a vacuum of car engines and tyre tracks, two vacant people in my confined space.

What am I doing? Where on earth am I? My hands cover my eyes and silent tears fall, trickling in between my fingers, soaking my cheeks. I can feel my scar, its rough edges impossible to ignore.

I'm not supposed to be here. I'm supposed to be with Nick.

From fighting, to fainting, to figuring out how to leave Liverpool, there hasn't been any time to grieve the loss of my love, or what I believed was love, until now. The mop is in some strange old woman's house. And my heart is aching.

God, it hurts. It really hurts.

It should be Nick inside this cab with me, not Jim. We should be on our way into central Liverpool, to some place called the Pier Head where he wanted to take me on a ferry across the Mersey. Apparently, that shows the city in its finest glory. Then, we were going to go to a Lebanese restaurant on Bold Street – wherever that is. Nick wanted to take me there for our first date, hoping I'd find the food authentic. Except he'd had no intention of taking me on a ferry and eating shawarma with me, had he? He's a total liar. Were the signs always there, just like Mary had suggested?

'You alright, love?' the driver asks, looking at me through his rear-view mirror.

I dab my cheeks and nod, not wanting to indulge, as the tunnel comes to an abrupt, but most welcome end. I close my eyes, too, thinking it best to avoid seeing the scene of my crime, and possibly my abandoned little Peugeot. It must still be there. I'm tired, so, so, tired . . .

Next thing I know, the driver shouts 'wakey, wakey', and demands to know how to get through the gate.

The gate?

I bat my lashes, stretch. We're stopped before a set of electronic double gates with a fancy sign on the front saying, 'White Oaks'. Through the intricate metal frame, I can see the house in the distance, standing tall, wide and ever so grand behind a huge sweeping driveway, complete with a round, manicured lawn, a fountain in the centre of it.

Jim leans forward to speak to the driver.

'Gimme a sec, mate,' he says. 'I'll get the gates open.'

He gets out and walks to the intercom. The gates both scroll aside, making an opening for the cab to drive through. The driver whistles again, but this time it isn't to any tune on the radio. He's as impressed as I am. Although the fountain is beyond tacky. White cherub statues are so Eighties.

'That's twenty-five quid, love,' the driver says.

Oh yeah. This is on me.

The house is more of a mansion. Many of my friends in Dubai live in villas of a similar size, but they're rented, or company owned, plus space is just cheaper out there. My mom's house in the states isn't much smaller than Jim's, but that's also a standard East Coast family home. Not a Victorian, brick-built double-fronted delight that oozes money. Only those with excessive cash have two lifesize gold-plated lion figurines on each side of the front door. I linger on the door step, my bags by my side.

'Wait here,' Jim tells me.

I'm a little taken aback. It's freezing and this is Jim's house, so I'm essentially a guest.

Still, I'm not here to be invited in for coffee. We're rushing against the clock, on a tight deadline, and all Jim has to do is grab some keys and get a car out of the garage. Oh, the garage. What an understatement. Five cars are sitting on the driveway, none that would look out of place cruising up and down the beach road in Dubai. Behind the two convertibles is a garage to rival an aircraft hangar.

Jim doesn't fumble for a key or ring the bell. The front door swings open.

'Jim-Jim!' A lady says with a musical accent – possibly Portuguese – wearing sweat pants, t-shirt and flip-flops. She throws herself at Jim, giving him a hearty hug. I kind of want one, too.

'Hey Gloria,' Jim says, kissing the lady on the cheek.

'Jim?' I ask, before he leaves me outside in the cold. 'Can I use your bathroom?'

Jim looks at Gloria, who covers her mouth and tries to hide behind an unsubtle giggle.

'Please?' I ask, rage beginning to simmer.

'Is that okay, Gloria?' Jim asks.

What an odd question. Although what Jim's doing now is even more odd. He's placed his hand on my lower back. I'm convinced he has no idea he's doing it. Yet, there it is, his hand lingering, touching me.

'Will you show her the loo by the study while I go and grab the keys I need?' he says, darting off.

Gloria claps her hands in front of my face. 'Come in, darling.'

'Excuse me, just one minute.'

I open one of my suitcases. I want to get out of my damp clothes, the ladder in my tights spreading longer, wider. Taking out a pair of black skinny jeans and a pink sweater printed with zebras, I also grab some clean pants, socks and a bra, and my toiletries bag.

'You got a lot of stuff, darling.'

'Well, it's *all* I've got,' I say, and follow Gloria indoors.

The interior isn't surprising. In fact, it's exactly how I predicted it would look from the second I saw the cherub fountain. Everything from unnecessary sculptures to heavy mahogany furniture shiny enough to act as a mirror, a black and white tiled marble floor dancing through the wide hallway and a double staircase leading to a mezzanine with lots of fresh, colourful carnations in large vases. There's no style to this place whatsoever. Just lots of big, clean things. If I were Jim, I'd spend less money on flashy cars and pay an interior designer to do something special with this place.

'Through here, darling.'

Gloria leads me through a study, fitted with thick beige carpet and a giant desk, plenty of filing cabinets and shelves filled with photographs, golf trophies and model cars. I roll my eyes – then hope Gloria didn't notice – and scurry into the bathroom and lock the door. Catching my reflection in the mirror, I gasp, shocked at the state of my face. Jim had told me I looked 'great' at the train station. I let the cold water run and splash my face, removing the traces of mascara from beneath my eyes and injecting some life into my cheeks. I change quickly, not wanting to be the reason I miss my own flight.

I do dawdle back through the study, keen to catch a glimpse of the photographs on the shelf. Jim's chatting away to Gloria outside, telling her how he's taking a 'mate' to the airport as a favour. Gloria asks if he wants dinner when he returns. He declines, but not without praising her cooking, which does smell delicious, zesty spices filtering from the kitchen. The photos are mostly from a wedding on what looks like a beach in Bali, the couple a bit older, as if they're perhaps getting married a second time around.

And there's Jim.

A teenage Jim with that strange blend of puppy fat and gauntness around the face, but so clearly Jim. His messy curls have stuck around for twenty odd years and he's doing that one-sided smile, unsure about committing to being happy or not. He's pictured with three other boys of a similar age, maybe brothers, but more likely to be cousins or friends. One, with jet black hair, is holding a guitar up in the air. They aren't in Bali. That photo looks like it was taken in a British pub.

'Zara,' Jim's voice shouts. 'Ready?'

I roll my damp clothes into a tight ball under my arm.

'Ready.'

Jim hugs Gloria again, and she points to her cheek indicating her desire for a kiss.

'Tell your mama I say hi,' she says.

'Will do, Gloria. Thanks.'

'How is she?'

'She's been better, but she's also been worse.'

Gloria brings her hands to her heart and gives Jim a slow, sympathetic nod and all I can do is wonder. What is wrong with Jim's mom?

'Hop aboard,' Jim says.

'Really?' I ask.

He's lugging my suitcases into the back of a vehicle that isn't one of the sports cars or SUVs. Instead, the back doors to a minibus fly open, the back seats pushed down.

'We're going to London in that?' I ask.

'Not good enough for you, your highness?'

'Don't start that again.'

'Come on, girl, I can't go more than seventy in this thing so we better get a move on.'

I wish I could be subtler, but like magnets, my eyes are drawn to the array of cars standing motionless to my right. I don't even care for fancy motors, so why am I giving off the air that I do?

'You don't even have to sit by me,' Jim says, climbing into the driver's seat. 'Take your pick, get some kip, spread your legs . . . I mean put your legs up. Sorry, love.'

'Are you blushing, Jim?'

'Get in the bus.'

I laugh and open the passenger door, settling beside him up front.

'This is the only thing I'm insured on,' Jim tells me.

'Oh, of course. I don't care.'

'You do.'

'No, I don't.'

'You wanted a lift in the Audi TT.'

'I don't even know what that is.'

'Sure you don't, princess.'

'You know what, don't start the engine yet. I think I will sit in the back.'

'Be my guest.'

'Ha,' I huff. And I clamber between the passenger and driver's seat, taking the double seat on the second row. 'I'll get some sleep. Wake me up when we get there.'

But strangely I don't feel tired. Hugging my knees to my chest, I stretch my pink sweater over them, the zebra print stretching. My mom always told me off for doing this, for ruining my clothes.

'I like your unicorns,' Jim says, looking at me through the rear-view mirror.

'They're zebras.' I'm shocked he's noticed I changed.

Jim fiddles around with a few leads, takes out his phone

and plugs it in, keeping it on charge. Sensible. At least one of us now has a means of communication. It was kind of Jim to offer to get my phone back earlier and I didn't react graciously, I know. But I'm glad he didn't get it; there's no way I could have allowed him to venture over there again. A lost phone is nothing compared with what I've actually lost today, and besides, who do I need to contact? Katie, so she can gloat and tell me she told me so? Trawling through social media will depress me: far too many people relishing in gin o'clock and Nick's favourite word; Fri-yay. And I bet Abi has unlocked my phone by now, anyway, her supportive girl-friends all plying her with white wine, telling her again and again what an ugly whore Zara Khoury is. Oh, how the photos of her husband's cock will shock them all.

As we drive away from Jim's house, the electric gates open to begin our journey, and Jim's phone rings. He puts it on loud speaker and continues to drive.

'Hey Mam, what's up?'

'What's up with me? Don't you mean what's up with you?'

'Me phone was dead. That's all.'

'I thought *you* were dead.'

'Don't be soft.'

'I'll give you soft. Soft lad.'

I can't help but snigger, for that's such a great expression. *Soft lad.* Jim's mom's voice is melodic, filled with warm gravel. I can imagine her with a rolling pin tight in her grip, using it to threaten her son.

'Mam, I'm coming over.'

'Why?'

'Yes, why? Don't we need to get to London?

'I need to make sure you've taken your tablets, that's all.'

'Ethel's here, son. You know, Ethel Barton?'

'Yeah. Of course, I know Ethel Barton.'

'Her daughter Yvonne's here, too.'

'Quite the party.'

'What was that?'

'I said, it sounds like quite the party.'

'No, the party is tonight. Yvonne's sixtieth. You coming with me?'

'No. I'm busy . . . Look, have you taken your pills, all the blue ones?'

'Yes.'

'And the white? The big tablet ones?'

'Four already.'

'Good.'

'Ethel knows, she's here.'

'Yeah. You said. Well, don't forget. And make sure Ethel doesn't forget either.'

'I won't. Love you.'

'Love you, too.'

Jim hangs up and turns the radio on. I'm a bit disappointed. I'd been quite enjoying listening into that conversation. It was so real. I've honestly never spoken to my mom like that before, or my papa for that matter, never finished with, 'Love you, too.' And Jim is so concerned, so focused on making sure his mother is okay. I've been stuck with him for five, almost six hours and I have to admit, it's nice to see this side of him.

'Hey,' I shout over, from two rows back. 'Is your mom okay?'

He catches me briefly in the rear-view mirror.

'Chronic irregular heartbeat,' he says, his diction strong on each syllable.

I don't want to shout, though, I want to talk. Why was I so hasty to move here, to the back of the minibus? All Jim had done was call me a princess. And as far as insults go, I could be given a lot worse.

My mom was young when I came along and seriously messed up her plans. On a good day she affectionately called me 'her little mistake,' and on a bad day I was 'an inconvenience.' Then she became a new mom for the second time around.

'I'm sorry,' I said to her, before attempting any sort of salutation. I was fourteen, freshly expelled from boarding school, and just landed at Boston Logan where my mom had had to drive four hours with a three-month-old baby to come and collect me.

'Let's just get to the car,' my mom said. 'I need to feed Paige.'

'I feel awful, Mom. I didn't do anything wrong. I promise.'

'Well, if you didn't do anything wrong, why do you keep saying sorry?'

I sat up front of my mom's car in the airport parking lot while my mom nursed Paige in the back. I listened as my mom cooed and sang 'You Are My Sunshine', softly, a little out of tune, so clearly enjoying motherhood now that she was ready to embrace it.

Unlike the first time.

She was April Abbot, a young flight attendant stationed in New York City for only six months when she fell pregnant to a charming salesman for an international oil and gas company. Samir Khoury's dark, handsome features and French Arabic accent were simply too irresistible for a small-town girl from the coast of Maine. They married quickly, quietly, and I was born in the Big Apple.

'I wanted to see the world,' my mom had told me, often. 'It didn't seem fair that your papa got to live his life to the max, but I had to stay home. I didn't want to become my mother. Or her mother.'

So to make up for that unfairness, my papa hired a nanny.

And my mom got exactly what she wanted.

She returned to flying and got to accompany her husband on certain business trips. But his job was demanding and we had to move to Hong Kong when I was two. Another nanny was hired, followed by another when the first quit due to me biting her. Obviously I don't remember doing that. Then we moved on to Singapore, on to Dubai, and as the number of nannies increased, so did the number of hobbies my mom took up. Tennis, pottery, yoga, volunteer work, all to fill some sort of gaping hole in her life.

'I see the way you look at other men,' my papa would say, as I hid in the bathroom, listening to their arguments each time they came home late from dinners, from galas, from those many occasions where my mom looked so enchanting, like a movie star with invisible wings. 'How is all this not enough for you, April? Tell me?'

One of the 'other men' inevitably ended up lighting a spark in my mom and my parents divorced. My papa stayed in Dubai and I went with my mom back to her home town of Rockport, Maine. At first, I was delighted about this new arrangement, believing I'd get a whole parent to myself. My mom was infinitely happier, keen to show off her new fiancé – an ear, nose and throat specialist called Hank – to old friends. It's always baffled me how adamant she was to see the world. I mean, my papa gave her that on a plate, and yet, she ended up settling in the lobster town where she was born.

There was a lack of affordable nannies in Rockport, and the last thing a woman preparing for an East Coast white wedding needed was a ten-year-old not settling into the local elementary

214

school. All the other kids had been attending since they learnt to write their name and I was the new kid. The one with the weird accent. The one who asked too many questions.

'I've spoken to your papa and he wants to help you,' my mom told me, smiling. 'He's going to let you go to boarding school in England. This is every little girl's dream. I couldn't get enough of *Malory Towers* when I was your age.'

Malory Towers it was not. I lasted a few years before I was kicked out.

With Paige settled and asleep, my mom began the long drive north to Rockport.

'Paige is really beautiful,' I said, secret code for another apology.

'She's an angel, isn't she?'

'I can babysit her whenever you want. You know, whenever you and Hank wanna go out to dinner, or to a party, or something?'

My mom shifted in her seat, adjusted her breast within the bra cup, then the other side.

'That's better,' she said to herself.

'I really like babies,' I continued.

'There's more to babies than just liking them.'

'I know. They're hard work.'

'They can be.'

'But liking them's a pretty good start, right?'

'You also like ballet, Zara. It doesn't mean you're Anna Pavlova.'

I counted the gas stations, the motels, and waited for my mom to ask me about what happened at school, why I was forced to leave. Paige needed feeding again, so I decided to make myself scarce and hung out in a roadside McDonalds for a while, picking at some nuggets, licking the salt off the fries.

215

'Are you okay?' my mom asked when we started the final stretch home.

I shrugged. 'I don't know.'

'What do you mean, you don't know?'

'If I was okay, people would want to be around me. But they don't.'

'Zara, that's ridiculous. You choose the wrong people to be around, that's your problem.'

'But, I don't mean to choose the wrong ones. They always seem so nice.'

'And a teacher old enough to be your father? That didn't seem wrong to you?'

'He was nice to me, Mom. That's all.'

'I don't want to hear it, Zara,' she snapped, holding her hand up to my face. 'I only asked if you were okay. Why can't you just be okay?'

'I was only being honest.'

'And that's fine, honey. But, I can't get into this right now. I need to concentrate.'

Paige woke up, started crying, but the road leading into Rockport was congested and there was nowhere to pull over. Leaning across into the back seat, I found the pacifier and slipped it into my baby half-sister's tiny mouth, but Paige spat it out, unable to be soothed. The radio crackled, the country song playing becoming disjointed as the singer sang about loving you forever and ever, Amen. My mom started crying, too.

It was never going to work.

It wouldn't have been fair on Paige. She was a blank canvas, whereas I was spilt paint, too much of a mess to start cleaning up amongst diapers and lullabies. So, it was back to Dubai where I could attend a school with a British curriculum, picking up at the point I was booted out, my papa once again giving my mom exactly what she wanted. Freedom.

But it wasn't freedom to see the world.

It was the freedom to become a good mom; to get it right this time.

The journey to Heathrow continues smoothly.

We're making good time, hitting no congestion, not getting slowed down by the bad weather, which has cleared up a little further south. I've been attempting to paint my nails with the polish Marina gave me as a leaving present. 'To remind you of me, Zara-Baby,' the card had read, attached to the gift box containing three bold colours. Marina frequents nail salons at least once a week and occasionally invited me along. It was our bonding time, a chance to talk, except Marina always ended up talking to the nail technician (rudely) or to the woman beside her (in Russian).

I abruptly jerk forward, drawing a line of Purple Mystery down my left hand, the little bottle spilling its contents all over the thigh of my black jeans. Jim has pulled over into a gas station, various food outlets welcoming us to eat, drink, rest.

'I need petrol,' Jim says, twisting around to look at me. 'Would you mind . . . ?'

I fish out my purse. A deal is a deal.

'I'll fill up and wait here,' Jim says.

It amazes me how men never need to use the bathroom. I'm bursting and run across the parking lot into the main hub, enjoying the chance to stretch my restless legs. It's heaving, a long line of hungry travellers streaming from Burger King, from KFC, from Costa. A small, dark arcade jingle-jangles in the corner, a few truckers leaning against the one-armed-bandits, throwing away their money for no reason other than to feed their addiction, a kid crying because his dad won't let him go on the Postman Pat ride. I buy two tuna melts and two cappuccinos to go.

When I return to the minibus, I slide the side door open and get back into my seat, two rows away, and lean over to give Jim his snacks. Silently, he gives me a double thumbs up and I realise he's chatting on the phone.

'Come on, Snowy lad, what's the big news?'

'Get your arse round here, mate,' the voice is shouting back through the loud speaker.

'Just tell me now while I've got you on the phone.'

'Where are you, mate?'

'Doesn't matter. Spill the beans.'

'Okay . . . okay . . . okay . . .'

'Go on!'

Whoever 'Snowy' is falls silent, a hiss of air crackling through the speaker.

Jim lowers his voice a touch. 'Is Helen pregnant again?'

'Jimbo. Helen'd rather take a vow of celibacy than get preggo again. You know what she's like, mate. Christ! You know what the twins are like.'

'So, what's the big news?'

'James. I've bought a ring.'

'A ring? As in jewellery?'

'I'm gonna ask Helen to marry me.'

Strangely, my heart skips a beat when Jim's glance catches mine in the rear-view mirror. His head falls back onto his headrest, releasing a long, silent sigh.

'Jimbo? Did you hear what I said?' Snowy shouts.

'I did.' Jim swallows.

'I'm gonna propose to Helen.'

218

'I got that. Fucking congratulations, mate. I'm – I'm made up for you.'

'And so you should be. You better start writing that best man speech.'

'No pressure then?'

'And, I was thinking, we should reunite! The band! Do a turn at the wedding, like.'

'What? "Video Killed the Radio Star"?'

'Yeah, Jimbo, haha! Now, come over. The bubbly's on ice.'

'She hasn't said yes yet.'

Snowy laughs – a hearty, explosive laugh – and it travels through Jim's phone and bounces off the soft grey interior of the minibus. Jim joins him, and I almost do, too, for this Snowy guy's laugh is infectious. I bite into my tuna melt, burning the roof of my mouth.

'I'll come over after work on Sunday, mate,' Jim says. 'I've got a lot on at the mo.'

'Since when have you got a lot on?'

'Look, piss off and go and make an honest woman of your girlfriend.'

'Are you with a bird?'

'No, I'm not with a—'

'HELEN! HELS!' Snowy was shouting. 'Come here! HELS—'

'Snowy, stop it . . .' Jim says, trying clumsily to take his handset off loud speaker.

I can hear a woman in the background telling Snowy to shut up or he'll scare the kids.

'HELEN, OUR JIMBO'S GOT A BIRD.'

Jim grabs his phone. 'I haven't got a bird, mate.'

But, Snowy hangs up and Jim tuts, putting the phone back in the dock.

Another minibus loaded with children in matching sports kits parks up beside us and I clock a bunch of kids banging on the window and pulling faces. I go all cross-eyed and stick out my tongue back at them. One kid gives me the finger. I'm actually way more offended than I expect to be. Embarrassed, I take my tuna melt and my cappuccino and warn Jim that I'm changing seats, coming to sit up front with him.

'Christ,' Jim says, aloud but not directly at me. He's staring at the signs ahead for Burger King, KFC and Costa, but seems a million miles away. 'Snowy and Helen are finally gonna to do it.'

'Congrats to them,' I say, getting myself settled in the passenger seat. 'And sorry for listening. Your friend was kind of loud.'

'You're not wrong there.'

'You don't seem too happy about it.'

'What?' Jim turns to me. His eyes are narrow, scowling.

'Oh, I'm sorry. I just spoke when I shouldn't have . . . I do that. Sorry.'

'I am happy,' he says, his tone quite the polar opposite of happy, as he starts to drive off. 'I'm very, very happy.'

'Yeah, you sound it.'

'I'm just, you know, under a bit of fucking pressure now.'

'Okay . . .'

'I mean, I'm gonna have to stand up and talk about Snowy to a room full of people. That's not easy, like. And I'm gonna have to tell the very best – and the very worst – tales about him to the likes of his nan.'

'Yeah, I'd hate to be best man, or maid of honour . . . well, no I'd actually like to be asked to be maid of honour, I've never been a bridesmaid for anybody. But hold on. Forgive me for overhearing, but did Snowy mention you guys used to be in a band?'

'Nope.'

'He did! Don't deny it. Come on, tell me. You were in a band?'

'Okay, fine. Yeah. I was in a band.'

I fight the urge to laugh as an obvious tint of red rises from Jim's neck to his cheeks. He must have been the lead singer. With that hair and that smouldering glint? I remember the photo I'd seen back at his house. Jim was head and shoulders above the other three guys when it came to looks.

'I bet you were the lead singer, right?'

Jim gives a small groan.

'Oh, Jim, I'm not asking you to reveal your inner secrets to me, I'm just making light conversation about a band you were in. Don't be so uptight.'

Jim's mouth drops open into one large, round O.

'Well, you are uptight,' I justify. 'You've been uptight all day.'

'You don't know the half of it.'

'No, that's right. I don't. Because you haven't told me.'

'Look, I'm bad at hangovers. Okay?'

'Where did you go last night?'

Jim winces. 'The Titanic. It's not a ship, it's a—'

'A hotel,' I give a little whistle. 'Yeah, I saw it when I was looking for somewhere to stay last night. That place was way over my budget. You don't do anything by halves, do you, Jim?'

'Not anymore, it seems.'

I hang onto Jim's words, hoping for an opening, or just more of a chat. I turn in to face him, lifting my right knee and getting comfy nuzzling into the passenger seat, holding tight onto both cappuccinos. He puts his foot down and speeds up, overtaking the slow lorry ahead of them.

221

'Why are you watching me?' he asks.

'Why do you turn my every move into something sinister?' I cry, quite eager to spill his drink into his lap. Why is he so damn difficult? And besides, the tuna melts are going cold. If I make a choice to eat carbs and cheese, then I want them piping hot and juicy. Instead, I can't find a cup holder so have to sip my cappuccino whilst also holding Jim's, offering it to him now and then. My stomach rumbles as the delicious smell of hot bread gives way to a warm odour of cooling cheese, and eventually, just stale fish. The radio doesn't even work in this minibus. The luxury of that BMW is sorely missed.

'You wanna know about me?' Jim asks suddenly, although the way he says it makes me not want to know. 'Well, guess what? There's nothing to know.'

'Bullshit.'

'I don't do anything, haven't really done anything—'

'That's totally impossible.'

'It's not.'

'How did you get a car like a BMW if you don't do anything?'

'I don't wanna talk about the fucking car.'

'Okay, fine. I get that. It's a sore point. But how do you not *do* anything? What does that even mean? You live, you breathe, you have a mom, you have friends, how does any of that mean you do nothing?'

'What I mean is . . .' But Jim tails off.

He opens his mouth to speak again, yet no words come. Jim bites his lip, his frown apparent, even through the hair that tries to hide it. He looks stuck – incredibly stuck – as though he's working out an illogical equation.

'You wanna know what I think?' I try, aware that I'm on thin ice. 'In the time I've known you, I've seen two things.

One, you're super nice to the people who know you well; your mom, your friend, your maid—'

'My maid?'

'Oh, I mean your housekeeper, Gloria. Sorry, "maid" is a very "expat" thing, and it's not supposed to be derogatory. But, back to the point. I've seen you be the good guy to these people, these people who *know* you. And I've also seen you be the good guy to complete strangers, myself not included, because I fucked up your car.'

'I love it when you admit that.'

'Shut up. Let me finish. Mary, you were so sweet with her. And that bachelorette party, although I won't ask why you so willingly took your shirt off for them, and even when you bought me those potato chip things, I could see you through the window, chatting away, being so nice to the guy serving you. All these people you charm. But you also know you're never gonna see them again.'

Jim shakes his head, making out like I'm talking nonsense.

'So, my point is, I think you're afraid of getting to know new people.'

And Jim glances across at me, then back to the road.

'I could be wrong,' I say, throwing my hands up in defence. 'I usually am. As your good self has witnessed. But I'd like to think I got something right today.'

As expected, but not hoped for, Jim doesn't respond. Maybe I should've stayed sitting two rows away. At least the cappuccinos are empty now and I don't have to nurse his caffeine. The raindrops on the window of the minibus dance in zigzags downwards, landing onto other raindrops, all adjoining or diving off into new directions. I think about where I can head on to next, after this impending flight. My papa's villa in Dubai will be empty again. He's in Saudi this time. Marina's in Moscow for the weekend. Sammy recently started boarding school in Australia, the likelihood of him being expelled at zero. He's too good at rugby. So I have space. Possibly the last thing I need.

'Would you mind passing me that?' Jim asks.

'What?' I blink, hearing but not comprehending. 'I was lost in my thoughts.'

'The butty.'

'Sorry?'

'That. The tuna butty. Ta.'

I take a cold tuna melt out of the paper bag and hand it over. I might as well pick at the other one. Silence between us stretches as we chew, passing cars filling in the blanks. Jim takes large bites, with his large mouth. There's definitely something a bit Mick Jagger about him. Just *something*. Maybe it's the whole band thing.

22

Jim

'Video killed the radio star . . .'

The words aren't very coherent, but I make them out.

Again.

'Video killed the radio star . . .' Zara's only started bloody singing, hasn't she? Quietly, her mouth stuffed with tuna butty. I've finished mine and scrunch the empty paper bag into a ball with one fist.

'Video killed the radio star,' she sings again, a touch louder now.

I toss the ball towards her feet and she sings a little more. She clearly doesn't know any of the lyrics other than the title words of the song, so she's making them up, some mumble jumble of 'mi-mi-mi' and 'ma-ma-ma', with a 'doo-doo-doo' and a 'da-da-da' thrown in. My head's still banging from last night, and I'm trying hard to ignore her. I catch my reflection in the rear-view mirror. Ha. I look like a bad actor doing some serious driving-acting. I mean, I like a bit of a sing. Who doesn't, eh? But, not now. Not here.

'VIDEO KILLED THE RADIO STAR,' Zara ups the volume. 'Come on, Jim! VIDEO KILLED THE RADIO STAR. DA-DA-DA and DOO-DOO-DAH, MA-MA-MA-MA-MI-MI-MA-MA. OH! OH-OH-OH!'

'Shut up, Zara.' Please.

'Ah, was that a smile I just saw, Jim?'

'No, you're giving me a headache—'

'VIDEO KILLED THE—'

'Agh! You're tone fucking deaf, girl!'

'MA-MA-MAAAAH!' she wails. 'Oh! VIDEO KILLED—'

'The radio star,' I sing, involuntarily, teeth gritted. I do NOT want to be doing this. But fucking hell, if you can't beat 'em, eh? I'm singing. So, what? I'm singing. 'Video killed the radio star. In my mind and in my car, we can't rewind we've gone too far!'

Hey. At least I know the words.

'Woo-hoo!' Zara cheers. 'Yeah!'

Great. And now I'm blushing. I can feel that hot tingle in my cheeks and my face is breaking into a smile completely against my will. I don't want to smile. This is so lame. Zara's pure buzzing though, and still out-singing me in the volume category, which is fine. I'm not competing with that. I just continue to sing in my own way, and she carries on badly, making up loads of her own words as I sing the correct ones. Okay, maybe I am accentuating my diction here. Just a bit, like. And we come together during the 'Oh-a-aho oh' parts, bopping our heads in time to the beat we've created. As we reach a natural finale, Zara gives a huge round of applause and drum rolls with her feet.

'You're such a dickhead,' I say.

'That's the nicest thing you've said to me all day,' she says. 'So, what were you called?'

'What?'

'Your band. What were you called?'

'Oh. The Dentists.'

'WHAT?'

I give a shrug. What's her problem?

'The Dentists?' she cries.

'Yeah. It was funny. You see, Snowy and the others, Mikey and Griffo, they all wore them train tracks.' I flash my teeth and point to them. 'But, me, I had naturally straight pearly whites. See? Never needed them. And . . . what? What the fuck you laughing at?'

'That's NOT funny,' Zara howls.

'It is! It was!'

'You called your band THE DENTISTS 'cause you had perfect teeth? And your bandmates had braces?'

'Ah, fuck.' I slap my forehead. 'It's not fucking funny at all.'

And I laugh so much that it hurts my sides. Christ, I'm struggling to catch my breath, and Zara's laughing beside me, wiping away tears. Eventually, we slow down with a sigh, then another. It's quiet again, but, I have to admit, a whole lot better than before. Nothing about today can be described as easy, but right now, it's easier. Just a little.

'You okay?' I ask, a few miles further.

'At least I'm not dead,' Zara says.

'That much is true.'

'I mean, imagine if I'd died in our crash today.'

'Bit morbid, girl.'

'Not only would I be dead, but I wouldn't have achieved anything.'

227

'Sounds like you've done a lot to me.'

'How?'

'You've seen the world.'

'Been dragged around it, more like. I'd rather keep still.'

I shake my head. What I'd give to swap.

'I thought I was home,' she says. 'I thought I had it all sorted.'

'Not 'cause of Nick?' I ask, aware of how me saying the word 'Nick' sounds like I want to be sick. The sick bastard. I hope that somehow gives Zara a bit of comfort, if she noticed.

'Well, he was a damn good liar. But, I had more than just romance pinned on this trip, you know. I was hoping to go back to university, too, finish my degree. I've always regretted dropping out. A stupid snap decision. But, everyone on my course was either so damn talented or so sure of themselves, I couldn't keep up. My papa called that my excuse for being lazy. And guess what? Guess whose bright idea it was to go back and complete it?'

'Nick's?'

'Got it in one.'

'He's not the boss of you.'

'What do you mean?'

'I mean, just 'cause he's a total bellend doesn't mean you can't go back to uni.'

'No way, it's a sign. This whole day's been a sign.'

'What were you gonna study?'

'Art. Well, illustration. Which is such a pipe dream of a subject anyway.'

'That attitude'll get you nowhere, Zara.'

'I'm being realistic.'

'You're being depressing.'

'Realistic IS depressing.'

I laugh out loud. 'Bloody hell, girl.'

'What?'

'I only asked if you were okay.'

She finally finishes that tuna butty and dabs her mouth with a brown serviette.

'We're making good time,' I assure her. 'We should be at Heathrow in about an hour.'

'Are *you* okay?'

'Why?'

'Oh, just because of . . . everything. Today. And . . . Oh, it doesn't matter.'

'You're not making any sense, love.'

'You seemed a bit *upset* after you spoke to your friend on the phone,' Zara says, a careful tone to her voice, tip-toeing on egg shells. 'I'm sorry. I could be totally wrong again, or maybe it was me that you were pissed off with . . . under-standably . . . and I—'

'You weren't wrong.'

'Oh.'

'That was me best mate on the phone,' I swallow. My words rich, precise. 'And he's marrying me ex.'

'Helen?' Zara asks.

'They've got two kids.'

'Twins?'

'You picked up a lot from that conversation, didn't you?'

'Small details are one of my few skills.'

'They've been together years, like. With me blessing,' I tell her.

'But?'

'But what?'

'I sensed a . . .'

'A but?' I sigh. 'Nope.'

229

I sit forward, my eyes on the road as we cruise down the middle lane.

'It's just a bit – I dunno – weird?' I ask myself, aloud.

'Complicated?'

'Yep. Complicated.'

There's an open end to this conversation, but definitely an end.

Heathrow's getting close; a relief for both of us.

'You wanna know why I got expelled from boarding school?' Zara asks.

'I've a feeling you're gonna tell me anyway,' I say. 'Fire away, love.'

23

Zara

The navy-blue blazer lined with yellow ribbon, matching socks pulled up to the knee, was more costume than uniform. The straw boater only stayed on my head thanks to a string of thick elastic, so tight that it created a deep dent beneath my chin. In the heart of a Berkshire village, the school's main entrance stood regal like a medieval castle, with smaller Victorian houses dotted around the premises; a quaint village of premium education. The acoustics of the main hall created decadent sounds, lush with pure echo and vibrating a grand warmth, whether from the headmistress addressing the school on Monday mornings, or from choir practice in the build-up to the annual carol concert.

My imagination went wild at first. What a novelty – the *Malory Towers* dream. But it all wore off as quickly as chocolate pudding was devoured on a Friday lunchtime. Teachers were strict, girls could be mean. It became stifling, no room for escape. Whichever corner I turned, I was still in school.

One novelty, however, remained.

His name was Adam Jeffrey Blackmore, head of Art and Design in the lower school, known to the pupils as Mr Blackmore, but known to me as AJ. He wasn't that old, late twenties at most. To a girl in Year Nine, that should be considered ancient, but when the majority of faculty were women with children old enough to be having children of their own, Mr Blackmore – with his thick blond curls and clean-shaven jaw – stood out like a fresh daisy amongst wilted daffodils.

All the girls looked forward to Mr Blackmore's lessons, even the ones who couldn't sketch a smiley face without it looking distorted. It became a game for us to vie for his attention, to get him to roll up his shirt sleeves to the elbow, lean on our desks and help us stroke our paintbrushes with a perfect water-to-paint ratio. The pretty girls, those who could pass for eighteen and smoked out of the dorm windows but never got caught, flirted unashamedly, undoing the top buttons of their white blouses to flash a dash of trainer bra, batting their eyelashes caked in clear mascara. Those who were awkward, riddled with acne or hanging onto much-loathed puppy fat, those with crooked teeth awaiting braces, or those who excelled in mathematics and found endless excuses to skip sport, oh how they blushed a deep purply rouge at Mr Blackmore's very presence.

For a kid like me, I was neither one nor the other. Accepted by both the popular and unpopular, I hovered in the centre, not part of a group but not a clear outcast. I wasn't attractive enough to be a part of Octavia Langford's gang, but I wasn't smart enough to keep up with the discussions that Ruth Gilbert's clan had over cheese sandwiches and green apples. So, I never participated in outrageous flirting with Mr

Blackmore, nor did I shy away behind the easels. Art happened to be the one subject I enjoyed. And I was good at.

'Zara Khoury, I'd like to see you after class,' Mr Blackmore said.

Whoops and laughter followed; a massive lack of subtlety.

'You have a talent,' he told me. 'An eye for detail, for colour.'

'Thank you.' I beamed. Praise was quite alien to me, and I was forever seeking it, trying a little too hard in areas where I had never shone, such as drama or debate class, or tricking my parents into ruffling my hair, the way moms and dads do to their kids in movies. 'I like art because I don't have to think.'

'That's not true.'

'How?'

'You are thinking, you're just utilising a different part of your brain.'

'Really?'

'Of course. You choose what colour, what intensity, what stroke. It's just coming to you effortlessly compared to other subjects, perhaps.'

Whether this happened to be true or not, I didn't care. I was bowled over by his kindness, how he spoke to me like an equal, his clipped English accent crystal sharp. I joined the art club, and worked on an intricate lino print that required more hours than the weekly extra-curricular activity offered.

'Can I work on this during lunch break?' I asked.

'Of course,' Mr Blackmore replied.

Lunch breaks progressed onto Saturday mornings, when I'd usually only be tagging along with other girls into town on the bus to buy clothes from Miss Selfridge. Many of the British girls went home for the weekend.

'Zara Khoury is having an affair with Mr Blackmore,'

Octavia Langford announced to the dorm. 'He makes the paint on her canvas ever so moist.'

'You're filthy,' Ruth Gilbert stuttered, aiming at Octavia, but shooting a quick dash of disgust my way.

In truth, I played up to both teams. I giggled and blushed when Octavia patted the seat beside her in the common room, desperate to show me how many dirty words she knew and how she strung them into sentences that mentioned Adam Jeffrey Blackmore, her posse surrounding us both, some twiddling my wild untamed hair, some offering me a Skittle. And when Ruth Gilbert pointed out that my mixed-medium still life of a boudoir dresser was 'accurate yet magical, giving a rather shallow item a blast of personality,' I lapped up the chance to discuss art in detail, convincing my peers that I really was putting in the extra hours for my work, and only my work.

But Mr Blackmore contributed much more to my world than watercolours and acrylics. I had a friend; I belonged. When I worked on my creativity, I wasn't trying to be as cool as Octavia or as intelligent as Ruth. I wasn't figuring out ways to make my nannies desert me, or shaking my jazz hands to play the star in the school musical, anything to make my parents give me more attention.

'You never take a break,' I said, one lunchtime when February's snow sat thick on the windowsill, the girls outside squealing as they slid about on the ice, arm in arm, over-reacting to the minor danger this weather could impose.

'Believe me, this *is* a break,' Mr Blackmore said. 'I can sit here in peace, eat my lunch and encourage young talent, or I can drown in Mrs Llewellyn's cigar smoke, trying to look interested in staffroom talk about baking bun loaves or how quickly arthritis progresses.'

'Mrs Llewellyn smokes cigars?'

'Can't you smell it on her?'

'I never get close enough.'

He never suggested I call him AJ, although when I pointed out his initials on his leather art folder, he told me that's what his mates at uni had called him. I just started calling him that, and AJ never corrected me.

We worked in silence often, and I loved how he wasn't the kind of teacher to just sit behind his desk and pretend to mark things, the way others did during detentions. He was always working on a project of his own, usually sketches in charcoal or oil pastels, using the edges of his fingers to smudge or define. We commented on each other's art, then carried on without fuss, or sometimes struck up conversations that enthralled me.

Once, it was about how the ending of *A Chorus Line* was more terrifying than uplifting, how the dancers became identical, lost all sense of their beautiful individuality in order to get the job, and how that happens too often in all walks of life. Another time, we discussed abortion, and I didn't feel uncomfortable in the slightest. One particular chat that unfolded came after I'd taken photos on a disposable camera during a weekend trip into town. I'd snapped three homeless people in the doorway of a closed-down video shop. The shutters hovered a few feet above the ground, creating the opportunity for a den of sleeping bags and cardboard boxes. It inspired a collage of snaps and sketches, a chance for me to try out charcoal, too.

'It's sad, isn't it?' I ran my fingers over an image. 'Makes me feel lucky.'

'These people might have been lucky once upon a time,' AJ said. 'Depending on your perception of luck. Not only those without a physical home are homeless.'

'You mean like people who don't know where they belong?'

'Do you think that's what I mean?'

I pondered his question. He was always encouraging me to see beyond the 2D. He tried to get his classes to do the same, which usually ended in titters or smart-ass comments.

'Well, it makes sense,' I said, nodding thoughtfully.

'How?'

'It's cheesy but home is where the heart is, right?'

'Clichés exist for a reason.'

'If you don't know where your heart is, where you're loved, then you can't call a place home, can you?'

'And how does a young girl like you come to that conclusion?'

'Because I don't know where I belong. I never have. I mean, I really loved living in Singapore because my school was awesome. But we moved, and I always knew we would move, so I never felt like I could relax or make friends because I knew I'd have to say goodbye to them. It made it easier that other kids were in the same boat; you know, expats.'

'I've always been intrigued by the students here like you, the expats.'

'Why?'

'I was born in Kent, grew up in Kent, I even went to university in Kent. Moving to this school was like taking a rocket to the moon.'

'You see, I'm intrigued by that. You must love Kent.'

'Why do you say that?'

'Because you know it's yours.'

AJ laughed. 'So, Zara Khoury, are you telling me you're homeless?'

'Privilege and material things aside, then yes. I'm a home-less bum.'

236

'And what about this school? Don't you see this as home, for now?'

'AJ. You just answered your own question.'

'I did?'

'You said, "home . . . for now". Surely home is . . . what's that word that means forever?'

'Permanent?'

'Yes. Home is permanent.'

'You've never had that, have you, Zara?'

I shook my head. I'd also never completely realised any of this until I'd said it out loud. Mr Blackmore had helped to discover my talent, but AJ was helping me to discover who I was.

'We can display these prints for parents' evening,' AJ told me as we both admired the finished pieces hanging to dry on clothes pegs across the art room. 'Like a mini exhibition.'

'With my name above them all?'

'Of course!'

I thought nothing of throwing myself at AJ, my arms wrapping around his middle.

'Oh, thank you,' I cried. 'That's the best news ever.'

He hugged me back, no hint of stepping away. His hand fell upon my head and he tossed my hair, roughly yet meaning well.

'You deserve it,' he said. 'Your parents will be proud as punch.'

'My parents won't see it. Unless we take a photo.'

'They aren't coming?'

'Nope. My mom's heavily pregnant, so she can't fly. And my papa is too busy, but I don't blame him, he's got to work. It's cool.'

What wasn't cool was Octavia Langford witnessing

that *hug*. And informing Mrs Llewellyn. I was no longer allowed to engage in extra art sessions unless it was during scheduled art club. AJ was issued with a warning, something he told me when we met in town every other Sunday afternoon to sketch in the park. Sometimes I played around with the landscape, but when I felt particularly inspired, I created cartoon strips, breathing a fantasy into the world I knew. The forbidden friendship lit a fire within me, gave me a deeper understanding of what made me tick, and nothing became more important than finding ways to keep AJ in my life.

Until AJ fell in love.

He met the owner of an independent bookstore in the village close to the school's grounds. How painfully romantic. He introduced her to me once, and never arranged another Sunday afternoon session again.

And, it embarrasses me to admit, something deep within me cracked.

I persisted in trying to get one of our meetings arranged, or perhaps to start lunch sessions again because, 'Octavia's stupid snitch was months ago – surely no one cares anymore!' and when AJ said no, I cried, broken hearted at the loss of my first true friend. Well, at least that's who I thought he'd been.

Mrs Llewellyn found me in tears outside the art block.

The stout woman, who did indeed reek of cigar smoke, became a mother figure to me for this long, strong moment, just as she vowed she would be to all her girls when they enrolled at the academy. I relaxed into tears as Mrs Lewellyn held me tight, walking me slowly to her office where she allowed me to pour my heart out over a cup of English tea and a digestive biscuit.

'He was so much more than a teacher, Mrs Llewellyn. And I was so much more than a student. To him. I felt it. And I've never felt anything like that before.'

I wasn't allowed to discuss it any more. Mrs Lewellyn instructed me to go to class and 'perk up' because I'd gotten everything off my chest. She said it wasn't an admirable quality to wallow.

A week later, I found my dorm cubicle raided and a series of sketches resembling a cartoon strip – complete with my initials on every loose page – scattered all over my bed. The strip featured the intimate adventures of a small white cat with the letter 'Z' hanging from her pink collar, and her affair with a big black dog carrying a teacher's cane, his fur splashed with spilt paint. Not one student took the blame for invading my personal space, nor did any of them pin blame on another.

Adam Jeffrey Blackmore resigned from his position with immediate effect.

And I was put on the first flight to Boston.

24

Jim

So, Zara got to go to Hogwarts but didn't learn to fly.

I wonder how a girl like her would have survived in my school. It was Catholic, but about as religious as a packet of prawn cocktail crisps. The girls rolled their skirts around their waists so many times to show off their legs that sometimes you could see their knickers. The lads would stand around in large packs, hardly speaking, wide stances in Kickers boots and hands stuffed into the pockets of Berghaus or Helly Hansen jackets, too expensive for most families to buy their sons, but they found a way anyway. It was either that or the bullying would kick off. The girls approached us way more often than we approached girls, the gender split across the school yard as bold as a lightning strike. Christ, it must have been hell on earth for the misfits.

I was lucky, I had good mates.

Then, when we got a bit older, I had Helen.

When you coupled off, and it was serious, it was a thing

to stand off behind the science block, arm in arm. The daring ones would cop off, and yeah, Helen was daring. We'd kiss for the length of a lunch break, my balls aching to explode, the afternoon a fucking bastard to get through.

I was clever though. Not bragging, like. My reports and exam results can prove that.

But, hey, I wonder where I'd be now if I'd had the chance to go to Hogwarts.

25

Zara

'Wow, I just talked a lot,' I say to Jim, after a beat.

He blows his lips out. 'Sounds like you were better off out of there.'

'You're kidding, right?'

'Why?'

'It was one of the world's top boarding schools. Still is. That stigma stays with you. I'm not blaming my lack of career on something that happened when I was fourteen, but—'

'You are.'

'I guess.'

A sign for Heathrow airport indicates we're getting close, although traffic is building up, moving, crawling, then moving a touch faster again.

'Shall we play a game?' I suggest. 'To pass the time?'

Jim nods.

'A–Z of a TV show?'

'Which one?'

'*Friends*?'

'What is this? 1999?'

I scoff, a little shocked by how retro *Friends* has become. '*Breaking Bad*?'

'Good choice. Me first. A – Albuquerque.'

'B – Bryan Cranston.'

When we reach the letter 'Q' in our third round of the game, the latest topic being classical literature (Jim's choice), the minibus crawls into gridlock.

'It's as if everyone has just accepted this is the way it has to be,' I complain.

Jim switches the engine off, folds his arms across his chest.

'Honk your horn, Jim.'

'What good'll that do?'

'Nobody's honking.'

'It might come as a shock, love, but that won't budge the traffic.'

I check the clock on the dashboard again. Thirty minutes ago, I was expecting to arrive at Heathrow precisely two hours before my flight is scheduled to take off. Now, I'm cutting it fine and moving nowhere fast.

Jim closes his eyes, resting up.

'Jim?'

'Hmm?'

'I'm going to miss my flight.'

'It'll move soon, girl.'

'This is so frustrating.'

'I don't know what your problem is. Can't you just read a book?'

'A book?'

243

'Yeah, if I wasn't a slave to this wheel, I'd just sit back and read.'

'Oh, sure. And where do I get a book from?'

'You mean you haven't got a single book in all that stuff back there? In your life's belongings?'

'No, books are too heavy.'

'Not even one paperback?'

'No, Jim. Not even one paperback.'

'You'd find that time passes by quite beautifully with a paperback.'

'Beautifully? Seriously?'

'In fact, here you go.' Jim reaches down into the shelf in his door. 'Read this. It's the book Mary gave me. It's more the sort me ma prefers, but hey, a book's a book.'

I accept the book, some sort of thriller with the silhouette of a child dragging a teddy bear up a hill.

'You brought this with you even though you knew you were driving?'

'I always have a book with me. Always.'

'You didn't have one with you before we got to Mary's.'

'I did. I had the Gene Wilder autobiogr . . . FUCK.'

'What?'

'I left it in the fucking BMW.' Jim slams his palms against the steering wheel.

'Guess you'll be needing this back, then?'

And Jim snatches back my offering, smoothing the crease in the cover, and returns it to the little shelf inside his door. As angry as he is, I have to admit that his temper is quite cute, how he cares so much for something as trivial as a book. I imagine drawing a little monkey with a red face, holding a bunch of books close to his chest, perhaps with a scholar's hat and spectacles. Or, perhaps not a monkey. A frog. Yes, a little green frog, all protective about his precious paperbacks, hopping on them to mark his territory. That would make a great sketch.

'Look, you've got bags of time,' Jim says.

But he's wrong. Check-in will close in fifteen, maybe twenty minutes and although we're just a handful of miles from the airport, we aren't within walking distance. We're trapped.

'Wasn't there a better route you could've taken?' I snap.

'Ah,' Jim sighs. 'I forgot this'd be my fault.'

'Can't you ever answer a simple question?'

'Can't you ever stop being such a demanding little princess?'

'Fuck you, Jim.'

'Oh fuck you, Zara. Fuck. You.'

My mouth hangs open. How dare he. How DARE . . .

'Stop gawping at me, Zara.'

I turn away, keeping a tight hold of my disgust.

'I didn't cause that accident down there, or road works, or whatever's going on, like. Don't blame me. God, you can be so fucking childish. Did you know that?'

If my intestines could loop into a knot, they would do so right now. I despise being called 'childish', a word my papa likes to use whenever things don't work out for me. Like when I defended my expulsion, or dropped out of university (a course he also referred to as 'childish' because 'drawing is for pre-schoolers'). He even called my relationship with Zein 'childish' because I never had a ring on my finger. To give him some credit, he did show fatherly concern about my scar, and lowered my rent when I couldn't get a job. But when I cried he reminded me not to be so 'childish' because like all wounds, it would heal.

Damn it, Jim's right this time. I am being childish.

'You think you're the only one with problems, don't you?' he says through gritted teeth, almost as if he didn't want me to hear him. I peer across, feeling as though I'm spying on him as he leans over to his phone, scrolls through recent contacts and clicks on, 'Ma Home'. The loud speaker rings out and Jim snatches the handset, bringing it to his ear, keen for some hint of privacy.

His mom doesn't answer.

Jim taps the wheel with his free hand, his foot revving unnecessarily. He hangs up and tosses his phone aside. It lands between my feet. I bend down and pick it up, placing it on the seat between us with care.

'I'm sure she's okay,' I say, delicately.

'How would you know?'

'She's gone to a party . . . a sixtieth birthday party. She told you, earlier.'

Rain batters down on the windscreen. We left one storm in Liverpool, and after driving down the spine of the country through wintry drizzle, we've hit another storm in London. The minibus rocks from side to side as enormous winds show the motorway who is in charge here. The traffic starts moving again, slowly, and as Jim edges forward, stopping, starting, stopping, starting, visibility is beyond poor and it's a miracle he doesn't drive into the back of the car in front.

'Yvonne,' Jim says, eventually, breathing a small sigh of relief, and although he's speaking loud enough for me to hear, it's clear he's talking to himself. 'She's gone to Yvonne's sixtieth birthday. Ethel Barton's daughter.'

And in complete silence, we make it to Departures at Heathrow. Twenty minutes too late.

* * *

246

'Check-in is closed,' the grounds staff inform us.

I'm pulling endless reasons from the air as to why they should allow me to check in. From inventing a terminally ill grandmother, to pretending I'm a journalist keen on publishing a high-profile article on how airlines treat their customers, to yelling that the damn plane won't be taking off for another hour, I fail on all accounts.

My luggage is battered, tired, sitting on an empty line in front of an empty check-in desk, Jim resting upon it. He looks as worn out as the jeans on his long, skinny legs and I can only sympathise. The man, for all his faults, has done his best. He tried with impressive effort to get me here on time, and despite it costing me a small fortune, I just can't remain angry at him. It's too exhausting. In fact, he looks as disappointed as I feel.

'What happens now?' he asks.

'I'm on stand-by for the next flight with availability. Tomorrow morning . . . if there's a spare seat.'

'Do I get to go home now?'

'I guess.'

'You gonna be alright?'

'I think so.'

Jim stands, overbearing in height next to me. I'm longing to brush my teeth, take a shower, lie down, and no doubt Jim feels exactly the same. Twisting my hair around and around, I secure it into a messy bun with the band around my wrist. And he smiles, just on that single side. It's infectious, and I smile back. Our journey could have been a whole lot brighter if moments like this weren't so far apart. Just that morning, I'd woken up in a cheap youth hostel beside a pub already swarming with students drinking pints for a pound. My heart had been totally broken, and it's Jim who has been by my side.

'You know what would be cool?' I say.

'What's that, love?'

'If we met by chance in say, a few years from now . . . a good chance, like—'

'Like if I drove into the back of *your* brand-new BMW?'

'Ha ha. You really should leave your mysterious empire and go into comedy, Jim.'

'I'm thinking about it.'

'But, what I'm trying to say is, it'd be cool if we met and I wasn't a heartbroken wreck, and you weren't hanging on death's door with alcohol poisoning. We might have a shot at being friends. Maybe.'

'It's definitely crossed me mind that you were sent from hell to torture me.'

'Oh, me too. Likewise.'

I hesitate, but decide to reach out my arms towards Jim and his shaggy tattered hair, his thickening stubble. A small chuckle escapes from me first, then another followed by him, and he steps forward, accepting my farewell embrace. He's all skin and bone beneath that dated old fleece he's been wearing all day, his long arms wrapping firmly around my small back. I thought he'd feel damp, kind of cold, as his appearance presents. But he's warm, like a gentle fire burning beside a thick woollen rug. I squeeze him tight. God. I could've done with a decent hug like this hours ago.

'Well, if we don't meet by chance again,' Jim says, not fully breaking away, his hands resting on my lower back. 'I hope that heart mends. It's wasted on that lying bastard scumbag. You're worth more.'

Breathing in a little through my nostrils, I swallow the lump that's popped up in my throat. Tiny tears prickle around the corners of my eyes and I wonder why more people in my life can't decide to say such nice words to me.

He's leaving, backing away, except he reaches one arm out and I presume he's about to give my shoulder a gentle punch, say something along the lines of 'hang on in there, kiddo,' then I remember he isn't an American jock. Instead, he squeezes my shoulder and moves his hand towards my face, and with absolute tenderness, strokes the patch below my scar and says, 'All the best, love.'

At the check-in, a new line of passengers starts to form, ground staff now at the desks. That brief stillness within one of the world's busiest airports has come to an end, and hustle returns to greet bustle. I sigh, preparing myself for the long, lonely night ahead of me as Jim gives one wave, a single salute, and walks away. The sliding doors to the terminal's entrance are opening and closing with haste, a gush of angry wind slipping through and blowing in lingering dead leaves, a discarded sandwich wrapper, a loose luggage tag. Jim takes a quick step backwards when the wind sends a hit his way, before continuing onwards, forwards, outside.

'Jim!' I call, and follow him, my bags trailing behind.

He stops, turns around.

If any words were about to fall from his lips, they would be, 'What now?', except he just looks too jaded to speak.

'I need your bank details,' I tell him. 'So I can transfer the money I owe you.'

'Right,' he says, as if he'd forgotten, which is hard to believe after the almighty song and dance he'd made out of it earlier. 'You got a pen?'

'I do, with my art things. I have a pencil case.' I crouch down and start to unzip one of my suitcases. 'Not this one. One moment, let me look in the other one . . .'

'Zara . . .'

Another gush of wind attacks, the shrill whistle of its roar loud and strong.

'Oh, Jim. You can't drive in that atrocious weather. You're pooped. It's dangerous.'

He raises an eyebrow and if I could read his mind, I'd guess he was wondering why I'd changed the subject. But I'm not backing out of our deal. I have a better idea.

'I need to get home,' he says. 'To bed.'

'Reverse that. You need to get to bed. Then go home.'

'I can't—'

'You can. Look, I'm not sleeping on an airport floor, so I'm going to have to get a hotel room, one of those Travelodge places across the way. You should do that, too. They'll have pens and paper galore, and actually, they'll have Wi-Fi. I can get my laptop out, transfer the money to you there and then.'

'Zara, I can't.'

'Jim, you can. And you will.'

'Who are you? Me ma?'

'I hate the way you do that.'

'What?'

'Make out like I'm being a nag when I'm just protecting you.'

Jim narrows his eyes, cocks his head to one side.

'What if you fall asleep at the wheel?' I say.

'I won't.'

'Or what if another car skids into you because they can't see the road clearly? You might not be as lucky as you were this morning.'

'Lucky?'

I look at my pile of luggage and back to Jim.

'Well, for the very, very last time . . . can you give me a lift?'

There's only one room vacant.

Sitting behind the reception desk of the Travelodge is a middle-aged woman, her uniform tight and stretched across her chest, her eyeliner drawn thick and wonky below each eye, her name badge simply stating *Manager*. A young guy, skinny and camp with huge hands flapping about, is working beside her and telling a most animated tale. His badge says *Kyle*.

I greet them. Where I'm getting my chirpiness from, I don't know.

Kyle pauses mid grand gesture, unleashing a sigh of disgust at being interrupted.

'Only one room?' I repeat what he tells me.

I might have missed my flight to Dubai, due to take off any second, but many other flights to various towns, cities, countries have also been cancelled due to the gale force winds. Sure, we could hop back into the minibus, drive around to the Premier Inn, to the Ibis, to the Radisson, but as Kyle informs us with a smugness that I find both unnecessary and unhelpful, other hotels are likely to be fully booked tonight, also.

'No bother, I'm going home,' Jim reiterates, stepping away from the suitcases, checking I've got all of my things safely with me. 'I wanna wake up in me own bed in the morning.'

I point towards the entrance, to the rain being swept sideways by the harsh winds.

'You're not driving all the way to Liverpool in that.'

Kyle volunteers to agree. 'She's right, you can't drive to Liverpool in that.'

'It's a twin room,' the manager pipes up. 'Plus, there's a chair. And a pouffe.'

Chuckles erupt from the pair behind the desk, Kyle's eyes streaming with tears as he holds onto the manager's hand, her face all screwed up as if she's trying not to wet her knickers. Jim walks away, clearly too cool for this. Handing my passport over as identification, I pay for the room upfront as Jim flicks through leaflets advertising West End shows and London attractions. The manager starts typing away while Kyle spins around in slow circles on the chair beside her, studying his fingernails.

Is Jim really going to drive all the way to Liverpool now? In that storm?

Or is he going to share this room with me?

I've shared tents at festivals with people I hardly know, hostels with backpackers I didn't know at all. What's the big deal about this? We've been in close confinement all day long. Still, there's a stigma with hotels, an intimacy, or sleaziness, or both. Jim walks towards me, fanning himself with a leaflet for the London Dungeon, keeping himself awake, I suspect.

'I'm gonna sleep in the minibus,' Jim says, yawning.

'Don't be stupid.'

'I'll recline the back seats, it'll be dead cosy. Like camping.'

'I can't let you do that.'

The manager stands. 'Actually, *I* can't let you do that.'

'Why?' both Jim and I ask, in unison.

'Because our parking is strictly for guests only.'

'Come on, Jim,' I say. 'It's a twin room. No point in wasting a good bed.'

Jim takes hold of my suitcases for the umpteenth time that day. Anyone would think he was being marched to the room with a gun to his head, not being given a comfortable space to sleep for a grand total of *free*.

Stop it, Zara, I tell myself. Shake it off. An opportunity for company has arisen rather than spending the night alone. *Be grateful, Zara.*

As we both trudge my belongings down the corridor, I get distracted by the hum of a vending machine. I stop and toss some loose coins in, choosing a few bags of potato chips, a couple of Snickers. The thrill of the items slowly twisting from their shelf and tumbling into the tray never fades, no matter how old I am. What does get boring, however, is hotel key cards not working. After a few fumbles, I allow Jim to take over, so he enters the room first.

He pauses, and I bump into him.

'Oh,' he says.

'Oh, what?'

I have to jump to peek over his shoulder.

'Ah,' I say.

'Hmm.'

The twin beds are not twin beds at all. They are one. An inviting kingsize.

Jim puts the cases down and lets out a long, drawn sigh, then leaps forward and dives onto the bed, flopping out like a starfish. It looks like such a great idea that I copy his actions and flop down beside him.

'You have no idea what boundaries are,' Jim says.

'Do you wanna take a shower first?' I suggest.

'Do I smell that bad?'

'No comment.'

The two unopened bottles of Shiraz in my suitcase are begging to be drunk. There are no wine glasses, so I pour wine into the two white coffee cups sitting on white saucers

253

beside the little kettle. I flick the plasma television screen on. A music channel churning out hits from the Seventies and Eighties is playing 'Sweet Dreams' by the Eurythmics.

The patter of the shower sounds, steam misting from the bathroom door which Jim has left slightly ajar. I blush, and sip my wine generously. When Jim emerges after a few minutes, just a towel around his lower half and dripping water all over the thick carpet, he looks so different with his long hair flat and wet, stuck to his rather chiseled face, that I feel very grubby. Grabbing my toiletries bag, I take my turn to shower and slip into my PJs, little grey shorts laced with a pink frill, and a matching t-shirt with 'AMOUR' printed across the chest. I brush my teeth – oh, heavenly! – but curse my scar, so red without make-up, then wrap my hair up into a towel.

'Exotic, isn't it?' I joke, twirling around the Travelodge room.

'It's more upmarket than a chalet in Rhyl,' Jim says, helping himself to more wine.

'Where's Rhyl?'

'Wales.'

'Where's the most exotic place you've ever been to?'

'Rhyl.'

'Ha ha, very funny.'

Jim flashes me his half smile. 'What about you?'

My passport is hanging out of my canvas tote bag and I pick it up and toss it to him. He catches it sharp with one hand. He sits on the corner of the bed and flicks through it as if it's an illustrated storybook. Nodding consistently, he studies the various stamps with an almost geeky interest. Then he finds my photo and laughs – standard procedure – holding it up to compare with my face now. 'Zara *May* Khoury', he reads out. I was twenty-six on that photo, four years ago, with bleached blonde hair and a glowing tan from long days doing very little in the South East Asian sun. I spent four months there after things ended with Zein. Jim closes the passport and hands it back to me, as if he's read my mind.

'Wanna know the real reason The Dentists never hit the big time?' he pipes up with.

'Absolutely.'

'Well, me mate Griffo, his dad got us a gig in Puerto Banus for his mum's fortieth birthday party, except I never had a passport. And I sort of only admitted that when it was too late.'

'How late?'

'As we were all leaving for the airport.'

'Why didn't you just Fast Track, get one of those premium appointments?'

'I was fifteen. I didn't know.'

'But, what about the guys, the ones with the awful teeth?' I tease.

'Oh, they went. They called me a wanker, got themselves a free holiday. And me, well, I stayed behind in Liverpool.'

'Did they play without you?'

'They might've called me a wanker, but they're not wankers. Besides, none of them could sing. Even Mikey, he's a music teacher now, he's got great rhythm, but he's tone deaf. Like you.'

'Video killed the—'

'STOP. Anyway, when they came back, all sunburnt and full of lies about sleeping with loads of women, we decided to just stick it out as mates. To be honest, I think that's why we're still so tight. The Dentists going platinum probably would've torn us apart.'

I drag the towel off my head and, shaking it out, I lay it out on the carpet. Taking the opened bottle, the unopened bottle and remaining snacks, I place them down upon it. I grab a couple of pillows and the cushions that decorate the bed.

'What are you doing?' Jim asks.

'Isn't it obvious?' I say. 'We're having a picnic.'

To my delight, Jim plays along.

'I don't even know your surname,' I say, crossing my legs as Jim outstretches his, both of us using pillows and cushions to slouch against.

'Glover,' he says.

'Great. I can find you on Facebook now.'

'I'm not on Facebook.'

Once again, my perception skills fail me. I've lost my touch entirely. Of course Jim isn't on Facebook. I bet he's never even considered it.

We open the second bottle and Jim refills my cup.

I notice a hole in the back of his t-shirt and am tempted to poke my finger in, just for fun, but I eat the Snickers instead. Jim hadn't been wearing this t-shirt this morning when we crashed because I seem to remember a camper van print, which is now replaced with some beer brand I've never heard of. I bet he got changed when he picked up the minibus.

Blondie is singing 'Call Me'.

'Jim Glover?'

'Yeah?'

'Do you believe everyone has a soul mate?'

'Oh, Jesus, girl. You're asking *me*?'

'I wanna know your thoughts.'

'Okay . . . fuck. Erm. Well, to be honest, yeah, I used to believe that. But now, I dunno.'

'Helpful.'

'Look. We live in a mental world, everyone running around like every minute's about to be their last. No one's taking the time to get to know anyone anymore, it's all rushed.'

'You mean dating, all those apps, swiping and scrutinising everybody's faults?'

'Hmm. Maybe. I don't know much about apps and shit. But I do think people used to tolerate each other more than they do today. They allowed their love to grow. Sometimes it worked, sometimes it didn't. Finding love . . . and by "love", I mean the kind classic movies portray, or the "love" our grandparents told us about when we were kids . . . well, today it's different. The world's moved on, it got batteries, it goes faster and faster. It's all so instant. No one allows anything to grow. Love included. If a relationship shows a hint of needing a bit of watering, people are quick to get the fuck out. I'm guilty of it meself.'

'Or maybe you just haven't found The One.'

'Cheesy, like. But, I reckon, when you know you know.'

'Oh, I love that notion, Jim.'

'God, you are a hopeless romantic, aren't you, girl?'

'Hopeless.'

Cyndi Lauper appears on the screen. 'Time After Time' fills the room, the space between us. It's nice to sit back and listen, enjoy the sensation of the wine, take a moment. The conversation has dried up, but that doesn't matter anymore.

'I might have to hit the sack, love.'

I agree, struggling to keep my eyes open, too. The bed is beckoning.

But neither of us move.

I decide to break the silence at the exact moment that Jim does.

'You can have the—'/ 'I'll sleep down here—'

'Sorry what?'/ 'What? Soz.'

'I don't mind—'/ 'You can have it—'

'We can share—'/ 'We could share—'

'Sorry,'/ 'Sorry.'

So, since I'm not sure of anything Jim is saying, I presume he feels the same way.

'It's big enough for a whole family,' I manage, although a little too loud for my liking, my eardrums tingling at my own shrill.

'You won't even know I'm there,' Jim says, a mock yawn prompting me into a genuine one.

He's still wearing his t-shirt, his ripped jeans, and I feel quite naked in my PJs. Like a married couple from one of those old sitcoms, we each climb into opposite sides of the bed, the only thing missing being rollers in my hair and a pair of striped pyjamas on Jim. I plump up my pillows and he lies flat as if his body is displayed in an open casket. Cyndi Lauper hits the high notes with 'I will be waiting' and I giggle to stop myself from cringing. I catch Jim smirking, too. The music is invasive, if not corny.

'Shall I turn it off?' Jim asks.

I nod, snuggling downwards.

He points the remote towards the TV, but it doesn't turn off. Stretching his arm out further, screwing up his face to somehow help him press down harder, he tries again, calling the remote control a 'lazy bastard'.

'If you're lost, you can look, and you will find me . . .'

The duvet flicks back and he swings his long legs, still wearing his ripped jeans, out of the bed.

'No, wait,' I say, sitting up and pulling his shoulder back. 'Let me.'

258

I swing my bare legs out of bed now, standing, but Jim also stands and says, 'Nah, you stay where you are.' Both of us are moving, both speaking simultaneously yet again, neither hearing the other one's words.

'No, it's fine,'/ 'Get back into bed,'/ 'I'm closer,'/ 'I'll turn it off.'

And now, we're both standing at the foot of the kingsize bed, so close, inches apart.

'. . . If you fall, I will catch you . . .'

I can feel Jim's breath warming the top of my head.

We freeze.

Neither of us are making any effort to turn the TV off. My eyes are fixed on the blue speckled carpet. I make my move, turn towards the TV and switch it off from the main button on the side. A deeper darkness clouds the room, the only light passing from the bathroom door which remains ajar. The intensity has passed, we can get back into bed now, fall into a desperately desired slumber.

I sit down on the bed but Jim takes my hand in his, pulling me back to standing upright, before him.

I dare to shift my gaze upwards, a lightness in my toes, my knees, my heart, as I take in his hair, his jawline, his lips, anything but his eyes. A strand of my still-damp hair is caught in my eyelashes, and I fidget a touch, pushing it out of the way. Jim lifts his other hand to assist me and allows it to linger in my hair. I look into his pale, narrowing eyes and we are locked together within a bubble of stillness, ready to bounce, ready to burst. What will happen if I blink? It's all I can do to stop myself.

So, I move . . .

. . . Take a little step in towards him . . .

No.

This isn't supposed to happen.

Just because I'm stuck in a hotel room with Jim, doesn't mean I have to . . .

. . . But I want to. I want him.

And God, my fear of getting hurt is as powerful as the heat intensifying between us.

This isn't supposed to . . .

It is happening. I falter, as if I'm standing at the beginning of a long tight rope. Can I do this? Can I fall into him? What if he doesn't catch me? The feel of his fingers interlacing with mine sends a shockwave of electricity buzzing through me. He lowers his head further and I raise my chin, our lips inches apart.

Getting closer.

Closer.

And closer.

Unexpectedly, Jim steps back, abrupt, as if he's been pulled out from the water.

His phone's ringing.

'It's an unknown number,' he says. 'I've got to take it . . . Excuse me, love.'

Then, as Jim leaves the room, he mouths, 'Sorry', and goes out into the corridor.

I sit on the edge of the bed, anticipating his return, unsure of what to do with myself. Good God. We almost kissed. We very nearly, absolutely, totally almost fucking kissed. Jim! I can't kiss Jim, can I? Will I kiss him once he comes back into the room? Is that what's supposed to happen? The urge between us had been real.

I flick on the lamp and take a look around, the white bed sheets enticing me. I can hear Jim's voice outside, a muffled distant echo of a half-audible disjointed conversation. Perhaps he says, 'Helen'. And again. Whatever he's saying, there's no laughter and a certain urgency, the words, 'Stop', 'Calm', 'Listen', all repeating often. Then, even those words filter into distortion until they're small noises too far away for me to hear at all.

The room falls quiet, the glow of the lamp a bright reminder of being alone. Of course, I can turn the TV back on, catch up on the news, wait for Jim to return. But what if he doesn't want me to wait? What if nothing happening between us is exactly how it should be?

I pick up the towel from the carpet, fold it onto the chair. Then I place the empty bottles and snacks into the trash. I brush my teeth again.

The silence beckons me to darkness, to bed.

I wait another minute, maybe two . . . And then climb beneath my half of the duvet, switch off the lamp, and fall sound, sound asleep.

Daylight isn't the only thing to wake me. It's also the need to drink some water. The wine helped with the deep sleep, but I feel groggy, a dull weight sitting between my eyebrows. I don't want to wake up properly just yet. My thoughts are quite consumed by Jim; I'm anxious to open my eyes and find him beside me.

Unless I've been dreaming. The kiss . . . no, the almost kiss . . .

What will I do once I open my eyes; once Jim opens his? How my heart flutters.

Turn. *After three*, I say to myself. *One, two, THREE*.

But all I'm faced with is a sea of white cotton, Jim's side of the bed still empty, the pillows missing. The bathroom light is on. I somehow recall turning it off, falling asleep in complete darkness, which means Jim must be in there. I sit bolt upright in bed, my ears sharp to welcome the shuffle of a towel, the flush of a toilet, the dripping of a tap, but I hear nothing. His pillows are on the carpet, a few bath towels discarded at their side. The room is etched with stillness, not a human sound other than my own breath.

The clock tells me it's nine forty-three. Wrapping the duvet around myself to keep warm, I get up and circle the room. Jim wouldn't leave without saying goodbye. But there isn't a sock or a shoe or a pair of jeans here that belongs to anybody other than me.

Jim Glover has gone.

And I'm back to being where I should be, on my way to the airport.

26

Jim

The luxury of choice wasn't available. There was no deciding whether to stay, whether to go. I could only go. And Christ, I didn't want to wake Zara up. She'd slow me down.

It's nine in the morning. I've passed Birmingham, the Saturday-morning quiet giving me a much-owed favour. The minibus is hanging in there, pushing seventy, hitting eighty with a rattle. And so what? I'd take another busted vehicle into my responsibility if it means getting back to Liverpool in record time.

'Come on,' I will the accelerator.

Of course, Zara wouldn't mean to slow me down. She'd only ask questions because she cares, probably would've poured me a glass of water, held out my fleece to help me into it, and, well, get smack bang in the middle of me having to make a swift exit. All of this would've taken time. Time which I don't have.

Why am I so far away from Liverpool? Why? Of all nights to be away from home, why this one? I'm never away from home, never. The motorway's beginning to feel like quick-sand, dragging me under. If only I could see its ending.

Hurry, hurry, please.

And God, how my neck aches when I move it slightly to the right. Ouch. A never-ending ripple of creaks and crunches patters down my spine as I twist, stretch, trying to iron out the stiffness engulfing me. I slept on the floor last night. It was only fair that Zara got the bed to herself. She'd paid for the bloody thing.

Sixty-nine miles to Liverpool.

Come on, hurry.

When I finally got Helen off the phone – not an easy task since she was a) crying and b) pissed as a fart – Zara was fast asleep, tucked up in the bed beneath the duvet. I stood for a moment, watching her, that sweet face cuddled into a pillow, her pink lips slightly parted, her breath light. Her scar was hidden behind a curtain of her hair and I felt the urge to sweep it out of the way, stroke her cheek, but I didn't want to frighten her. Bloody hell, we'd almost got off with each other. What's more, I wanted to. I think. Maybe it would've been the final piece to the mind-boggling puzzle that was yesterday, but I'll never know now.

Helen had called me from her mate's house, an unknown number. She'd been fighting with Snowy – again – and wanted me to pick her up in my BMW.

'That's impossible, Hels.'

'Nothings i-poss-ble, Jimbo.'

'Me car's in the pound.'

'Liar.'

'I'm not even in Liverpool, love.'

'Fucking LIAR.'

And so on.

If Helen had used her own phone, would I have answered? Or would I have let it ring out? Would I have kissed Zara? I recall my stance, how I'd bowed my head, angled it to the left a bit, leant in. My lips were a second away from touching hers, maybe less.

But the moment was missed.

Gone.

All that remained was the floor, beckoning me to sleep. I woke up around six, nature calling. On instinct, I checked my phone, on silent after Helen's call. There were four missed calls, all from an unknown number, and thank God, a text message from Snowy.

Jimbo. Pick up your phone. Your ma's in the ozzy.

I wanted to tell Zara I had to go. I did, honestly.

I'm going to be honest, right. I hated her at first, for obvious reasons. Then I resisted liking her until, hand on heart, it became completely impossible. But the rush of pleasure she'd made me feel smacked me in the face like a harsh, cold gust of wind. I'm needed at home. Urgently. Yet this morning, I was more than two hundred miles from home, from my ma, and Zara bloody Khoury was the sole reason for that. She was the root of all my problems, growing deeper, branching out further. So, I scribbled a quick note before dashing off into the bitter dawn.

I had to go.

The wheels beneath me can't go fast enough.

'Ah, come on!' I yell, bashing the dashboard with my fist. 'Hurry. Please.'

I go over that text message again and again, the vision

giving me a headache. If Helen hadn't been such a pain in the arse last night, I would never have put my phone on silent. And if I'd never met Zara, I wouldn't even be in this situation.

It was a blessing I'd needed a wee at six in the morning.

Thirty-three miles to Liverpool.

The unknown number had come from Ethel Barton's home phone. Ex-directory. Luckily, she knew Snowy's ma and was able to get a message to her, and she passed on the message to Snowy. I saw the text just before returning to my makeshift bath-towel bed on the floor of the Travelodge room.

I tried calling Snowy back, standing in the Travelodge car park, the dull fuzz of planes flying low overhead. The frost bit my toes within my trainers, my fleece just not cutting it in the Baltic early morning. I watched my breath condensing in the air as each ring repeated itself, a hamster wheel of frustration. Snowy never picked up. At least he'd sent me Ethel's number.

I got inside the minibus, called Ethel Barton.

'Ethel? It's Jim,' I said, throwing the van into gear.

'Where the hell have you been?'

'What happened, Ethel?'

'It's a good job I was there, you know. A good job I found her, you know.'

'Found her where?'

'Where are you, Jim?'

'Shut up and tell me what happened to me ma, Ethel!'

'Well, I can't tell you if you want me to shut up, soft lad, can I?'

'Ethel.'

'Do you know what time it is? I never got to bed 'til gone eleven, you know.'

'IS SHE OKAY?'

Ethel let out a long sigh. 'Yes. She's okay.'

'Is it her heart?'

'She fell. Getting out the bath.'

'Were you there?'

'No, I wasn't there, soft lad. Your mother had this God-awful idea to get in the bath on her own. On her own! For the rest of me days, Jim, I swear I'll never understand what the bleeding hell compelled her to do it. She knows not to get in the bath on her own, never mind get out of it. I said to her time and time again, you know. I did, you know.'

'So, how did you find her?'

'Well, I sensed something wasn't quite right when she didn't come to our Yvonne's sixtieth, didn't I?'

'She never went?'

'No. I waited 'til the buffet opened and thought, it's almost nine, it's not like your mother to be late. She'd booked a taxi for seven, you know. Seven.'

'And you waited 'til nine to realise something wasn't right?'

'I had to wait 'til the buffet opened. The cling film doesn't come off the plates by itself.'

'Fucking hell, Ethel.'

'Jesus Christ, Jim. You've got a dirty mouth.'

'So what happened after nine?'

'I told our Yvonne to give me a lift to your mother's. But she was well away. It was quite embarrassing, you know. A woman of our Yvonne's age, drinking like a teenager, you know. So, I dragged her husband away – he's teetotal, you see, since his bypass – and God love him, he took me to your mother's.'

'And she was . . . where? I don't understand, Ethel.'

'Lucky I had that key, Jim. I went straight upstairs and there she was on the floor.'

'Oh, God. Me mam? On the floor?'

'She'd been there since tea time.'

'She could've caught pneumonia.'

'Well, the heating was on full blast, you know how careless she is about that.'

'Thank God.'

'So I called an ambulance and she was whisked in. She needs a hip replacement.'

'But her heart?'

'Her heart's fine, love. It's . . . fine.'

'You don't sound so sure, Ethel.'

'I called your sisters. Although, I hate to think what my phone bill's gonna be next month. They're on the next flight home.'

'Oh Christ, Ethel,' I say, my throat tight, dry. 'What does this mean?'

'Just get yourself to the hospital.'

'I'm on me way.'

'If I hadn't left our Yvonne's party, you know, I hate to think what would've happened.'

And if I'd truly let Helen go all those years ago – with my blessing like I said I had – I'd already be at my ma's side.

It was supposed to be a beating, not a blessing. Pushing ten years ago, roughly.

Snowy had asked me to meet him in the Old Ship, the sort of pub where you went once, but never twice. A blend of damp and piss reeked from its walls and although dry roasted peanuts were sold behind the bar, nobody dared to eat them.

'What the fuck are we doing here?' I whispered, although we were the only customers present. 'And why are you dressed like a mef?'

Bulked out in a multitude of layers, Snowy was sporting jumper upon jumper and three beanie hats. His short arms stuck out by his side and as he sat at one of the many empty tables in the pub, he gave a little knock on his shin to reveal a shin pad. He looked ridiculous.

'In answer to your questions,' Snowy began, a wobble in his voice. 'We're here so you don't get barred from the Pacific Arms, 'cause it's our local, and I'm dressed like this 'cause you're gonna beat me up. And I'm a wuss.'

I rolled my eyes and bought us both a pint. I'd had a long day in the mailroom followed by another rejection from the editor after asking if I could write a feature – just a short one and not on company time – to go in next month's issue. Snowy's cryptic behaviour was amusing, if anything, but not what I fancied putting up with this evening. I sipped my pint and, with respect, tried not to wince at its bitterness. Snowy necked half in one swift go, then cleared his throat.

'Jesus, I'm sweating me tits off.'

'You reckon?'

'I need to ask you some questions, Jimbo. You ready?'

I let out a big sigh.

'Good. When did you last have sex with Helen?'

'Y'what?'

'You heard.'

I scratched my head, lowered my voice. 'Dunno. Ages ago. Why?'

'Ages ago? As in years? Months? Weeks?'

If only the ale tasted a fraction better.

'Jimbo, please.'

'About two years ago,' I lied. It was more like two months ago.

'But you split up three years ago?'

'Four.'

'Okay. Who broke up with who?'

271

'You know that.'

'Well, we all know it fizzled out, but someone must've pulled the plug.'

In all honesty, I don't know the answer, it's foggy. There were endless moments you could say me and Helen became no longer me and Helen. Like how she didn't let me inside her house for months after the abortion. Or when she decided it'd be best if I wasn't invited to her sister's wedding. And there was that fella with the Honda Civic who drove her to work. And picked her up. Steve.

'Hold on,' I said. 'When have I ever beaten anyone up? Why am I gonna—'

'Next question.' Snowy started to rip up his soggy beermat. 'Do you wanna get back with her?'

The doors into the Old Ship swung open and an old fella shuffled in, paper beneath his arm, a nasty cough rattling around his chest. A silent nod to the barmaid indicated his usual and he continued to shuffle, heading straight for me and Snowy. We edged our low stools out of the way as the old fella squeezed between us and plonked himself down on the sofa against the wall. Evidently 'his spot'; no compromise was going to be made just because we were in its vicinity.

'Well?' Snowy asked. 'Do you?'

Braving my pint, I took a huge gulp. It was kind of Snowy to show his concern for me and my wishy-washy love life, but that's all it was. Kind. No offence to Snowy, but I didn't need kind right now, I needed a lucky break. Maybe I would write the feature anyway, print it in bold (and a huge fucking font) and staple it to the editor's desk.

'Do you wanna get back with Helen?'

'No,' I said. Surprisingly.

'Why?' Snowy asked, concern draining his usual cheery face.

'Snowy lad, you know why. We don't work. We're not right for each other. She's here,' I unfolded one hand, and then the other, 'and I'm there. And we just can't seem to . . .' and I tried bringing my hands together, but couldn't, as if a magnet was keeping them apart. 'I mean, I love the bones of Helen, I do, and I care for her. We all do, don't we? But, Christ. Can't believe you're making me say this out loud, lad, but she's not . . . she's not me girl.'

Snowy removed one beanie hat and mopped between his thick black eyebrows. I snatched it and, scrunching it into a little ball, threw it into Snowy's face, a subconscious attempt to lift the atmosphere. I didn't enjoy how the words I'd just spoken rang in my ears, how they now hung inside the Old Ship. There was either a great amount of dishonesty in them, or an over-bearing truth, one I wasn't ready to admit. Four years on.

Four years.

Christ. I'd always presumed stuff with Helen'd work itself out.

'So, you're not *in* love with her?' Snowy asked.

I shook my head, slowly. 'No.'

'Phew,' Snowy said. ''Cause I am.'

The old fella stood, shaking the table and pushing his way past. I tried to work out what Snowy had just said, but caught a glimpse of the old fella pointing a finger towards the Gents', so I gave him a thumbs up. Me and Snowy watched him shuffle into the loo, the door swinging open, then swinging shut with a slam. It echoed. We couldn't exactly sit and wait for him to emerge. Nor could we order another pint. Our stomachs wouldn't be able to cope. So, we returned to face one another.

'I'm in love with Helen,' Snowy confirmed.

'And is she . . . ?' I asked.

'She doesn't have a clue. I've never . . . I wouldn't ever . . .'

Snowy pulled off both beanie hats and wiped his whole face. I'd never seen my best mate so serious before. Even when his nan died, Snowy wore a smirk beneath his tears, thinking of the mayhem she was causing up above. But not now.

'Go on, mate. Hit me,' Snowy said, bracing himself. 'Hit me, Jimbo.'

'Behave. I'm not gonna hit you.'

'I'm so sorry, mate. But I've got to tell her. It's eating away at me and I need to just, you know, unleash the demon. Get it out there. So I can move on.'

'Move on?'

'She's gonna reject me, right? So, I might as well get it over and done with. Hear her actually say no.' Snowy flicked away some long, imaginary red hair. '"No, Snowy. I don't want you".'

'Good impression.'

'Thanks, mate.'

The old fella returned and the barmaid brought him a second pint.

'What are you waiting for then?' I asked.

'Your blessing, of course.'

I wished we were in the Pacific Arms. At least I could've cleared my head with another pint and a few rounds on the quizzie. I didn't want to give Snowy my bloody blessing – as if it were my God-given right – to have Helen Gladstone. She wasn't a puppet with strings controlled by me. She could do whatever she wanted. As could Snowy. As could I. I wasn't going to be the bastard who tried to own his ex. That was the sort of crap Mikey Farley did, every time, and made a misery out of everyone involved.

Besides, I knew Helen.

Snowy was right. She would say no.

'You've got it,' I said. My words lay thick between us, hovering.

The tightness across Snowy's neat face began to slip away, his laughter lines reappearing, his cheeky grin poking out. The bright wet glisten in his eyes lost its balance and a couple of tears ran down his cheek, relief literally pouring out of him. He offered his hand, a formal move between two best mates, so I accepted with a grab rather than a shake. We laughed and pulled each other in, turning the moment into a hearty hug.

'Take them stupid layers off, you fat bastard,' I said. 'And go on. Piss off!'

Snowy stepped away and, shooting a salute to the old fella, galloped to the doors.

Then he stopped, but didn't turn around, his gaze glued to the frayed leftovers of carpet.

'Jimbo? What if she says yes?'

A shiver encased me, so cold that I wanted to rip a jumper off Snowy's back and wrap it around myself like a blanket.

'Like I said, mate.' I swallowed. 'You've got me blessing.'

My ma's on a ward with three other ladies. She's propped up in bed eating wine gums, picking out the yellow ones and putting them to one side. They're my favourite and this is something she's done since I was a kid. Her face is pale, the shock of her fall still fresh in her mind as well as her body, and she's refused to eat the toast brought to her earlier because she only likes it with that marmalade from the Asda.

An apology from me wasn't allowed; she slapped my hand, told me to shut up. But I'm still fraught. If my ma had died alone, just like my dad, how could I ever forgive myself? Still, she's much more interested in where I was last night, wanting to know all the details as if I'm about to reveal an upcoming plotline from *Corrie*.

'I was just helping a mate,' I say.

'I know when you're lying.'

'I'm not lying.'

'What's her name?'

'Mam!'

'Come on, son. It'll make me feel better.'

'That's blackmail, and you always told me blackmail would send me to hell.'

'I told you a lot of things.'

I pop a yellow wine gum into my mouth, then another. She gives me a little shake.

'I promise you, I was helping a mate. Who happened to be female. She needed a lift.'

'A lift? In that bloody big car you won?' My ma tuts, as if that bloody big car is a prostitute who shows up to Sunday mass with her skirt tucked into her knickers.

'Kind of,' is all I can think to reply.

'I told you that car would bring you nothing but bad luck. Remember the lottery winners?'

I nod. 'I remember. I do listen to what you say. Hold on. Why are you saying that? Why are you presuming the car brought me bad luck?'

''Cause of the look in your eyes, the weight of the world on your shoulders.'

'I think that's got something to do with you being here in the ozzy.'

My ma releases a weak raspy laugh.

'Jim. I know you got a fright, me falling. But I know you better than anyone. Something else has happened to you, son. You seem different.'

I just long for some colour to appear in her cheeks, a little more volume to escape from her lips, any hint of recovery going in a good, sharp direction. She's almost seventy-five, which isn't that old in this day and age, but she's fragile. My hand's in hers again, and I run my index finger over the veins and knuckles, her paper-thin skin delicate, precious. I'm scared. I'm downright lost. But my ma won't put up with anything soppy. She never allows a sentimental moment to last longer than a flicker.

'I think you should see her again,' she says, pulling her hand away from mine.

'Who?'

'Don't play games with me, soft lad. You know who.'

'Get some rest, Mam.'

Disappointment washes over me when she doesn't argue back. She closes her eyes and falls deeper into her pillows. I sit back in the plastic armchair, watching her chest move up and down.

Once my ma is sound asleep, I leave the hospital and call Griffo.

'Where are you, mate?' I ask.

'Home, lad. Where are you?'

'On me way back from the ozzy. Griffo, I need to drop your dad's minibus off.'

'Sound. Now?'

'Yeah.'

'Sound.'

'And then I'll need a lift back to mine. Is that okay, mate?'

'Sound as a pound.'

Mrs Wong isn't too pleased to see me when Griffo drops me off. She stands behind the deep fat fryer, two customers awaiting their food, and huffs enough to set the place alight. Her antisocial kids are sitting on the stairs playing Uno and don't say hello or bother to move out of the way to let me past. When I find my front door ajar, I understand why Mrs Wong is so pissed off with me. Her kids must've tried to get into my flat to watch Netflix, but they were too late. The living room is already occupied. With Helen.

'What are you doing here?' I ask her.

'Nice to see you, too, Jimbo.'

Her maroon Doc Martens are off and her stockinged feet are resting on my tile-and-teak coffee table, a mug of instant coffee in her hands and a huge woolly jumper keeping her warm, some B-list romcom on the telly. Anyone would think she lives here.

And for a moment, I like it.

Coming home to nobody is tiresome. After a long day in the toll booth or a heavy night in the Pacific Arms, or even after a weekly shop in the Asda, getting home is always a great feeling. But once I shut the front door, take off my trainers, whack the kettle on, life can be unbearably lonely. My paperbacks are sacred, my love of films a God-send.

'Hels, I've had a fucked-up few days—'

'Jimbo, stop. You don't need to explain.' She places her coffee on the table, spilling a little over the rim, and stands up. 'I just wanted to say sorry.'

'It's okay.'

'It's not. I was drunk, I didn't mean to be such a pain.'

'Sit down, will you? You're making the room look untidy.'

Helen allows herself to smile and sits back down, taking her coffee and curling her feet beneath her. I wonder if Snowy has popped the question yet. She's not wearing a ring. She rests her head against the leather settee and closes her eyes, sighing.

'You look like shite,' I say.

'Look in the mirror.'

I flop down next to her, take the coffee mug from her hands and swig.

'Do you wanna tell me where you've been?' Helen asks, her eyes still closed.

'Haven't got the energy, to be honest, girl.'

'You alright, though?'

'Me? Yeah. 'Course. It's me ma I'm worried about.'

'How's she doing?'

I put the mug back onto the table and hang my head over my knees. Helen places her hand on the small of my back, reminding me I'm not alone, that I've got a friend.

'Ah, Hels. I'm sorry, girl. I'm a right mess.'

'Don't be daft.'

'She's so frail, Helen. She's so small and frail, and I wanna help her. But, I can't. I can't do fuck all. She's me ma, and I can't do anything to fucking help her. Me dad'd be ashamed of me.'

'Oh, Jimbo, don't torture yourself. Come here,' she says, letting my head fall into her lap as she strokes my hair, holds onto me tight. 'You're amazing with your mum, the best son she could ever wish for. And your dad's looking down on you so proud, Jimbo, I promise. Me own mother always says so, you know. She does. She says "Roy Glover'd be so proud of that lad. He's watching from Heaven".'

'Bloody Catholics.'

I break away, stand, stretch out. I can't sit around moping all afternoon. I've got to sort myself out, get back to the hospital, find out when my sisters are arriving in Liverpool. Christ, our Lisa and our Emma are coming home. What will I make of them? Bloody hell, what will they make of me? Exactly the same as when they left, only older and a hell of a lot more broke.

'It's not true,' I say, pretending to read the small-print credits on a framed poster of *True Romance*. 'Me dad. He'd never be proud of me. This life, this isn't what he wanted for me. Or where I saw meself ending up, if I'm honest.'

'But, you're a good man, Jimbo.'

'Am I?'

'Of course!'

'Am I?' I turn around, lock eyes with Helen. 'Really?'

She looks away, uncurls her feet and starts to loosen the laces of her Doc Martens to make them easier to slip back on.

'Look at me, Helen.'

'Jim . . . The kids are with me mum 'cause Snowy's at the match, and I only popped in to say sorry. For ringing last night. But, you know what? I think I should go now.'

'How am I a good man when I kissed me best mate's girl the other night?'

'I'm getting out of here—'

'No, Hels. It's alright for you to corner me when you're pissed, to ring me, to pour your bloody heart out when you need it, but where does that leave me? Good ol' Jimbo. Always here for you. But, it's not good, is it? It's fucking toxic.'

'Stop it, Jimbo.'

'No, I won't stop anything. 'Cause all I've done is sit in that fucking toll booth for years and feel sorry for meself, waiting for some lucky fucking strike, and you know what? It's bullshit. There's no such thing as a lucky strike. I won a BMW, out of the blue, and look where it's got me. You make your own luck in this world, and I should've been clever enough to know that.'

'Jim, calm down. You're upset about your ma—'

'What are you actually doing here, Helen?'

'Seeing if you were alright!'

'Oh, really?'

'Bloody hell, Jim, you never go anywhere and then you disappear? No one can get hold of you? Griffo tells us your car's been stolen, you needed a minibus to get somewhere? Come on, Jimbo. This isn't normal behaviour from you.'

I'm about to lash out again, tell Helen to shut up. But, instead, I laugh. Not in a happy way, or a tickled way. No, it's more of a bitter realisation. I sigh, a "ha" and an "oh", the words "brilliant" and "of course" tumbling out, too.

'What's so funny? So "brilliant"?' Helen asks.

I can't contain myself.

'Jim?!'

'It's not normal, is it?' I manage. 'For me. It's not normal. Because I'm so predictable.'

'Well, yeah. You are.'

I nod and let out a big sigh which not only controls my laughter, but kills it.

'Derek bloody Higgins was spot on,' I say. 'When he said I was going nowhere.'

'Your boss? When did he say that?'

'The day I won the car.'

'You should've told him to fuck off,' she snorts. 'You're wasted in that job. We've all said it. If I were you, I'd tell your boss where to shove it.'

'Yeah, the old me, maybe. But I can't be that person anymore.'

'Why not?'

'It's impulsive.'

'It's passionate, Jim!'

'It got me nowhere and . . .' I trail off. I don't have a clue where I'm going with this response, this feeling of fight. I so desperately want to be the man I envisioned myself being back when I was too young to understand the bite of reality.

I could've been a journalist – even an editor by now – maybe living away somewhere, like London. Watching my sisters both rise from their working-class upbringing to achieve their dreams and ride off into the sunset set a benchmark, one that was filled with hope, the possibility of success. Only they did it before getting a toe stuck into the rut that I quickly became buried in.

Then again, look at Zara and the opportunities she's had given to her on a gold plate. Those stamps in her passport. And yet where's she? Still sat alone at Heathrow waiting to be told when she can get on a flight? God. How I suddenly want to hold her, tell her how I understand. Or at least tell her that I believe I might understand. I was pretty awful to her, wasn't I? All she'd wanted was a friend. Someone to talk to. I could've easily provided that. Easily. For God's sake, that's who I am. Everybody's bloody friend. And the girl who seemed to need me the most, even just for a day, well, I let her down. There isn't much I can offer to people, but I could've offered Zara my friendship. It wouldn't have cost a penny.

But I judged her. Scrutinised her every word, her every breath. Is it because I envy the privileged life she's had? Or is it because she's different to anybody I've ever met before?

'Jim?'

Helen.

I almost forgot she's here.

She's got her car keys in her hand, jingling them in that way people do when they're eager to leave, get a move on, get the fuck out of where they are.

'Jimbo!' she says, maybe for the third or fourth time, and claps her hands to snap me out of my daze. I sit down on my settee, pat the seat beside me for Helen to sit down, too.

'Are you lost or found?' I ask her.

282

Helen scrunches up her face.

'What I mean – without sounding all hippy dippy and shit – is, do you honestly think you're living the wrong sort of life, with everything you've got? Or do you believe that you're exactly where you should be?'

'Where else would I be?' She shrugs, matter-of-fact.

I nod, her question a direct answer.

Putting her hand over her mouth, Helen starts to giggle, her whole face blushing. She makes some comment about not really knowing why she's laughing, but I know why. She's been caught off guard, sober. I place my hand on her knee to calm her and although it works, she leans in and I naturally follow. Then hesitate. No. Helen slips her hands and then her arms around me, squeezing me into the comfort of her woolly jumper.

She kisses me.

I pull back, but don't resist enough. Helen launches herself forward and pushes me back into my settee, climbing on top of me, straddling me, kissing me. She reaches down and holds the crotch of my jeans. Physically, I can feel Helen. The shape of her curves, more substantial in recent years, her skin still as soft. Her weight comfortable around my hips, against my chest. Coarse strands of thick red hair tickling my forehead, my eyelids. Yet I feel nothing.

As quickly as it all began, Helen stops. She breaks away, stumbles a little, tripping over her Doc Martens, strewn on my living room floor. She pulls her woolly jumper down, stretching it towards her knees, then puts her hands to her cheeks, her forehead, finally resting them on the back of her neck.

'No more,' she says.

I sit still. Listening.

'You're not right for me, Jim,' she says, that unmistakable

lump appearing in her throat. 'I thought you were, but you're not. You were kissing me – fuck – touching me as if you were a stranger. Like you've forgotten me. You're not my Jimbo anymore.'

'I haven't been for years, Hels.'

It's Helen's turn to laugh; just one short *ha*.

'We both know that ain't the truth,' she says.

I stand up, ever so carefully, not wanting to upset Helen any more than I'd want to wake a sleeping baby. Fat, fast tears bring her silent sobs into the room.

'I never meant to lead you on,' I whisper.

'You didn't. I just kept hanging on.'

'I think we both did.'

And I take her into my arms, as any good friend would, and hug her tight. She hugs me back, a final line now drawn in permanent marker.

'So, come on,' she says, wiping her tears on her sleeve. 'Who is she?'

I'm not sure that one of my heart-to-hearts with Helen is what I should be doing right now, but we can't change a lifetime's habits in the space of a few minutes. So I give a slight nod, ready, perhaps, to admit who's at the absolute forefront of my mind.

'Zara.'

27

Zara

Right. I'm almost packed.

I feel fresh, rested. What would this morning have been like if I'd woken up beside Jim, naked? Oh my God. My stomach does a whirl like a ferris wheel in overdrive. What a relief, surely. A random fuck with the guy whose car I smashed up wouldn't have solved anything. Would it? Even if it had been wonderful; the most memorable sex of my life; the sort that makes my heart race like it's doing right now?

Stop.

Maybe sex was never on the cards. Just a kiss. And what if that kiss had been awkward, the kind where we each predicted the wrong rhythm? What if it was sloppy? He might be the kind to get his teeth involved; his perfect teeth. Then again, maybe it would have been soft, delicate, and completely in tune with my desires. The flutter of something special on the horizon . . .

Oh, stop!

Snap out of it, Zara. Now.

It's not as if I can endure another long-distance relationship, one that will no doubt be as unsuccessful as the last. We can't make promises that neither can keep. Even with the best intentions in the world, these things just never work out. I've learnt this the hard way, and Jim watched the entire lesson being taught. This is obviously why he's left without saying goodbye. Our meeting was an accident. A bad one that ended quite well. But it has ended.

I give the room a final check. All clear.

Except on the dressing table beside the empty wine-stained coffee cups. A note.

Sorry got to dash. Forget the money, life's too short. Have a good one, Jim x

Ha. He doesn't want the damn money after all. That's a relief. I guess.

No, of course it's a relief, and actually, quite a nice – no, generous – gesture. But . . .

Have a good one.

HAVE A GOOD ONE?!

Jeez. Same to you too, Jim.

'Nothing until tonight,' I'm told at the airport. It's noon.

I accept a seat on tonight's flight and leave my suitcases and broken holdall in the airport's storage facility, not before layering myself with an extra two t-shirts beneath my zebra print sweater. I remember a cream beret that I packed. What a shame I hadn't thought of that yesterday. I pull it over my clean, blow-dried hair.

I buy some glossy magazine and a Kinder Bueno and head

to the London Underground. I haven't been to Covent Garden since my boarding school days; a trip to see the matinee of *Miss Saigon*. Killing time in the West End is going to be much more interesting than sitting around the terminal, waiting all day to check in. Settling on the tube train, I open the magazine and nibble the chocolate. But the latest weight-loss tips and reality-star scandals won't distract me from yesterday, from last night. I zone out.

Oh, Jim. Jim Glover. Who's not even on Facebook.

'There's no going backwards,' I murmur, aloud, not giving two hoots how crazy I might seem to my fellow passengers. 'Only forwards.'

'Deep,' some guy says, sitting opposite.

I nod, agreeing, although deeply wishing I knew where the hell to go forwards to.

Ah, damn. I miss my stop.

I get off at Kings Cross St Pancras to change trains, but God, there are SO MANY people. It's stressful and hectic. I feel the need to get out of the Underground, and fast, so I wander into St Pancras International.

For a train station, this is a delight.

I sample all of the Jo Malone fragrances, and as a result smell like a walking, talking florist. I buy a Chanel lipstick for Katie, my way of saying sorry, you were right.

But what I really need is a drink.

I don't fancy the rowdiness of a British pub, so I go to the champagne bar.

'A Merlot, please,' I say, pointing to the second cheapest on the wine list.

It's delicious. And it's going down too quickly.

I've got a lot of time to pass. A. Lot.

Jim went on and on about how time passes by beautifully

with a book. I don't mind reading, especially by the pool or on the beach, but today I've been struggling enough with the most banal celeb gossip. I'm not sure I could focus on a book. Although . . .

It's still another six hours until my flight.

I finish my drink and head to WHSmith, browsing through the A–Z of fiction, reading the back of anything that catches my eye. There's a theme unfolding; I notice anything with the words 'lie', 'deceit', or 'stranger' in the title. Hmm. The more blurbs I read, the more all the stories start to sound the same. I move on to fact. Some healthy lifestyle hardbacks: interesting. I read a few vegan recipes. Everyone will be vegan one day, so this book tells me. Then, I find all the biographies. Who was that guy Jim had been reading about?

Oh God. Zara!

Why is everything I'm thinking directed towards Jim? Why? Yesterday morning I'd been in love with Nick, and now I'm pining after Jim? What will tomorrow bring? Tears over letting *another* random guy slip through my fingers? I need to stop this train now before it derails – let's face it, I'm already on slippery tracks.

'Can I help you with anything?' a shop assistant asks.

Startled, I pick up the first book I can get my hands on, lying in a pile on the table beside me.

'Found it,' I say. 'Thank you.' And I make my way to pay.

It's a biography, paperback, about an old movie star, Judy Garland. It's only when I've already paid for it that I realise I know who Judy Garland is. Well, was. She was the actress who played Dorothy in *The Wizard of Oz*, one of my favourite childhood films. This could be kind of cool. Maybe I should tell Jim about it when I've finished.

Oh, wait. Jim's gone.

Have a good one, Jim. Kiss.

Kiss?

No, I'm reading far too deeply into a simple goodbye note. A *goodbye* note. And what did he mean, 'have a good one'. Have a good what? Flight? Life?

The champagne bar beckons me. I climb up onto one of the high stools and order another glass of Merlot, large. I open the first page of the Judy Garland biography, attempting to let some words sink in. But, oh, here I am, flying back to Dubai tonight, only a day after arriving in the UK. I'd been so sure about leaving Dubai, and now I'm completely unsure about returning.

I know what I need to do.

I need to speak to somebody *in* Dubai. Tell somebody I'm coming back. That might make me feel better, or at least give me a sense of purpose; a genuine feeling that I'm going home.

I'll have to use a payphone, though. How retro.

Does this train station even have a payphone? Are they still a thing? Will I need some money or can I use my card? And who should I call? It's quite intense, calling a pal long distance from a public phone. Of all the ways you can make contact with people these days, a phone call now seems the most drastic. The least breezy. If I'm going to call anybody, I guess it should be Katie, but I'd much rather see her face-to-face, and all will be super between us after thirty seconds. Besides, she won't answer her phone. She'll see some long, unknown number from abroad and think it's someone cold calling her about insurance.

Agh. Hold on.

I don't even know Katie's phone number. I don't know anybody's phone number because all of my numbers are still in my phone.

God, I'm so directionless. So pointless.

I open my passport and turn to the back page. My next of kin; my papa. His number is written there in black and white, to be called in case of an emergency. Is this an emergency? Holy crap, I'm crying. I'm drinking wine, one page into the life of Judy Garland, and crying. And I can't stop them flowing, the tears, they're just falling, falling, running away from their ducts. I'm not even making any noise; I'm barely breathing. Seriously, I'm just so desperate to know where the fucking hell I belong.

Oh, look.

There's a payphone. Beside the bar.

I'll call my papa. Yes. I'll let him know that I'm on my way back, and say that maybe once he arrives back from Saudi, we can all go to dinner somewhere fancy.

The payphone accepts card; wonderful. I dial the number written in my passport.

It's ringing. I hear his voice.

'Samir Khoury. Leave your name and number and I'll get back to you.'

The tone beeps, and I intend to leave a message. Except I can't find the words, not even a simple *hello*. It feels so damn forced. There's nothing for me to do other than hang up and return to my bar stool.

'Another?' the bartender asks.

'There's a reason he left so abruptly,' I say.

The bartender looks down at the empty stool beside me.

'Oh, no. Not here,' I assure him. 'This morning, at the hotel. There has to be a reason.'

Yes, I know. I'm back to thinking about Jim again.

But last night something almost happened, I'm sure of it. A window opened.

'I think he's loyal,' I say to the barman. 'Jim. I don't think he'd leave without a reason.'

'Okay. You just let me know when you'd like a top-up, madam.'

'Oh,' I sigh, a little whiney. 'I was hoping you'd say something more profound than that.'

'Profound?' the barman asks, like he's never come across that word before.

'Yeah, like, "Go after him, tell him how you feel!"'

'Go after who?'

'Jim!'

Unlike the stereotype, this barman is clearly not an actor. His blank expression tells me there's no chance he's going to indulge in my fantasy Hollywood movie scenario. He wipes the bar down, keen to stick to his true role, bar tending.

'Anyway,' I say. 'I can't go after him.'

I wait for the barman to ask why. He doesn't, but he does pause to raise an eyebrow.

'I've a more than good reason not to go after Jim Glover. And that reason is called Nick, or Greg, or whatever the fuck he's called.' I look up apologetically, not meaning to swear before this perfect stranger. He softens a little, still listening. 'I can't possibly do it again.'

Two ladies are waiting to be served and I lose the barman to them.

I think of Zein, my first boyfriend. I'm sure that was love, in some way. Except neither of us ever made a leap; we always kept our gestures small, our decisions on the line. Maybe Zein wanted me to go with him when he studied in Europe; wanted me to initiate. I just sat back, though. I let him go, let him leave me. Any hurt I'd felt from Zein meeting somebody else, well, I blamed on myself for never committing to him fully. It was easier to be happy for him.

The barman returns.

'Should I let Jim go?' I ask, taking a huge gulp of wine. 'Or will I always wonder?'

My new book is on the bar. I could pass the time *beautifully* by reading this. Or I could go after Jim, take a leap of faith.

I gently edge my empty glass towards the barman.

'Well?' he asks.

'I'm gonna make a move,' I reply. 'Or I'll always wonder.'

Yes, I'm going to do it. I am! I'm going back to Liverpool, today, now. Right now. I arrived in this country with a plan, didn't I? And true, that plan has not gone how I'd originally hoped, but it was a plan nonetheless to go to Liverpool and make a new life for myself. Perhaps the plan is still in motion; it's just taken a different direction. Screw my things. They'll be safe in Heathrow, surely? Somehow, I'm going to go and find Jim Glover.

Katie will crucify me for this, but I don't care.

And this time I've got no mop to drag me down.

I get to Euston station, where trains go direct to Liverpool.

I stand beneath the vast timetable and see the next train to depart is 17.07. There's a long queue at the ticket office, but there are also plenty of self-service machines free. They're pretty simple to work out. I put my card into the slot.

I hover over the square on the screen that says 'Buy Tickets'.

Press, press, press . . .

Hmm. What I'm doing is nothing short of crazy, right? To go all the way back to Liverpool, after such an epic journey getting away from the place? This is totally fucking crazy.

And what's more, I'm going to find the guy who brought me on that epic journey?

An energetic ball of nerves performs somersaults in my stomach.

We almost kissed . . . we . . .

Yes! I want to see Jim. Yes! I *want* totally fucking crazy. Otherwise what's the point in living? I haven't found what it is I'm looking for yet, so what harm can it do to keep trying, to give something else, something potentially wonderful, a damn shot? I have nothing to go back to Dubai for other than a nice room in my papa's villa for a half decent rent, so why not? Why the hell not?

All I have to do is press the button, buy a ticket, get on a train.

I press. My finger presses the screen in front of me and I wait.

Nothing happens.

I press again, a little harder, but it's quite obvious that the goddamn screen has locked. I look over my shoulder, trying to find a station attendant, somebody to help me. The screen flickers, briefly, and it seems like it might be working now.

'Buy tickets'.

I hover. Again.

Attempting to pull myself together, I feel a brush across the heels of my suede sneakers. A faint apology ensues. I turn, but nobody is there. Twisting around the other way, I see a lady mopping the station floor, cleaning around the bottom of the self-service machine beside the one I'm standing at.

A mop.

How did such an object, used to eliminate crap off the ground, once play a major role in my life? The fire in my belly is drenched, sodden. I can see the front door to the house on Clifton Crescent opening, those little girls staring at my witch's broom. I can see Abi's cold recognition of who I must be. I can see Nick. *Greg.* The story I'd participated in. The happy ending I'd gotten oh so wrong. And I see George, laughing; another story I'd read back-to-front.

I won't do this again.

I won't turn Jim into another story, one to tell Katie and the latest gang of expats. I won't ridicule myself in the Irish pub, drowning myself in enough tequila shots to feel confident, to be funny. I can just picture it, the drunken rounds of pitying applause, Katie howling, 'You did it again, Zara! You hopeless fecking romantic!'

Hopeless.

It has to stop.

I have to stop.

A beep beeps from the machine and my card ejects. I've hovered too long.

I back away, avoiding the lady with her mop, and meander down the escalators, deep into the London Underground. Just over an hour later I'm at Heathrow again, and this time I check in. I'm handed a boarding pass for the next Emirates flight to Dubai International Airport. In the departure lounge, I buy my second tuna melt of the day and pick away at it, sitting amongst the crowds and wiping the tears that fall down my cheeks with a brown paper napkin. On the plane, I read a few chapters about the early life of Judy Garland, drink more red wine and, inevitably, cry.

Night turns into the brightest of mornings as the grand A380 touches down onto the hot, dry runway. The Dubai sky is so perfect, such a beautiful, confident blue, that there's nothing to dislike about it. The warmth outside is delicious.

November is the expats' favourite month. Inside the airport, a member of the ground staff catches my eye, smiles and says, 'Welcome, ma'am.'

Maybe I am home after all.

Maybe.

28

Jim

The seat in my toll booth today has seen better days. The yellow sticky sponge is emerging from the plastic faux leather cover. My high-vis jacket scratches my neck, something that's perhaps always happened. I can't quite remember.

'Y'never heard of a barber, mate?'

It is – of course – the fella in the Ford Focus. Connie and Carl's laughter about something not likely to be funny blasts through his speakers and I'm reacquainted with that aftershave; too many spices for a Monday morning.

'Have a good day, mate,' I reply, handing over the change.

'Nice one.'

And with that all-too-familiar unnecessary rev, the Focus speeds through the tunnel. I'm doing my utmost to deliver decent customer service today, but I'm forced to multitask, exchanging coins while reading messages appearing on my phone from my sisters.

Jim! Landed. We've hired cars. On the motorway. Emma and co in the car behind. Heading straight to the hospital. ETA 9.40 rush hour traffic permitting. Meet us there. Love you. Lisa

Hey little bro!! We absolutely can't wait to see your hairy face. Sienna, Mason and Bree can't believe they're going to meet you in the flesh. Well, Bree doesn't really understand but we think she's got a high IQ for a 6 month old. A bit like her Uncle Jim, eh?! She slept for the whole flight. If only she'd do that on land haha. See you soon. Love ya loads. Em x

Oh, I forgot to say Jack's super excited to catch up with you. Like you, he's from a whole family of sisters haha. Love ya loads. Em x

Relief wafts into my nerves. I've been kind of dreading seeing my sisters and hearing about their dramatically changed lives, but these messages already confirm they haven't changed too much. Lisa's always the practical one, straight to the point and never afraid to offend so long as the job gets done, and she gets her way. Emma never stops talking.

How was Mum yesterday? In good spirits? I don't want us all to overwhelm her in the hospital, she hates fuss. Do you think Lisa and Paul should go first and then I take the kids in with Jack this afternoon? Lisa thinks we should all go right now. What time are you getting there? Or are you there now? Love ya loads. Em x

I hand change to the person waiting in the car below. The

messages stop and I take a moment to glance away from my screen and engage in being friendly. The fella in the driving seat looks ever so bloody pleased with himself. And with good reason, too. He's driving a clean, white BMW M3. I can't exactly mistake it. Its whole shape will be imprinted in my mind forever. The fella's eyes meet with mine through his smart specs. Pity oozes from them.

Pity for me. Fucking hell.

By the way, Mum mentioned to Lisa on the phone that you've met somebody. What's her name? How did you meet her? How long have you known her? Sorry about the fifty zillion questions but I'm hoping you're easier to get hold of when I'm actually in the same country as you. It drives me nuts how impossible you are to get hold of (GET A FACEBOOK ACCOUNT FOR GAWD'S SAKE!) and your Skype connection sucks. Ok, lecture over little bro. Who's the girl? Love ya loads. Em x

The BMW M3 speeds off, the noise of its engine ringing in my ears like Fleetwood Mac playing live. Christ, this high-vis jacket is taking the piss. My neck'll be raw red by the end of my shift.

They've only been back in Liverpool five minutes and already they're bickering with my ma. I can hear them from the corridor.

'I'm not having it!' my ma's protesting.

'You bloody well are, Mum,' Lisa dictates.

'I said NO.'

'And I am saying YES.'

'Who do you think you're talking to?'

Emma's intervening with 'Stop it' and 'Listen' and 'Can I get a word in?' and 'Nobody ever listens to me', getting trampled over with words like football studs on a freshly mown pitch.

Griffo, who's kindly given me yet another lift, stops in his tracks in the corridor. He wanted to say hiya to my sisters, especially Lisa, his first crush; his mouth would drop into a giant O, iced with a bit of dribble, whenever she used to barge into the room. But he hands me a selection of magazines for my ma that he picked up on the way.

'I'll leave youse to it,' he says, pressing his lips into a thin smile and narrowing his eyes.

'Mate, ta for the lift. Again.'

He punches my upper arm. His hair's combed over with gel and his whole appearance is flabby around the edges. Middle age has hit him earlier than most would welcome it. Griffo doesn't seem to care in the slightest, though; if anything, he embraces it. He's even started drinking bitter.

'I'll be an independent human again soon,' I wince. 'Promise.'

'Pacific Arms tonight? After visiting hours?'

'You're joking, aren't you?'

'Pints are on me. I know this is the last thing you wanna hear right now, mate, but a new contact of mine just paid me three grand cash for . . . well, something.' Griffo laughs, just like a stupid kid who's let off a stink bomb, which looks creepy coming from his puffed-up, grown-up face. No wonder Griffo never got himself a proper job. His dad's keeping him close to protect his blabber mouth. Maybe not close enough, though.

'Surely you've just given me too much info there, lad?'

He mouths a silent *oops*. 'Pints on me. See you in the Pacific later.'

'You're impossible,' Lisa squeals at my ma from around the corner, the staff on reception glancing away from their screens in disgust. I close my eyes and frown, anticipating the response.

'Well, well, well,' my ma says, her voice sounding much stronger at least. 'Living in the land of the bloody free hasn't changed you one bit. Still a bossy madam if ever there was one.'

Griffo backs away, reiterating 'pints' and 'Pacific', then does one.

I head into the ward with the magazines. All day, as I've taken fivers, tenners, twenties and exchanged them for coins, my left hand turning bright pink with cold, I've been feeling sick at how it might be, seeing our Lisa and our Emma and their big fat American life in the humble surroundings of an NHS hospital. Yet, hearing their voices, I actually feel okay, as if stuck in a time warp, and I wish I had a paperback beneath my fleece so I could sit in the corner and blissfully ignore them all. I left Mary's thriller in the bloody van. I need my head screwing on.

'Yo,' I say slowly, unsure of where the 'yo' came from.

Emma jumps up first and starts to flap and clap. Her many movements make way for Lisa, who simply stands and embraces me with a warm hug. She breaks away, looking into my eyes with a closed-mouth smile, then takes in my forehead, my hair, my chin. Christ, she's so dramatic some-times. Where does she think she is? Little House on the bloody Prairie? Luckily Emma drags me away and between hugs and kisses introduces me to Sienna and Mason, ushering her weary kids to hug me, too. I mess up their hair before I'm whacked – well, smacked – on the back.

'Alright, Jack?' I say, bracing myself for a strong handshake, only to be pulled into him.

'HEY, BROTHER,' Emma's husband yells, suffocating me with his huge body and arms. 'Glad to see you, it's been too long.'

'I'm Paul,' Lisa's husband says, with a lot less volume yet equal enthusiasm. I take in his neat haircut, his side parting. Finally, I'm meeting the hot-shot lawyer who got hitched to our Lisa in Vegas. He was knee-deep in a case for our Emma's wedding here in Liverpool; same again for my dad's funeral, apparently. 'Apologies. My hands are kind of tied here.'

Paul's sitting in the plastic armchair, the youngest member of the family, baby Bree, sat upon his knee chewing on a rubber giraffe. Bree is actually Emma and Jack's third kid, and I think of how Lisa and Paul have been trying to conceive for years, IVF having failed twice. I instantly warm to Paul, The Good Uncle. He could teach me a thing or two.

Making my way past my suddenly huge family, I manage to give my ma the magazines and a peck on the cheek. 'From Griffo,' I tell her.

'Oh, Griffo!' Emma exclaims. 'He was so in love with our Lisa, wasn't he?'

Lisa blushes and perches on the armchair beside Paul and Bree. A short breath of silence follows and I'm able to take in the whole picture. Emma, Jack and their kids look as though they've walked straight off the set of a made-for-TV family movie, all jumpers and beige 'slacks', a song escaping their mouths rather than speech. Lisa and Paul look expensive, their jeans, their boots, their white shirts and sleeveless body warmers all screaming designer labels. But, really, my sisters seem the same as always. Just with better teeth.

'Dare I ask,' I say, 'what you're all bickering about?'

'We're not bickering,' Lisa says, to nobody's surprise.

'Everyone's getting on me bloody nerves, son,' my ma says.

'Look,' Jack says, taking centre stage with his massive hands. 'Allow me to intervene. It seems to me, from my recent

301

observations, that there is a whole lot of misunderstanding going on here. My sister-in-law – your ever-so-wonderful sister – has made your mother an offer she can't refuse. However, your mother – this incredibly fearless woman – is finding ways to refuse because she believes the offer will cause problems. Only what your mother – whose strength I admire from the bottom of my heart – doesn't seem to understand is that there is NO problem. None whatsoever. In fact, there is more of a problem if she . . .'

And Jack keeps talking.

Words bubble out of him like Niagara bloody Falls, leaving me feeling soaking wet.

Bree starts to cry, prompting Jack to speak louder, and slower, so our Lisa picks her up and bounces her in a different direction. I can't speak for anybody else but my guess is nobody, not even Emma, is listening to him.

Then, my ma hurls a magazine across her bed, target unspecified, hitting me in the head. I tell myself to be grateful that the woman's getting her strength back. Shame she couldn't have aimed it smack bang into Jack's mouth, though.

'I'm not going to America,' she says.

I pick the magazine up off the floor and roll it into a baton.

'America?' I ask.

Jack's hands are still splayed, but his words – thank fuck – have stopped.

Lisa passes Bree back to Emma and straightens her super-expensive body warmer, smooths down her sharp mid-length haircut. As always, she stands poised with her feet in a ten-to-two position, unable to shake off the dancer within.

'Jim, I've been suggesting it for years,' she says. 'And now I'm not suggesting it. I'm enforcing it.'

302

'Enforcing?' I ask. 'What is this? An episode of *Law & Order*?'

Sienna and Mason repeat my words to one another in a bad attempt at the Queen's English, saying 'lore and ooordare' over and over. Emma pushes their heads down and they hide out of sight beneath the bed. Which is sort of where I feel like I should be, along with my dignity. It's supposed to be me taking my ma to Florida. That was the deal, the promise *I* made to her. The happiness she exuded when I'd twisted her arm into going – it was me who'd been there to witness that, me! Not them. But I can't take her anymore, can I? Should I be relieved that they've come, riding in on their metaphorical horses to save the day, bailing out their hopeless little brother?

Lisa rolls her eyes at me. 'Trust you not to understand.'

'Understand what? Try me, sis.'

'You've never told Jim about this?' Lisa says, looking at my ma.

'There's nothing to tell,' my ma says. She closes her eyes, pretending to want some sleep.

Jack's hands start up again. 'Allow me to—'

'Jack, not now,' Emma says. 'Jim, we've been trying to get our bloody mother to come to stay with us for years. She can stay for six months on a tourist visa and if she likes it, Paul can arrange for her to live with us permanently, can't you, Paul?'

Paul replies, apologetically. 'Indeed I can.' If he was wearing a tie, this would be the point where he loosens it. I imagine he does that often. The capable guy who never gets the praise, just the penance. Not that I've got much sympathy for him at this moment in time. I'd promised my ma a couple of weeks by a pool. This lot are promising a lifetime.

'Hold on,' I say, waving my baton. I'm interrupted by Emma.

'Jim, Florida is awesome for old people – sorry, I mean people like Mum. The sunshine, the lifestyle, and she'd be around her grandkids all the time. It'd feed her soul, don't you think? And Paul can make sure she gets the best health care. Isn't that right, Paul?'

'Indeed it is.'

I step back and hand the magazine baton to Jack, who takes it and swings it like a baseball bat. Standard.

'So, let's get this straight,' I say. 'First of all, you two bugger off to America and don't come back for eight bloody years. And second of all, you whizz back to steal me ma and take her with you, against her will? Don't you think that's a bit greedy?'

Paul clears his throat. 'I'd say it was generous, over greedy.'

'Thanks, Paul, mate. But is anyone gonna tell me why it's taken eight years to check we're okay? Which we are, by the way. Aren't we, Mam? We're O. Kay.'

'We're okay, love.'

'Really?' Lisa huffs. 'Sure you are.'

'You know what, Lis,' I say, pointing my finger with menace. 'You're actually doing me fucking head in.'

'Language!' Jack sings.

'Soz.'

Emma grabs my fleece sleeve, tugging it and resting her head on my shoulder. The dancer in her is also still apparent: her movements so graceful, it's as if she's about to haul me into a waltz.

'Little bro, you know why I never came back. We talked about this so many times – I feel like it's all I ever talk to Mum about when we call. But she's always said she under-stood; that you both understood. Tell me you do, please.'

I do.

304

Of course I do.

'Can you all keep your bloody voices down?' my ma stage whispers. 'Them in the beds next door are gonna be having a field day with all this going on.'

Emma had been pregnant with Sienna at my dad's funeral. She'd been expecting twins, but one died in the womb and the remainder of her pregnancy was complicated. The doctors assured her this had nothing to do with flying, nothing whatsoever, and it would have happened anyway. Then Mason came along soon after Sienna and with two small children, she never found the confidence to fly again. Hypnosis started to help, and she was never shy to admit how much she wanted to visit home, something I perhaps tend to forget. It makes me dislike pieces of myself more and more. I can't be sure what Lisa's reasons are for not coming back sooner, but I've always presumed it's a mixture of being there for Emma and trying to start a family of her own. Plus Lisa isn't good at going *back*. If only I could follow in her footsteps, just a bit, like.

'You can't just take her away from her home,' I say, quietly.

'What's she got here?' Lisa asks.

Emma squeezes me, slipping her hand into mine.

'She's got me,' I say.

Then Lisa takes my other hand.

'But, what have you got here?' she asks, the bluntness in her voice now softened.

Nothing, I think.

And that's just what I say. Nothing.

It's not ideal to go out drinking the night before an early shift.

And with no money.

But when Griffo says he's paying, he always pays. I don't like taking the piss though, and won't be staying out long.

After the family meeting of the decade, I just need a stiff pint. And maybe a shot of JD.

Lisa and Paul drop me off at the Pacific Arms on the way to some big Victorian house in south Liverpool they've rented on Airbnb, sharing with Emma and her brood. Paul expresses his love of the decor and despite it having five bedrooms, calls it 'quaint'. Lisa doesn't speak much during the journey apart from asking the odd question about my job and my flat ('Still there?' applying to both). She makes a remark about how I shouldn't be renting, it's such a waste. I hear her complain to Paul about the weather, saying something about how she doesn't miss 'this'.

'Don't they have rain in Florida?' I shout from the back seat.

'Shut up, Jim.'

'Sorry, it's just I'm sure I read somewhere that Walt Disney invented big heavy rain clouds to appear once a day so it pisses down and makes everywhere look green and lush. Is that not true?'

'Just shut up, Jim.'

Griffo's got a pint waiting for me. I almost cry with happiness.

Snowy leads us all in a 'cheers' and gives a short speech about something and nothing. He's wearing the latest Everton shirt and his trackie bottoms, his usual attire for mid-week drinking unless we go into town. Griffo keeps his smart coat on, long and bulky, which I always like to believe has pockets filled with wheels and deals. In school, he used to keep Refresher bars in his blazer and sell them for 7p. He insisted he was making a profit and we had no reason not to believe him, as much as Mikey tried to prove him wrong. And now, with his loose tie patterned with Pooh Bear and honey pots,

Mikey's still in his teacher's uniform, glasses resting on his nose. I remove my fleece and tie it around my waist.

'Aaaannnnd!' Snowy goes on. 'Drum roll, please!'

We tap our hands on the table we're sat at, our spot, in the corner next to the quizzie. Tonight we've got our pick of tables, it being a Monday. The place is dead except for a few old regulars at the bar, sipping a bitter, reading the paper, watching the footy news. Snowy blows a pretend trumpet with his fists and gives one final bang on the table, prompting us to stop and listen.

'Now's the time for us all to open our ears – and our hearts – to hear our very own Jimbo's story about . . . Zara.' Snowy waves his hand above his head, painting an imaginary rainbow, and repeats Zara's name as if she's some sort of moon goddess.

How does he know her name?

Oh.

Shit.

Helen.

What else has Helen told Snowy? I hope his intentions to propose haven't been ruined by . . .

No. No, no, no. She would never. I know Helen inside out and she'd never tell Snowy about us, or about what could've been us. Of that I'm sure. Snowy's elbowing me over and over to the point where I want to wallop him.

'Jimbo,' Mikey says. 'Spill. I need a bit of juice. Not only did I have to do detentions after school today but Tori's giving me grief about me not wanting to go to her ma's for Chrimbo. It's November. Who talks about Chrimbo in November? Who? I'll tell you who. Crazy bitches. That's who. And now I've got to commit to listening to her and her ma slag off the Queen and get all teary over *Call the* bloody *Midwife* when all I wanna do is sit in me own chair, in me own house, drinking me own ale.'

Snowy slams his hand down again.

'Have you finished, Michael?'

'He's never finished,' Griffo laughs.

'Fuck off, Griffo.'

Then, my three mates turn their entire focus onto me. I've got two choices here. One; tell them to shut up and mind their own sorry business. Or two; tell them the truth.

'Zara is . . .' I begin. This is awkward. I should just change the subject. 'Lovely.'

'Ahhhh,' they all sigh, to my surprise.

'Fit?' Mikey adds.

'Mikey. Shut up,' Griffo and Snowy both say.

I swig my pint. 'She's about this tall, or should I say, short? Fits under me arm, like. Never stops gabbing, in this not quite American, but definitely not English accent.'

'Sound.'

'Boss.'

'Boss.'

'She's seen the whole world. Well, not the whole world, but you know what I mean. She's one of them expats. Travelled, moved around, got a shit load of stamps in her passport.'

'Come on, mate,' Mikey sulks. 'More juice.'

This feels so pointless, such a waste of my – and their – time. And yet my best friends look like puppy dogs, eager for a bone. The last thing I want to do is piss on their chips.

'She's got a nice tan,' I say, trying to jazz up my description. Christ, for someone who prides themselves on reading a lot, it seems I've dumped any eloquent vocabulary I know in a nearby wheelie bin. 'And sort of dark hair with loads of them highlights, and she winds it up into a little knot on her head when she's in the middle of talking, then pulls it out again. I wonder how her arms don't get tired.'

'Long hair? Sweet.'

'Boss.'

'Sound.'

'And you know what? She's kind. Like, she tries so hard to be nice and be good that it seems to backfire, like she's just a bit too soft for this world. But, I don't mean *soft* . . . 'cause she's strong, stronger than she thinks. She's brave. Yeah. That's it. She's brave.'

'In what way?' Snowy asks.

'She just – I dunno – jumps. Goes for stuff. Almost without thinking.' I laugh inwardly, enjoying how much I know about Zara Khoury. 'She follows her heart, which is big, fellas. It's one big old heart and she follows it. Hasn't brought her much luck, though.'

Mikey groans. 'Look, lad, this is all getting a bit, like, fucking mushy. Get to the good stuff.'

'Michael,' Snowy says. 'You are a pervert. End of.'

Griffo leans in, lowers his voice. 'Jimbo, this is the closest you've got to a girl in years.'

'Eh, I'm not a prude, lad,' I say, in my defence.

'One night stands don't count,' Snowy says. 'So, come 'ead. Dish!'

I shrug. They want more, but I don't have more to give.

'That's it,' I admit. 'Sorry, lads.'

'That's it?' Mikey asks, almost crying in pain.

'Well, she lives in Dubai. I'm not likely to ever see her again, am I?'

'Why not?' Griffo asks, but I shoot him a filthy look. Money is no object to Phil bloody Griffin. Mikey takes out his phone and starts messing about on Facebook. 'Does she like you?'

309

'Dunno,' I say. The Zara I'd gotten to know seems to like everyone. 'At first, her positivity made me think she was nuts. But, as the day went on, I found it admirable, you know, a better way to get on with the daily grind of life, that's for sure. You should've seen the way she enjoyed every bite of this tuna butty in the minibus, and her sheer joy in forcing me to sing—'

'Ah, mate, I miss you singing,' Griffo butts in.

'Shh,' Snowy says, gesturing me to continue.

'We talked a lot,' I say. 'Well, I'll be honest, *she* talked a lot. It actually made me sad to hear her sadness, like it should be against the law for someone who tries so bloody hard to be happy. She was fucked in so many ways, and yet she kept smiling, unlike yours truly.' The lads nod, groaning in solidarity. 'So yeah, I'm confident she liked me. You happy now? You mad sods. You've bled me dry and that's it.'

Except that's not it. Zara also thinks I'm a great many things that I'm absolutely not. How could I have told her I wasn't successful? That failure's all I know, laced with lost drive. How? If I were to ever see her again (which is absurd), I'd have to tell her the ugly truth. And it's so very ugly.

'That's it?' Mikey checks.

'Yep,' I say, finishing my pint. 'Anyone else got any stories they'd like to share or is it alright if I scrounge some money to win back a few on the quizzie?'

'Whoa, whoa, whoa.' Snowy stands. 'Not so fast, mate.'

'Ah, what now, lad?'

'We've covered Zara.' Snowy counts out on one finger. 'Ish. But this is just the start, Jimbo. We need to know what happened to your car.'

Ah.

The car.

'Well,' I start, unsure how to begin. The thought of it all still frazzles my insides like a newspaper being set alight. 'Zara kind of crashed. Into me. It's, erm, how we met.'

Snowy's head is in his hands. Mikey's mouth is flopped open and Griffo keeps his poker face straight. Something tells me they weren't expecting that. In fact, I've shocked myself. I overlooked how Zara and I met to tell my mates what I liked about her. I feel sick. Not the bad kind of sick, but sick nonetheless.

Snowy's harping on.

'Now me mind's blown here, mate,' he says, tugging on his short hair. 'You told Griffo's dad it got stolen, 'cause Griffo's dad told Griffo. But you never told *me* that, did you, mate? When you finally rang me on the way to see your ma in the ozzy, you told me *you'd* fucked up. "I. Fucked. Up," you said. And you said the car'd been taken to the pound. So, come on. Spit it out.'

Blowing out my lips, I ruffle my hair and scratch my scalp.

'It's in the pound. Illegal parking, no insurance. I don't wanna talk about it.'

Griffo's stroking his chin, looking eerily similar to his dad.

'It's still rightfully yours, though,' he says. 'At least that much is true.'

'Griffo, what good's it doing to me half smashed up in the pound?'

'It's still rightfully yours.'

'Yeah, I heard you the first time, mate.'

'What's her name?' Mikey chirps, eyes still glued to Facebook. 'Zara what?'

'Khoury,' I say.

'Curry?' Mikey asked. 'As in curry and chips?'

My voice is croaky, so I clear my throat trying to remember

311

how I saw her name spelt on her passport. 'No, K-H-O-U-R-Y. I think it's Lebanese.'

'Boss . . . okay, is this her?'

Mikey flashes his phone into my face and yes, there she is, sunglasses on her head and standing on a beach with her arms outstretched, that iconic Dubai hotel shaped like a white sail in the background. Beside her photo is the option to 'add friend'. I've never joined Facebook – I originally thought it would be a stupid fad. And how people seem to use and abuse it makes me want to steer even clearer of it.

'Mikey, you're a total stalker,' I say. 'Put it away.'

'All I did was type in her name.'

Snowy grabs the phone to take a look. I insist they all leave me – and Zara – alone.

'Mikey, you've got a mutual friend,' Snowy says.

'What?' Mikey asks, peering over Snowy's shoulder and trying to get his own phone back.

'Who's Leon Taylor?'

'Snowy lad, gis me phone back.' Mikey snatches it and looks closely, clicking away and scrolling through. 'Leon's a mate I went to uni with. How does he know Zara? Small world, innit?'

'I swear to God,' Snowy says, standing up to go to the bar. 'Every time I get a new Facebook friend, I've already got mutual friends with them. Fucking weird. Like the whole world's interconnected. I befriended this fella in Tenerife when me and Helen took the kids there last year. Turns out our mutual friend is me Aunty fucking Eileen. His ma used to work with me Aunty Eileen's second husband, Frank. Weird, eh?'

I'll be honest, I don't really have much of a clue what they're talking about, but Snowy and Griffo seem to understand and

312

are sharing similar stories with enthusiasm. I go to the bar instead, ordering a round and putting it on Griffo's tab. I'll be getting paid in four days and I'm counting. Good job I've got a large bag of pasta in the cupboard at home, although the opened jar of pesto now seems extravagant. It wouldn't be a bad idea to try and win some money on the quizzie. I return to the table expertly carrying four pints in my hands and four packets of crisps in my teeth. Mikey's talking about Leon Taylor.

'And here's me, stuck in a freezing cold classroom, giving meself piles from sitting on a bloody radiator teaching little shits about crotchets and quavers, and there's Leon fucking Taylor in fucking Dubai. I bet his classroom's got a chandelier. You know what? I'm gonna go home and tell Tori we're moving to Dubai. I'm gonna say, "Babe, pack your bags, we're moving to Dubai." If Leon Taylor can get a job in some fancy international school, then Mr Farley can, too.'

'At least you won't have to go to your ma-in-law's for Chrimbo,' Snowy says.

I spit the packets of crisps into the middle of the table.

'How's your Lisa?' Griffo asks.

I just shake my head, roll my eyes and to my relief we mutually agree it's time to have a go on the quizzie. Well, three of us anyway. Nobody can tear Mikey away from his phone, stalking Leon Taylor on Facebook and obsessing about how to ask Tori if they can move to Dubai.

29

Zara

'You decide yet, ma'am?' The nail technician grins.

Well, if a grin could kill.

I apologise and shuffle in my flip-flops. No, I haven't decided yet.

A woman waiting to pay taps her credit card on the reception desk while the other nail technicians ignore her, chattering amongst each other and pretending to look busy. She checks her phone and releases a heavy sigh. I can see how much she's trying to be patient. Customer service is excellent in Dubai. When you demand it.

'Please,' the woman says, squeezing a polite smile. 'I haven't got all day.'

I catch her eye, give a sympathetic nod, but in truth I'm envious of her. Not because of her glorious height or even the brilliant bling shining from her left hand, but because this woman doesn't have something I've got. All. Damn. Day. I wouldn't be killing time in a nail salon with Marina otherwise.

Analysing my mood, I run my index finger across the rainbow of colours. Something with a sparkle? No, something pastel, like lemon or baby blue? Oh, no. Perhaps, a blast of shocking neon? Or, how about plain old red? Standard pink? Black? I go back to the beginning again, then make a decision. White. The label beneath the bottle calls it 'Blizzard'.

'This way, ma'am.'

I'm led into a clinical white-tiled room by a nail technician with the name badge Rubylyn, and settle myself into a big white chair. Music trickles through the speakers, pleasant sounds strung together to make some sort of relaxing noise, rather than a tune. Not that any of the women getting treatments are listening. They're all wearing headphones and watching the plasma screens hung upon the white walls playing episodes of *New Girl*. Or they're like Marina, who's reclining on the chair beside me with a whole entourage of technicians painting fingers, toes, threading eyebrows, waxing upper lips, fitting eyelash extensions . . . the list goes on. And, due to the amount of staff tending to Marina, just one lady is assigned to do my feet first, followed by my hands.

'Not a problem,' I say. 'I've got all day.'

Rubylyn doesn't offer me any headphones so I take out my new phone, a gift from my papa. It's a gift out of guilt rather than kindness. When I arrived back at his villa a couple of days ago, it was a surprise to find him there, lounging on his leather sofa in golf attire, having flown back from Saudi early. Apparently it was a public holiday, announced at short notice and not uncommon in the United Arab Emirates, but news that had slipped off my radar due to being out of the country.

'Where've you been?' he asked me.

I was speechless.

'Looks like you're moving out,' he laughed. 'Why so much luggage?'

'I *was*,' I said.

'You *was* what?'

'Doesn't matter.'

I decided to take my things up to my room, one suitcase at a time.

'Hey.' My papa stopped me. 'I know when my daughter's upset. You're upset.'

'Oh, really?'

'What's with the attitude?'

'Papa. I *was* moving out. Remember?'

He removed his glasses, narrowed his eyes as if calculating numbers in his head.

'I told you.'

'Told me what? When?'

'That I was going to live in England, Papa. You took Marina and me for dinner at the Sheraton, that Thai place with the jumping fish, and I told you about how I'd—'

'Wait, wait, wait. Slow down, Zara.' He stood up, switched the TV off. 'What's the jumping fish got to do with anything?'

Again, I struggled to find the correct response. Hoisting my suitcase up the marble staircase, I couldn't believe that my own father had forgotten. Actually no – I could totally believe it; as clear as the sky is up and the sea is wet; my own father had forgotten.

Well, at least I've got a phone now. A good one, too.

I open Facebook, like a few photos, comment on the odd amusing status. The massage taking place on the soles of my feet is heaven, so I put the phone down, reminding myself that a bit of much-needed pampering isn't killing time, it's

316

making good use of it. Marina is the only person I know in Dubai who doesn't work during the week. The whole place is so work hard, play hard, all my friends – well, acquaintances – do long, stressful hours and release all their tension by partying at the weekend. Sure, there are plenty of women like Marina; housewives, stay-at-home mommies, but I'm not in those circles. I wonder where the party will be this weekend, where I can let my hair down and forget.

About Jim.

Oh, Jim Glover. Why am I still thinking about him? Four thousand miles stand strong between us and that's nothing compared to the strength of my head telling me this is a No Go Area. The last long-distance attempt resulted in disaster and I must, must, must learn from my stupid mistakes. I need to find a job, and fast. Throwing myself into some sort of work will be the best solution and, of course, a great way to meet new people. Maybe I should just put it out there and ask the universe (well, social media) if my services are needed? It's knee-deep into event season here. Surely some companies need an extra girl to dish out a shot and a smile?

I peep down at my toenails, transforming into flawless white, smooth and party ready.

Maybe someone's having a pool party this weekend. The weather is perfect for barbecues, too. And isn't it that girl's birthday, the one hosting the yacht cruise on Friday afternoon? What's her name, Layla? Lola? Or is it Nayla? Friend of a friend. I'm sure I've seen an invite to that in my inbox.

'You want headphones, ma'am?' Rubylyn asks, a little late into the treatment.

'I'm good,' I say, the spacey ambience kind of working for me.

I start to type a status before my fingers are preened and

317

polished, attempting to find out if any of my Facebook friends can point me in the direction of some work.

God, I sound so needy, though. Delete, delete, delete.

I try again.

And totally sound like a prostitute. Delete, delete, del—

BEEP.

I click on my new notification; an invitation entitled *Brunch . . . Because.*

Dubai has a slightly different take on the wholesome late breakfast, early lunch ordeal, with hotels offering customers a deal on unlimited international cuisine and unlimited alcohol every Friday afternoon. These events are often extravagant, luxurious, littered with expats from all corners of the globe, and, of course, a perfect way to make new friends.

I read through the details.

At 'Oceanic O', the new beachside/poolside restaurant in the new Marriott. 10 live cooking stations, cocktails on tap, a purpose-built chocolate room, ice sculptures, stilt walkers and live jazz band. Because it's Friday. Because we can. Who's in?

When? This weekend.

The guy inviting me isn't somebody I know well. In fact, I can't work out how I even know him at all. Most probably a previous brunch. That's how the expats roll, isn't it? I know a handful of people who've already said yes to attending so it should be good fun, a chance to throw myself back into the social circuit. I no longer have the option of hanging onto my laptop in my PJs, looking forward to a Skype call from Liverpool, and besides, I can't hide away forever. Never, ever again will I jump into a relationship unless its flesh and blood and bones are within my physical grasp. So I have to get out. I have to say yes.

Rubylyn starts to massage my right hand, leaving only my left hand free to keep browsing. I'll take some time to think about how to write my job-hunting status, maybe come up with something catchy, witty. Then my heart sinks. The date for the brunch isn't *this* weekend. It's the following weekend. Right, I'll update my CV and contact all the promo companies I worked for last year. They might let me wear a mask, or face paint. Or maybe they just won't care. And I'll draw. I've got a new sketchpad waiting to be put to use. It won't amount to anything, but it's something to do, something I enjoy, at least. I sit up straight.

'Relax, ma'am,' Rubylyn snaps.

I say sorry and receive a tut, then a tug to my index finger. Using my left hand, I accept the invitation to brunch. Yes, I'll definitely go. And I spend the rest of my manicure trying to remember how I know the guy who's invited me. A guy called Leon Taylor.

30

Jim

In the booth, I open the paperback I took from my ma's house last night when I nipped in to grab some essentials she wanted bringing into hospital. About the comic genius of Dudley Moore, it'd been one of my dad's books and I was thoroughly surprised to find it there on the shelf, having never noticed it before.

Two sentences in, I've got to explain to a driver that she can't pay on card.

'Why not?' the woman asks.

'Cash only, love.'

'But, I wanna use me card.'

'You'll be able to use it soon.' I attempt a smile.

'But, I wanna use me card now.'

Dudley Moore's story'll have to wait.

Ah, what a difference a week can make. Or not. Exactly one week's passed since I received that phone call from Connie and Carl on Mersey Wave 103.4 and yet, despite the pandemonium over the past seven days, here I am again, in the toll booth, reading a paperback, getting stiff knees. The BMW's still in the pound. I'll have to put a few quid aside over the next few months before I can think about getting that back, if it's even worth bothering. Only yesterday, as I sat in the canteen to eat my ham and pickle on brown bread (courtesy of the tenner I won on the quizzie at the Pacific Arms), Derek Higgins had swung by to remind me about the card-payment training day.

'How could I forget, Derek?'

'I hope you know this is a privilege.'

I opened my packet of Cheddars and crunched one slowly.

'You're The Chosen One, Jim.'

The woman wanting to pay the toll fee on her card seems to have finally comprehended that she can't. Gayle Freeman's in the booth beside me, and being the perfect team player, she's waving all cars over to her, allowing the woman to reverse without commotion. Really, Gayle should be The Chosen One.

A welcomed lull encases me and I delve into the first chapter about Dudley Moore. I make it through three full pages before I've got to give change again.

Our Emma sends me a message.

Hey little bro!! What time do you finish work today? We're doing tours of both footy stadiums today (Jack's idea obviously!) and then going for food at the Albert Dock before going to see Mum. Wanna join us? Lisa and Paul are coming too. Love ya loads. Em x

No, I don't want to join and listen to Jack harp on about *soccer*. I mean, don't get me wrong, I'm glad they're making the most of their time in Liverpool. Emma's kids are sweethearts, and they've warmed to their Uncle Jimbo since I gave them a Mars bar the other day. Plus, their politeness is bloody astounding, a million miles from the Wongs' anti-social kids. Well, four thousand two hundred miles to be almost exact. I message Emma back to say I've got errands to run and to have fun without me this afternoon. In truth, it's the perfect opportunity to go and visit my ma. Alone.

'Y'never heard of a barber, mate?'

He's late today, the fella in the Ford Focus. I laugh, as usual, wishing him all the best.

Then I get another message, from Mikey.

Ring me now.

Can't mate. Working. I reply.

Fuck work. Ring me now.

Something up?

Quite the opposite.

It'll have to wait. Speak to you later mate.

Twat.

BEEP!

I apologise to the driver waiting for his change and tend to the queue that's built up within a matter of seconds. I catch Gayle Freeman's chin sinking into the many rolls of skin surrounding her neck, a look of disapproval beaming from her eyes like headlights in fog. She does such an excellent job of being efficient and pulling faces simultaneously. Really, quite a talent. The queue disappears almost as quickly as it began. Gayle leans out of her open window, calls my name.

'What's got into you?' she yells.

My response is a shrug and a one-sided smile. I'm wondering the same thing. At least I'm not predictable anymore.

I receive a series of angry doorbell buzzes at my flat above the chippy. It had totally slipped my mind to speak to Mikey after work.

'What's your problem?' I ask Mikey, who's also been banging on the door, too.

'I can't stay long, I'm parked on double yellows.'

'What's going on, Mikey?'

'I knew if I sent you another message, you wouldn't reply. Ungrateful bastard.'

'So, you've come over to insult me for . . . what exactly?'

Mikey undoes his Goofy tie, sits on my settee, then stands again. I don't sense that he's in any trouble, that his haste is any cause for concern. In truth, Mikey seems excited, like a kid waiting for his turn on the bouncy castle. Maybe he's been bumped up to Head of Music, but why that'd be of any interest to me is a mystery. Or perhaps Tori's pregnant again.

'Jimbo,' Mikey says, taking a deep breath, a twinkle in his eyes behind his glasses. 'You can go to Dubai.'

'Oh? Can I?' I say with a chirpy sarcasm.

'You can thank me for it later.'

'Again, can I?'

'Do you not wanna know how?'

'I can hardly wait.'

Mikey throws back his shoulders and splays his hands. For a moment, I think he might burst into some sort of Andrew Lloyd Webber song, but he simply says the name, 'Leon.'

'Right . . .'

'Leon!'

'Means nothing to me, mate.'

'Wrong. It means everything to you, Jimbo.'

'Y'what?'

'Leon Taylor.'

'Your old uni mate?'

'Spot on.'

'The fella you slagged off for the best part of an hour at the Pacific Arms the other night?'

'Didn't.'

'Okay, lad. You didn't.'

'Leon's sound,' Mikey says, his voice ringing into all corners of my little flat.

'Sure he is,' I say, calming my mate down by gently pressing my hands onto his shoulders and edging him back into the settee. 'For a fella who can't header a ball and falls asleep at the table after four pints. According to you, that is.'

'Well, he did used to fall asleep after four pints. Doesn't mean he isn't sound.'

'Never said he wasn't.'

Mikey grabs my arm and pulls me down to sit beside him. The heavy bustle from the flyover outside causes the windows of the flat to rattle, a noise I like to drown out with the velvet tones of vinyl. Mikey's still holding onto me with a tight grip.

'Jimbo. Leon knows Zara.'

'You mentioned.'

'He's gonna set you up.'

'Y'what?'

'He said you can stay with him.'

'Oh, can I?'

'Yeah. He's got a spare room. Says people stay all the time.'

'I bet.'

'He loves having people over, showing them around Dubai.'

'Who wouldn't?'

'He was a bit like that at uni.'

'I can see how Huddersfield and Dubai'd be similar. From a tourist's point of view, like.'

'You're a massive twat, Jimbo.'

'Oh, so you *were* coming over to insult me?' I laugh, breaking my arm free.

I fall right back into my settee, fold my arms.

'You heard me, Jim,' Mikey says, pointing his finger at me as if I'm one of his unruly pupils. 'Leon Taylor said you can stay at his place in Dubai. In fucking *Dubai*, mate. For free. I mean, buy him some duty-free ale or something to say thanks. You know the score.' And Mikey cups his hand around his ear, sticking out his head. 'I'm listening . . .'

'Listening? For what?' I ask.

'I can't hear you,' Mikey sings. Patronising bastard.

'Mikey, why are you really here?'

'Fuck's sake, Jimbo. I'm not saying it again. Thank me another time. You piece of shit.'

Straightening his tie and his glasses, Mikey heads to the door and opens it, the Wongs' antisocial kids peering from the stairs. I try to follow him but the kids block my way, eager to go inside and watch Netflix. I call out to Mikey just before he reaches the back entrance by Wong's kitchen.

'Mikey, don't take the piss. You don't seriously expect me to go, do you?'

But Mikey's getting into his car.

'What's your excuse?' he asks.

'Y'what?'

Mikey slams his door and turns the key. The window slides down.

'There's always an excuse with you, Jimbo. What is it this time?'

This silences me. What does Mikey mean by that? There's always an excuse?

'We all have it hard, mate,' Mikey says, revving. 'But, when you want something, you go for it. Well, some of us do, anyway.'

The revs add to the deafening noise from the flyover. One of the Wongs' antisocial kids darts past and dumps a load of potato skins into the wheelie bin, its stench filtering outwards. A few loose skins blow into the wind, dance around my trainers.

'You honestly think I can just pack me bags and go to the other side of the world to stay with some fella I've never met?' I yell. 'Get set up with some girl I hardly know?'

Mikey revs harder. 'Yeah.'

'Do you realise how fucking crazy that sounds?'

'No.'

'Mikey, lad. I've got no money. None.'

'We thought you might say that.'

'Well, I haven't!'

'So sell something.'

The car window squeaks on its way upwards, Mikey's face becoming a blur behind the rain-speckled glass. I run my hands through the hair hanging over my eyes and then through my stubble, the beginnings of a beard. Does Mikey really think things are as easy as that? Just sell something – something?! – and piss off? To Dubai? And what the hell would I tell Zara, if she did actually happen to know this fella, this Leon Taylor, and agree to meet up? 'Oh, hiya Zara.

Remember me? The fella you thought was a rich entrepreneur? Well, I'm skint. Pure skint. And that's just the beginning, wait 'til you find out where I live . . . oh, and by the way, love, can you buy us a bevvie?' I batter on Mikey's window, willing him to understand.

'I haven't got anything to sell,' I cry.

But Mikey's indicated and slowly starts pulling out, away from Wong's, away from the potato skins, away from me. And my string of tiring excuses.

She's in the day room watching *The Chase* when I arrive at the hospital. I greet her but get shushed because she's playing along, trying to answer the questions Bradley Walsh is asking against the clock. I wait with patience, offer 'Tom Hanks' as the answer to one question and get an almighty evil look from her in return.

The Chaser wins.

My ma calls it 'scandalous' and tells me to switch the bloody thing off. Then I take a seat in the plastic armchair beside her. We're all alone, the ward quieter than usual, a lull during staff changeover.

'They're letting me out tomorrow,' she says, as if it's top secret.

'Well, you look superb,' I say, and mean it.

'I feel it, love.'

Her new housecoat, peaches and cream and lined with satin, matches her new cosy slippers, a gift from my sisters. The colour has brought out a natural blush in her cheeks, somehow turning her greying hair to silver. I wish I had a bag of Minstrels for her, or some Revels. She's such a chocolate fiend and I want to give her whatever makes her smile, even if it is just a packet of sweets.

'That fall might be the best thing I ever did,' she chuckles.

'Don't say that.'

'Why not? It's only brought us all together again, hasn't it?'

I don't say anything. The day room's vacuous silence isn't pleasant and although I'd been looking forward to being with my ma away from the commotion my sisters like to create, the quiet moments now feel long, and rather bleak.

'It's almost as if they never left,' she says, relieving the sterile air.

'I feel like a kid again.'

'Wanting to hide from them every chance you get?'

'Not half.'

'Is it bad that I forgot how shrill our Lisa's voice can be? Me own daughter!'

'It's not bad that you forgot at all. It's miraculous.'

We both share a laugh, a sneaky one, as if the nurses are being paid to spy on us.

'Eh, Emma's husband knows how to be heard, doesn't he?' She grins.

'My ears are still ringing from when he first opened his gob.'

'Do you think he's one of them Trump supporters?'

'I'm marching our Emma to the divorce courts if he is.'

'And the other one, Paul, is it just me or are his eyes a bit too close together?'

'You think he's a bit inbred?'

'I imagine his mother married her cousin.'

'You're terrible!' I cry, my stomach aching from trying not to laugh out loud. And my ma, God, she's sniggering so much, I actually just saw her slobber. She shushes me, although really she's shushing herself.

'I think the most hilarious thing,' I say, catching my

breath, 'is that they all thought you'd go across the pond to live with them. I mean, can you imagine? Putting up with all that twenty-four seven? They must think you're crackers.'

It's my ma's turn to catch her breath, too. And she sighs, a sing-song of a release.

'I am.' she smiles. 'Crackers.'

'Well, yeah. That part's true,' I tease, winking at her.

She grabs my hand. Well, my wrist. Something firmer than another blip of affection.

'No, son. I don't think you understand.'

'Y'what?'

'I'm gonna go.'

'Where?'

'Where do you think, soft lad? I'm gonna go. With them. To America.'

'Are you messing?'

'No, I'm not messing.' She fiddles with the satin lining on her housecoat. 'Our Lisa's been going on about it for ages. Thought it'd finally shut her up.'

'Ages?'

My ma looks at me, apologetic. If I could replace that thick silence from earlier with the eerie fuzz surrounding me now, I'd do it in a heartbeat. The words 'go' and 'them' and 'America' hang above my head, pressing down like a cloud awaiting the storm to begin. What confuses me the most, though, is the lightness in my ma's voice, her positivity.

She's leaving Liverpool.

And going to America.

'You can't be serious, Mam?'

'Tell me why not, love?'

I can't. There's nothing I can say to stop her because there's nothing stopping her. Only me. A million reasons for her to

329

stay bounce through my mind, but none translate into actual words. And maybe it's because those reasons are not actually reasons. They're excuses. Mikey was right.

My ma's eyes look bright and yet they're shadowed with frailty. She has something to live for. Only not enough time to enjoy it.

'I don't like admitting when I might be wrong,' she says.

'Wrong?'

'That car. It brought you some luck.'

The painkillers she's on are clearly strong; she seems a bit delusional. I can't recall if she knows about my car misfortune, or if I'd mentioned it and she's forgotten. The last few visits run through my mind. Now's not the time to break the news that the car brought me the very opposite of good luck.

'You'll have to send me a postcard,' I joke, desperate not to get choked.

'The kids said they'll show me how to get an email address.'

'I can show you how to do that.'

'Don't be daft. What do I want an email address for?'

'Postcard it is, then.'

'Postcard it is.'

Another quiet moment passes, but it's not as heavy as the previous, as if a window has been opened. Even the faded curtains seem to sway, a sense of life in a somewhat lifeless room.

'Shall we put *Corrie* on?' my ma asks.

I seize the remote and switch the telly back on, the familiar theme tune blasting out.

'I wonder, will I be able to watch *Corrie* in America?'

I don't want to give her an excuse not to go.

'You can watch pretty much anything from anywhere these days, Mam.'

'Isn't that marvellous?'

And we're sitting here together, just like any other Wednesday evening.

'Oh, hold on,' my ma says, tapping her hands on the chair's wooden arms with a sudden burst of excitement. 'Go into the ward for me, love. In me bedside table, there's a packet of Minstrels. Ethel Barton brought them in this afternoon.'

With a firm nod, I do as I'm told. Good old Ethel Barton. She's come out alright in the end.

In all the years that I've worked in the toll booth, I've never been able to work out whether I prefer the sunny days, the blue sky and sharp edge to the fume-ridden air, or if a typical rainy day is better, the grey grumpiness being a more understanding ally, befriending the high-visibility jackets dotted around.

Today, most people would call it lovely. It's a lovely day. Not a cloud in the sky, as the song goes. Ed Sheeran's coming from the silver Nissan Micra and the chatty girl's wearing her sunnies. On cue, she dips them.

'Hey you,' she says to me, a little subdued.

'How was your night out in Oxton last week?' I ask.

'Oh, fine. You mightn't see me much anymore.'

'Why's that, love?'

'I'm selling this car. Gonna be getting the train instead.'

Now look, I don't know anything about this girl other than she drives a Nissan Micra. There's no time to find out why she's selling, or even ask where she would be getting the train to, but one question does spring to mind.

'How much do you reckon you'll get for it?'

'Few grand. Why, you interested?'

'It's quite old, right?'

The girl huffs. 'It's not an old banger. But, yeah, it's old. I didn't actually think I'd get that much for it, but my brother said the parts are all in good condition and parts can always be sold separately. To be honest, I wasn't paying much attention—'

'There's a queue, love.'

The girl puts the car into gear, gives a friendly honk partnered with a pouty sad face, and waves goodbye.

The yellow sticky sponge peeping through the seat of my chair is coming loose on my navy trousers. They really ought to invest in some new furniture. It's the only essential the staff require. I give the back of my irritated neck a quick itch, shuffle to get comfy. Then I open up my book, but my focus isn't on the words on the page. It's on something Griffo said to me in the Pacific Arms.

A new 'regular' pulls up.

Once again, smugness shines and unless I'm imagining it, he pities me. It's the fella in the white BMW M3, of course, an almost-replica of the one that had once belonged to me.

Counting out the coins before handing them over, I hesitate.

'What's the holdup?' the fella asks.

I lean out of the window, peer down upon the car, eye its length, take in the tyres. It's not an almost-replica of the car that once belonged to me. It's an almost-replica of the car that *still* belongs to me. Enough is enough.

'You having some sort of problem up there?' the fella asks, his tolerance level fading.

I am, yep. One hell of a problem, in fact. The high-vis jacket is digging into the back of my neck like a flea biting for the title. I can't stand wearing the bloody thing for a minute longer. So I'm taking it off. Now.

I leave it hanging on the sad excuse for a chair and walk away from the toll booth, across the tarmac, not looking over my shoulder once.

Because I, James Anthony Glover, am never going back.

I quit.

There's method to what many – Derek, Gayle, amongst others – believe to be my madness. You see, while I've been sitting in that toll booth, there's a car out there sitting in a pound belonging to nobody else but me. Yes, the car, with its sorry, crumpled arse, isn't a pretty sight, and if I want to drive it anywhere, I'll have to endure embarrassment, questions.

But I don't want to drive it anywhere.

In fact, it's the last thing I want to do right now. Because I want to travel in something much more adventurous than a car, or a train or even a boat. I want to stop making excuses for the sad little life I've created for myself and get on a plane. I've got an idea, and it could be totally bonkers, a reason for my mates to laugh at me or even frown upon me, but it's an idea. It could work. And if it does, then, I'm going to go to Dubai. I'm going to see Zara.

I ring Griffo. Ask for help. Four minutes later, Griffo calls me back.

'Meet me at Haddon Park Way tonight at midnight,' he informs me.

'You think it'll work?' I ask.

'Wear something dark.'

'Of course.'

That's the easy part.

31

Zara

The Dubai Mall. The perfect way to kill time for anybody who loves to shop.

I'm on the top floor of one of the planet's largest indoor shopping arenas watching animals in the wild leap across the latest LED plasma screens.

'Can I help you, ma'am?'

I blink, snapping myself back into the bright lights of the electronics store.

'I'm just browsing, thank you.'

I love to shop, but one thing I'm not is a window shopper. There's very little I can shop for without a job securing my purchases. I take out my phone, hoping Katie is on the move. She's meeting me outside the mall to watch the dancing fountains, a pastime that never tires in Dubai, only she's stuck in traffic. In the car with her are two mutual friends of ours that I've done a variety of promo work with. Despite the scar sunken into my cheek, I'm wearing a bright yellow off-shoulder dress and tan wedges, hoping that a mint lemonade and a catch-up might persuade them to put in a good word for me.

My phone flashes with a notification, but it's none of the girls. It's just another marketing email from Liverpool University. I'm losing my patience with all this. Why did I ever bother entering my details into their system? I've been getting bombarded with emails ever since. The last email was the top ten tips for how to be vegan on a tight budget. Super.

I make my way through hordes of shoppers, following the pristine walkway through the mall, down the escalators, past an array of food courts and outside to the waterside viewing deck where the dancing fountains are currently on a break. A plethora of eateries surrounds me, from international chains to independent restaurants, all spilling with a multi-cultural blend of locals, expats and tourists. It's as if the whole world has gathered right here, right now. To my right, my eyes scan from the ground up, up, upwards, taking in every inch of the Burj Khalifa, a shimmering rocket kissing the Arabian night sky. Families pose for photographs, whoever is taking the picture crouching as low as possible, trying to get the whole tower in the background. Many more are taking selfies. The warm atmosphere has an edge, that feeling that something exciting is about to happen, like when a crowd awaits a rock star's appearance onstage.

A short, dead silence falls across the vast exterior of the mall. The Burj Khalifa is flashing like a giant Christmas tree, indicating that it's time. Gasps and sighs break the silence across the ever-so-still manmade waterway. Then Andrea Bocelli's 'Time to Say Goodbye' blasts out through speakers as hundreds of powerful water chutes catapult into the air, choreographed perfectly to dance in time to the music.

I smile, tickled. I like to imagine that each shoot of water is real, like a person, a dancer. Before the music begins, as the crowd waits in anticipation of the fountains starting, I have this image of the 'dancers' being in grand dressing rooms below the waterway, sitting there and having a cigarette, taking five before their performance. Silly, I know. But what the hell.

Now, the water is dancing in all directions with emotional, graceful movements. Some spectators have even started to cry. It truly is spectacular. It's water. And it's dancing. Reaching its finale, water shoots upwards to an almighty crescendo, followed by raucous applause.

And as quickly as they gathered, the crowd disperses.

I catch my breath, remain still. I have no desire to follow anybody in and get caught in the stampede. At least there's some space at the edge of the waterway now. I had to stand up on my tiptoes to see the effects of the 'Time to Say Goodbye' routine, and now I can bag myself a good 'seat' for the next song. The 'dancers' are on their break again, but they'll be back soon.

Leaning against the rail, I get my phone out and scroll. Still no word from Katie. I click on the email from Liverpool University, wondering what enlightening information it's offering. Maybe a discount from a clothing store I'll never visit, or five shots for the price of one in some bar I'll never drink at.

Only it's not from the student union, or the marketing department. It's from admissions. I skim-read. Oh, for God's sake. Seriously. The irony of the timing. Just as I arrive back in Dubai, the possibility of a life in England behind me, the damn university wants to confirm that I've been offered a place to finish my degree, starting in the new year. For some reason, this news makes me think about one of my suitcases, still unopened in my papa's villa, full of warmer clothes for winter. I haven't bothered to unpack it yet, although the task will undoubtedly kill some of the oodles of time on my hands. Tucked into one of the pockets is some stationery: a new pencil case with a unicorn plastered across the centre. How embarrassing. How old do I think I am? All in anticipation of having a first day back at school, my new boyfriend waving me off from behind the wheel of his car?

The image of that new boyfriend isn't Nick anymore. It's Jim.

My thoughts are becoming jumbled. Everything and nothing makes a whole lot of nonsense. I've been hanging onto the Jim part, perhaps as a tool to help me get over Nick. Perhaps not. But, you know, it's easy. Hanging onto Jim, I mean. How he might watch me enter the main doors of the department as I look over my shoulder, hoping for a nod of encouragement, a wink to reassure me that I'm doing the right thing. And he's looking at me in the same way he did that night, in the hotel, just before that almost-kiss. I'd been safe, exactly where I was supposed to be.

Before the moment passed.

The crowds are gathering close to the waterway again, the surge of selfies going crazy. Being alone amongst thousands of other people is so much lonelier than simply being alone. My imagination is exhausting me with fake scenarios of somebody being here beside me, of Jim Glover looking up at the Burj Khalifa, his hands gently on my waist. Still, a warm smile spreads through me like a much-needed hug, until I'm thrown out of my daydream by a push from the family standing beside me. I brush off their series of apologies politely. It happens. Everybody wants to get a decent view. Kids get excited.

Oh my God.

I can't believe who I spot. The reason the family had pushed into me. He's at the front now, having barged his way to the railing, and he's stretching his arm around the woman he's with. I'm all flushed, and then ever so suddenly feel my blood run cold, almost as if a sharp blast of the mall's air conditioning has hit me, thrown over me like a bucket of water.

George.

The guy responsible for the fucking hole in my face.

'Hey,' I find myself saying. And again, louder. 'Hey! George.'

He turns around, looking rather pleased that somebody has noticed him. I've got no intention of actually talking to him, hearing his pompous voice, so I honestly can't fathom why on earth I want to grab his attention, but somehow, I do.

I just want him to look at me.

At. Me.

And he does. His eyes fall upon mine, and all too soon, they fall upon my cheek. The only thing left to fall is George's face. Which does. To the floor.

I wave, a spontaneous reaction at seeing someone familiar and yet without an ounce of friendly intention. The woman beside him smiles, unknowing, and waves back to me.

The heat returns to my body and just seeing George falter, so incredibly unsure of himself in that simple, small moment, brings me huge comfort. Perhaps the thought of Jim behind me is helping, although I'm not going to rely on that or give a figment of my imagination the credit for the strength I'm now feeling. A funny term pops into my head, one that sums up George to perfection. I can't work out where I heard it. George is a total bellend.

Oh how I'm trying not to laugh.

Where did that expression come from? It's not something I'd ever say.

George moves from the railing. He ushers the unknowing woman away, leaving space for the children in the family to spread out and get a much better view of the impending fountain display. I glance down at my phone again, the email from Liverpool University still hanging there.

Jim!

It was Jim who had called Nick Gregory a total bellend, during our journey to Heathrow.

'... *just 'cause he's a total bellend doesn't mean you can't go back to uni.*'

Yes, that was it.

I read the email again, this time with full concentration.

I have been accepted into the school of Art and Design to complete the second and final year of an Illustration degree. Not Nick, not George, and not even Jim. Just me, Zara Khoury. It's here in black and white. This news, coming through to my private email address, has nothing to do with any guy, or anybody other than me.

Why can't I go back to university? Does a man define my right to complete my studies? No, of course not. Never.

A wave of disgust hits me, ashamed at how thoughtless I've been towards my own true self. All those sketches, all those comic strips – hilarious according to the few people I've dared to show – have come from my mind, my hands. Nobody else's. Even my papa, who disapproves of the arts unless it suits his mood, found the meerkat in the jacuzzi sketch amusing and had been the one to suggest I 'put it on a t-shirt or something', planting the idea of getting it printed onto a canvas tote bag.

But I've lost my inspiration so many times. I'm so easily led by others. What if I fail again?

Silence strikes, broken by the twinkle of lights and awe of the spectators. A tremendous chute of water powers into the sky accompanied by traditional Arabic music, bold and dramatic, its energy blasting across the heart of the Middle East's modern metropolis. It's the perfect soundtrack for this dance as I watch the water swirl and swoosh, around and around, with as much attention as I'd given the second reading of my email. Because this will be the final time I watch the dancing fountains. I'm going to leave Dubai for good.

And go back to Liverpool. Definitely.

32

Jim

Haddon Park Way is where my car sits stationary in the pound.

Griffo's used his dad's contacts to find out this information behind his dad's back, so no matter what the outcome might be from the task ahead, I'll be forever grateful – and owing – to my old pal.

'This is so fucking exciting,' Snowy says, like a balloon on the verge of popping.

He pulls a balaclava over his face and does a series of punches that can only be compared to a Power Ranger. Griffo's dressed for the part, minus the balaclava, and his height and width make him look like a doorman for a dodgy club. Mikey, in general dark stuff, just looks pleased with himself.

'I knew you'd think of something,' he tells me.

'Even though I'm an ungrateful bastard, a massive twat and a piece of shit?' I ask, just to be sure.

'Keep your voices down,' Griffo says.

'POW!' Snowy says, bending his knees and elbows like a ninja. 'Soz. Couldn't help meself.'

It's impressive how Griffo's learnt to speak clearly, yet with minimal volume and no movement of either his upper or lower lip. He gathers all of the Dentists in.

'Now, has anyone done this before?'

I break away from the huddle with a highly offended 'NO'. Mikey and Snowy also step back and scoff, Snowy protesting, asking Griffo what the hell he takes us all for.

'Fucking stereotypes!' Snowy cries over being hushed. 'Just 'cause we're Scouse lads you reckon we've done this before? We're not all dodgy like . . .'

Griffo raises his eyebrow.

'Like me?' he asks.

'No, no,' Snowy stammers. 'I mean, yeah. No offence.'

'None taken,' Griffo says.

Mikey's fuming. Pure FUMING.

'But we're playing up to the stereotype, aren't we?' he remarks, breathing heavily. 'All that shit that's said about Scousers, and yet here we are about to . . . We can't. We can't do this—'

'Look. Stop it,' I whisper as loud as possible. 'For starters, you can all do one. I'm here now, after you planted the seed in me head, Michael – thanks very much, mate – and I can do this alone. You all think I'm so full of excuses, well, I'm about to show you I'm not. This is *my* solution, not yours. If you don't wanna help, leave now. I won't blame you.'

They seem to have listened, and they nod. We were united once as a band, and now we're what? A band of criminals?

'And this is *not* a crime we're committing here,' I say, convincing myself, too. 'Technically.'

'He's right,' Griffo chips in.

'All I'm doing is taking what's rightfully mine. That's what you said, Griffo, isn't it? In the pub. The car's still rightfully mine. And those tyres, those beautiful nineteen-inch diamond-cut alloys, are mine. Won fairly and squarely. And that is what we're taking, and that is what I'm selling.'

Snowy raises his hand for permission to speak, then speaks anyway.

'Can't you just get the car fixed? Pay the fine? I'll lend you the dosh.'

'I already suggested that,' Griffo says.

'Alright, big fella,' Snowy snaps. 'No one likes a showoff.'

'Lads,' I go on. 'If I paid the fine, paid for insurance, then on top of all that, paid for the repair, it'd cost more than it's worth for me to keep the bloody thing. What if it's written off? I don't know the extent of the damage; I'm no expert. It'd probably cost less to buy meself a second-hand car. And it's not about driving around Liverpool or having me own wheels, is it? I don't need a nice car. Or a shit car. I need money to get out of here. And if I don't do it now . . . Look, I understand if you don't wanna help me. But, lads, I could really do with the help.'

Mikey pats me on the back. Snowy follows, patting into a drum roll that develops into a quick hug. Griffo delegates.

'Snowy, you're on watch.'

'Why him?' Mikey scowls. 'He'll blow our cover.'

Griffo sighs. 'He's loud and he's fast. He can shout if someone's coming and run away to hide quicker than you, you slow-arsed little turd. Now, shut up and listen.'

Mikey's the one to climb the chain link fence first, boosted by me and Griffo. This way, I'll have a mate on both sides when I climb the fence, for physical support. You see, if I fall and break my leg, the whole Dubai trip is fucked. But, if

Mikey falls and breaks his leg, he'll get sick pay from the school and a few weeks off. No contest. Griffo's confident enough to climb it without a boost. His dad's taught him well.

Thankfully, we all get to the other side without breaking any bones and go in search of the BMW M3. Griffo's got the registration number and the tipoff as to where it should be. It's not difficult to spot. The boot is a massive giveaway.

'Fuck me,' Mikey says.

'Ouch,' Griffo says.

'Tell me about it,' I say.

As far as crimes go, according to Griffo, removing a tyre is speedy. This *isn't* a crime, I tell myself over and over. I'm taking what's rightfully mine. Griffo reckons he can get a grand in cash for all four tyres plus alloys on the black market, which is enough money to book a flight and spend a week in Leon Taylor's place.

Griffo shines his phone's torch over mine and Mikey's heads as we remove each tyre using the tools Griffo brought along. Due to the sensible fact that we're wearing gloves, it isn't as easy as we expect. Still, we manage it, and each of us carries one tyre back through the pound, back to the fence where Snowy's waiting for us. Griffo directs me to boost Mikey up onto his shoulders, then I use all of my strength to hand each tyre to Mikey, who throws the first one over the fence and almost knocks Snowy out.

'Watch it!' Snowy yelps.

'Watch the tyre!' I shriek. 'Sorry, mate.'

The next two tyres are thrown over in the exact same manner, Mikey clearly seeing this as a bit of a joke. Nobody else finds it funny.

'Now, Jimbo, go back for the last tyre,' Griffo tells me.

So, back I go through the pound, tracing our steps back to my car. The quiet surrounding me is eerie, a slight squeal of wind blowing amidst the stillness of the vehicles. I'm all alone with my prize, for the first time since moments before the crash, when Elbow had been singing 'One Day Like This' on the radio.

'Hey,' I say, feeling like a dick for talking to a car.

I circle it, gloved hands stuffed into my fleece, taking it all in whilst ignoring the boot. The sides, the bonnet are still perfect. A bit of dried mud splattered from the rain gives the white finish some freckles. My ma was disgusted by it, wasn't she? Her first thought was what the neighbours'd think. How she disappeared into its leather racing seats! The sound system's top class; music never sounded so good. So fucking good. Saying goodbye is harder than I imagined. On the passenger side, I peer in through the window. A bow tie lies on the floor, fallen off that bloody mop. A part of Zara's past.

I remember her bravery. Her absolute will to try and make her life better.

For all her faults and failures, I admire her. A chill runs down my spine at the prospect of how Zara's likely to react to my own faults and failures, the ones I never admitted to. Her innocence handed me a fake identity on a plate and I made no effort to correct her. How can I be sure I'm doing the right thing?

Well, I can't, can I?

I rest my gloved hand on the roof, give it a gentle pat.

'Ta-ra,' I say.

Getting over the first half of the fence is tricky on my own. Mikey and Griffo have already clambered over, awaiting my return with the final tyre which I have to throw over with a fuck load of strength. The second side is easier, my best mates all there to catch me. We pile the tyres into a van belonging to Griffo's dad, one we've never actually seen before. The 'crime' is completed with a distinct lack of drama.

'He's going to Dubai!' Griffo shouts, speeding out of Haddon Park Way. 'Woo hoo!'

'Thanks to Mikey,' I say.

'Why Mikey?' Griffo asks.

'Well, thanks to you, too, Griff. For sorting tonight out, like. But it was Mikey who got in touch with that Leon fella, had the idea that planted the seed—'

'Nah,' Mikey says. 'Wasn't me. I was roped in.'

'Oh?'

I turn to my favourite, my very best mate, sitting squashed up beside me.

'You?' I ask Snowy.

Snowy grins, raises his eyebrows, although he's missing his usual spark.

'It was your idea for me to go and find Zara?'

'It was indeed,' he confirms. 'I mean, how else was I ever gonna keep you away from Helen?'

God. I feel my heart collapse inside my chest, a million apologies etching into my face. Snowy smiles at me, perhaps acknowledging my guilt, or perhaps because he's finally getting the girl he wants all to himself.

'Mate . . .' I try.

'Nah,' Snowy says, dismissively.

Everything's out in the open now and there's no going back.

33

Zara

I'm all checked in at Dubai International Airport. Again.

I'm travelling light this time. My spirit, too. I'm practically floating through passport control. I'm going back to England, sticking to my original plan. Yes, sure, there's another man in the picture, but he's not my sole reason.

I don't think, anyway.

I've gone over this with myself a million times, questioning my actions. Is the man the main deal here? It's possible. But it's not the *only* deal.

I am sure of one thing, though. Jim Glover couldn't have been just a chance meeting. His voice, his face, his attitude is imprinted within me, spurring me on to do this. I know where he lives; I've been there. That will be my first point of call. I've got nothing to lose, and everything to gain.

Oh, that night in the hotel! The *almost*.

There's no way I'm going to let that pass. No way. And I'm also not going to pass on this opportunity, shining like

347

a laser in my face, to go back to university. The stars are finally, finally, finally aligning and the universe is totally giving me the signs to go for it.

I took a taxi to the airport. Nobody was home at my papa's villa to give me a ride, to wave me off. The goodbyes were completed a short while ago, before the first trip to Liverpool, and in truth, they'd failed to have any sort of impact on anybody. Including me.

My life has ended in Dubai. I should never have come back.

'Never go back,' I say to myself, handing my passport over.

Then, I stop, keeping a grip on my passport.

'You okay?' the guy on the desk asks.

Never go back. My own advice. And yet here I am, going back.

I close my eyes, think about the dancing fountains and recall that wonderful feeling of warmth as I listened to the music, made that decision, envisioned Jim behind me, urging me on.

'Everything's fine,' I say.

I release the passport.

I never did catch up with Katie, but we chat on WhatsApp. She's being positive about my decision, in a polite, two-dimensional way. The chat is pretty boring, if I'm honest. She's engaged to the 'lettuce', which is nice. I'm a bit upset that I found out on Instagram and not from her directly, although I know it's nothing personal. It's the modern world, isn't it? In the staged photo, she's kissing her guy, her hand stretched out to the camera as if to say *talk to the hand*, but her palm has 'I said yes!' written across it in black marker pen, a retro filter added for a whimsical touch. Like I say; nice. That's her life.

Mine is waiting for me in Liverpool.

I board the plane.

34

Jim

I'm fucking terrified.

Thirty-three years of age and I've never been on a plane before.

Two days ago I was stealing from my own car and now I'm jetting off to the Middle East. My head's wrecked. It doesn't soften the blow having everyone I know waving me off from Manchester Airport. I've been silent the whole way, sitting up front as Griffo drives the minibus, letting my league of Scousers gab away to each other in the back.

Helen was gabbing away to Lisa, who was trying to entertain Maisie, who was stealing crisps from Rocco, who was crying. Emma was listening to Snowy relive tales from his tour-managing days, revealing that whatever happens on tour doesn't actually stay on tour. Mikey and Tori were arguing, kind of about the same thing, him saying how he wanted to move them all to Dubai so he can teach music at an international school and Tori yelling at him to sort his life out and move them all to Dubai so he can teach music at an international school.

The Americans stayed behind with the kids, and of course, my ma.

It seems to take forever to check in, the queue moving ever so slowly. My entourage are waiting in the Costa, but the very thought of caffeine gives me the jitters. My fingertips are sweaty, my knees like jelly. A dryness coats my throat and droplets of sweat dance around my brow. I should've got a haircut.

'Is there a bar in there?' I ask the fella in front.

I don't want to be scared. But, Christ, I am.

The fella looks befuddled, and I realise that maybe he doesn't speak English. But he indicates his head to the signs pointing to the departure lounge and nods. This relaxes me, for a short while, and gets me through the last part of the queue.

My hand trembles as I take hold of the paper boarding ticket. I drop my passport not once, not twice, but three times whilst waiting for my suitcase to plod along the conveyor belt. I'll be surprised if they let me on the bloody plane, the way I'm behaving. I look dodgy as fuck.

'No going back now, lad,' Snowy says when I join them all in the Costa.

I pull him to one side, eager to know.

'So?' I ask, quietly.

Snowy gives a slight shake of his head, glancing towards Helen. 'Bottled it, mate.'

'Right, this is where we leave you,' Lisa says.

She stands up, gives me a hug, a single kiss and steps away to allow the next person to have a go, as if saying ta-ra to me is some sort of dance ritual.

'Hold on,' I say. 'Why are you leaving me here?'

Nobody answers my question, and if anything, they ignore me, gathering their bags and putting their coats back on, telling Maisie and Rocco to put the empty cups in the bin like it's a game they'll enjoy.

'No, I'm being serious,' I reiterate. 'Aren't you coming in to have a pint with me?'

Emma squeezes my arm. 'We can't do that. Passengers only.'

Well, at least she's remembered I've never done this before.

Showered with hugs and kisses, I disconnect myself from everyone and tell them I love them.

'Now, piss off,' I say. 'The lot of you. Piss off. I'll be back in a week.'

Christ, they're all getting on my bloody nerves. And guess what? They won't even piss off. They just carry on faffing about, Helen wanting another coffee and Snowy thinking he's lost his wallet before he realises Rocco's sitting by the bin with it, shaking it like a tambourine. Lisa's flirting with Griffo, oblivious to how obvious she is. I'm just going to have to go. I can hear an out-of-tune sing-song of 'safe travels' behind me, but I walk on, waving one arm and refusing to turn around.

Once I've got a pint in my hand, I feel okay. More than okay. Boss.

I like it here, in the airport. There's a buzz mixed into the boredom that's lit a fire in my belly. It's fun wondering where everybody else is going. This is such a different sort of wondering to the one I've been used to in the toll booth. This time, I'm not watching, I'm doing. Just like every other person here, I'm bloody well going somewhere. I'm going to find Zara. I'm not going to get all cosmic or anything; that's all bullshit. The fact is, *she* crashed into *me*. And yet I made a lot of decisions that day. Some were forced upon me, yeah, but they were decisions all the same. It's led to something bigger. It's getting me out. Maybe we did crash for a reason.

A second pint confirms my feelings on that point.

I'd been anxious that I'd get a bit lost in the airport, not know how to find the correct gate, board the plane in time. But, I have to say, the whole experience has come to me with ease. Even getting onto the plane itself (which I thought I might chicken out of) is a breeze. The tunnel is a boss trick, you don't even realise you're on the plane until you're, well, on it. Christ, them pints have gone to my head. I should've eaten something.

As I work out how to fasten my seatbelt, I find myself chatting to the woman in the seat beside me. She's Iranian, married to an English fella, and they've lived in Dubai for two years. They like it a lot, says it's an amazing place to raise a young family. She's got two sons.

'Why Dubai?' I ask.

'My job, actually,' she tells me. 'But my husband found work easily, too. There's plenty of opportunity. Is this your first time to Dubai?'

'It's me first time flying.'

'Oh my God. Really?'

'Yep.'

'So, I should ask *you*. Why Dubai?'

I give her a smile with one side of my mouth.

'A girl?' she asks.

'Sounds daft, doesn't it?'

352

She returns the smile. 'Good luck.'

My comfort zone has been left behind on that shabby seat in the toll booth. The plane taxies to the runway. It powers its engines and roars forward, tilting back and shooting into the sky. What am I doing? Jesus Christ.

What on earth am I actually doing?

35

Zara

Learning from my mistakes, I knew to fly direct from Dubai to Manchester this time.

I'm so exhausted with travelling. I'm not sure when I'll finally grind to a halt. This isn't like hopping on a bus in Thailand with just a backpack and a plan to get drunk, jiggling about for half a day across bumpy roads to get to Laos with more drinking objectives. Nor is it like being passed from one parent to another, seven thousand miles apart. Yo-yoing to and from Liverpool has made me so drained, it keeps my nerves from spinning out of control. Perhaps all this to-ing and fro-ing from here to there and back again has just become the norm; an intensified version of my whole life, really.

That's not to say I don't get pangs of fear. Whenever this happens, I return to people-watching – those with their own hefty suitcase or a stroller or just a takeout cup of coffee – working out who they might be, where they might be going.

Except my instincts are blank. My soul aches for a final destination.

The taxi driver is super nice and we chat the whole way to White Oaks. I give him a good tip before getting out and buzzing the gate.

This is it. I've arrived, and the whole world shrinks into one small space; the one I'm standing within right now. My body feels light, but the thump of my heart is heavy. God, this moment is long.

I await Gloria's voice.

'Hallo, yes?'

'Hi, Gloria? This is Zara, Jim's friend. We met last week.'

'Zara, yes?'

'Is Jim home?'

'Uh, I don't know.'

I pause. 'Can you check, please?'

'I can't do that.'

'Oh. Why not?'

'Because I don't know where he is.'

'You mean he's not home?'

'I don't know if he's home, but I don't know where he is.'

This is rather confusing. Gloria's first language is not English, but surely what I'm requesting is coherent? The intercom fizzes with muffled chatter. I'm hoping that Gloria will at least buzz me in to get me out of the rain.

'Zara?' Gloria's voice says.

'Gloria?'

'Mr Griffin is here.'

'Okay . . .' I don't have a clue who that is.

'He wants you to come inside.'

'Great!'

The gates to White Oaks open. After getting myself back to Liverpool and remembering Jim's address without a hint of trouble, a moment of doubt has dared to creep in. I throw my shoulders back and grow tall. Pulling my single suitcase behind me, a notification alerts my phone. As I wait for Gloria to open the double doors in front of me, I check my messages to distract me from the cold.

It's a private message from Leon Taylor.

Hey lady, long time no see! Looking forward to seeing you at Friday brunch. You still game? Should be a good'un. X

Raindrops splatter onto the screen of my phone. I smile, a warmth tickling my nerves. I'm so glad to have an excuse, to tell Leon I can't make it. Something else has come up. I'm sure it will be a 'good'un'; those sorts of brunches usually are. But this time, I will have to pass. Zara Khoury is busy.

Gloria answers the door and ushers me in swiftly. I slip my phone into my canvas tote bag and make a mental note to reply to Leon later. There are more important things happening right now. Jim is either home, or will be soon. And I'll be here waiting for him.

36

Jim

I watched three full movies and drank double measures of Jack Daniels with Coke, surprisingly never feeling beyond merry, if a little tired. The food was pretty decent, too. I don't know why so many people moan about it. It was like a hot school dinner, without semolina.

And now. Jesus actual Christ. Dubai International Airport is something else. Ha. And I'd thought Manchester was a bit of alright. The floors are so clean I can see my own sorry state in them. The carpets are so thick they could be trampolines. A giant fountain welcomes me and my fellow passengers into the arrivals area. Still, all of this is nothing compared to the rows and rows and rows of palm trees. *Indoors.* Palm trees inside a fucking airport.

'I mean,' I say to myself, 'what the . . . ?'

Once I collect my luggage, I meander around Duty Free. Having done my research on the local currency and worked out how many dirhams there are to a pound after spending

357

seven hours drinking bourbon, I select a couple of bottles of wine to give to Leon Taylor as a thank-you gift. It's overwhelming, all the booze shining brightly from bottles and fancy boxes, but the price tags aren't so bad. I just hope my GCSE maths isn't letting me down.

Leon Taylor is waiting, holding up a piece of A4 paper with 'JIMBO' scribbled across it. Nice touch.

Leon's handsome in the way a straight fella can't deny. Every angle on his face is chiseled to perfection and he smells so fresh that I feel compelled to kiss his neck. But I don't, obviously. We have a brotherly hug, a sort of any-friend-of-Mikey's-is-a-friend-of-mine hug.

'I love airports, man,' Leon beams in his home counties accent, confidently dropping in the American slang, as he heads towards his white four-by-four, dragging my suitcase with little effort. I follow, carrying the duty free. 'I mean, everyone's so happy, innit. Everyone coming, everyone going. Look at us, I never met you before in my life, man! And yet here we are, bro.'

'Here we are.'

'I love people coming to visit. Me and my wife, we love it.'

'I'm dead grateful, mate. Honest.'

'I love Scousers, man.'

'Cheers. I love . . .'

Luckily, Leon laughs just hard enough for it to be infectious, so I laugh too, shaking my head and throwing my hands into the air, declaring that I'm tired, or something. Leon tells me he totally understands, totally, totally, totally, as he closes the boot and climbs into the driver's seat.

'And wait 'til we take you to brunch!'

'Brunch?' I ask.

'Yeah, man. Did Mikey not fill you in on the brunch?'

'Erm. You mean like breakfast before lunch?'

Leon bashes his steering wheel and wipes the tears from his eyes, laughing harder.

'It's so much better than that,' he says. 'I'll tell you *all* about it.'

I gaze out of the window to see the first country I've ever been to outside the UK. It's night-time and as we drive across the six lane flyover, I take in the thousands of rooms lit up inside huge hotels, boats floating on a stretch of water below us, all decorated with fancy lights. Everything's so big. In the distance, I can see the skyscrapers, getting larger and larger the closer we drive. Apparently Leon lives on the twenty-second floor.

'You know who's gonna be at the brunch on Friday, don't you?' Leon asks.

Christ, I can't even think what day it is today. Wednesday. Leon looks across at me, eager for my answer. I guess correctly, of course.

'You've got one hell of a story to tell us, man,' Leon says. 'We need to get back to my apartment, get on the balcony and crack open some beers.'

I laugh again. Yep. That's exactly what we need to do.

Already, this trip to Dubai is the best thing I've ever done. Ever.

37

Zara

He introduces himself as Richard, holds out his hand.

It's as if I'm at White Oaks for an interview.

He leads me into that study, the one with the garish gold trophies and model cars, and gestures for me to take a seat on the leather Chesterfield. He swivels in a chair behind the vast desk a fair distance away. Broad and bald, he seems in a hurry to be somewhere else.

'I'm gonna make this quick,' he tells me. 'James Glover is a liar.'

That single word, *liar*, cuts me like a sharp knife.

Richard drops his pen down and stands up, starts to count on his fingers. 'If James Glover told you them cars are his, he's a liar. If he said the minibus is his, he's a liar. If he gave you the inclination that he was me, or anything like me, he's a liar. And if he told you that this house is his house, well, sweetheart, he is a liar.'

It's such a dirty word, *liar*.

I shudder. If Jim has lied about all of that, then who the hell is he? How could this happen to me twice? What is wrong with people, telling fucking lies?

'Excuse me,' I say, tears choking me, that dirty word *liar* hammering into my head. I notice the door to the small bathroom ajar and run towards it, locking myself inside. That man, Richard Griffin, is terrifying. His bald head shines pink and he speaks through gritted teeth. I don't want to ever hear him say the word *liar* ever, ever again. I'd happily escape out of that tiny bathroom window, like a runaway bride, if only my damn suitcase and canvas tote bag weren't in his study.

Splashing my face with cold water and dabbing it dry with a freshly rolled hand towel, I stare at my reflection, tired and beaten. How far have I come since the last time I stood in this exact room, doing pretty much the exact same thing? Thousands of miles, and yet a million steps backwards. How much longer can I keep doing this?

I see my reflection again, ignoring my scar with all my might. My dark eyes are glaring back at me. The last time I was here Jim changed his t-shirt. Except he didn't. Because this house is not Jim's house. Which means he changed it somewhere else.

I remember sitting in his car, the rain battering down, the ladder in my tights. The smell of the grease, the grey of the flyover. I have been to Jim's home, haven't I? But it's not White Oaks. It's somewhere very different indeed.

I unlock the bathroom door to find Richard Griffin opening a package with a Swiss Army knife, reaching into the box and lifting out a small glistening red Ferrari. He holds the car up to his face and kisses it, unashamed that I'm watching him.

'Jim didn't,' I say.

Richard places the car down onto his desk as if it's a newborn baby.

'Hmm?' he mumbles.

'Jim didn't lie about anything.'

'Good.'

'It's quite simple really,' I say. 'It was me.'

'You lied?' Richard scowls, and I feel quite afraid. It's time to go.

'No, Mr Griffin—'

'Richard.'

'Richard. Jim never lied. I never lied. What I did was presume. I presumed that he drove fancy cars and lived in this fabulous house and enjoyed some sort of charmed life. No offence.'

'None taken.'

'Jim never told me anything. He just helped me.'

'That sounds more like our James.'

'I have to go. But thank you.'

'Do you know where you're going?'

'Yes. I believe I do.'

I turn to leave and find Gloria hovering at the bottom of the staircase, dusting things that already look sparkling clean. Smiling, I ask her politely if it would be possible to call me a taxi.

But there's one obvious question I haven't worked out the answer to.

'Richard?' I call.

Without making an appearance, he answers back with, 'Yep?'

'Where did Jim get his car from? *His* car?'

Three words echo down the hallway.

'He won it.'

38

Jim

Today, I chilled on a beach which was impressive, if not natural. Skyscrapers stood proud against the backdrop of the bluest sky as I lounged on a sunbed, sipping a Long Island iced tea. Between chapters of a cracking book about the Coen Brothers I picked up at the airport, I watched skydivers parachute down to soft landings. Feet away, an infinity pool rippled, inviting me in for a dip.

I'm back at the apartment now and Leon's arrived home from work buzzing with that Thursday feeling. The Dubai weekend has started; business hours are Sunday to Thursday here. We've decided to take it easy tonight, just a few drinks on the balcony (again) because tomorrow is the big brunch day. Leon's wife, Cheryl, has invited a few friends over and we're ordering in. Thai. Apparently you can get any sort of cuisine delivered here, twenty-four seven. I wonder if you can get a roast dinner.

Although this is supposed to be a quiet night in, already

I can feel the vibes of a party on the horizon. The tunes are on; Leon's playing DJ as he sorts people with drinks, gets the plates and cutlery out ready for when the food is delivered. Upbeat music bounces from another apartment in the building opposite, another group of expats with the same idea as the ones here.

I'm just embracing it.

Tomorrow's going to be . . . well, I don't know what it's going to be.

I've never done anything as crazy as this in my whole life. I'm going to see Zara, the girl who crashed into my car, in a fancy five-star hotel on the other side of the world. And why? Because I've made it happen. Yeah, my mates gave me a kick up the arse, but they've kicked my arse a lot over the years and I always told them to do one. Every date they set me up on, every girl I chatted to in the pub, Christ, the pressure. It's all they wanted, for me to have a girl, any girl. And it's what I wanted, too. But I want more than any girl. I want *the* girl. I've never gone out on a limb like this. Something's always blocked me, never felt right. When you know, you know, eh? It's a good job that Leon's ploughing me with cold beer otherwise my nerves'd be shot.

What if she annoys the living hell out of me, just as she's done before?

I can't quite put my finger on it, but there's something about Zara Khoury that I just can't shake off. She's unlocked a little door within me, already made me step outside and see what can be found. It's only going to be brilliant tomorrow. Boss. It can go no other way.

'SHIT,' Leon shouts from the open plan kitchen lounge. 'OH. SHIT.'

Cheryl shushes him and asks him why he always has to

be so dramatic. I step in from the balcony, wondering if he's smashed some beers on the floor and needs a hand cleaning up. Leon and Cheryl are squabbling over something, her hand covering her mouth in disbelief. She's kind of laughing . . . or crying? No, laughing.

Leon, however, is not laughing. At all.

'Everything alright?' I ask. I place my half-drunk beer onto the kitchen bar, catching a glimpse of my freshly tanned arm. Christ, I might look pretty healthy after this trip, less like a vampire.

'She's probably joking,' Cheryl's saying to Leon. 'How well do you know her?'

'Well enough to know she wouldn't bail on a brunch,' Leon replies.

'Er, what's going on?' I say. For the first time since I arrived, I feel as though I'm standing in the wrong place, that I need to disappear. There's an edge to the atmosphere, a haze of things being out of joint. Cheryl and Leon are talking aloud but it's as if they don't want me to hear. Their friends are still out on the balcony and although I could easily rejoin them, I'm eager to know what the problem is. And there's clearly a problem.

'Look, man,' Leon says. 'Zara ain't coming tomorrow.'

I shrug.

Okay. Maybe I expected too much.

It's fine.

But, fuck. The sudden nausea I'm experiencing isn't nice. It brings my high crashing down to an awful low. I tell myself to get a grip; that things never usually go to plan.

'Well, it was probably quite likely,' I say, holding it together. It's hard. 'I was taking a bit of a mad risk.'

'She said she's in England,' Cheryl says.

I snort a short laugh, pick up my beer and swig. 'Of course she is.'

'Man, I am so sorry,' Leon says. 'Unless she's talking shit.'

'Nah. God knows what she's doing, but from what I know of her – and it's not much – she doesn't ever seem to be in the same place for longer than five minutes,' I sigh. 'Christ almighty. What the hell's she doing back in England? And what the hell am I doing here? Ah, for Christ's sake.'

Here I am, surrounded by a couple of bloody strangers, in the fucking desert.

Cheryl reaches out, compelled to give me a hug. I'm not too comfortable about her doing this. I stiffen up. This is just weird.

'There's only one way to find out,' Leon says.

'Find out what?' I ask.

'If she's talking shit. I'm gonna video call her.'

'Leave it, mate. If she doesn't wanna come, she doesn't wanna come.'

'Are you serious?' Leon cries. 'Ah, man. This is your girl. You're her guy. You can't give up now. Let's find out what's going on here. And look, if Zara's just making up excuses, seeing you here's clearly gonna change that. Okay, so the surprise won't happen how we planned it tomorrow, but come on, who cares? Right?'

This is all a lot of faff; a lot of fuss. Leon and Cheryl's attention was welcoming at first, maybe due to the jet lag or the excitement of actually getting here, but it's making me feel super claustrophobic now. If only I could just close my eyes and open them to find I'm back in my living room, watching my telly, drinking instant coffee and eating toast, waiting for Snowy to drag me out for a pint.

Except, no.

That thought, so comforting when I used to sit in the toll booth, doesn't give me that warm and fuzzy feeling right now. It makes me feel cold, and it's nothing to do with Cheryl keeping the air conditioning at Baltic. I don't want to go home. I don't want to sit alone in my flat above the chippy. I want to stay here. With the dry desert heat and the sandy floors, with the powerful sunshine and the bold moon, with the adventure and the ambition. It's all-encompassing. Although I'm sweating from my pores, I don't want to escape before I've even experienced it.

'Go on then,' I say. 'Let's do it. Call Zara.'

39

Zara

Wong's is open and busier than when I'd sat outside in Jim's car. Perhaps because it's later in the day, and the dark evening is enticing locals to get themselves a chip shop dinner; fish and chips and mushy peas, or something else from the extensive menu lit up on the wall, mainly featuring Chinese dishes and British food deep-fried in batter.

'Yes, love?' the Chinese man behind the counter asks, after I've waited my turn in the queue. He's working super efficiently, shovelling large portions of fried potatoes onto white paper and drowning them with salt and vinegar before wrapping them up into tight parcels.

'Does Jim live upstairs?'

The man smiles, nods many times, and acknowledges the suitcase I'm lugging behind me, so he opens the hatch on the counter allowing me to pass through. He's already started to serve the person who's been waiting behind me when a Chinese lady steps out from behind the large metal refrigerator.

'Back door!' she shouts into my face.

'Oh, I'm sorry, I didn't know where the—'

'*My* kitchen. Not Jim.'

I point at the Chinese man and try to explain that he sent me this way, feeling terrible for passing the blame, getting the poor guy into trouble. It's too late, though. The lady has stomped over to him and is yelling at him in Chinese. They both continue to serve the customers whilst arguing, so I go on ahead past the kitchen. I find myself with nowhere to go other than through a back door or up a staircase.

I leave my suitcase at the bottom, making sure it's pushed against the wall safely.

Up I go.

Pieces of mismatching carpet sit frayed on most steps. On others, the wooden floorboards peep through. The walls drip with grease from the deep fat fryers downstairs and there's no light bulb hanging from the single wire dangling from the ceiling. At the top of the stairs are two doors. One is covered in paper decorations with gold Chinese symbols, red tassels hanging from the frame. The other is painted black, in the middle is a single brass '1'.

Is this it? The end of my journey? Please, let this be the end. I knock.

The second time, I knock so hard that I realise the door is already open.

'Hello?' I call out, taking a small step inside.

The TV is on and I can hear signs of life, fidgeting, re-adjusting on what sounds like a leather chair. My heart is racing, pumping blood to my cheeks, my head, every inch of me feeling so alive I think I might explode. This is so intense. I've finally arrived. Every step I take into Jim's flat, this tiny, yet – wow – neat flat, is taken with caution, with a calm breath, because perhaps this will be one of those moments to cherish forever.

Four doors branch from the miniature hall, with just enough space to hang a mirror and a poster of *Pulp Fiction* in a clip frame on the wall. All doors are open wide, displaying a clear view of each small room. Nothing is out of place; everything is in order. It's obvious where the sounds are coming from now, so I edge towards the lounge.

Some cartoon is blaring from the TV. I'm greeted by not one, not two, but three shocked faces, all wary of this strange woman towering over them. The faces belong to the children of, I suspect, the Chinese couple downstairs serving food. There are two boys, both of a similar sort of age, both protectively grabbing tight hold of the younger sister. With slippers on their feet and wearing what looks like pyjamas, these kids aren't unfamiliar with their surroundings. I must have made a mistake. I'm in the wrong flat.

'Hey!' I say, giving a double wave with the enthusiasm of a kids' TV presenter.

The three children don't respond, barely blink. The boys squeeze the girl tighter.

'I'm looking for Jim?'

The oldest-looking boy jumps up from sitting to his feet in one fast move. He points the remote at the TV, switching it off. As silence bolts the room, the children all scurry past me like mice. By the time I turn around, the front door has slammed shut and they're gone.

Okay. So this *is* Jim's flat.

The film posters, the vinyl; do these portray an image of Jim Glover? I'm not sure. But the bookshelves, filled with creased-up books that have definitely been read and aren't placed there for show; yes, they must be Jim's. God, there are so many; a whole wall covered in bookshelves, so many paperbacks crammed in tight. He always has a book with him, that's what he told me. Always.

I can sense him.

A smell. Nothing bad – or good, even – but an aroma. Familiar.

'Jim?'

I go into the kitchen and notice the photo collage on the wall. Jim's face is featured multiple times, along with the faces of the boys in that photo in Richard Griffin's study, and a striking girl, woman, her hair shocking red, sometimes ginger. Helen. A microwave sits on top of the refrigerator, which is covered with postcards – mainly from Florida – all lined up neatly in rows. The kettle stands beside a gas cooker, a mug tree with six mismatching striped mugs hanging to its right. A long red roller blind with an oriental pattern hangs from a sash window; a wooden table with two chairs is snug against it, with a red swirl tablecloth covering part of the wood, a half-burnt white candle positioned centrally in a holder.

I'm in the right place.

Come home, Jim. Come home.

Despite the warmth of the flat, the home he has made for himself, it feels wrong to continue snooping without him here. I'm an intruder and for all I know, those kids have run downstairs to tell their parents to call the police.

But I don't want to leave.

This flat is lovely. Every corner is complete, every item has a place.

A home.

God, it feels like home.

And anyway, where else should I go? Right now? Surely Jim will be back soon, and without doubt at some point tonight. I'm so tired that the thought of traipsing back into the city and showing my face at that hostel again is too much to fathom. I might even have to share a dorm! Besides, I can't handle any form of transport that isn't my feet dragging me to a bed. Not tonight.

Sitting back into Jim's sofa, I let my eyes close over. But my phone rings.

It's one of those video calls.

Hm. Why is Leon Taylor calling me? I messaged him back to say sorry, I can't make the brunch. What does he want now? Unless he's calling me by accident. I look at the screen and laugh, because of course, of course, of course it's a mistake. This guy has never called me in his life. Generic brunch invite, yes. Normal. A video call? No. He must have knocked his phone while it was unlocked, for sure. I let it ring out.

Closing my eyes again, sinking deeper into the sofa, I enjoy the near-silence, traffic echoing outside. I'm all safe, cocooned inside this darling little flat.

My phone rings again.

'What the—' I say, and decide to answer. 'Hello? Leon?'

The screen is pixelated and a delay causes a rustle of feedback before I hear, 'Zara? Is that you?'

'Of course it's me,' I laugh. 'You called me. Who else would it be?'

'Zara, can you hear me?'

I still can't see him properly on the screen. The sound quality is bad.

'What did you say? Leon?'

The camera shakes, then comes into focus.

I sit up straight and hold the phone before my face, staring into the screen. With a white wall, a white tiled floor and a large grey L-shaped sofa visible in the background, there's no denying that sort of apartment. Clinical, ultra-modern and drenched in Ikea, furniture bought to be temporary. I take in my own surroundings. This is a prank, surely. It's a prank. Only who's playing it on me? And why would they? Unless I fell asleep just moments ago and I'm caught in the middle of a bizarre dream.

'No . . . it can't be . . . Jim?'

'Hiya, love.'

40

Jim

As soon as Zara answers the phone and switches on her camera, I know where she is. I know every crease in the back of that settee. There's a Lightsaber behind her, resting against a cushion, and I know it belongs to the Wongs' antisocial kids.

'Jim? Am I seeing things?'

'Wait, surely I'm seeing things?'

'You're in Dubai?' she shrieks, but I can't help cutting in.

'Zara, hold on. Why are you in me flat?'

'Because, because . . . no, *you* hold on. Why are you in Dubai? What the hell, Jim?'

'I came here to . . . oh, I dunno. Fucking hell, Zara!'

'What?'

'What do you mean, what?!' I tug at my hair, my finger-tips cold from the fierce air-conditioning. Words fail me; my insides squeeze into knots. Oh, how familiar these feelings are at simply hearing Zara's voice, and yet I can't bear the sharp blast of disappointment that's just hit me. Why isn't she here? Why the holy almighty fuck is she there?

'You came here to . . .' Zara says, repeating my words. 'To what?'

'I said I dunno!'

'Stop shouting!'

'I'm not shouting!'

'You are!'

'Well, so are you!'

The lens focuses – or the connection improves – and Zara's face suddenly becomes even clearer, bringing her closer to me. Yet she's so very far away.

'I did what I *do*,' she says.

I squint. 'Go on.'

'What?'

'Elaborate.'

'Oh God, Jim. You know!'

'Do I?'

'Yes! I did what I *do*, I came to find you, to surprise you and . . . No. No! This doesn't make any sense. Why are you in Dubai? That's where I live. Or lived. Oh, I don't know anything or what to think. Agh!'

Her mouth hangs open and for a moment, I wonder if the screen has frozen.

'Zara?'

'Yeah?'

A sigh escapes me.

'I don't believe this,' I say.

'Well, neither do I.'

'You're in me flat?'

'Yeah.'

'In Liverpool?'

'Where else would I be?'

'But how did you know where I lived? Have you been stalking me?'

'What?! No. No, Jim. I have *not* been stalking you.'

Honesty washes across her face, and Christ, it's such a sweet face. I want to break the screen, reach through the cracks and touch it, tell her not to worry, to calm down. I'm here for her, after all. Oh God. I'm *here* for her. And she's fucking *there*.

'So, how did you find out where I lived?' I ask.

'I just did. But, Jim, seriously. Why are you in Dubai? Are you with Leon Taylor?'

'Well, yeah, obviously.'

'You know him?'

'I do now.'

'This still doesn't make sense.'

'You're telling me.'

'Jim, please. Why are you in Dubai?'

I pause. Her frantic blinking attacks me like strobe lighting.

Why am I in Dubai? The answer is clear, simple. I've got to tell her.

Tell her!

It's not as if I can run or hide, or invent some crazy story that turns this situation into a coincidence. We're two people who met by accident. Only a calculated plan could bring us together again. These are the facts. Zara deserves them.

'Zara, love. I suppose I did a *you*.'

'A *me*?'

'Yep.'

'I don't understand.'

'I did what *you* do.'

A gasp, so light, so delicate, escapes her. 'You came to find me?'

'I did.'

'Oh my God.'

'I know.'

'Oh, Jim.'

'Yep.'

'So we both . . .'

'We both.'

Zara's hands clasp her mouth and I let my head hang, my shaggy curls falling over my eyes. On impulse, I find I can't stop myself from silently laughing, trying harder and harder not to, in fear of upsetting Zara. Through the speaker of Leon's phone, I can hear her, too, sniggering. We both shake our heads, laugh out loud, and I'm grabbing onto my side where a stitch has formed. Zara tries to say something, but she's taken over by a fit of giggles and this tickles me even more.

'Why?' she suddenly bursts out.

'Honestly, girl. I'm not entirely sure.'

'You know what, Jim? Me neither.'

We laugh some more and naturally it filters into a long, long sigh. We could laugh about it all night. Except this isn't a joke. It's a total shambles.

'Look, Zara, I'll come straight back. Tomorrow.'

'To Liverpool?'

'Where else?'

'Okay . . .' she says, breaking eye contact. She glances to her side, to where I know the window overlooks the flyover. The scented candles on my windowsill are unlikely to have been lit and I can smell the deep fat fryer from Wong's chippy as if it were in Leon's kitchen right now. Zara switches direction, her focus now towards my bathroom, a space so small that I feel squashed just thinking about it.

That flat, that life, that person called Jim Glover, isn't anything she would've imagined.

377

'I was gonna tell you. I wanted to tell you. But . . .' I'm a coward, I want to say. To admit.

'I like it.' She smiles.

And for once, I don't get that knee-jerking urge to argue with her.

'Don't come back tomorrow,' she says. 'Enjoy Dubai. You've never been to Dubai, right?'

I bite my lip. 'I've never been anywhere, love.'

Zara doesn't seem bothered by my embarrassment. In fact, she's not even taking any notice; she's clapping her hands, her eyes glistening and growing huge.

'I just realised,' she exclaims. 'You're going to the brunch, aren't you? Tomorrow! This is why Leon invited me to that brunch. So, hold on, *how* do you know Leon?'

'Ah, I'll tell you another time, love.'

'Tell me now.'

'Well, it does involve some stalking. Not from me. Me mate. He's a bit of a—'

'Stalker?'

'Yeah.'

'Jim, you *have* to go to brunch tomorrow.'

I shrug. Surely brunch is just overpriced eggs three hours late.

'Experience it, lap it up, go crazy,' Zara goes on. 'Make weird friends. Contacts.'

'Y'what?'

'Expats, Jim. Expats LOVE a new kid in town, you'll have a ball. Trust me.'

'It's that good, is it?'

'It can be.'

'No, Zara. I should come back. I mean, you're in me flat, girl. I need to come back.'

378

'No! I'll come back to Dubai instead. I'll meet you there.'

'At the brunch?' I ask, not proud of how keen I sound. 'Is that even possible?'

Zara chuckles. 'No. In a few days.'

'Well, in that case, I'll come back to Liverpool instead.'

'Please, stay there. You see, I can't come back to Dubai tomorrow.'

'Why?'

'Well, I guess it doesn't really matter anymore . . .'

'Eh?'

She slaps herself across her forehead. 'No. It does matter, actually. It does.'

'You're making a whole lot of nonsense there, Zara.'

'Sorry. I've got a meeting, like a meet and greet thing.'

'In Liverpool?'

And she gives a shy smile. 'At the university.'

'Whoa, that's boss. How come . . . oh, Jesus. Really?'

'Yeah!'

'You're gonna do it?'

'I think so.'

'No, I *know* so. Zara, you have to do it.'

'I know.'

'You're gonna get your degree,' I cheer, and then hold Leon's phone at arm's length to raise my free hand. 'Go 'ead, girl. Gimme five!'

Zara's hand plasters the screen as she laughs, giving herself a little whoop.

'Look, love, you're more than welcome to stay there in me flat. Use whatever you need.'

'I can't do that.'

'You bloody well can.'

'Well . . .'

'Zara, just stay and do what you need to do, sort your uni stuff, make yourself at home.'

She skips a beat. 'Thank you, Jim.'

'Don't be soft. I'll do this "amazing" brunch, or whatever, and then come back to Liverpool in a few days once you're all sorted. You've got to give this all you've got, girl.'

'I feel kind of bad, though. I should really come back to Dubai. I mean, you went all that way!'

'So did you.'

I bring the phone close to my face, as if somehow that means bringing Zara nearer to me. It must have startled her because she pulls back into my settee, stretching her phone away from her. Whether it was the jerk movement, or the internet playing up, her face has now become pixelated.

'No, Jim. I'll see you in Dubai in a few days,' she says, filtering through after a slow delay.

'Zara. Shut up. I'll see you in Liverpool in a few—'

The connection is disrupted. Zara's sweet face fizzles into a disfigured freeze. I press to call again, but it fails, and fails again. The battery is low on Leon's phone; just three, no, two per cent remaining. I stare at the handset, a ringing in my ear confirming the immediate lack of Zara's presence in the room.

She's gone.

She was never even here in the first place.

And now I'm on the other side of the world, so far from her. So far from home.

Outside, it's hot, humid, a sandy breeze creating a perfect outdoor evening temperature. Everything about it is so incredibly un-British, so unfamiliar to any climate I've ever experienced. A sea – in which I can swim – is a stone's throw away, the desert imminent. The actual desert. With actual camels.

What the hell have I done?

'Jim?' Leon's head peers around the glass door onto the balcony. 'Everything alright, man?'

The party's in full swing on the balcony.

I should ask Leon for his phone charger, try and call Zara back.

'Grab yourself a beer, man. Come join us,' Leon calls, before getting dragged off by one of his mates. A wave of laughter ensues, a joke shared amongst friends, a most enjoyable time being had out there, just feet away from me.

I should socialise.

I look down at Leon's phone, the screen black, the battery dead. A dark heaviness falls on my chest and I slump downwards. What are the chances? How am I here, in Dubai? How can the one person I came here to find be there, in Liverpool?

A bang brings my awareness back into the apartment, my attention drawn to the windows. Lights dance through the sky, giant palm trees dangling, accompanied by shooting stars. Another delightful squeal, a further bang.

I smile, one corner of my mouth rising, the steady beat of my heart returning.

Fireworks.

These don't half beat the ones in Snowy's back garden. I wonder what the occasion is, but then again, I'm in Dubai, aren't I? From what I've learnt so far, this place doesn't need much of a reason to throw a celebration. I laugh, allowing the phone to slip from my hands and land on Leon's sofa safely. Christ, there really are worse places that I, James Anthony Glover, could be right now.

It feels right to socialise. And I'll tell Leon to charge his phone.

I can speak to Zara again later. Or tomorrow.

Or one day very soon.

41

Jim
20 months later

The boutique hotel on the corner of Hope Street fizzes with celebration, a sense of achievement breathing across the lobby. On my way to the reception desk, I zigzag through families meeting other families, friends sharing in-jokes with one another and making fun of the gowns draping over their unfamiliar formal attire. I straighten my black tailored jacket and loosen my silk tie a little. July's not the best month to be wearing a suit.

'There's a thirty-minute wait for taxis,' the receptionist informs me.

I know I should've hired a car at the airport, but it wouldn't have been responsible. I'm an emotional mess and not afraid to admit it. Christ, I only arrived in Liverpool from Dubai last night, desperate to be here days ago, but work had my passport while they were renewing my bloody visa. I mean, talk about timing.

'You're best hailing a black cab on the main road, if you're in a hurry?'

Exiting the main entrance, I step out into Hope Street. Concrete slabs lie beneath my feet in the Georgian Quarter, home to a fusion of classic exteriors and modern interiors. A mother stops me, asks if I'll take their photo. Her family position themselves on the steps of the French bistro next door, the graduate in the centre looking almost as pleased with himself as his parents do.

'Of course,' I say. 'Now say *fromage*.'

The family crack up.

I can't help but look down at the mother's shoes, wonder if she's bought them especially for today. My heart swells and a lump crams into my throat. I hold the phone steady and capture the moment. The whole family thank me for the photo.

'All the best,' I wish them.

I walk down Hope Street, towards the Anglican Cathedral. The sun is high, beating down upon my head and although I'm used to a hot climate now, it's uncomfortable here, as if the air isn't ever prepared for it. I stop to put my sunnies on, glad to have an excuse to hide behind the polarised lenses. The Anglican Cathedral grows larger with every step I take, a giant icon standing strong and sure of itself. Behind me, the Catholic Cathedral, its crown pinching the clear sky, shrinks, although the stained-glass panels dance in the sunlight. My ma always felt guilty for preferring the Anglican over the Catholic, by design only, of course. That's Catholics through and through, though, isn't it? Even the postcard, the one tucked inside my suit jacket pocket, is riddled with guilt. My ma feeling awful about enjoying herself so much in Florida whilst poor Ethel Barton was having (another) hip replacement.

'It just doesn't seem fair,' my ma had written.

I approach the main road on a hill. Many families flood the cathedral's entrance, a crossover of ceremonies. Everybody looks so happy. I want to tell them all to stop, just for a moment, to acknowledge that the world isn't spinning the right way around today. But even if they did, and a magical minute's silence ensued, it's not going to take my pain away, is it?

A rush of panic seizes me as I hail a passing cab. It drives straight past. I hadn't noticed the light was off, passengers already inside. This gives me a quick sense of relief, buying me a little more time before I've got to say goodbye. I drag my eyes away from the road and let them wander up to the top of the cathedral and down again.

And that's when I see her.

Throwing her mortar board into the air and catching it.

I blink hard. Perhaps it's not her. She can't catch to save her life.

'Zara?'

I remove my sunnies, but the sun is so bright, I've got to squint. It makes my eyes water, so I put them on again. Amidst the many graduates, all dressed identically, I find her again.

It is.

It's her.

Zara.

She's stood in the middle of an older couple, one arm around each, and smiling, whilst a younger girl – maybe seventeen or eighteen and bearing a striking, natural blonde resemblance to Zara – takes a photo. A small gang appears and jumps into the photo, all wearing the same gown and mortar board, and raucous laughter follows. Two of the gang pick Zara up, as light as she still is, and she sits upon their shoulders, posing for even more photos. The woman is embracing many of these graduates whilst the man shakes their hands. Zara's doing some sort of dance with the younger girl. Some of her pals joining in.

Christ.

I wonder if she still lives in the flat above the chippy.

I recall the view from the front window; the flyover, a far cry from my current apartment overlooking the golf course, a myriad of modern architecture framing the green horizon. Only Zara could manage to find beauty in that flyover. The rattling of the lorries, the swish of the rain, the whistle of the wind. It helped her to zone into her work without ever feeling alone. Her words, not mine. I remember seeing an easel grace the corner beside the DVD shelf. String hung from wall to wall, her drawings attached with wooden clothes pegs like bunting floating above my leather settee, my tile-and-teak coffee table, my record player. She listened to David Bowie on vinyl, sometimes Fleetwood Mac. She'd picked up a Supremes LP from a charity shop for three quid. I found it adorable that Zara had started to call a pound a quid. It had only taken her a couple of weeks to settle in, just as I was doing in Dubai.

'It's my urban art haven.' She'd smiled at me across the screen, bringing her shoulders up to her ears as she snuggled into a giant woolly jumper, once belonging to me. 'Minus a bunch of pretentious hipsters and artisan coffee.'

'If I hear Wong's has become vegan, I'll come after you,' I'd told her, winking.

'No you won't, Jim. You already did that once.'

I feel a shiver beneath the heaviness of my suit, despite today's warmth. It's been a while since I've thought about that particular conversation. The last time Zara and I spoke.

It was the day I'd been offered the package; visa, healthcare, the lot. And all because of that one article.

'You have to take it,' she'd said; no hesitation, no plea.

I knew I'd have to take it. And we knew she wasn't leaving Liverpool either. As always, the screen froze mid-conversation and we only picked it back up in pieces, to break free from the disjointed cyber cords of a long-distance twenty-first century relationship.

I take a step towards the cathedral.

I start waving.

And Zara stops dancing.

The sun slides behind a light cloud giving me an opportunity to take off my sunnies.

She could be the girl on the side of the road again, not far from the tunnel, in shock at the car crash. Her mouth drops open, her eyes pop out. Walking towards me, her cheeks rosy, her scar almost faded away, she's as bright as the sun, a bounce in her stride.

We arrive face to face.

And I don't know what to say.

Neither does Zara, so it seems.

A silent *hello* ensues, a wordless *how are you?*

A puzzled look washes over Zara and she stutters as she speaks.

'So, are you . . . ?' she asks. 'Here for . . . ?'

'No,' I confirm. 'Not this.'

'Oh?'

'Me ma. She . . .'

Zara takes in my black suit. 'I'm so sorry, Jim.'

'Me too.'

We stand in silence again, looking into one another's eyes.

My hand brushes hers, our fingers interlacing slightly, naturally. Just for a moment.

It's the night in the Travelodge once more.

'Well, are you good? Happy?' I ask.

Zara releases a laugh and sighs, throwing her head back, but her mortar board slips off. As she twists, stumbles and tries to stop it falling to the ground, I catch it. She covers her face with her hands and laughs again. I laugh, too.

'Soz, bit of a shit question,' I cringe, then mock myself with a squeaky voice. '*Are you happy?*'

She accepts the hat back, twirling it back and forth in her hands.

'Remember the meerkat in the jacuzzi?' she asks.

'How could I forget?'

'He's about to take the app world by storm, I hope.'

'Really? How?'

'I've been working with an animation studio, here in Liverpool. I'm joining the team full time next week. There's a new game being launched soon, so keep your eyes peeled. And that's all I'm saying.' She grins.

'You're not spilling the beans?'

She puts her hat back on, and holding onto the top, she pouts, shaking her head.

'Bloody hell, Zara, it's not like you to keep quiet.'

'And it's not like you to pry.'

And just like that, the emptiness between us starts to fill. Not having to rely on the strength of the local Wi-Fi really does make a difference. Zara had been right to end it. Not that I hadn't understood her reasons. Her scar was a glaring reminder. Still, it hadn't been easy to accept, to switch her off. Literally.

'I've read your stuff online,' Zara says. 'I follow the mag.'

So, she'll know I've been kept on as editor. I'm pleased. I don't like to brag.

'I told you, didn't I?' Zara smiles, knowingly. 'The pace in Dubai is fast. You either run with it or get left behind. It's so great that you ran.'

'You mean that?'

Zara pauses, inhales her surroundings.

'Of course I do,' she says. 'How long are you back for?'

'Just a week.'

'Your first time back?'

A dormant ache squeezes my chest, my face flushing hot. I'd meant to come back sooner. I'd meant to go to Florida. She'd been doing really well in the sunshine, my ma, and kept telling me to focus on my job, to make a life for myself just as she was doing. She sewed sequins and frills on little Sienna's dance leotards, watched her recitals. She said she liked the beach – a shocker, but she swore on my dad's grave. In the end, it was her heart that packed in and she went suddenly. Quickly. According to our Lisa and Emma. A small, small comfort, overshadowed by a regret I'll never overcome.

'Things . . . escalated,' I say.

Zara nods. She'd been the first to read that article, telling me it was 'right on the mark'. I'd written it on a whim, alone in Leon's apartment, sat at Leon's spare laptop, after being unable to get hold of Zara to find out how her meeting at uni went. So, I wrote. My first impressions of the futuristic metropolis had inspired me somehow, perhaps after visiting a cheap Pakistani restaurant on the other end of town, devouring the delicious food amongst a very different crowd to the brunch crowd. Dubai has stories to tell. The surface can be scratched. Anyway, I emailed my article to some fella I'd met at that first brunch, chatting about everything and nothing beside the frozen daiquiri stand. I'd been using that fella's business card as a bookmark for my Coen Brothers book, the one I was reading by Leon's communal pool.

Turns out that fella liked what I'd written.

Two days later, he took me out for dinner, introduced me to shisha. An official interview took place the following week, thanks to Leon lending me a suit. And now here I am – in my own suit – nearly two years later, back to before. Almost.

I'm aware of how close I'm standing to Zara, how I tower over her, and I look down, see that she's wearing little shoes with a wedge, although she doesn't seem any taller than I remember. Like a little doll. The clouds pass and I'm about to shield my eyes with my hand, but Zara lifts her arm at the same time, on the verge of speaking, and our hands meet again, only in an awkward fumble. We laugh, exchange sorries.

'May I ask you a question?' she says.

I shrug, unsure of why I don't just say yeah.

She laughs.

'What?' I ask.

'*This* is the Jim I know and love. The one who makes me work so damn hard for an answer, the one who has so much inside him but won't let any of it out.'

I smirk, then give her a broad smile.

'What's your question, love?'

'What – what was your mom's name?'

I swallow. 'Patsy.'

And whatever strength has been holding me together completely falls apart.

'Ah, shit . . .' I say, because I'm choked, eyes welling up. 'Sorry, love.'

Zara reaches out and grabs my left arm with her right hand, giving it a squeeze.

'Oh, Jim. Why didn't you call?'

''Cause you told me not to.'

'I know, but I didn't mean you couldn't ever call me again. Like, ever.'

'You said no more. It wasn't working.'

'Well, it wasn't!'

'And I respected that.'

'Our calls were hindering us. We survived together in a car, but we were never going to survive over a screen, over the damn internet. This was the only way,' she says, her gaze locked into mine, nothing whatsoever between us. 'It is the only way.'

'I know . . . Which is precisely why I never called.'

I look past Zara, to the crowd she had been standing with.

'Is that your dad?' I ask.

Zara rolls her eyes a little, accepting my diversion.

'He took me for dinner last night,' she says. 'Told me he was proud of me.'

I feel my heart tighten, hard, followed by a release so large, so weightless.

'This is their first time to Liverpool,' Zara goes on. 'That's my mom, and my sister, Paige. Quite the reunion, which is going okay. I think. Papa's not doing so good, he's going through his second divorce, which is why my brother isn't here. They aren't talking. Anyway, I'm taking them on the ferry this afternoon, and my mom's dragging me on the Magical Mystery Tour tomorrow. Such a tourist.'

'You know, I've never done it,' I admit.

'Seriously?'

'I'm not a tourist.'

'Neither am I.' She smiles.

'Yeah. Eh, did you know George Harrison's uncle used to drink in me local?'

'The Pacific Arms?'

I laugh. It sounds funny in her accent; a bonkers blend of regal fantasy, a true world away from my lot and how they talk. But I'm touched that Zara Khoury knows the name of the pub that holds a million memories of mine, most of them bog standard pissed-up nights, but many highs and a fair few lows.

The chatter around the cathedral seems to heighten. Another graduate skids past and clasps Zara with a high-five. She passes some comical remark, a private in-joke perhaps, and Christ, I realise I'm about to lose her all over again. Somebody calls her name and as she turns to acknowledge them, I notice a cab with its light on and back away, giving the driver a gentle thumbs up. It's time to go.

'Anyway,' I say, placing my hand upon her shoulder, just gently. 'Congratulations, love.'

And a smile encases my heavy heart watching Zara skip away, a spring in her step but with roots firmly planted. I clamber inside the cab and I'm right where I should be, going home. Life – its journey and beyond – is awaiting me.

42

Zara

My jaw is aching. For the first time in my life, I don't think I'd like to get married, or at least have a wedding. Not only am I tired of the endless posing and pictures, but my parents are starting to drive me crazy. I guess I could always elope.

'Zara has made a reservation at an Italian place, Samir,' my mom is telling my papa, although my papa is wafting his hand in her face, as if her words are creating a pungent odour.

'The Hilton has a steakhouse,' he says, loosening his tie further and yet refusing to remove his jacket. 'Let's just go there. It will have air conditioning.'

Paige reminds us all about how she doesn't eat animals. We're crammed together around a small table in the Philharmonic, a grand old pub famous for its even grander washrooms, over-populated today by gangs of friends hanging onto their last few hours of student life, and, of course, by other bickering families. The ceremonies are over and everybody is hot and hungry. My friend, Dom, is at the bar after insisting on buying us a round of drinks.

'Who is this Dom, anyways?' my papa asks. 'Your boyfriend?'

'Papa, hush.'

'So he is. He's your boyfriend.'

My mom gets the chance to waft her hand back at my papa.

'Samir, when will you grow up?' she says. 'Dom is not Zara's boyfriend. He's just her lover.'

'Mom!' I say, along with Paige.

We blush together and giggle, a real sister moment if ever there was one. Actually, there have been a few of these moments over the past couple of days, natural, uncanny and comforting. Thanks to her tagging along with my mom to my graduation I no longer feel like that distant relative, the one who once gave her a My Little Pony when anything from *High School Musical* would have been more appreciated. Until Paige takes out her phone to document what just happened with GIFs and emojis and her perfect pout. She looks exactly like our mom, an all-American girl with well-maintained teeth and flowing natural blonde locks, the only major difference between them being Paige confidently exposing her midriff whilst our mom's toned figure is covered demurely with pastels and pearl. Paige shows me the image of us both that she has posted to her four thousand plus followers. I'm unmistakably Samir Khoury's daughter, with his short height and long nose, thankfully minus his bulging belly and sweating temples, which he is currently dabbing with a napkin.

'Forty likes? Already?' I ask, impressed.

'That's nowhere near enough,' Paige sulks, then snaps her fingers repeatedly. 'The pace needs to pick up if I'm to be an influencer.'

'Remind me, what is it you want to influence people with again?'

'Anything. Everything. I mean, I don't care!' She looks upwards to find inspiration and then turns her attention back to our picture. 'That's definitely your best side, Zara.'

Dom arrives with a tray of drinks, his energy refuelled from a double vodka Red Bull. He twists his pointed beard, arguably his most favourite thing on this earth, before planting a wet kiss on my cheek. My mom creeps me out by winking at me, like she's pretending to approve. God, she really doesn't know me at all, does she?

'The steakhouse has good reviews,' my papa pipes up again. 'And they do fish.'

But a commotion by the bar drowns out his restaurant pleas and we all look in the direction of the students – well, graduates – doing some sort of buddy ritual, downing shots and making one hell of a noise in doing so. I think about Jim, how I hope he's in the company of his own buddies, perhaps in the Pacific Arms, drowning his sorrows with them all.

Oh, Jim. Jim Glover.

There've been times when I've wondered whether we even met at all. It was all so brief, you couldn't even describe it as whirlwind. Yet, somehow, he opened a door for me, and I guess I opened a window for him to escape. To think that I'm just here, and he's just there . . . Wow. I never got to think like this before. It was always me being here, and Jim being way, way, way over there, beyond Europe, across the desert, up a skyscraper and heavily pixelated due to an illegal VPN.

I hope he's okay. God, I really hope he's okay.

And his poor mom; his 'ma'. Patsy.

'Zara! Zara!' Dom says, yanking the straps of my dress.

'Sorry,' I say. 'I was a million miles away.'

'Your dress is soooo pretty,' he says.

I smile. It is pretty, second hand with a vintage floral print and damn comfortable, too. I planned that carefully, knowing I'd be sitting down for three solid hours on a wooden bench waiting for my name to be called out. I wish I'd been as smart about my sandals. I thought wedges were supposed to be comfortable.

But Dom's clearly drunk too much on an empty stomach. He's harmless, if a little too keen. And definitely too young for me. He tickles my bare arm and tries to take my hand, but I pull away.

'Cheers,' Dom says, raising his glass a little too abruptly and spilling beer onto his Hawaiian shirt, worn in solidarity with his four housemates. 'To us.'

We clink and I gulp, the red wine feeling sticky in my throat. It's bizarre to think that I'm drinking in a pub in Liverpool, and Jim probably is, too. If only it were the same pub. Would we talk? I laugh. Of course we would talk.

'What are you laughing at?' my mom asks.

'I was just thinking about a friend of mine,' I say. 'It was his mom's funeral today.'

'That's not very funny.'

'Oh no! That's not why I was laughing.' Because it wasn't. Yet I'm still laughing. I'm just sitting here, thinking about Jim and all I can see is us screaming at each other at the side of a road, in the damn rain. And this makes me laugh even more. And I remember him sitting in that old lady's house . . . Mary? Yes, Mary! And reading her book on her rocking chair because I had fainted, and . . .

'What's wrong with Zara?' my papa asks, perplexed.

'She's thinking about her friend,' my mom shrugs.

'Good God. Another boyfriend?'

Dom sits up. 'Huh?'

'Look, Zara,' my papa says, unaware that he has just banged his fist upon the table. 'Let's go eat. Even if it's your cheap Italian, I don't care. I just need to eat.'

I drink up my wine, a little too fast, and stand up. My family follows suit and we face the gauntlet of people, squeezing and sidling through the Philharmonic until we're outside. It's still sunny, although it's almost seven. Dom is lingering in the doorway. He asks if he will see me tomorrow before he heads home with his parents to Somerset.

'I'll try,' I say, honestly. It will be nice to say goodbye.

Paige gathers us all together for a final selfie outside the pub and I lead the way down Hope Street towards the main road. Except instead of turning right and heading towards the 'cheap' Italian, as my papa calls it, I stop on the corner.

'Mom,' I say. 'Would you be offended if I wanted to call it a day and just go home?'

My mom smiles. 'Of course not, honey. You tired?'

I nod. 'It's been really great.'

'But what will you eat?' my papa asks.

My mom places a hand on my papa's back. 'She can feed herself, Samir. Don't worry.'

'I'm within my rights to worry about my own daughter, aren't I?'

'Papa, go to the steakhouse. Spoil yourself.'

And we stand on the corner of Hope Street, all kissing each other's cheeks and saying goodnight, and I watch my family walk away from me, together, perhaps to even eat together. Whether they do or they don't, I guess it doesn't matter. Today has been good.

And tonight?

Well, I told a lie.

I'm not tired. And I'm not going home.

I hail a black cab.

'Where to, love?'

I get inside and slam the door.

'The Pacific Arms, please.'

The Pacific Arms is only about a five-minute walk from my little flat above the chip shop, although I've never been inside. I always meet friends for dinner or drinks in town and the bus stop is in the opposite direction to the pub, so I've no reason to go in there or past there. Besides, drinking in Jim's local without him being there would be totally weird. I'd miss him, which sounds silly, especially since I live in his old flat, but I would.

I thank my cab driver and stand on the sidewalk, looking at the pub in all its faded glory. The windows have intricate globes carefully designed into the glass and a neon orange poster saying 'Karaoke Wednesdays' has been not-so-carefully taped against it. The doors are all open, more to allow a cool breeze to enter than invite a crowd, so the mumbled chatter of punters and sports commentary filter towards me.

I step inside.

There are two guys sitting in silence with their arms folded watching the big screen; some sort of track athletics. A much older gentleman is standing at the bar, sipping his beer. Beside the flashing lights of a quiz machine is a gang of men and women, a similar age to me. They could be the after-work crew, all smart shirts with top buttons undone, smart dark trousers and little black dresses. Except their attire isn't from the office.

'Whose round is it?' one guy asks, knocking back his whiskey. He yanks his much shorter friend into a headlock. 'Come on! Your turn.'

'No way, Mikey lad. You haven't bought a drink all day, you stingy fucker,' the shorter guy shrieks.

Another guy – wearing a long black leather coat, despite the heat – drags himself away from the quiz machine, offering to keep the peace and buy the round. The door to the ladies' room swings open and a woman with long red hair emerges, marches straight over to the short guy and whacks him across the head. His response is to pull her towards him and smack a kiss on her lips.

Of course, I recognise this gang. Their smiling faces were hanging on the wall of Jim's kitchen before it became mine. I've always wondered if and when those pictures would come to life: perhaps a chance meeting in the queue of Primark or waiting for the 87 bus. Maybe we've all been at the Baltic Triangle together, drinking craft beer and eating sourdough pizza, but I just didn't notice them amongst the crowds. I want to say hello. I want to ask, where's Jim? But, I linger, like a ghost haunting a past I almost had. Almost.

'Where's Jim?' I hear, but it's not my voice speaking. It's the woman, Helen.

'Left ages ago,' the shorter guy says. There's no mistaking that's Snowy.

'Should we ring him? Check he's okay?'

'Leave him be,' the guy in the coat says, who must be Griffo. He's aged the most from the youthful faces I was accustomed to seeing whilst waiting for the kettle to boil, before I packed the collage into a box to be shipped to Dubai. 'If Jimbo needs time on his own tonight, then that's what we'll give him.' And he swings one arm around Helen and another around the most drunk of them all, Mikey. They both lean their heads on Griffo's big shoulders.

'No!' I hear. Oh my God. It's me. I've spoken out loud.

Helen catches my eye before I shoot my glance to my painted toes popping out of my sandals. I've just forced myself into a private conversation between a gang of strangers, and why? Because I selfishly want them to call their grieving friend so I can . . . what? Catch up with him? Until today, Jim and I hadn't spoken in more than a year and a half. We never parted ways badly, because we'd already parted. We never broke up, because we never got the chance to be together. We never did anything, because in many ways, we gave each other everything we ever needed.

So this, whatever I'm trying to do right now, is a mistake.

'Are you alright, love?' Snowy asks.

I smile and point to the big screen. There is a woman from Finland doing the pole vault and the slow-motion replay is showing her failure. I've never been more grateful for somebody failing.

'Oh, no,' I say, giving a terrible acting performance. I even slap my palm to my head. 'I'm devastated for her.'

'You American?' Mikey asks.

Griffo gives him a shove with his elbow.

'No, Mikey,' he says. 'She's Finnish.'

It's my cue to leave. I am wonderful improvising with a pencil, but not with my words.

'Bye,' I say.

Helen narrows her eyes, but the sing-song of 'ta-ra' from the guys allows me to leave the Pacific Arms with a small spot of dignity remaining. If I could only leave. I reach the open doors and stop, deflated from my spontaneous idea not working out. It's been a while since I've felt this way and I don't like it, don't appreciate how it's making me feel. I shouldn't have come. I stopped putting myself in situations where the likelihood of disappointment was far greater than the wish. And it's worked for me, so far.

For me?

Who did I come here for? For Jim? Or for me?

And if Jim was here, what good could come from us seeing each other anyway, when we live so far apart? I mean, perhaps it would have been lovely to sit down face-to-face over a drink. But when it comes to Jim and me, it's always been perhaps. Which is why it never was.

The sun has started to lower. Through the pub windows it casts a sharp orange hue against the overbearing greyness of the sidewalk. I twist around, catch a glimpse of the gang again, all talking loudly over one another. I'm going to go home and pour myself a nice cold gin and tonic, add a slice of lime, open the windows and put a record on. Fleetwood Mac, maybe.

I leave the Pacific Arms, and there, on the street; there he is.

'I would say, fancy seeing you here,' Jim says. 'But, you live here.'

'And you don't,' I say.

He's holding a portion of chips from Wong's wrapped in paper, a salty warmth that I'm more than familiar with lacing the short space between us.

'Hungry?' I ask.

'Not particularly. Mr Wong only gave them to me when he realised I'd been waiting so long.'

'Why? Is Wong's really busy tonight?'

'No, love,' he says, taking a step closer to me. 'Wong's isn't really busy tonight.'

'Oh. So why were you waiting so long?'

Jim gives me that one-sided smile and I can't work out whether he's amused or irritated.

'Oh!' I say.

'Yep,' he says.

'You weren't waiting for chips, were you?'

'Nope.'

And as we stand there between the pub and the chip shop, in a place that we've both had the pleasure of calling home, there is no almost. There is no perhaps.

All there is is now.

Acknowledgements

This book was born from a journey in itself, from taking a risk after being stuck in a rut and turning that risk into a whole new life. So an eternal thank you must go to Dubai, the United Arab Emirates, for becoming my second home for seven years. To all the wonderful expats I lived and worked amongst, from the forever friends to the acquaintances; we made memories to cherish always. All of you opened my eyes and my heart to something new, something different. Thank you.

And, of course, thank you to the city of Liverpool, a place I'm lucky to always call home.

A huge thank you to Camilla Bolton, my agent at Darley Anderson. Camilla, you got me. To the Rights and TV/Film team at Darley Anderson; Mary, Kristina and Georgia, and Sheila in TV and Film; to Celine Kelly, for your initial belief in this story, and to Roya Sarrafi-Gohar for reading with such a sharp eye for detail. Thank you all so much. To Helen Huthwaite and her lovely team at Avon, HarperCollins, thank you for welcoming me to your family with so much warmth and smiles.

Thank you to David Runacre-Beck for the broken brain-storming chats between chasing toddlers around London; to Owen Walters for his super-sharp and efficient advice on flashy cars; to DC David Purcell for the facts and helping to keep them creative; to Rose-Mary and Luca and their delightful staff at Two Spoons, Honor Oak Park, where I endlessly wrote over brunch, lunch and coffee (decaf while pregnant!).

For supporting and believing, I'm eternally grateful to my Scouse family. Angela and Paul – my mum and dad – you allowed me to dream whilst keeping my head screwed on.

And thank you to Oli, who I dedicate this book to. My husband, best friend and wonderful daddy to our bears, you've been by my side long before the first word and you're always on the journey with me.

An unforgettable love story that will grab
your heart – with a twist to break it.

Could two imperfect people
be the perfect fit?

Very Nearly
Normal

Hannah Sunderland

Coming May 2020.